W9-CRN-399

World History of Erotic Art

Primitive Erotic Art

Philip Rawson

Primitive Erotic Art

G. P. PUTNAM'S SONS   NEW YORK

© Philip Rawson 1973

All rights reserved. This book, or parts, thereof,
must not be reproduced in any form without
permission.

Designed by Rod Josey

Library of Congress Catalog Card Number: 72-94433

SBN: 399-11108-5

Printed in Great Britain

Contents

Foreword

The word 'primitive' in our title is easily misunderstood. It is a hangover from self-righteous nineteenth-century materialism, and has been taken to imply that peoples or stages of culture labelled 'primitive' are less 'advanced', and hence less valuable, than 'us'. They could therefore be destroyed without compunction, and with all the attendant savagery towards other peoples which has been the hallmark of European culture. Western sexual neuroses, especially those from which Christian missionaries suffer, have sanctified the repression of many exotic sexual customs, evolved through millennia, which were held sacred by 'primitive' peoples. Some have been allowed to survive in the shadow of Western colonialism, remodelled in the grim and hypocritical image of European prostitution. And this cheerless image has been used to taint, in the minds of Westerners, many sexual customs which in their own societies are or were a source of joy and cultural affirmation. We are even obliged to use the word 'prostitution' to designate customs to which it has no real relevance. Whole populations have been deprived of their own culture and given nothing to replace it. Symbolic of Western attitudes is the fact that numberless museums in Europe and America contain works of art made in 'primitive' societies, from which the genitals have been lopped. The number of works of sexual art we know to have been burned, smashed or castrated is so appalling as to numb one's mind with shame at our civilization's mania for destruction.

When we confront this prurient crime, prolonged over centuries, and ask ourselves how on earth it could have happened, something important emerges. The very existence of this book bears witness to the fact that at least some of us now recognize such crime to be a horrible mistake. There can be no doubt at all that most people with any insight into our present-day dilemmas realize that populations and cultures once labelled 'primitive' could have something very valuable to give us. This does not simply mean material objects of art, which we may seize and accumulate, but living thoughts and attitudes which are expressed in living arts.

It is very improbable that any of us would be able to live tribal, 'primitive' lives, trying to heal our own psychological wounds by, so to speak, dressing ourselves up as 'primitives'. But the truth is that we actually share far more of the world of the primitive than we care to admit. The destructive hatred which our own cultural representatives directed against primitive culture was, of course, integral to the development of their own culture. The hatred was aroused by, and really directed at, parts of their own humanity which seemed to be obstructing the development of that world of emotion-free, abstract and quantified concept which has become our false god and our prison. It is a well-known psychological pheno-menon that people project onto outside scapegoats hatreds whose true object is part of their own characters. We have chosen to believe that we can be primarily 'scientific brains', whose only realm of operation is 'objective fact'. And so we have tried to devalue our emotions, sensation and intuition as meaningless in modern life. We have relegated them, at best, to the marginal regions of art and entertainment, at worst to oblivion, where they do not vanish but remain un-consciously and devastatingly at work.

It has been amply demonstrated by Cassirer and others that even the most abstract symbolism rests, at bottom, in a bed or matrix of analogy-patterns which are formed from infancy onward, in every person's mind, by means of those very functions which we now culturally devalue. So unless we want to live in our present state of miserable divorce from the roots of our own worlds, which effect-ively prevents them flowering, we must keep open our channels of communication with those roots. If we do not, our societies become the victim of erratic and dangerous symbolisms (such as obsessions about short and long hair, or white and black skin) with which they cannot cope. Outside our tidy world of useful logical concepts (which are not realities, but conventionalized mental shadows of reali-ties) uncontrolled neuroses flourish: especially in the realm of sex, that most potent of human experiences.

Now that we are free to appreciate 'primitive' sexuality and its imagery, we will find that it should rather be called 'primary'. It lies, in fact, at the basis of our own thoughts and language, not only about sex itself, but about our world, its creation and our own psychic energies. A developed symbolic and metaphorical imagery, based on feeling and sensation, is what we need above all. To explore these depths of analogy, especially those revolving around sex, can vitalize vast reaches of our own experience, which otherwise would lie atrophied and dangerous within us. This book, therefore, is not a mere accumulation of facts for the conscious con-ceptual filing-system, but an exploration of the tissues of sexual-imagery woven by 'primary' men.

In fact, many of the works in these illustrations may not at first seem erotically stimulating to us. They are in no sense obviously titillating in the manner of girlie magazines. They all refer, in one way or another, to the direct inward experience of sexual arousal and activity. Often they also refer to the outward, tactile experi-ence of other people's sexuality; for touch is a realm which primary art knows intimately. Primary people use their hands actively and constructively, not like inert flippers, as so many Westerners do. But each of the works illustrated here is an invitation to every reader to explore all the corners of his own memory, to search for echoes from his own past experience, and enrich his present knowledge of himself and his world.

PHILIP RAWSON

1 Early History of Sexual Art

Philip Rawson

Primitive people do not see themselves as separate egos moving in an abstract pattern of society. Their sense of identity is found within groups through which their whole environment finds its meaning. Among the American Zuni, for example, the individual belongs to a number of overlapping family and social groups, such as kinship, dance and warfare societies. Most important in all societies are totem groups. Each of these, one might say, is a kind of concrete universal image of all the kin, past, present and future, of the human group combined with and symbolized by the totem species. This group binds men into a unity with their natural environment in the most objective possible way, through a compound of ritual, i.e. things done, legend, i.e. things spoken, and art, i.e. things used. When a concrete image is presented to the eye of a primitive it refers much more directly than we can believe possible to real experiences, to memories of acting, feeling and sensing. The elements of the structures expressed in primitive societies are not known conceptually, but through symbols based on mythology and custom, which are imbued with strong feeling, since they have been fortified by lived ritual. Primitive people have had immediate personal experience of relatives enduring disease, dying and being ritually despatched to the beyond; they have experienced many times the profoundly moving performances of ecstatic shamans; most have themselves been through initiations in the course of which they endured privation and pain in the presence of masked supernatural beings, and ceremonies in which blood was shed. Such people attach a far more potent and immediate meaning to the notion of life than we can ever imagine. And if we believe that by calling some of their images, in our own tongue, 'ancestors' we are expressing their true meaning, we deceive ourselves.

Meaning arises from the contents of the beholder's own mind and memory. Even though tangible symbols may indeed be a first evolutionary step on the road to abstract thought, each primitive man brings to the interpretation of his visual imagery a complex chain of direct experiences, all the more powerful for being unclouded by intervening abstract concepts, which we cannot share. An image, when its field of reference is well understood (i.e. conventional) can become for that very reason especially potent. Its broadly conceived metaphorical shapes are enough. It does not need an elaborate infrastructure of 'realistic' forms to make it intelligible to the people for whom it was made.

Even a quite 'abstract' sexual symbol must, to primitive peoples, have had a powerful 'content' of immediate feeling. This is especially important in dealing with sexual imagery that has a serious intent, in connection, for example, with funereal monuments. For most primitive people simply do not share in our sense of an invisible but absolute barrier between what is seriously religious, and what is sexually stimulating and delightful. Certainly there are many serious occasions upon which sexual intercourse is taboo, and sexual enjoyment forbidden. But that does not mean to say that the sexual symbolism used on serious occasions is deprived of its sexual connotations. The truth is that symbols only live by virtue of their chain of experience-content. The more intensely the content is 'realized' in memory, the more potent the symbol. And primitive peoples are very much concerned with potency, at all magical levels. There is no reason at all to suppose that the experience-content of sexual symbolism is ever deprived of its full range of reference in any primitive culture; although, of course, particular local customs may add specific overtones and qualities to any imagery. Thus an ancestor-image which exhibits a large and decorated phallus is supposed to remind people, male and female, of real experiences of the phallus; with in addition any special factors, such as beliefs, say, about the relationship of semen to vitality, and perhaps memories of initiations in which phalluses, real and artistic, figured. What *we* have to do is to use our knowledge to try and discover what kind of thoughts, sensations and experience we must add to our own responses when we study the imagery of primitive peoples. First of all we need to realize how greatly the responses we are bringing to their arts are impoverished and diluted.

One way in which they are impoverished is in the tactile sphere so vitally important to all erotic and sexual art. Unfortunately it is extremely difficult for us in the West to understand this aspect of aesthetic meaning, largely because we live our lives in a culture dominated by graphic media (including film and TV) which devalue and inhibit tactile experiences. Our society does not encourage us to explore by touch either our environment or other human beings. We only experience a few items of our food by hand. In commercial stores and in museums, for valid reasons in both cases, we may not touch the things on display. Our notions of visual *chic* in furnishing and clothing are aimed solely at the eye; the hand is repelled by machined finishes. And to attempt human contacts with our hands can lead to social ostracism or even criminal prosecution. Only our pets will tolerate our fondling them; and our lovers. This defect of tactile experience is now quite widely recognized in psychological contexts. But as yet the full consequences for art have not been drawn.

The chief of these is that, whereas we are able to recognize visual forms as constituting a structured world of reality, we are unable to do the same for genuine tactile forms. Indeed few people are aware of the possible existence of an intelligible world of tactile reality at all. But there is such a world, with its own language of communication. This consists of sets of hand-grips and clasps, related to each other by intelligble transitions and sequences of shape which only reveal themselves completely to the moving hand exploring a pattern of grips. One of the most serious defects of our modern museum display methods is that they address themselves to the eye alone. For a very large part of the world's three-dimensional arts are actually addressed to the hand quite as much as – in some cases more than – to the eye. This is well known to be so with Japanese tea-ware pottery, for example; but less known with African and South Seas wooden sculptures. No one who has had the opportunity to hold and consciously to explore by hand the forms of such works can ever forget the sense of live communicating surface under his palms and fingers. The form-sequences of African and South Seas carved figures gain a complete extra dimension by being followed through by touch. Still more interesting, perhaps, is that the same is true even of many of the best Western sculptures originally made to be placed far out of reach in a church or on a façade. All sculptors have, in fact, worked to their own hands far more than the Western gallery goer can recognize or believe. He never has the chance to find out.

Primitive peoples have not laboured under these disabilities. They have a rich fund of emotive tactile memory and coordinated tactile experience upon which to draw. They can communicate by tactile symbolisms which gain their meaning from the way they refer to this fund, evoking echoes and responses from the whole sphere of touch. Many works of art which to us may seem visually either insignificant or pointlessly extravagant may yield a wealth of touch-forms to the hand. This kind of tactility, of course, has nothing to do with the generalized polished smoothness of nineteenth- and twentieth-century sculptured surfaces. In fact, roughnesses and abrupt transitions against which the hand comes to a stop, as well as hollows or channels whose true forms the eye cannot see but which the fingertips can appreciate, may be important components in an artistic touch-structure. Important elements in primitive art may aim, not at analogies in the world of visible forms, but at analogies in another world of experienced forms the eye has not ever seen, nor ever can; for they belong to the memory-repertoire of touch. Even the act of finger or stick-painting may embody tactile overtones the eye cannot perceive directly. And we must not imagine that primitive peoples have had the same incentives as we have had to make their arts measure up to (or even, as with modern 'abstraction', deliberately avoid measuring up to) a visual norm or erotic ideal. For when we grasp some form only with the eye, we may well be missing the principle tactile point, even though tactile forms can also have an incidental, visually appealing freshness. Certainly the visual and the tactile do complement each other. But there are many experiences, especially sexual experiences, which the eye is totally inadequate to render. Now that sexual photography, both still and moving, is quite readily available, its sensual inadequacy as an art is becoming easy to check.

It was hinted above that the one occasion in contemporary Western life when tactile intimacy is acceptable is between lovers. And this can make sexual art a particularly significant point of departure for a tactile aesthetics; this is the one region in which we Westerners may be able to call up sufficient touch-experiences to start bringing the touch-metaphors in primitive art alive. In fact there are quite a number of apparent stylizations in for example, the features of African masks, which have distinct sexual references especially *via* the sense of touch.

All of this should make it clear that the simple distinction often made between sophisticated erotic forms and primitive sexual art may not be well-founded, and that we must be prepared to accept that works of art had a directly stimulating quality for their makers which we cannot see in the photographs with which this book is illustrated; for the book itself is a product of that very graphic culture which helps to inhibit our world of touch. Its pictures are shadows of shadows.

Of course the races of primitive men are immensely diverse. Some of them have left sexual art; very few have left written documents. Much of our information about some of the most important traditions comes from hostile European sources. Concerning the magnificent erotic imagery of the Peruvian Chimu and Nazca peoples, for example, we have no information at all as to what it meant in its cultural context. So anyone who sets out to do more than merely describe physically a sexual art and the conditions in which it was founded is obliged to call upon comparisons and parallels from other cultures which are better known. In this book the aim is to interpret the meaning of each art, often by comparison with others, rather than simply to catalogue it.

Sexual matters have been either ignored or meagrely studied for many peoples; and because the ideas of many surviving primitive groups have been contaminated by Western ideas, a great deal more imaginative reconstructing by similarities and parallels is necessary than for many other aspects of primitive life.

If we are to understand any kind of primitive art we must have some conception of the way primitive thought operates. It works, like all thought, on a basis of analogy; but among primitive peoples these analogies are direct and concrete. Two or more things which are like each other can stand for each other; and once an analogy is entrenched, to refer to one is to refer to the other. We must never underrate the feeling–content of primitive symbols and the power of the emotions lying behind them. One thing certainly they never are: abstract. The things done in primitive ceremonial, the emblems made by primitive art, precede and probably condition formulated theoretical belief.

Our modern equipment of high-level conceptualized mental forms is, of course, a special cultural construction, evolved in the course of its relatively recent history by Western civilization. It is possible to study the evolution of symbolism in the early civilizations of Mesopotamia and Egypt. We find there that concrete things embody what we would call conceptual ideas. In Sumerian inscriptions what we mean by 'kingship' is represented by the principal concrete emblems held by kings shown in art, the measuring cord and rod. Concrete facts directly indicate the idea, to which they are the only key. The same is true among all primitive people. Concrete realities or their representations combined into metaphors convey complex ideas; by relating, in ritual and art, those concrete realities or their images, ideas are related. This is how ritual acts and how works of art gain their meaning.

The concrete realities may be objects like shells, blood and parts of the bodies of animals; these the ritual, mythology and art bring together in significant ways. The meaning they bear rests on deeply entrenched and compelling analogies which produce in combination a vivid form and density of meaning which words and concepts never can.

The point is that our own structure of mental abstractions is based upon an accepted group of first level analogies, which even precondition our perception. These analogies between concrete experiences may be quite different from those we have canonized in our own perceptual–conceptual and language structure. But they may be of the same kind as those our poets and artists deal with. Primitive peoples inhabit a spiritual region where objects, metaphors and ideas are interfused, and are not differentiated into concrete and abstract components as they are with us. Objects have meanings everyone understands; meanings can be expressed by adapting objects. Events have meanings; clear but otherwise indefinable meanings can be conveyed by controlling events. Among ourselves a degraded vestige of this way of thinking survives in our 'language of flowers' for various occasions, and our languages are full of dead and petrified metaphors.

Among primitive peoples an overwhelmingly important place in the scheme of concrete metaphor is played by sex, and all its processes. The duality can supply the basis for that essential dialectic of opposites upon which all thought-structures rest. Many kinds of life-meanings can be embodied in male and female attributes and activities. Deep-rooted, compelling analogies, such as that between the female

4

body and the earth, or between the male sperm and irrigation, can give rise to a wide variety of ritual and artistic expressions. And what Victorian writers like Frazer interpreted as 'sympathetic magic', i.e. immature and inadequate science and technology, can best be understood as expressions of underlying metaphors which our superstructure of abstraction and calculation has disqualified, though they may express undoubted analogical truths. Sexuality, with its functions and related images, serves primitive people as it can serve us, to symbolize thoughts beyond the reach of conscious rationalisation. It may be a source of imagery to deal with those mysterious and unintelligible experiences which we can only describe in such vague terms as 'origins', 'time' and 'life-energy'.

All primitive men share a number of beliefs or assumptions which are so deeply entrenched and so much taken for granted that they need never be explained or criticised. They may emerge, for example, in turns of phrase or in rituals which are explained by a seemingly casual story. The first and most fundamental is the belief in something we, because of our own cultural heritage, by analogy with the breath, call 'spirit'. This has produced a wide variety of expressions, some of which are, in our context, extremely important. The primitive man's notion of 'spirit' is most clearly seen by any person when someone he knows well, and loves, dies. A kind of equation forms itself in his mind:

This dead body $=$ the live body I know, minus X

$\therefore \quad$ X $\quad =$ the live body minus the dead body

It is that X upon which an immense quantity of human ingenuity has been spent, to define by analogy its nature and presence, both as alive in society, and as ghost. Sexuality has been the chief ingredient in this great web of symbolic speculation. For that X was recognized as emerging from the womb and 'growing' its body, and gaining with the grown body an identity of some sort with its group-kin. This identity was not, of course, purely personal. For the primitive notion of spirit does not imply our notion of the separate individual as the highest criterion of value, the ultimate construct. The X within the human being was conceived not as separate for each person, but as a kind of communal living stream in which individuals participated, and which they helped to perpetuate by their own sexual activity. This itself was something in which everyone had a stake, in one way or another. And we must always remember that the elements in the web of analogy woven around the X are never in the first place ideas or concepts in our sense of those words. Objective sexual symbols were themselves the primitive form of the 'idea' of spirit. Primitive men did not conceive an abstract idea of spirit and then cast around for suitable symbols, deliberately choosing sexual ones out of a number of possibilities. Long and slow evolution had crystallized into the symbols what we must call ideas, aggregating around the symbolic foci as unities in their minds. In experiencing the symbol they were aware of the idea not as a limited and defined concept but as an unbounded chain of experiences and memories. Without the symbolic form the idea could not exist. And the idea focussed on the symbol was a kind of amorphous accretion, not clearly defined by limiting borders which separated it from other ideas. It was inclusive, not exclusive. Its scope could extend wherever analogy led. Eroticism in the primitive context was thus a real and powerful force; its significance was never confined to individual and personal passion.

We must not believe that sexuality and the erotic for primitives were limited solely to the experience of intercourse and orgasm. In practice sexuality, and especially female sexuality, is functionally expressed in pregnancy, birth and suckling no less than in intercourse. It is the male, whose sexual function is completed in orgasm, who tends to focus his sexual imagery upon the act of intercourse, whereas the female sees sexuality and the erotic as embracing a far wider functional spectrum.

By a web of meaning working through analogy, the sexual image extends itself into the world of nature. 'Spirit' at the human level was naturally identified with that continuing vitality which manifests itself in sexual feeling and activity, pro-creation and birth, with the 'stuff' of inheritance and family identity. It was not limited to the sexual urge alone, though that was one of its major analogical com-ponents. By a wide variety of ritual and artistic symbolisms and structures its force was harnessed to the major human activities such as hunting, war and agriculture. But in addition, primitive men perceived and accepted a powerful analogy between the inner sexual forces which impel the human being and those which impel events of the natural world. They explored a wide variety of the implications in this analogy, especially in terms of those things which mattered most to them, in con-nection with food and the social structures which give them their sense of identity. The human phenomena of sex have often been used to symbolize and to take inward possession of the outer phenomena they symbolize by means of rituals in-volving sexual acts. This analogy will be found buried at the root of a vast range of religious and artistic expression, Indian, Chinese and Japanese, as well as our own. Virtually all the peoples mentioned in this book have operated in this way. This indicates why it is wrong to talk of ritual magic in terms of our ideas of simple causality. The primitive aim was, in some sense, to possess and identify with, not simply to control and dominate.

There is implicit in the term 'primitive' an evolutionary sense. We may never be able to fill the enormous gaps in our archaeological knowledge of human evolution, for we will certainly never find written documents from most vanished societies; but it is possible to trace the evolution of deep-laid human thoughts about sex and the erotic through art, particularly by comparing ancient arts with the arts and customs of modern primitives, belonging to similar stages of culture, whose cultures have been studied by modern scholars. In particular, the evolution of sexual art can be correlated with our maps of human distribution from palaeolithic times down to the present. We may, perhaps, never be able to assess the extent to which the common factors between customs and art among people living so far apart as South America, Melanesia and Scandinavia are due to either the migration of peoples or the migration of culture. Both must certainly be involved. There is a general picture of human and cultural evolution and distribution which is now fairly generally accepted. It can serve as a background, linking together the different manifestations of sexual art with which this book is able to deal into a kind of evolutionary tree, whose branches are represented by the different traditions of art.

Palaeolithic Age

The trunk of this tree is Palaeolithic, its root the hunting-culture of peoples using stone tools and implements of bone, antler and tusk. We believe that the human race emerged something like 2,000,000 years ago on this planet, and that the ancestors of modern man, *homo habilis*, emerged as the successful type using stone tools. By about 40,000 BC in Western Europe Neanderthal man, with his Mousterian culture and flake-tools struck from tortoise-cores, was burying his dead in shallow graves under the floor of his cave living quarters. Most important of all, he tied up the dead body in the crouching position, and sometimes either painted or sprinkled it with natural red ochre. The same custom among surviving primitives is explained as being a recreation of the foetal posture, the ochre a reference to life-blood. The conclusion is unavoidable. The dead man is being returned into the place from whence he came. Hence the earth is even at that early date in some wide and general sense analogised with the womb. The ritual acts testify to the power of the analogy. It would be going too far to attribute any specific 'beliefs' about birth, re-birth and death to these people, who never walked wholly upright. But the dead were also given their weapons; and the first hint of art occurs in the form of an artificial cup-shaped depression on the underside of one of the slabs used to cover a Mousterian burial in the Dordogne, at La Ferrassie. Such cups, in later art, seem to have a generically feminine significance. There can be no question that here we can see the earliest appearance of what became one of the deepest underlying themes of primitive art, the feminine sex of the earth, which is so often marked later on in more specific ways. It is possible that the Mousterians had learned their burial custom from more advanced Cro-magnon contemporaries who shared the sub-glacial environment with them, and who carried on developing the theme of the feminine earth after Neanderthal man had become extinct.

During the Lower Pleistocene period the last great ice-age was in progress, and the human race which lived purely by hunting was distributed along the lower fringes of the colossal northern ice-cap in what would have been a temperate climate. Principal remains come from China, North India, Iraq, Palestine, Spain, France, southern England and North Africa, as well as from further south in Africa and Java: a relatively restricted range for a not very numerous race. The characteristic art of this epoch mostly comes from Western Europe, though some important pieces come from southern Russia. The successive cultures which trans-mitted the stages of the art of the early hunters are as follows. First the Aurig-nacian culture (c. 34,000–30,000 BC) ranged probably from western Asia to the north and west into Europe, and east into Afghanistan. Its art is confined to simple geometric images on stone and bone objects, and to finger tracings on the wet clays of certain cave walls. From it evolved the Gravettian culture (30,000–25,000 BC) which extended from southern Russia to Spain. Probably inspired by the art of this culture, which includes the famous stone and mammoth-ivory 'Venuses', as well as very fine geometric symbols, the Solutrian (c. 20,000–15,000 BC) and Magdalenian (c. 15,000–10,000 BC) cave artists of France and Spain – whose normal expectation of life was, as the skeletons show, little more than twenty years – developed their magnificent style of animal art, the so-called 'hunter-style'. They probably initiated the herding of animals. After about 8000 BC, when the ice finally retreated, the herds of wild game vanished from the European–Russian plains, giving way to forest. The majority of the human race on the fertile land-masses of Europe and Asia adopted new modes of life revolving about food gathering and an agriculture based on Middle-eastern food-plants, supplemented by herding and hunting. It seems certain that it was during this stage that a new, masculine, sexual element was added to the ancient persisting female religious image, as we shall see.

The hunter cultures, however, did not die. They spread out along the fringes of the retreating ice to the north, and southward in Africa and Australia. In the North the ancestors of the Eskimo had entered America probably by about 20,000 BC. The Eskimo today live primarily from fishing and hunting especially seals, walrus and bear, though their art and ideas have been contaminated by medieval Christian contacts from Iceland and Greenland. The Eskimo were followed by the tall Red Indian races, who gradually populated the Americas from the north. The animal mime-dances of the Plains Indians, centred upon cabins painted with animals, and the rituals of the New Mexico Indians carried out in the presence of animal totems in a chamber, echo the Palaeolithic painted caves. The hunters and herdsmen of Siberia, such as the Yakuts and the Tunguz, the Ainu of north Japan and the Lapps of Scandinavia, preserve ancient hunter customs and art. In the south, hunters of Palaeolithic type survived until recently in the now extinct Tasmanians, whose equipment had Mousterian affinities. Probably between about 14,000 and 16,000 BC the aborigines entered Australia, perhaps intermarrying in the south with the Tasmanians; their progress may perhaps be traced in the Lower Pleistocene types of tool appearing along the southern coasts of Asia, through southeast Asia. Today their culture has some Magdalenian features, though Neolithic types have intruded from southeast Asia. They used rock and cave paintings, significant incised stones, and weapons resembling those depicted in caves of the Dordogne. They use a type of 'X-ray' representation in their painting which also appears widely distributed among the hunter populations. And they produce as well a variety of arts in impermanent materials, some showing sexual images, which are all consistent with their Palaeolithic culture, and help to suggest the kind of background of cult and ritual which may have inspired other ancient arts which have been destroyed by time. Another important surviving group of artistic hunter peoples is the Bushmen of southern Africa, who were driven by the nineteenth- and twentieth-century wars of extermination into the Kalahari desert, and there hunted like game by European settlers. Their magnificent ancient rock-paintings can no longer be interpreted properly by the survivors, though they are known to be religious, and associated with masked dances. One of the last men to be shot in the last war of extermination was a painter, with horn-tubes of colour, resembling known Aurignacian paint-tubes, slung around his waist. Painters and sculptors among them were initiated castes. It is interesting that human skeletons of both Eskimo and Bushmen kin-types have been found in European Palaeolithic graves.

About 6000 BC a new kind of rock-painting appeared in the western Mediterranean which was in a hunter animal style, but contained well conceived, elegant human figures in movement – earlier hunter human figures had been far less developed than the animals – derived from the Anatolian city art at e.g. Čatal Huyuk. This second hunter style spread from North Africa into the Sahara region – where it produced some fine sexual images – into Sicily, Spain and even into Australia.

From this point it will be possible later to pick up the outlines of those various branches of hunter eroticism and art which spring from the trunk of Palaeolithic culture. The development and spread of agriculture with Neolithic–Megalithic and Bronze-Age life-styles introduced a new dimension into sexual imagery which will also be discussed later. But it must be remembered that early layers of hunter imagery lie buried but active everywhere under the layers of more sophisticated imagery, which have been imposed upon them by evolving civilization and cultural exchange. When we discuss all this material we must be prepared to take enormous leaps through space and time, even into our own epoch; for the persistence and distribution of basically similar imagery is truly staggering.

The sexual-erotic imagery of the hunters emerges from that original equation of earth with womb. There is, perhaps, a danger of our taking this too casually, and failing to see how vital it is, since the cliché 'womb and tomb' has already passed into our popular and degraded psychological jargon. The mythologies which we shall discuss will make the importance of the equation clear. The experience of rock caves must have been imbued with this image for early man. But it is important to recall that neither the great Palaeolithic underground caverns of Spain and the Dordogne, nor the rock hollows painted by modern primitives, were used as tombs. They clearly had a special kind of sanctity which went further than an interest in merely human origin and end. Palaeolithic men seem to have been particularly modest about themselves. They certainly regarded the animals off whom they lived as more potent than they. Men might be born on, live and die on and then be buried under the floors of their rock shelters. But the great painted caverns, especially, testify to their interest in the earth as the sacred womb out of which emerged the kingdom of the animals, that realm of abundant life upon which the life of man itself depended. The painted halls in the great European caves are extraordinarily difficult for us to reach; to enter them must have been even more difficult for Palaeolithic men. Only after a formidable and exhausting journey, groping their way by the light of fat and mosswick lamps along endless narrow, clay-slippery corridors, where they might encounter at any moment the giant cave bear or lion, down chimneys or waterfalls, through vaulted chasms and tiny crevices barely passable by the human body, perhaps for three hours or more, could they reach the halls and corridors where the painting was done.

It is clear from the customs of modern primitives that the long winding magical journey to encounter sacred objects is an integral part of ceremonies meant to rehearse the pattern of Creation. And the Palaeolithic caverns were clearly intended as creative ritual centres. The visitors, probably for the same reason as modern Australian aborigines do on their sacred rocks, impressed their hand prints as testimony to each individual's right to enter, not simply because it 'identi-fied' him like a fingerprint, but probably because (as Professor R. B. Onians[1] and S. Giedon[2] have shown) the hand is to primitive people directly linked with a human's personal spirit. The entrance to Pech Merle, 'guarded' by two enormous sculptured female reliefs, actually looks like the entry to a womb. And the evidence all suggests that the caves were thought of as the creative centre of the fertile earth, the womb from which animal creation mysteriously sprang. The ritual journey to the spiritual source is a characteristic of the religious phenomenon still known today among the hunter peoples, called Shamanism.

The shaman is a specially gifted individual, sometimes also a magician, occasion-ally a chieftain, who undergoes catastrophic experiences, often including simulated death, loss of identity, change of sex; after long training and many initiations, by performing magical dance-figures and by virtue of magical equipment including animal heads and skins, or bird costumes and ritual drums, he is able to visit the world of spirits either for purely religious purposes or, for example, to discover how a disease is to be cured. Among the Siberian, Eskimo and southeast Asian peoples the shaman visits the spirit world only in trance. He may describe to his audience in a special voice his visionary experiences. But since many even more primitive hunters actually perform ritual journeys in the body, either alone or in ritual groups, to visit specially sacred spots, such as caves, rock-clusters, mountain tops or even man-made shrines, it is more than probable that the visionary journeys described by modern shamans follow patterns based upon actual ancient ritual journeys.

One of the classic documents on primitive religion, *Black Elk Speaks*[3], records the memories of an aged Dakota Sioux shaman, which go back to the period before the decimation and genocide of the Sioux after the Wounded Knee massacre of 1890. On one occasion on Harney Peak Black Elk called out a long prayer to the

'Grandfather, Great Spirit', which was recorded. Among the phrases in that long prayer was '. . . to the centre of the world you have taken me and showed me the goodness and the beauty and the strangeness of the greening earth, the only mother, and there the spirit shapes of things, as they should be, you have shown me and I have seen'. The whole amounts to an incredibly precise, long-range, traditional record of a journey, led by an ancestral representative, to a cave in Mother Earth filled with 'spirit shapes' – a most accurate term for the incised and painted animal forms in the Palaeolithic caves of Altamira, Lascaux, Les Trois Frères and Font de Gaume. Dr H. Kühn noted that 'haunted' rock pictures were mentioned in a play by Lope de Vega in 1598. They were re-discovered in 1909 in the Las Batuecas country. And when Dr Kühn visited the Valltorta paintings in 1923 the villagers would not go with him, for fear of spirits. Pope Calixtus III (1455–58), who came from Valencia, pontifically forbade religious rites which were still being celebrated in his day in a Spanish cave decorated with pictures of horses.[4] It is thus not at all fanciful to see the way in which the incised reliefs and paintings appear on the walls of the great caves, often defining the natural humps and hollows of the mother-rock into animal forms, as an imaginative reading of the propagation of animal spirits within the earth-womb itself, by the 'blistering' or 'bleeding off' of spirit shapes from inward membranes of the earth, very much as beings are propagated, but outwards, from the skin of the Maori creator-god Tangaroa (who may, incidentally, retain vestiges of a pre-Palaeolithic, pre-sexual symbolism). Such art, to its makers, must have been a profoundly creative spiritual activity. This idea is supported by other evidence which we must be careful not to interpret in terms of our own narrow, abstract, economic concept of cause and effect. The Mandan Indians, for example, were pleased to see the paintings George Catlin did, because 'they brought the bisons'. The Australian Karadjeri retouched the cave paintings in their sacred rock-chambers seasonally, to help the reproduction of the animals. The Cora Indians of Mexico put clay images of animals in their caves for similar reasons; there is a pair of coupling bison in the Dordogne's Tuc d'Audoubert cave. But the Karadjeri went further. They retouched paintings in their Gallery of the Female Rainbow Snake specifically to cause spirit children to be found by fathers and incarnated by mothers. Retouching, also practised in the European Palaeolithic caves, was believed by these West Australians to preserve the continuity of power flowing from the ancient mythical pictures. This procedure is perhaps, from the symbolic point of view, far more satisfactory than the repeated re-making of ritual paintings on impermanent materials, such as bark or cloth, practised by many primitive peoples. There can be little doubt that hunter rock-paintings were meant not only to be looked at, but to be repeatedly retraced as part of an active ritual, which involved what can only be called a mystical communion between the men and the course of animal life which nourished them. For the cave pictures represent mainly game beasts, rather than predators.

Into this context the sexual imagery of the Palaeolithic caves must be set. Far the greater part of this is female. And it is often said that people in a Palaeolithic stage of culture are not aware of the fact of physical paternity; that the women have continuous sexual relations as a matter of course, and so their periodic pregnancies are not attributed to paternal insemination. This is sometimes held to be the reason for the preponderance of female imagery in Palaeolithic art. It may be that certain Australian aborigines do not recognize paternity. In fact, however, there is abundant evidence that ancient Palaeolithic people saw a connection, but not in the heavily masculine-oriented conceptual cause-and-effect way in which we see it. There are plenty of male sexual symbols in the great caves; and plenty of hunter peoples know the facts of generation. But they do not see them isolated in the same scientific sequence, with the heavy value-weighting on masculine seed, as we do. Instead they recognize propagation as essentially a feminine activity, aided and abetted in a variety of different ways by the male with his own genitals – which, after all, were always familiar visitors to the depths of the feminine body. Since in the caves themselves the overwhelming analogy is between womb and earth, it is natural that the feminine predominates; and most of the surviving masculine emblems are portable, made of antler or bone. They can in fact be most beautiful and elaborate. The organs of both sexes are drawn on the magical costumes of some Siberian hunter shamans, and on their ritual drums, indicating that sexual images, both male and female, were felt to convey active spiritual force, producing ecstasy not merely in our degraded meaning of that word, but in its original sense of 'standing outside the body', i.e. in the spiritual realm.

If, however, Palaeolithic peoples did not isolate in their idea of generation the semen as alone responsible for fertility – which seems most probable – they may well have identified the male contribution to the propagation of offspring as having to do with the active friction of the male organ inside the female. There is a good deal of evidence to suggest that this was so, both in anthropological reports and, for example, in an ancient Sanskrit text which analogizes conception with the fire produced by a hardwood rubbing-stick working in the slot of a softwood stick. A similar image, on a broader scale, is illustrated by a northwest Australian hunter custom first recorded in the mid-nineteenth century. The men of the tribe performed a ritual dance around a trench dug in the ground and 'decorated' with bushes. They at first held their spears up between their legs like phalli, and later they stabbed them repeatedly and vigorously into the trench. This, unfortunately, is all the record tells. Incidentally, such a notion of what the male contributes to generation adds a dimension of movement to primitive sexual symbolism which sophisticated eroticism might envy. And it seems clear that the essence of the masculine symbolism is not merely subordinated to the birth-female complex, but involves sexuality as a whole with all its proper overtones of pleasure and ecstasy. It is legitimate to speculate that identification of the semen as the only true male contribution to generation is analogically, and possibly hence historically, connected with the development of crop cultivation and the sowing of seed. This analogy will be discussed later.

Before going on to discuss Palaeolithic art in detail there is one complex point that must be made. It applies to all primitive arts; but it must be made especially in connection with those arts for which we have no documentation or records. It is that, whereas nowadays we tend to see visual art as a separate and isolated activity, with a line of significance all its own, each primitive art is merely one single aspect which would have been combined with others into a thoroughgoing life-activity manifesting itself in many ways: through rituals involving, for example, blood letting and smearing, through dances that mark out patterns in space, through postures and gestures, cries and songs, stories and mime, stylized acts of all kinds like laying on hands, exchanging food and gifts, as well as through visual-plastic forms. In fact any object we might think of primarily as a work of art may have been only one element in a complex activity involving many of the things listed above. Where only an impressive art in permanent materials has survived, as in the great caves, we could easily be misled into believing that this particular art was in some sense 'primary' in its culture. There may be a few traces of the rest of the range of symbolic activity to which the pictures contributed, such as the winding traces of dancing feet impressed in the clay of the Pyrenean cave Tuc d'Audoubert, but the customs of modern primitives make it quite clear that even the most impressive visual arts are only a part, never the whole, of any symbolic structure. In addition we have to remember that there are types of possible symbolism other than pure form incorporated into primitive arts. There may have been a symbolism in the material itself, in the substances in which it was executed, in things which were originally added to it or smeared onto it, such as, in particular, blood or excreta human and animal, semen, fat, feathers or bodily organs, including the sexual organs. In all modern primitive cultures one finds these substances used to convey complex expressions of meaning by direct action; as, for example, when a blood-smeared churinga is thrust between the legs of a clay-painted boy initiate at a certain stage in an Australian aboriginal ceremony. Most such substances reflect, in one symbolic way or another, the overriding concern of all primitive societies with vitality, energy and active growth, as will appear. Vivid sexual desire, and all evidences of its presence and fulfilment, do precisely that. For primitives in general believe that the physical world is full of signs addressed to men, to remind them of their spiritual roots. These signs they continually actualize and rehearse, to keep alive their sense of their meaning. They exalt the sense of life, and elaborate a mystery cult to conserve and renew it, thus giving the individual a high sense of his worth, both in the human sexual flesh and in the spiritual flux. The terms in which this complex notion is crystallized are regarded as so direct and obvious that they need no argument to justify them. The analogies that underly them are felt as entirely positive.

Everyone who discusses Palaeolithic sexual imagery must be profoundly indebted to S. Giedon, whose magnificent book *The Eternal Present*[2] has become a classic. Here what we can do is to add a superstructure of speculation and opinion to his ideas which will connect his discoveries with the innumerable later manifestations in art of deep-laid sexual symbolism.

Perhaps the most primitive, in the evolutionary sense, and the most obscure in meaning of all the female sexual emblems are the cup-shaped hollows which appear in so many Palaeolithic contexts, and the associated ring-holes made by pairs of addorsed cup-holes in opposite sides of a flat slab. Both cup and hole are to us so common and obvious that it is hard for us to imagine such simple things as having a symbolic significance. But to Palaeolithic man, who had no practical but only a symbolic reason for making them, they certainly did. To begin with, they were difficult to cut, taking a lot of focussed effort, and they were placed in such significant positions that their meaning is fairly clear. Their most obvious characteristic is that they are the result of long-sustained boring activity with stone points. The chief analogue in primitive human experience, and that a most potent one, with such activity is the sexual act. In recent times in India visitors to many ancient shrines used to have symbolic intercourse with stone-cut female deities by thrusting their fingers into deep touchholes, worn by generations of finger-thrusters, at the deities' sexual centres.

The relatively small bored-through slabs, like those in the Aurignacian Labatut, Abri Cellier, La Quina and Cap Blanc caves may well be the ancestors of the great Menetol ring megalith in Cornwall, England, and the many goddess-emblem ring-stones in India and elsewhere. The large examples were used by primitives in rebirth rituals, when the person to be reborn crawled or was dragged through the hole. The custom survived as a 'superstition' into modern times both in Brittany and Cornwall. 'Scientific' archaeologists sometimes resist any suggestion that the portholes in the many 'porthole cyst' tombs at megalithic sites around the southern coasts of Asia may have a rebirth significance. This, however, is very much an open question. For there is a great deal of evidence suggesting a Neolithic–Megalithic tomb–womb association, as will appear. Cup-hollows are found on many sacred objects and places of all the Stone Ages, including the underside of grave-slabs, on the vulva-like rock-cleft in La Pasiega cave, Santander, and arranged in a row leading to the male organ of an animal incised on a stone slab from La Ferrassie cave, Dordogne. Solid evidence would be needed to dispose of the powerful underlying sexual–symbolic suggestions of the custom, even though we have no indications as to the precise circumstances in which the hollows were bored.

This is especially so in view of the enormous number of undoubted female vulva-symbols found in profusion in the Palaeolithic caves and on countless works of primitive art. At Aurignacian La Ferrassie, for example, unequivocal vulvas were incised onto a rock over already bored cup-hollows. Both vulvas and cups appear on and around the bodies of animals in many caves. It is generally taken for granted by Western scholars, who belong to a male-dominated society, that the great caves were made by and for male hunters as part of their killing-magic. But it is by no means impossible, in view of the caves' preponderantly female imagery and of the importance of female rituals among the less culturally contaminated aborigines of Australia, that cave rituals formed part of what Australian anthropologists have referred to as 'women's secret life-ritual'. This may help to explain both the importance of the female role in witchcraft survivals of Palaeolithic cults, and the customary adopting of female costume, life and sexual role by male shamans among certain recent hunter peoples. It would make sense to recognize that the vulvas may designate female ritual acts, performed by female hierophants who operated in the caves. But, of course, there can be no certainty; and it is possible to conceive some ways in which the vulvas could be male ritual. For it is true that male symbols are also found in a few of the caves. One should never forget the enormous stretches of time the caves remained in use – often more than 10,000 years at least – and perhaps allow for variations in ritual, whilst admitting that male symbols could indeed have a role in female ceremonials.

The vulva-symbols incised and painted in the caves follow a number of canonical patterns, nearly all of which can be demonstrated truly to signify vulvas by the fact that they remained in use into early historical times to represent the vulva at the right place on a figure representing a female. A. Leroi Gourhan has published a small key to the patterns.[5] Some of the examples actually incised on the rock walls resemble extraordinarily closely vulva-symbols still identified and reverenced as such today in India and Africa. Clearly they were connected in some special way with rituals for reinforcing fertility in the generic sense, for urging the animal spirit-shapes to multiply and come. It is from the vulva that the live child emerges, as well as the menstrual blood which so many primitive peoples regard as highly powerful and dangerous, and which some still hold to be the substance out of which the foetus congeals in the womb. It is well known that, for example, the Australian aborigines regard the pits from which they derive their 'magical' red ochre as menstrual blood-deposits laid down by legendary Kangaroo women. Bushmen and Hottentots have similar beliefs.[6] Among others, the vulva symbols in El Castillo cave, Santander, are painted in red ochre.

Perhaps the most important vulva-symbol is the downward facing triangle, with either a vertical cleft bisecting the lower angle thus ▽ or a loop opening it thus ▽. It may also appear the other way up. Occasionally the loop is developed as a bored cup-hollow. This also happens on some important works of South American hunter art made by the Chimane Indians in Bolivia in relatively recent times. On the height of a mountain pass, close to a source of rock salt, which for these Indians symbolizes an essential life-substance related to procreation, a number of rocks were found deeply incised with numerous precisely similar vulvas, with some phallic emblems, and a few crude human figures at the summits of the rocks. The ancestors of the Chimane, when collecting salt, wore masks and feathers, carried their whirlers (bull-roarers), and danced on this spot; their ceremonies are not unlike ceremonies of Australian aboriginal totem-groups. There can be little doubt that these rocks were once regarded as the mystical source of the Chimane's incarnate tribal spirits. They form a particularly interesting link in the early development of sexually symbolic Neolithic–Megalithic ancestor figures, which are often mistaken by Western anthropologists for purely personal memorials.

One especially interesting sculpture was found in La Ferrassie cave; a roughly carved beast-head, not identifiable as any particular animal, and never forming part of a complete stone sculpture. On its underside was an incised vulva. Its meaning is impossible to decipher, but can only be guessed at. Its closest analogue is in certain ancient stone heads of fantastic animals, complete in themselves, found on the Columbia river in western Canada, which the present day Indian hunters who live there cannot explain. All that can be said of these strange objects is that they suggest an early appearance of that association between the head and sexual vitality which becomes so important in later sexual imagery.

Another major type of female emblem involves an extra layer of metaphor. The earlier sexual images all attribute analogically, through their reference to sexuality, the faculty of 'generation' to the rock on which they are worked. The unconceptualized meaning they suggest derives from their makers' own inner experience of sexuality being transferred and attached to the rock-site, chosen out of all others to represent the creative womb in the body of the earth. There were, so to speak, three components to the metaphor: 1 sign; 2 selected rock-site; 3 unifying common form of sexual experience in maker and beholder.

In the other major but rare type of Palaeolithic female emblem the symbolism becomes at once more complex and more abstract, and introduces a constant theme in human symbolism which has lasted down to the present day. It is the representation of the shell as emblem of the vulva. By inserting an extra component in the series of analogues, the reference to sexuality becomes less direct and crude, becomes, in fact, a more complex metaphor and hence indicates a more refined notion. There is one extremely important example of this, not on rock but on a Magdalenian fragment of bone from Arudy in the Basses Pyrénées, incised with the design of a shaggy horse's head, its tongue extended and licking a curvilinear symbol. That this symbol is indeed a shell is borne out by an extraordinary coincidence. Virtually the same design, save that the head is a stag's and there are two, not one, unmistakable shells, is cut in relief on the girdle-flap of a colossal rough image of the ithyphallic god Min from predynastic Egypt (c. 4500 BC) in Oxford. This image is even pecked all over with cup-hollows. Another similar Min image in Oxford also has a phallic emblem with a single shell on its girdle-flap. The Arudy shell is smooth, whereas the Min shells are spirate. But shells of all kinds are recognized as vulva-symbols virtually the world over, especially those univalves with deeply involuted pinkish mouths, such as certain varieties of *murex*. The cowrie, which can be either large or small, is far and away the commonest. At the sexual centre of a Japanese Neolithic Jomon figure (c. third–second millennia BC), for example, a cowrie is clearly delineated in the terracotta. At the present day, cowries are used in the clay sculpture of West Africa to indicate the vulva as well as the eyes. Eye-shapes, when schematically rendered, may also be used to symbolize the vulva. In many high societies the shell is the emblem of goddesses of love and fertility; and even bivalves have taken on this symbolism, e.g. Aphrodite's scallop, or the Japanese awabi. This extra poetic layer of symbolism interposed in the metaphoric series must signify that not the *actual* vulva is meant but the *notional* vulva, i.e. not a human but a spiritual reference. At least some of the Stone-Age peoples, particularly those who knew the sea, must also have recognized that shells came from the sea. And this recognition must have added to the compound image some such further dimension as 'maternal waters'.

Another aspect of feminine traditional symbolism appears first in the Palaeolithic caves – the breast, source of nourishment. Only one certain Aurignacian case is known; but that is so striking that it must authenticate other less certain examples. In the part of Pech Merle called Le Combel is a low chamber whose roof is garlanded with stalagmites resembling female breasts, even to the nipples, and whose back wall is split by a vulva-like crevice painted with red discs. The breasts were painted in Palaeolothic times; and beneath them a complex of animals was also painted – a lioness with a rhinoceros and three antelopes. This must certainly have been some kind of fertility sanctuary deep in the cave, not only connected with generation, but also with the supernatural source of nourishment. Outside, on the wall of the approach corridor, a single stalagmite shaped like a breast is surrounded by a cluster of red dots, no doubt an access signal at the approach to the main shrine. This image of a multiplicity of breasts is also specifically identified in the eroded roof-forms of the Mala women's caves at Ayets rock in central Australia, that colossal mountain monolith with such a deeply numinous significance to the aborigines. It also appears in later symbolism, on, for example, Bronze-Age 'ceremonial beakers' from Sialk in Iran, on Iron-Age bowls from western Europe and on supposedly ceremonial wares from Nazca in Peru. As an irrational and archaic attribute it appears on one or two otherwise anthropomorphic Hellenistic images of a mother-goddess sometimes identified as Artemis or 'Diana of the Ephesians', whose upper bodies effloresce into ranks of fruit-like breasts, while animal shapes spring from the hips and thighs. These sculptures must embody echoes of that same ancient Mother of the Animals whom we can first identify in Pech Merle, and who is not herself an animal – these are not animal udders – but a humanized analogue of the earth. The animal part of the theme survived in bronze fountains of the Byzantine period, which appear as pillar-like spouts from which animals spring. The addorsed animal busts on the pillars of Persepolis may have a similar symbolic background. For in pre-Classical symbolism, e.g. on Cretan seals or on the lion gate of Mycenae, the pillar often serves as an alternative emblem for the figure of a goddess identified explicitly as Mistress of the Animals.[7] The breast element has, perhaps, an even more interesting inheritance into and beyond the Neolithic and Bronze Ages. For it seems indisputable that pottery food-vessels the Neolithic world over have been either obviously or obliquely interpreted as having an analogical affinity with the human breast. Many a cup is actually shaped as a breast, or a bowl adorned with vestigial nipples; the inflection in the shape of others also has an unequivocal feminine significance. It has long been recognized, as it still is today in countries with an advanced ceramic culture, that even where surface ornament is not in itself composed of suggestive female symbols (as it so often is), the 'potter's space' a pot contains is in some potent but undefined way related to the female 'receptive', 'nourishing' or 'creative'.[8] Magical cups and cauldrons feature as divine feminine vessels in many legends.

The last ancient manifestations of feminine symbolism we have to consider are perhaps the most important, the actual images of women – or rather of 'woman'; for they are never individualized. There are a few carved in caverns. Only two, from Magdalenian times, are directly associated with caves of any labyrinthine depths; these two are on either side of the vagina-like entrance to the inner chamber of La Madeleine (Tarn) in France. Like the fine Magdalenian sculptures of animals their forms are developed out of the slightly undulating natural protuberances of the rock by very light incisions. Each of them, however, has a very emphatic pubic triangle. They recline on one elbow, their breasts drooping naturally. Their heads are stylized into the same single rounded mass, pointed at the back, curved at the front, used to represent the generalized volume of hair and face on most of the other Palaeolithic images. Their figures are so lightly outlined that it is difficult to say much about them save that they are broad, fat and short-legged; and that they must in some way personify the power of the sanctuary which they announce, addressing the entering visitor with slightly parted legs. Although they are not aggressively sexual, they may be remote ancestors of the many overtly sexual images found at many later sanctuaries in India and Africa, and of the Sheelagh-na-gigs in Great Britain.

The most famous rock relief of 'woman' comes from a rock-shelter at Laussel, now in a museum at Bordeaux. She was carved originally on a block overhanging a sanctuary, and was probably Solutrian in date (46 cm tall). She had been coloured red, the colour of power and life. Once she hung suspended, curved forward, belly out, as if standing in space, her head turned off to our left towards her own right hand which holds a buffalo horn aloft. Her bulbous breasts, belly, hips and thighs, beautifully delineated, bulge with fat. Her own left hand rests on her belly. Her pubic triangle is emphasized. There can be no doubt at all that her attributes are from beginning to end sexual; what their meaning is will emerge in due course. Incidentally, there are at least two other similar horn-holding images, less good, on the undersides of fallen slabs from other sites. What they signify can be interpreted as an interesting and important part of the animal fertility cult. We have two clues which taken together are highly suggestive, if not absolutely conclusive. The first is the virtually universal primitive conception of the horn, outward manifestation of animal 'head stuff', as an instrument of superhuman power. The second is an African rock-drawing reproduced by Frobenius,[9] illustrating an archer shooting at animals (including an ostrich). He is connected by a line of magic running from his genitals to those of woman whose arms are upraised. The Laussel Venus is thus, most probably, a monumental record of the power of the female, embodied in the rock sanctuary as 'Mistress of the Beasts', through mystic coupling with whom comes the hunting success upon which the whole existence of the hunters depended.

There is one other enigmatic 'fat-female' relief about which archaeologists have speculated inconclusively. It is a shallow incision on a slab, enclosed in an oval frame, also preserved in Bordeaux, and hence probably from some nearby site. Its upper part represents a symmetrical fat woman, her hands laid out along her sides. The lower part, however, is damaged and difficult to decipher. The bulbous thighs seem to terminate in rounded curves, beneath and between which appears a shadowy largish bust, head down. A suggestion that this represents the act of birth, the newly born being more faintly illustrated than the mother, has often been questioned. It certainly may represent birth of some kind, perhaps even a ritual rebirth; for the strange treatment of the thighs is meant to show them as ending with fat, curved knees turned back up and out, without benefit of fore-shortening. It could, however, also represent a symbolic sexual union, and thus be related to a number of small apparently bisexual figurines combining emblems of penis, vulva and buttocks from Trasimeno (Italy), Weinberg Caverns (Bavaria), the Jordan Valley, and Pembrokeshire (Wales). This enigmatic image could be one of the most significant of all the 'fat-female' images of Palaeolithic times.

Complementing these images is the other Palaeolithic group consisting of miniature figures in the full-round, carved in stone and mammoth ivory, from many sites in Europe and Russia. They are all extremely small, mostly under eight centimetres, though one is twenty-two centimetres, and it is almost certain that they were in some sense amulets, though only one of them is actually pierced; many people, however, wear their amulets tied up in skin bags. And, of course, to all primitives amulets are reservoirs of supernatural power, with a far greater and more deep-seated significance than we allow if we merely call them 'charms'. Some of the female amulets may have had another function as well, as we shall see.

The most complete and familiar of these Venus amulets is the stone Willendorf Venus, reproduced in almost every book on early art-history. It was dug from a late Aurignacian stratum in Austria and is about six centimetres high, superbly executed in the complete full-round. Like all these amulets it fits beautifully into the hand, providing vivid tactile sensations. It is truly a masterpiece, in part because it is thoroughly conceived from every point of view, whereas most of the other amulets are not. The Willendorf Venus probably shows a complete version of a formal symbolism of the feminine which, being executed time and time again in perishable materials, survived virtually into modern times. She is outstandingly broad for her height. Her hair obliterates her face. Her little arms are folded over her massive pendulous breasts – a trait perpetuated in the fat female terracottas of pre-dynastic Egypt and in the stone images of Neolithic northern Syria. Her thighs are fat, with the pubic triangle marked between them. But the whole figure is dominated by a kind of continuous pannier of fat enveloping hips, belly and buttocks. A less finely worked but similar piece was found at Gargarino in Russia.

The fine mammoth-ivory Venus of Lespugue (France) lengthens the bust, thinning it from front to back, stylizing the vastly exaggerated breast, belly and hip-buttock forms into enormous bulbs. Many other Palaeolithic figurines develop and stylize attributes which in these figures are found combined. Broadly speaking, they pick either upon the side profile or the front profile to emphasize. Where the side profile is picked upon, the figures develop an enormous sideways protuberance of all those body characteristics identified with femininity whose symbolism is so important. The beautiful 'La Poire' of Brassempouy (Mandes) is perhaps the most 'realistic'. That of Sirenil (Dordogne) is more stylized. But those of Savignano (Modena) and Grimaldi (Menton), narrowed from the front view, show in profile an immense protuberance of breast, belly and especially buttock. Of the many stylized amulets following this pattern, like that of Petersfels (Baden: the pierced example), it is the element signifying an immense protruding pile of fat over the buttocks which comes to dominate the whole profile. This phenomenon in living humans is called steatopygy. It has given rise to some unsatisfactory speculation, and was until recently regarded as a highly desirable quality among large numbers of primitive peoples, including Hottentots and Bushmen, whereas a more generalized but also steatopygous bulk was required of Arab, Jewish and some West African women, as well as Hawaiian princesses.[10] From the statements of these peoples, and from philological hints contained in the languages of Europe, it is clear that these piles of fat were analogized with vital force or energy; and this was why it was so desirable. The fat of animals was eaten for the purpose of refreshing energy, and offered to the gods as their due. There was, it seems, a direct imaginative association between the generative vitality, which was expressed in bulk of fat, and sexual charm; the public value of fertility and the private value of sexual enjoyment were not separated. Indeed the buttocks have been regarded by many peoples as the seat of sexual potency in both men and women. Vestiges of this feeling survive in the eroticisms of some high societies, notably medieval India and Baroque Europe. In the Venus amulets the preternatural development of the buttocks and hips enveloping the generative region, as well as the protruding belly and nourishing breasts, added up to a massive emblem in human terms of the same kind of supernatural potency as the maternal caves expressed. This is why any argument as to whether these images are erotic or religious is beside the point. They are both. In the primitive context desire was not separated from power.

The traditional Venus types based upon the stylized frontal outline were those which eventually produced the Neolithic- and Bronze-Age waisted icons, familiar examples of which reproduced in many art-books are the Cycladic violin-shaped flat idols, some marked on one face with breasts and/or pubic triangle. From many places in the middle East and Bronze-Age India (Mohenjo Daro) come little terracottas, flat but hand-modelled, often with elaborately pinched-up stylized faces and hair, small breasts and pubic triangles; they may be given added projecting buttocks. Even in Assyria such small terracotta 'mother goddess' figurines were being mass-produced in the sixth century BC from moulds, hands squeezing their breasts and large pubic triangles emphatically marked. These are certainly sexual, but perhaps were not meant to be stimulating. There can, however, be no doubt that the superb fat ladies of Anatolian Hacilar, some of whom nurse children, and those from Malta, belonging to an early Neolithic culture, certainly preserve a deep sexual–symbolic impetus from far earlier times.

At the important early Anatolian settlement of Čatal Huyuk images dating from the millennium between 6500 and 5500 BC preserve and develop the image of the Palaeolithic fat Venus figure, casting a light of meaning back onto them. One represents a large, in baked clay, woman, vastly fat, squatting between two feline animals, giving birth. A greenish stone relief from the same site represents two such fat Venuses, one nursing a child, another being embraced by a male figure. A small Natufian sculpture in stone of the ninth millennium BC represents a couple in intercourse, and a Yarmukian clay head from Sha'ar 'Ha Golan on the Yarmuk (c. 5800 BC) illustrates a stage during the goddess's transition from Mother of Beasts to more generically Fertile Mother, which took place during the early stages in the evolution of agriculture. The crude, lumpy chalk figure found in the Neolithic flint mines at Grimes Graves, Norfolk, with its legs turned back up and its deep cleft vulva, may well be a gross and barbarous descendant of the same type. There is a large group of terracottas of similar date, notably those from Strelice, Moravia (fifth millennium BC), of extremely steatopygous female figures, whose heads and necks are worked as smooth phalli, some nine centimetres long. It seems quite probable – though the more genteel archaeologist may rebel at the suggestion – that the heads of these figures were actually inserted into the vulvas of women or girls in the course of initiations, for example, to 'incorporate' them with the image of the Fertile Mother. Comparable ritual acts are known from, among other regions, Africa and aboriginal India.

Among the rock-pictures from the Sahara belonging probably to the last hunter epoch, and including many superb human figures, there are a number of representations of sexual intercourse. These pictures would probably have been connected with rituals and stories similar to those collected from the aboriginals of Australia. In them we catch glimpses of the kind of activities which must have been carried out as part of the diversified expression of underlying currents of sexual thought. Certain of the images can be connected with specific surviving African customs; but perhaps the most important of the old pictures are those which represent sexual intercourse either in the presence of animals or as hunters return with prey. One of them has been mentioned already, that in which hunter and woman are joined at the genitals by a line of magic. Female figures not in intercourse but attending at the scene have cup-hollows at their sexual centre. They testify at least to some general connection between hunting success and intercourse.

There is, however, another group of most significant pictures of the sexual act at Ti-n-Lalan, Fezzan. Human figures wearing animal masks and endowed with immense phalli – one with a large belly – are represented in intercourse with females who wear elaborate ornaments. These and similar pictures in Tanzania have been connected with surviving rituals of defloration preserved among modern Africans, when the priest-king ritually deflowers girls before marriage. They may also relate to legends such as that told by the Fon of Dahomey, that they were sprung from a woman fertilized by a panther. Other peoples have similar human–animal ancestral legends. Such legends and pictures certainly belong in a somewhat different context from the Palaeolithic manifestation, and played a vital part in shaping later sexual mythology. Actual women looked on as incarnations of the Mistress of the Beasts may well have acted out with animals, or their masked and skin-draped human representatives, in the most ancient times, the ritual intercourse which actualized the mythic creation of the beasts. There are suggestions in many mythologies that such impersonation was indeed the case, the legends bearing out the significance of our images. And many modern primitives have dances in which the couplings of animals are acted through. The Saharan paintings cast an interesting light upon the possible significance of the famous masked and skinned male figures in the Palaeolithic caves, which have often been called shamans. For among the hunter peoples of Siberia a few surviving rituals preserve an extremely detailed sexual imagery describing the masculine shaman coupling ecstatically with a spirit wife or wives, who are representatives of the Great Mother of the Animals: thus persuaded, She grants the shaman's people the privilege of hunting and eating Her beasts. Among other Siberian peoples (e.g. the Kumandin) a horse-sacrifice is accompanied by a performance by masked men wearing huge wooden phalli, recalling a similar ritual reported by Catlin among the Mandan Indians. One point emerges from the many such performances recorded: that for the ecstatic rite to be magically effective the sexual feelings of all the participants must be stirred as powerfully as possible, and harnessed to the supernatural goal.

There are a number of animal-masked human figures in Palaeolithic caves. The most famous is painted in Les Trois Frères cavern: a human figure with broad animal belly, clad in an animal skin and wearing antlers, crouches, his genitals dangling, advancing behind two bison whose female genitals are emphatically drawn in. His costume is virtually identical (save for the dangling genitals) with that of a Siberian Tunguz shaman published in an engraving by Witsen in 1705. Also in Trois Frères is an ithyphallic bison with human legs; in Lascaux is the 'toppling' ithyphallic bird-headed human figure with a bird emblem by him. In the Abri Mère (Dordogne) are several small bison-men. There are also in the great caves a number of uncertainly drawn and damaged representations of half-human, half-animal creatures crouched behind and over each other so as to suggest the sexual mounting of animals. One is a bone engraving from the Abri Murat (Lot). In Pech Merle is a finger-drawing in clay of a woman crouched in a sexually receptive posture beneath animal-like lines. Incised on a bone plaque from the Magdalenian

Laugerie Basse a pregnant female lies on her back beneath a stag. Her legs are animal, her heavy body human. A number of strange beings have beast-like heads closely resembling the isolated stone head from La Ferrassie mentioned above, which is incised with a vulva. Examples are incised on the rock wall at Les Combarelles, others engraved on a pebble from La Madeleine. One, incised on a bone from La Madeleine, is ithyphallic. Distant in time and place, but probably semantically connected, is the bull-headed dancer illustrated on a seal from Harappa in India (*c*. 2000 BC), a related statuette having been ithyphallic.

Taken all together these images offer much material for speculation. We must remember that they come from periods of activity scattered over many thousands of years. But it is more than probable that they refer to ceremonies which took place originally in 'spirit' caves when the coupling of animals was in some way re-enacted by their human representatives. Comparable modern material will be discussed later on. But before continuing further with this line of thought some additional facts must be brought in.

As has been mentioned, it may be that Palaeolithic men did not identify a physical nucleus of paternity in semen. It seems, however, impossible that they were not aware of some relationship between the active coupling and the breeding of animals. This is borne out by the magnificent pair of bison, the male mounting the female, modelled in clay on a rock in the Tuc d'Audoubert (Ariège). It is even more forcibly borne out by the numerous representations of phalli from other caves. One phallic stalactite is in Le Combel, Pech Merle, pitted with cup-hollows and worn smooth by some kind of ritual attentions. There are others. But perhaps more interesting are the many phallic antlers and bones – the so-called *batons de commandement*. Horns, as we have mentioned, are connected in basic physiological mythology with spiritual-sexual potency. Today in China both rhino horn and deer antler are still regarded as aphrodisiacs. It is not at all improbable that antlers and horns, those impressive biological signals springing from the head of beasts such as elk, caribou, bison or buffalo, should have become identified with power in general, a human paradigm of which is sexual potency. Evidence will be adduced to show that in Neolithic and Bronze Age Greece and Europe horns were identified symbolically with a sexual substance 'stored' in the head, from which reservoir of sexual potency was ejaculated the semen. To judge from the surviving Palaeolithic designs men must have equated horns with potency, though maybe not with semen. If, however, one imagines the horn 'batons' being employed as symbolic dildos, perhaps ritually inserted in the female genitals, a new symbolic dimension appears.

Some Palaeolithic horn staves are shaped in the likeness of the male organ, including the testicles. One comes from Le Placard (Charente). From the Gorge d'Enfer (Dordogne) comes the wide, forked end of an antler stave each of whose branches is carefully incised on one side with a view of the phallus from above, on the other a view from below complete with testicles and glans, so as to convert them into a pair of phalli. From Bruniquel (Tarn et Garonne) come two undulant antler staves, their tips elaborately modelled as the glans. One is engraved on one side with fishes with forked tails, on the opposite side with vulva symbols. The other is deeply incised with a strange 'split' pattern that might, conceivably, represent a penis with the urethra opened by subincision – a custom still prevailing among certain Australian aborigines as a special high-grade and trans-sexual initiation rite. On a staff from La Madeleine (Dordogne) a long undulent penis emerging from a realistic vulva is being licked by a bear's head. Other staffs are incised with animal heads licking a feather-like emblem which is one of the Palaeolithic stylizations of the penis, also found painted among vulvas in La Madeleine. These probably relate to the phallic 'wands' mentioned later. Perhaps the most interesting of all is a design of reindeer incised on an antler from Lorthet (Hautes Pyrenées); along with lozenge vulva-symbols are carved fine salmon 'aimed' at the genitals of the beasts. It is easy to deny a sexual association in this last case, and assert that it is simply a picture of reindeer and fish. However, the appearance on a few other bones of incised designs representing animal heads licking fish tails supports the sexual identification with some force. The double assertion, however, of relationship between fish and penis can indicate how early established was this analogy, which later became so universal and compelling. The diagrammatic likeness is perhaps not so obvious purely from the visual point of view; although many later fish-phalli on fifth-century BC Greek red-figure vases, for example, are indeed visually emphatic. But if one imagines the analogy as holding not between visual sign and visual sign but between signified and directly experienced thing and thing, i.e. between live, slippery, gleaming and violently writhing fish as experienced in the hunter's hands, and the actively twisting human penis in the vagina, the metaphor becomes most vivid.

As to the beast-head which appears licking both penis and shell-vulva, its meaning seems rather obscure. The best explanation that we can offer is that it represents non-human (i.e. animal-spiritual) sexual stimulation. Certainly courting animals lick each other's genitals as a prelude to coupling. Sheer stimulation of sexual feeling was certainly an important ingredient in many ecstatic rites. And the tongue can often substitute, both in fact and symbol, for the genitals of the opposite sex. This licking symbol seems, therefore, to be one of those more complex sexual metaphors which are found worked out in the art of other primitive peoples in the early Neolithic stage of culture, in which the tongue figures.

A number of the known Great Mother rituals of surviving primitives can cast light upon the symbolic material so far presented and prepare the ground for what follows. Many hunter peoples in the Americas have spoken to Europeans of the Earth as their mother. A Sioux prophet retorted to a European, who was insisting that he take to agriculture, 'You ask me to dig in the earth? But then when I die, she will not gather me again to her bosom. You tell me to dig up and take away the stones. Must I mutilate her flesh so as to get at her bones? Then I can never again enter her body and be born again. You ask me to cut the grass and the corn and sell them to get rich like the white men. But how dare I crop the hair of my mother?'[11] A similar, but perhaps less intense feeling, analogizing the Earth with a mother and hence looking on her as a transcendent Mother, appears in many other parts of the world, in the middle East, the Mediterranean, India and non-Confucian China. It may not be correct to assume that this female symbolism was *the* original human idea of the divine, for we have no evidence bearing on human symbolic thought earlier than the Palaeolithic period; and human history extends back beyond that phase for over a million and a half years. But those most ancient symbolisms that we know convey a sexually conditioned feeling towards the earth and its creative wombs more powerful even than the Sioux prophet's. The Navajo Indians' term for the earth is 'the Recumbent Woman' – an accurate description of the ladies of La Madeleine who might almost be called 'names' for the cave. The Zuni call the four subterranean worlds from which creatures emerged 'the wombs of the Recumbent Woman'. The Zuni, however, are farmers as well as hunters, and perhaps for this reason they know the metaphor of the seed. They thus take the critical step beyond the Paleolithic view and envisage Earth and Heaven as having been produced from the Great Waters, which were impregnated by two seeds planted in them by a remote, high Creation God. They also know the image of Heaven impregnating the depths of the Earth, from which all creatures are born, clambering up through her chambered wombs. Navajo shamans, in some of their rituals, re-enact this process of Genesis, the concrete paradigmatic image which lies behind and vitalizes so many later personifications and abstractions, claiming also to remember the process of their own incarnation and physical birth as a re-enactment of the cosmogonic image. This pattern, *mutatis mutandis,* appears again and again in the religious and sexual imagery of humanity, perhaps even carried in their unconscious minds as an archetypal analogy, but certainly inherited from their Palaeolithic forebears. A. Deierich's great book *Mutter Erde*[12] contains innumerable manifestations. Men feel that they are 'earthborn' in the same way as rocks, trees and streams – as indeed they are, even in a chemical sense, through the intermediacy of the sun. A great many myths refer to stones as 'bones of the Earth Mother', and conversely to bones as the essence of the physical being of man, implying that from the earth's stones comes the essential framework of each man.

There are numberless folk tales and superstitions concerning babies coming from caves, clefts, rivers, swamps and meres, many of which give rise to sexual fantasies and rites. Most powerful of all, perhaps, is the feeling which some groups develop that they come not from just the earth in general but from a special place, a certain cave, rock formation, lake, hollow-hill, wood or ancestral site, where souls of the unborn wait for incarnation, and to which the dead return. Australian aborigines hold that the spirits inhabit stone churingas or kulpidji marked with magical devices – often spirals – which are kept at the sacred earth-source. The belief that women become pregnant when they approach these fertile reservoirs of souls is very widespread. For the souls, in fact, are felt to be already waiting in one of the earth's wombs; their human mothers are only, so to speak, surrogates acting on behalf of the Great Mother herself. The child when it is first born, according to a ritual found across the breadth of the world, is placed on the bare ground, to re-assert by contact its true ancestry. Similarly the dead are laid on the naked earth to be reclaimed, and often buried in the domestic enclosure – as were the Palaeolithic men whose bodies and implements buried with them were often washed with red ochre. In the context of this deeply ingrained feeling, which among primitive men is held explicitly and consciously, the facts of sex and erotic activity take on a new meaning. They become indelibly symbolic, and may well be structured by taboo. But this does not mean that they necessarily become either restrictive or merely dutiful. The reverse is usually the case. Sexual activity plays its part as a major element in a spiritual mechanism and as such it may well be controlled for special occasions by ritual continence followed by indulgence; but it must also be kept at a high level of efficiency, and pleasure is a measure of that efficiency. At the same time by a kind of feedback system, the underlying cosmogonic symbolism of sex present at the back of the primitive's mind both enhances the act and provides an incentive to make it as satisfying as possible to both partners. It has often been asserted that primitive societies do not know the Western phenomenon of chaste, unconsummated passion, of ecstatic physically unfulfilled desire as a spiritual experience. This may be so. But active consummated sex against the background of unquestioned myth may itself be a high spiritual experience.

This is borne out by the attitude of the aborigines of the Oenpelli–Golbourne Island–Liverpool River region of north-eastern Australia. Their sexual life has been studied by R. M. and C. H. Berndt in a monograph so far unique.[13] It illustrates how vivid and important a role sex plays in the life of the aborigines, and by implication, suggests how its everyday manifestations are linked with sacred cave

1 (*Opposite*)
Diana of Ephesus, goddess
childbirth. 1st century AD

22

2 (*Opposite*)
Black painted stalactites in
form of breasts, and triangular
opening, possibly a vulva. Le
Combel, Pech-Merle

3 (*Right*)
Aurignacian stone showing
vulvas and small cupules. La
Ferrassie

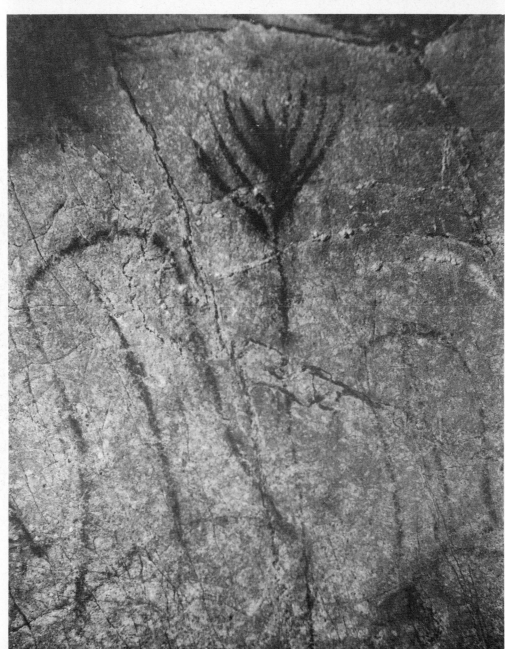

4 (*Right*)
Rock drawings showing
detail of two vulva symbols
and black feathered shaft.
El Castillo

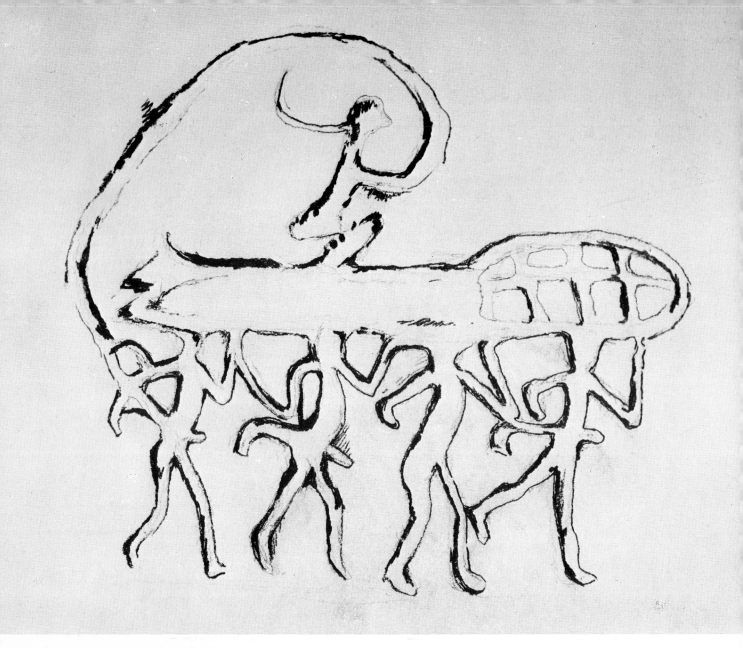

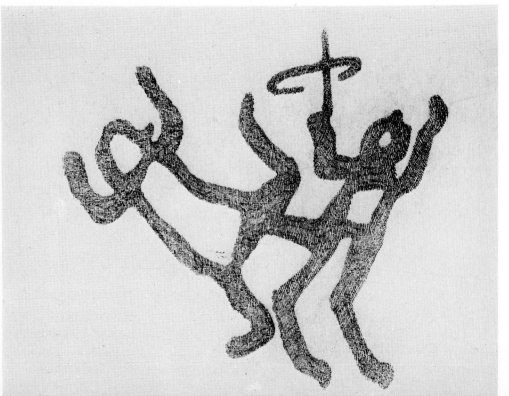

5 and 6 (*Above and left*)
Sandstone engravings, the
significance of which is
obscure. 7000 BC. Tel
Issaghen, Libya

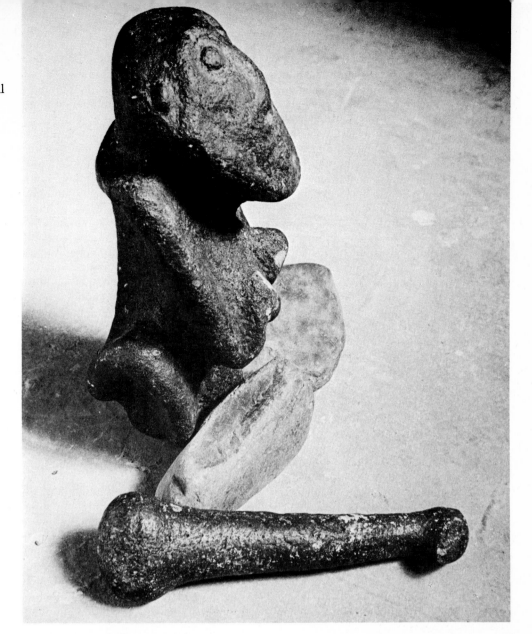

7 (*Right*)
Prehistoric stone figure, still used today as a symbol of power. New Guinea highlands

8 (*Right*)
Rock drawing, designed to promote successful hunting. Sahara-Atlas region

9 (*Overleaf*)
Cave drawings. Sahara-Atlas region

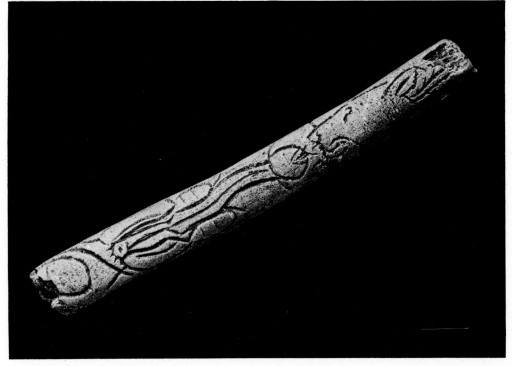

11 (*Above*)
Sepik pots with sexually
symbolic curvilinear designs

10 (*Opposite*)
Bark painting depicting the
story of creation. Arnhem
and

12 (*Right*)
Engraved staff with realistic
representations of a phallus
and a vulva. La Madeleine,
Dordogne

3 and 14 (*Opposite and right*)
Bark paintings, Australian
aborigine. Arnhem land

15 and 16 (*Previous page and opposite*)
Ritual fertility cult.
Arnhem land

17 (*Right*)
Sacred boards with totemic designs. Australian aborigine

18 (*Opposite left*)
New Guinea shield

19 (*Opposite right*)
Maori ornament shaped from a skull

and rock locations. By way of prelude it may be mentioned that it is well known that the Stone-Age Pitjandjara Australians (however 'missionized' they may be), in a way which epitomizes the attitude of many primitives, still feel themselves to be intimately related to the created world in which they live. Their totem system roots them to the creative birth-places of their animal ancestors and kin, who have their magical sites, caverns and boulders in the faces of Ayers Rock around its five and a half miles of perimeter. At these sacred places their kulpidji are stored. These, like the churingas of other tribes, are oval slabs incised with elaborate spiral and circle designs, and are conceived as concentrated masses of life-essence. Only fully initiated men are allowed to touch them in rituals and from mere contact draw a vast access of vitality. Women, and the uninitiated, do not know they even exist. The point here is that they 'belong' to the rock site where they are lodged, and draw their vitality from it. The rock itself, with its paintings, is the tap-root of the vital force. These pictures include today only a few schematic sexual designs – so far as is known.

There is, however, in the Oenpelli region a long series of sexual rock-paintings which have not (so far as we can discover) ever been photographed. They are rapidly falling out of use and either vanishing or being painted over with animals. But until recently they were used as a root-source of power in the carrying out of sexual magic. Paintings were done there, either on the walls themselves or on bark in imitation of the rock pictures, magically to 'realize' sexual wishes. We reproduce some of the bark paintings which have been collected. The pictures, carried out in ochres and blood, illustrate, to quote the Berndts' account, 'women with human, bird or reptile heads, severed arms, accentuated breasts, and elongated vulvae streaming with semen; women with babes suckling at their breasts, bodies of women showing (in X-ray style) foetal growth, women dancing, and men and women carrying out the sexual act'. There are four main types of drawing. The first, showing intercourse, realizes the desire of the artist. He draws himself coupling with the woman he desires. If it is a bark drawing he hides it carefully; the desired woman will then come to him at night and wake him up to make love. The second type aims at realizing pregnancy and making coitus easy. The third projects sexual hatreds and antagonisms, bringing pain and even death. Wives unfaithful by the liberal aboriginal standards, or unwilling lovers, are drawn with beast heads and pierced with sting-ray spines. The most popular type of beast-head is that of the Rainbow Snake, the archetypal patron of magic; and this shows that the meaning behind giving women such heads is to give power to the rite, and is not mere figurative name-calling. The fourth type is drawn as a threat to compel an unwilling woman to have intercourse with a man. 'If you don't come into the bush with me, I'll *draw* you' so as to cause pain and death.

Although these paintings are Australian, and are closely bound up with the customs of the given region and people, the fact that the customs they reflect are so extraordinarily similar to erotic witchcraft from very many parts of the world, including Europe, makes it virtually certain that comparable art of which we know next to nothing must have existed elsewhere. The special interest of these works is that they operated as a direct link between the transcendent Earth force and the immediate daily personal desires of the people. They also reflect and explain what art can mean in primitive societies: it is part of a mechanism of magical realization. It asserts, on the spiritual level 'such and such *is* now so!' 'The woman and I *are* having intercourse'. The corollary is that, once asserted as a proposition on this spiritual, i.e. metaphysical level, the act must occur on the physical. Since, as in all primitive art, form equals spirit, the propositions of art are thus equivalent to

(*Opposite*)
otongan god of
ivation and fertility.
ynesia

assertions that 'Such and such *is* the case'. To make the object as form makes it inevitable that the imaged event becomes reality. This explanation goes far closer to the truth than the old theory of sympathetic magic. For such 'making' does not express the mere wish, but states something as being already fact on the metaphysical level. All the sexual art illustrated in this book shares in one way or another in this function, stating spiritual propositions, not pious hopes. It may be helpful for the reader to review again in this light all the images so far discussed. For if we remember this in looking at each work, it can take on a new meaning.

We have, and can have, no evidence at all for the exact nature of ancient Palaeolithic ritual. The wealth and variety in detail among the particular legends and individual totem and shaman cults of modern primitives should warn us against being too precise in formulating theories about Palaeolithic beliefs. There is, however, one group of customs involving sexual symbolism which is so important, so widespread and self-consistent, and which also springs from Palaeolithic roots, that it is impossible to ignore it. This centres upon the labyrinth and the tomb-as-womb of the goddess.

To begin with we must recall two facts mentioned earlier: the long and winding underground journeys necessary to reach the innermost sacred caverns of Palaeolithic Europe; and the arduous ritual journeys undertaken by recent shamans, which probably reflect in some way those actual arduous journeys. To these we can add two further elements from the history of religion. First is the fact that following the analogy of the womb of the earth as mother, early peoples have consistently identified mines and galleries with her entrails.[14] Flints, fine vitrified stones, gems and minerals are, like organic nature, her embryos; but they must be exploited by man; they do not come to birth of their own accord. To simplify, one can say that from this fact, after the invention of metallurgy, comes both the strange charm and at the same time the spiritual danger of mining and metal-working, which make smiths and miners either greatly esteemed or outcast, and gives iron in Africa its extraordinary power. Embryo-ores were felt as being brought by human agency to birth in their smelting furnaces, second wombs. The chalk goddess from Grimes Graves in Norfolk, who is said to have been found set on a crude altar, was probably a placatory or ritual figure testifying to the sanctity of one of her own wombs. In addition we have to remember that primitive men most probably did not distinguish clearly between the female womb and other entrails. We, with our differentiated surgical knowledge, know very well that the uterus is a separate entity. Some agricultural African peoples know this too, and make womb emblems which are self-contained objects. But to the Stone-Age primitive the female vagina probably appears as the mouth to a labyrinth of entrails, analogized with the underground twisting and winding passageways deep in the earth. A clay plaque from Asia Minor *c.* 1000 BC, bears a maze-pattern, and the inscription in cuneiform reads 'The Palace of Entrails'.[15]

The second element from the history of religion is that numerous ritual dances of modern primitives, especially the Australian aborigines and the North American desert Indians, make a special feature of winding dances and processions during the course of ritual 'returns to the creative source'; and that the patterns of these dances are recorded in diagrams which feature deep undulations, spiral designs and concentric circles.[16] These drawn spirals, many of which are, in fact, developed into labyrinth patterns, are identified by the people who make them as representing the creative activity of a divine principle. The pathways the dancers follow back to the creative source trace the patterns of the currents of creative energy (so we conceptualize their much more concrete primitive notions) put forth by that source. The energy is represented by, or rather its presence is metaphysically asserted by, dramatically danced and drawn patterns. The circles and spirals punctuating the undulating path are said to be the places where spirit children of the clan were deposited by the mythical creative spirit, who is sometimes analogized with a magical snake.

The meaning of the large number of spiral, concentric circle, maze and labyrinth patterns used in the arts of many ages, including our own recent European past, is rooted in this ancient complex of analogies. The most sacred churingas and kulpidji of the Australian aborigines, long ovals of stone or wood in which the concentrated spiritual essence of the clan is stored, are all marked with such designs. The different patterns they follow are explained in terms of different totem birth and creation legends. Spirals in drawings of the Pima Indians of Arizona were explained in an eighteenth-century Spanish manuscript as representing the emergence of ancestors into the world. The flat stones inscribed and painted with designs from the Palaeolithic La Ferrassie, Labastide and Mas d'Azil caves have long been recognized as early relatives of the churingas. 'Macaroni' designs appear on the walls of some caves, usually by the entrance. The windings of the labyrinth as we know it in our cathedrals (Chartres) and initiation sites (St Catherine's Hill, Winchester) may indeed have lost their intestinal overtones; but by a long symbolic ancestry they are linked with the dialectic of the 'path to the source' and the emerging energy of the creative. A further element in the meaning of the undulant spiral may lie in its affinities with forms used in the so-called X-ray style of hunter art.

The origins and date of this last style are obscure; it does not appear in the Aurignacian – Magdalenian caves. But it is widespread in its pure form among the hunter peoples of the world, from Norway across Siberia into the Americas, and down into India, Malaya, New Guinea and Arnhem Land in Australia.[17] What it involves is that an animal picture includes, within the contour of each beast, illustrations of the vital inner organs and bones, as if seen by X-ray. This represents a kind of direct knowledge natural to the hunter accustomed to disembowelling and dismembering animals. And it seems that quite early on men identified the line of life with the branching complex of gullet, lungs, heart and stomach. Similarly the intestines were frequently represented by spirals or concentric circles. These designs, intended originally to indicate the internal facts, which to the hunters symbolized an animal's vital energies, were gradually converted in the sub-Siberian Ordos and Chinese Chou styles into external coils and whorls; some of these were interpreted in legend as additional wings or watery excrescences, and then modified by the process called iconotrophy. This term means that an icon representing a notion to one group of people, when it becomes the possession of another people who have forgotten the original meaning, or never knew it, reinterpret it in their own terms of analogy, reading into it what it suggests to them in their different culture-context. This may involve emphasizing one particular aspect of an originally broader icon-symbolism, subdividing a complex icon function into separate aspects, or transferring an icon to a cultural phenomenon which it was not invented for, but to which it is apt. The second population group may be descendants of the first, or people who have adopted prestigious motives from an exotic group. This process will play a very important part in what follows. In fact iconotrophy usually involves something being *added* to the meaning of a symbol, or its sense being particularized, rather than its whole meaning being lost. The original sense may certainly be overlaid, perhaps even bowdlerized or euhemerised, especially in the explanations primitives have given to Europeans; but the underlying analogy remains implicit in the symbolic complex, and can usually be deciphered.

It might also be as well to mention at this point that visual images as such have a strikingly independent existence. Once a potent symbol has been created it tends to travel far and wide, being adopted and repeated in a wide variety of different contexts, a corresponding variety of legends and stories being invented to 'explain' it. This is, no doubt, because the creation of a genuinely potent image takes not one but many generations. Even today artists are at work, quite correctly, on variants of the major sexual symbols of mankind.

The most vital and significant symbolic combination in which the undulant spiral appears is with the female body. A most important image was found in Čatal Huyuk, the large Neolithic site in Anatolia. It is a relief representing a goddess figure, her arms and legs raised and parted, painted in red with stylized designs. Her swollen stomach is so emphatically marked with concentric circles that archaeologists have come naturally to refer to her as a 'pregnant goddess'. The date is about 6150 BC. We must remember that, as primitive art never deals with mere facts but always with significances and powers, these red circles do not state the bare facts of the name we give her, but illustrate in red, that potent colour, the power of her more than human pregnancy.

This Čatal Huyuk icon is a version of a far older and very widespread cultural phenomenon. In a Gravettian context at Predmosti, Moravia, in Czechoslovakia, was found a mammoth-tusk incised with a design composed of concentric circles and rhythmically divided bands. It is easily recognized as a representation in incised line of the frontal view of a Palaeolithic fat female figure. The Venus of Laussel, for example, could be reduced, following orthodox modern artistic method, to a similar group of fluent enclosures. They indicate head, two enormous breasts, belly, vast hips and thighs. This is probably the earliest appearance of a type of image which appears constantly throughout European prehistory into our own historical period. It has many variants, some amplified or reduced, some – the most important – with the concentric circles converted into 'creative' feminine spirals. Those that we know best are incised on the great stones of the megalithic culture-complex ranging from Ireland through Brittany, Portugal, Italy, Malta, southern Arabia, India through Malaya, Sumatra, Indonesia and out into the islands of the Pacific. In the islands of the South Seas especially the symbolism passes through interesting phases of iconotrophy, combining with other symbolisms, but retaining some striking archaic manifestations as, for example, in the painted designs on some Trobrian dance-shields, which are virtually convoluted elaborations of glyphs representing the femal vulvo-anal region. Here we will concentrate at first upon the European manifestations of this female power imagery.

Neolithic–Megalithic Age

It was mentioned earlier that stones can be regarded by Stone-Age people as the 'bones' of the Earth Mother. On the analogical principle of the part standing for the whole, megaliths, dolmens, menhirs are naturally regarded as particularized manifestations of the deity herself. It is also a common feature of early levels of art the world over that designs incised upon a given substance illustrate a power felt to reside in the substance itself, of which it is symbolic. It is not surprising, therefore, to find innumerable spiral or circle images incised upon the enormous stone slabs associated with the Megalithic tomb cult (c. 3000-1000 BC). In some the spirals are reduced to a pair of circlets called eyes or oculets (e.g. Almeria, Spain). Such designs also appear on bones and antlers from Britain, on the Folkton chalk-grave drums, on the Aberdeenshire pebbles (also carved with bulbed volutes) and on pots found in the earlier passage-graves in northern Europe. More complete and complex versions of the same design executed on the walling slabs in the great chamber-tombs of Brittany, northern France, Ireland and Portugal show quite clearly that the circlets and spirals are still closely linked with the female body. Some, indeed, have projecting breasts. The great tomb-temples of Malta, with their feminine waisted ground-plans and open-armed embracing-crescent approaches, are dominated within by feminine emblems. Breasted pillars stand before the 'horned' tombs of Sardinia. A similar archetypal form – though the idea will certainly arouse objections – lies behind the Muslim mosque with its female mihrab–niche. Stylized mother-images reign in Anatolia. Undulant entries lead to such images in the inner chambers of Welsh tombs, just as they do in Pacific Malekula. All such imagery asserts for the first time a complete and deliberate association of the Mother Goddess with the dead. For the megalithic chamber-tombs, covered originally with great mounds of earth, and in Ireland at least with white quartz pebbles, were communal graves. These 'hollow hills' or 'glass castles' were still looked on in early medieval times with superstitious dread as the abodes of spirits, fairies, Morgain La Fée or the Queen of Elphame, with their sinister erotic overtones.[18] Earlier they were probably regarded by their original makers as magical reservoirs of dead souls waiting in the womb of the 'matrix' Earth Mother or Goddess of Death to be reborn. Numerous legends make it clear that, like the Australian churinga sites, the chamber-tombs were the places from which women derived their maternal power, becoming pregnant by visiting them at night – a thought which has echoes in the medieval witch-cult. They were to the Celts analogues of the halls of the after-world, where heroes sat feasting for a magically extended time with the supernatural Sidhe, enjoying intercourse with the daughters of the Sidhe, just as Indian epic heroes did with the Apsarases. A Celtic hero was persuaded to fight on behalf of a ruler of the Sidhe in return for the love of a divine woman. Both notions explain a number of sexual tombstone images. The maze spirals so many of the tombs bear are related to the wandering of souls in the Beyond, envisaged as maze-like creative passageways in the belly of the Mother. The world of the dead and the unborn was thus assimilated analogically with the mystical but actual journeys once paid by ritual visitors to the Palaeolithic cave shrines, and with the later ecstatic but imaginary journeys to the realm of the Mother of Beasts and Men taken by shamans.

It is quite clear that these mazes, meanders and spirals had come to symbolize what can be translated as the uncanny, numinous power of the transcendent realm, a power identified at bottom with the sexual energy of the earth in which women participated. They introduce the element of sequence and rhythm into visual art which would otherwise lack the dimension which musical and dramatic accompaniments normally give to primitive arts. During the Neolithic and Bronze Ages rocks, clefts and tombs were marked with emblems of this power, externalising and demonstrating their indwelling numen. Such are the Kerbstone at New Grange, Ireland, the Clear Island stone, and the later (La Tène) Turoe stone, Galway, Ireland. There are numerous examples in Scandinavia and Europe as well; for example, the Camonica Valley in northern Italy. It is a pure, but analogically quite justified speculation that the whole vast worldwide complex of spiral, maze and undulant ornament shares in this same underlying significance, most completely expressed in the elaborate vegetable and water volutes of Celtic La Tène metal-work designs and Celtic Christian manuscript ornament (eighth–ninth centuries). These must be distantly related to the surviving but archaic 'ornamental-fanciful' coils of Neolithic- and Bronze-Age southeast Asia, the Pacific islands and Maori New Zealand. It may well be that some related idea is conveyed by the meaning of the Nordic term 'wyrd', that mysterious power of destiny, so common in Northern poetry and from which comes our English word 'weird'. The torques and twisted ornament of the Celtic peoples, which we know were looked upon as charms, not mere ornaments, shared in this image of power. This undulant image of female fertility has another manifestation: in the coiling volutes of vegetation used to decorate so much architecture and sumptuary art all over the world. In India and southeast Asia its abstract form was adapted to the elaborate lotus rhyzome ornament which signified the fertility of the soil. In southern Siberia it was used, barely developed, to represent the tree of life associated with a goddess, on early textiles (c. AD 200).

Among the Celts of Europe, in France, Scandinavia, Germany and Britain we know that the cult of the Mother Goddess long survived, though a typical Indo-European masculine primacy encroached progressively upon it during the second and early first millennium BC. Most of the works of art which bear out our specu-lative knowledge come from post-Roman contexts and their iconography is confused by cultural mixture; but they tally well with ancient patterns. Artio was a Central European bear-goddess. The goddess called Epona either rides or is identified with the horse, and a horse figures in several legends as protector of the dead. There is evidence that in Ulster the king had symbolic union with a mare personifying the Earth's fertility. Something of this kind may be represented in a rock engraving from the Camonica Valley, showing a solar 'hero' coupling with an animal; and the phallic White Horse of Uffington may be an emblem of kingship by virtue of a similar sexual implication. Among the Welsh Celts, and still today among the Basques, a deity half female, half horse called Mari (among the Welsh Mari Llwyd) was a powerful spirit living in caves or the earth. A number of Celtic goddesses can be called divided 'functions' of the Mother Goddess. Such are Macha the fertility goddess in whose honour orgies were held, later a war goddess; Anu, whose paps are seen in mountains in County Kerry; and Brigitt, who became the Christian St Bride, goddess of abundance and marriage. The nearest, perhaps, to the original goddess herself was the Welsh Blodeuwedd, whose body was com-pounded, so legend describes, of flowers, the May Queen analogue of Roman Flora to whom Robert Graves' book *The White Goddess* is virtually dedicated.

We know, probably, a good deal more about the northern goddess Frig, whose mantle was later worn by a male version of herself, and whose name has passed into English usage as one of the terms for the activity of which she was always the patroness. Friday is also named after her. She is called in old Norse sources the 'Darling of the Gods', and many shrines to her must have been scattered about Scandinavia and Britain, to judge from the many place-names containing references to her. So far as the relative opacity of the sources tell us, she was the personi-fication of the fruitful Earth Goddess, and patroness of love in all its manifestations. In Denmark her sacred image used to be carried from an island shrine in a draped wagon drawn by cows, to circulate around the country and aid its fertility. Such ceremonial chariots were also used for other divine images by Scandinavian peoples. Wherever Frig's chariot stopped, so did war and work. The people aban-doned themselves to peace and pleasure, with ceremonial sexual orgies. Before the chariot departed, its secret contents were bathed in a pool. Such pools were sacred to the goddess, and offerings were thrown in. The slaves who performed the bathing were then slain in the same pool. There is reason to believe that, as happened elsewhere, priestesses of the goddess accompanied the chariot wherever it went and coupled in the wagon with local chieftains. In this way the fertility of each locality was related to the general source of all fertility. Sad vestiges of such sexual imagery probably appear in the little images of females with parted legs, their vulvas enlarged and often held open by their hands, which once survived on many of the churches of Celtic Europe, notably Ireland, Wales and – so James Boswell tells – in German Switzerland. In Ireland they are called 'Sheelagh-na-gig', and were interpreted as invocations of a generalized 'luck'.

These manifestations of superhuman sexual energy, however, all belong to phases of civilization into which agriculture had been incorporated, and those images of masculine sexual potency which are still familiar everywhere were gradually emerging. The earth as the mother of plants was known, by the epoch *c.* 6500-2000 BC in Western Europe, to need fertilizing by sown seed. And most probably there evolved at about the same time those compelling functional analogies which relate the penetrating impregnating male to the receptive but intrinsically passive wombs of the earth, and which resulted in so much elaborate sexual symbolism being expressed everywhere in cult and art. The penis became plough, axe, dagger and sword: semen the seed, rain, sun, snake and bird – obscure images for subtle inward energy as we shall see. The female principle became divided into separate divinities, each associated with an individual agricultural settlement. At each place the goddess seems to have become specific, spreading herself from her old rock and tomb hollows first into regions and fields, then into marshes, meres and springs, into towns and cities and ultimately becoming an anthropomorphic patroness of specific functions, such as childbirth, love and the hearth. The rituals of the Great Mother and her beasts were diffused into a degraded rustic imagery of nymphs and dryads who are the willing sexual prey of goat-legged satyrs. Some of the goddess's reflections retain in folklore their sinister overtones of death and the other world, like the taloned Lamiae originating in Mesopotamia but spreading into the Roman world, who steal men's vital energy away in sexual dreams, and the nixies who call them to an erotic but watery grave.

This whole complex of sexual imagery evolved along with new investments of masculine power. Rituals and belief concerning human ancestry and the fertility of the ground were externalized in elaborate sexual rites and images. It seems probable that in their earliest stages the evolving male-oriented religions and arts began by taking over older female imagery. For once a symbol has developed it can be applied to different functions in different contexts so long as its content remains alive. In Arnhem land today the aborigines still say that many of what are now men's customs were taken over from the women and modified. There are numerous instances of this happening in the history of the world's religions, and in Celtic art the female numinous spiral was adapted to a strongly masculine and warlike imagery. At the most primitive levels of Mediterranean religion can be found female cults adapted to masculine symbolisms, in different ways. We must not, therefore, be at all surprised at the many aggressively male megalithic menhirs, at the Celtic goddess becoming the Cross, at the Virgin Mary (Stella Maris) waiting so long in the wings of the Western Church to be recognized as the Theological Sophia, the maternal Complex of Categories.

As we go on to discuss the various manifestations of sexual imagery which seem on the face of it to be purely religious, we must always remember that among primitive peoples analogies work both ways. If they conceive ultimate religious notions clothed in everyday sexual terms, we will find that what *we* would see as everyday sexual facts are for them imbued with the charisma of ultimate religious meaning. The idea of the transcendent is enhanced by sexual sensation; sexual sensation is enhanced by the transcendent. The two components of the analogy are locked together in a structure of custom, legend and taboo. The ritual form is the generalization of what is always concrete experience. To remain healthy and alive a symbolism needs to realize both its unconscious matrix and its living root. Ritual acts, with which primitive art always deals, are never mere personal fantasies; they are distinct from everyday acts in the sense that their ritual exemplifies the meaning of the acts ritualized. Ritual connects up the manifestations which daily life scatters, gives them an ultimate context and a structure which is rooted both in the psychic ontogeny of each man and the phylogeny of his species.

The stages through which the fully fledged masculine phallic cult developed can be traced in the histories of primitive arts. Each one is represented by what may seem at first like a wide variety of customs and imagery. All, however, are rooted in a limited group of general notions and conceptions. Different stages coexist in the same culture, archaic vestiges often persisting for a long time, while certain particular manifestations may not appear everywhere. Needless to say, for the most remote cultures in time and place we have few documents, and speculation must be allowed to fill the gaps. We have also to remember that certain sexual customs from the Neolithic and Bronze Ages in Western Asia and Europe, which we are accustomed to regard as primitive in a general sense, were actually conditioned by the special social circumstances of life in early cities. Primitive population groups, such as islanders who lived relatively isolated from other populations, may never have developed these actual customs, even though they may have entertained the same generic symbolisms.

It was suggested above that the dominant analogy which led towards complete phallic imagery was that which identified the seed sown in agricultural practice with the male ejaculatory fluid, still called seed, or the same word in Latin *semen*. The analogy between the earth and the womb remained the compelling one, though a progressive domination of human institutions by male activities and symbolisms took place; this harnessed the basically sexual urge to broader cultural activities such as war, social construction and technology, a process which is now consummated in possibly disastrous ways. On the broad time scale of humanity's evolution, this idea is true. But there was an important intermediary stage. It is probably neither possible nor necessary to try and fix a point at which one could say men became aware of the physical facts of paternity. All the primitive people whose ideas have been recorded, whatever they may think about paternity as such, lay great stress of the sexual value of an opulent flow of semen. At the same time we know that most primitive groups were aware that the identity of the group, and its continuation in time, were due to a mysterious power which operated through a female bodily energy (also symbolized often by the moon, with whose waxing and waning the emotional life of women is intimately linked). There are, however, records of peoples who have taken what might be called the first step on the way towards differentiating this mysterious power from the female itself, and projecting it analogically into non-feminine natural forces, without relinquishing the idea that the source of what grows is within the female. In the early stages of agricultural life the first natural analogies for the force which impels the growth of plants are the sun and the rain, especially the latter. In both Australia and South Africa it has been recorded that women who wish to become pregnant lie in a shower of rain. This distinction may have become gradually more deeply ingrained, and identified with a complex of masculine symbols. The Chinese, for example, who have preserved very archaic images in their sophisticated Taoist symbolisms, refer to male orgasm as 'the bursting of the clouds'. Archaic Indian mythology equates the monsoon with male sexual fertilization. It is also known that some peoples have even identified the moon as masculine rather than feminine.

If they observe that the rain swells the seeds and sets them growing, people can take the first step towards the notion of insemination, even before the male semen is identified with the seeds themselves. In fact, of course, both rain and sun set growing those trees and bushes which flourish without human agency and were cropped by men long before human gardening reached the stage of seed-sowing. It would thus be natural for an analogy to be drawn between the fluid semen and the helpful fertilizing liquid of the sky well before any strict idea was evolved of an implanted second nucleus as the cause of life. Such an idea, however, although it did not entail abandoning the underlying image of the earth as fruitful Mother, nevertheless did involve transferring the idea of generic life-energy from the female to the male. This transfer must have taken place gradually, but once made, it was decisive. The widespread inner physiological imagery of male sexuality always remained dominated by the idea of a generic unparticled fluid power, even after the equation between semen and agricultural seeds was made. It was this power for which the snake became virtually a universal symbol, as will be seen.

Roots of European Symbolism

Men seem to have speculated concerning the nature of that fluid male generative power along lines similar to those implied in the cult of feminine fatness. Professor R. B. Onians [19] has amply documented the imagery in the case of archaic Mediterranean peoples; the objective symbolism of that particular complex – body-fluids, fats, head, spine, horns and snake – has so extraordinary a community with that of other peoples the world over that the fact cannot be without significance. It may constitute an important element in the Mesolithic–Neolithic agricultural culture-complex diffused after about 6000 BC both westwards into Europe and Africa and eastwards into southern Asia from the early farming communities in the middle East. It must be pointed out that, in the discussion which follows, Professor Onians' careful philological documentation has been treated as a point of departure rather than a limit for speculation.

Briefly the symbolism is this. First, the male semen which embodies the principle of life is held to be identical with certain particular body fluids; in them the vitality of the body itself is felt to consist, and they are identified as the transcendent, spiritual, non-earthly parts of the body. The old man, the sick man and the dead 'dry out' towards the bone. The spirit in archaic thought evaporates as ichor before it flies away as air. The fat, marrow and omentum in the bodies of animals and men are their 'life'. Anointing with fat and oils, as in coronation ceremonies, or as is done with sacred images the world over (e.g. Africa, India) is analogous to irrigating the anointed one with life-essence. Wine also feeds the moist spirit – while blood remains a feminine energy, and bone the earthly component. The white body-fluids are the masculine energy. The synovial fluid of the knee was closely related with the vital energies of man. But the most important of all was the cerebro-spinal fluid. And it was this which was believed to be within man the physical essence of the transcendent energy whose cosmic analogue was the 'fertilizing water' of the sky, channelled through the rivers of earth. The male semen was held to be a condensed form of this energy, passed out through the male genital machine to fertilize the woman. When a man died his escaping spirit was analogized with the evaporating fluid of his body, ascending figuratively on wings into the sky. The winged phallus, so widespread an image in Western sexual art from the large icons in the sanctuary of Delos (*c*. 500 BC) onward, is a symbol for a sexual–cosmic vitality at once human and superhuman. A very large number of varying burial customs of post-Palaeolithic humanity seem to indicate that the slow liberation of the fluid 'ghost' by decay is felt to be a troublesome time of limbo, which can be controlled or accelerated by the many different rituals such as temporary burial, dry and green funerals, discarnation or cremation.

The energy fluid is identified by many Neolithic peoples with ancestral power, the vitality which preserves the continuity of the tribe. And this probably explains one male initiation ritual, widespread among primitive people but rarely recorded frankly by Western observers – Layard is a notable exception[20] – during which adult male initiates have anal intercourse with novices. Among other peoples (e.g. in Tibet) potions containing the semen of seniors may be drunk by novices. These rituals must symbolize transmission into the new initiates, in its condensed physical form, of the vital energy which is seen as sustaining the group identity. Although there is no concrete evidence to prove the connection, such a custom may well lie behind the homosexual eroticism actively encouraged among the Classical Greeks. This phenomenon also helps to add a layer of meaning to the ancestor-images with erect phalli so extremely common in Africa, southeast Asia and other regions. Such images may thus be straightforward concrete symbols for an idea analogous to our 'ancestry in the male line', but with an extra dimension of sexual power added to the proclamation of spiritual identity, in which each ancestral or soul image subsists. Each image is also felt to constitute not what we would feebly term a 'memorial', but an active, positive and ontological reaffirmation of the continuing ancestral line of life in the face of individual death.

The association between the sexual energy-fluid in the cerebro-spinal complex and the head in particular is amply documented by Professor Onians for the Mediterranean. He supplements his information with references to Africa and the Semitic near East. An association between the head and the seat of the life-essence may at first seem so obvious and widespread as scarcely to warrant discussion. But this very obviousness demonstrates the power of the symbolism, even among ourselves. The expression of this notion in objective symbolisms is remarkably constant the world over. First there is the significance of the head itself, as a pure vessel of power; the practice of head-hunting once widely distributed all over the world and known recently in the Americas, southeast Asia, the Pacific Islands and Africa, is direct testimony to the notion that to possess a head is to posses its original owner's power. The cult of the ancestral head kept as spirit-counsellor and oracle was still more widespread, being known virtually everywhere. This includes Western Europe; for Greek and Celtic memories of the custom are preserved in the legends of, for example, the oracular heads of Orpheus and of the Nordic Bran. In certain Indonesian islands at the present day the Korvars, i.e. ancestor images furnished with actual ancestral skulls, may also be phallic. The widespread use of the mask as the prime vehicle of a spiritual entity needs no stressing.

Furthermore, Professor Onians has demonstrated that horns and hair in particular, because they are excrescences from the head, are generally interpreted as special manifestations of 'head stuff'. Since in animals horns were long known to have a sexual function, they were identified with specifically sexual 'head substance'. The exponential growth-patterns realized in the horns of cattle, sheep and goats have been explicitly recognized as powerful symbols by many peoples. William Fagg has often commented on their importance in African art. Male animals bearing these horns have been used again and again as emblems of supernatural power and fertility. Horns themselves have been used as shrine objects, embodiments of a power with strong animal significance, as in the temples at Čatal Huyuk (c. 6150 BC) and in Minoan Crete. Artificial additions to the head shaped as excrescences have been used in many different ways to express a superabundance of generic power with strong sexual overtones, such as horns on crowns or helmets, feathers (often associated with a celestial symbolism), crests and crowns.

There is one special excrescence from the face which, among some peoples, is especially exaggerated and associated with sexual energy. This is the nose. Everyone knows that folklore equates nose and penis. The red-nosed joke-mask is recognized everywhere as having a 'lewd' significance. Among the peoples of New Guinea, particularly in the Sepik river area, an outward and explicit identification is made in certain ancestor figures which have characteristically elongated and downward curved noses. These noses are sometimes actually connected to the genitals, penis and nose being fused into one form. When complex spiral or geometric designs are added to the faces of such ancestral figures and to the masks representing spirits, the compound meaning becomes very potent. It is not insignificant that these are made by people some of whom once wore long, phallic penis-sheaths, who elongated and perforated the septum of the nose to receive feathers and transverse slivers, and also used transverse penis pins to enhance feminine feelings during sexual intercourse. But this is only an elaboration of an extremely common identification between nose and penis, which some modern individuals certainly experience as a sensuous equation. Numerous masks from Africa (e.g. Baga fertility masks) make an association of the two members by using an explicit penis symbol to stand for the nose, the two eyes indicating its testicles. This was a theme Picasso took up from primitive art. Something similar can be found on semi-comical masks worn by European folk dancers, which have an ancient primitive ancestry.

Another highly suggestive feature of the head is the tongue. To stick out the tongue is usually regarded as a demonstration of some kind – apotropaic, rude or welcoming. There is one complex of thought in early Asia, including the primitive antlered heads from south Chinese Chang-sha tombs (c. second century BC) and similar modern carvings from Indonesian islands, in which an enormously extended tongue quite clearly manifests a special kind of energy. We have encountered the tongue featuring as a sexual element in Palaeolithic contexts; and in connection with these Giedon has adduced a typical northwest American Indian carving which represents an anthropoid creature and a frog lying together, the tongue of the former thrust into the mouth of the latter. To the Haida Indian this image may well have had a specific legendary explanation. But there is no doubt that the frog or toad may be recognized in some levels of culture as a womb symbol; it is thus not irrelevant to see the tongue, a primary agent of sensuous experience and pleasure, as connected in a significant symbolic way with vital energy. The mouth, in fact, may be recognized explicitly as female. Wooden masks, called 'torso masks', were carved in African Dahomey, in which the breasts of the female torso were interpreted as the eyes, the open genitals as the mouth. This powerfully suggestive motive is still often employed in painting the bodies of nude girl dancers in Western night clubs.

It will be obvious from the previous general discussion of symbolism and cult that the meaning which any phallic image had for the people who made it went far beyond what the mere shape itself could suggest. In practice most phallic emblems have been reinforced by vivid analogies with other impressive natural phenomena which formed part of their makers' experience. We have seen how the female sexual imagery of primitive man contained metaphors which were based not only upon similarities of shape but upon compelling similarities of function. The same is true, but to far greater extent, with male phallic imagery. First and most important is the fact that both to men and women the visual shape of the erect phallus always connotes a range of powerful inner experience, including the feelings of sexual arousal, active penetration and seminal ejaculation, with their accompanying sensations, emotions and fantasies. These may be symbolized by traditional images referring to things that have no obvious visual connection with the shape of the penis itself, though they may also be combined with overt phallic emblems. Such images, once they are elaborated, may be juxtaposed to produce a chain of oblique sexual references, enhancing and reinforcing each other.

One important complex of inwardly experienced imagery revolves about the identification of male energy with ejaculated liquid semen. As we have seen, historically speaking, the basis of the imagery was probably laid down in the very earliest farming communities during Neolithic phases of culture when the importance of fertility was becoming recognized. It has been shown by the Berndts that in the sexual life of the non-farming north Australian aborigines copious seminal ejaculation is especially valued by the woman as an important element in intercourse, yet at the same time the semen is not identified as a specific cause of an individual birth. Since the fluid semen came to be identified as the generic cause of fertility, it may well be that the identification of the sky as male, moistening and fertilizing a female earth, which appears in the oldest layers of so many literatures, took place during the very early stages of agriculture. It is also more than likely that a similar virtue was attributed to the seminal fluid of the male animals kept by cattle herding people, even by late hunters who had no developed agricultural economies. It must have been recognized by them that the females needed the male ejaculation to become fertile. The images of the sexually energetic bull, ram and buck, all horned herd-animals, must then have contributed their special overtones to male creative sexual symbolism. Some notion of the special sexual vitality residing in the 'king of the herd' who fertilized his females must have lain behind the custom of bull and ram sacrifice in the Neolithic- and Bronze-Age Middle East to justify the idea that his blood could fertilize the earth. Icons which testify to the importance and persistence of the seminal image are, for example, the great recumbent ejaculating figure with an animal's head in a Saharan rock painting published by Frobenius, and the ancient Egyptian images of the ithyphallic masturbating god Min of Coptos. The Egyptian Osiris, the corn god annually sacrificed and buried in the ground, who later on became patron of resurrection, often appears wearing Min's erect organ.

The fact that male energy manifests itself most obviously in the form of the special liquid which it ejaculates from the depths of the body prompted a two-fold speculation: first upon the source of this fluid within the male body itself, and second on its cosmic analogues. This double speculation is summed up in one of the most widely distributed symbols of psycho-sexual power, the snake, both the actual serpent and its artistic emblems. It is at first sight difficult to see why it should have the undoubted relationship to phallic symbolism it does have. Many writers have commented on its visual likeness to the penis, which itself may be called 'worm' or 'serpent' in vernacular speech. Some species of snake are able to erect their heads and wave them about. But this simple visual similarity is not enough to explain the meaning. In fact it is a more complex symbol than any of those we have so far discussed. For the snake may not itself be a primary component in the analogy, but a symbol for the common form uniting other components themselves compound, neither of which is a simple, objective, experienced entity. In practice, the common graphic symbols for the snake may resemble the symbols for the penis, for the undulant creative power which has been analysed previously, and for water trickling in rivulets and in curling rivers. The actual snake sheds its skin, and thus it is often said to be a symbol for repeated regeneration, either in the sense of regeneration of the spirit at each human birth among people with a strong sense of tribal identity, or in the sense of personal regeneration among people who have well developed initiatory or mystery religions. Some snakes may live in holes in the ground. All move with an undulant or coiling motion which is itself significant; and the bite of many brings death. The snake as symbol is thus felt to refer to a whole chain of linked and un-logical analogies combining sexual and genital energy, based on the notion of the fertility residing in water, especially by people inhabiting regions where water is not abundant or easily controlled. It is connected with the kind of energy involved in transformations; by the mere touch of a bite, without any gross injury, a man is made to die; water propels the growth of plants; human vitality leads to sexual propagation; or other-worldly energies are channelled into effects in this world. The kinds of symbolism in which snakes appear may be represented at the simple, phallic level by the numerous folk-tales in which the long, sinuous, snake-like penis of some legendary man creeps into houses or under the ground to have intercourse with women; at more elaborated stages it appears in the magical snake (e.g. the Rainbow Snake of northern Australia or the Indian Naga Vasuki) through whose agency all kinds of magic and medicine are effected and who is invoked by potent emblems and amulets. Early Greek mythology retains echoes (in a version of the legend of Tiresias) of the special significance seen in a pair of snakes coupling in the erect posture, as they also appear twined about the 'rod' of Hermes or the healing 'wand' of Aesculapius.

All these various images are united and authenticated by a widespread tradition of archaic psycho-physical medical thought, for which we do have substantial documents. This tradition symbolizes the vital energy within the human body as a luminous snake, usually thought to reside, in subtle form, in the cerebro-spinal marrow, whence it expresses itself in sexual activity. The snake is the form in which the soul creeps out of the mouth of the dead, lives in the snake sanctuary, and visits the houses of the living. Most important is the fact that this inward image provides the link between phallus and head as interrelated spiritual centres, which is such a common feature of the ancestor images of early farming communities. This symbolism was also known in many primitive city societies. In ancient Greece, the snake was also used to symbolize the infusion of natural fluid upon which the life as well as the fertility of both men and the earth depended. There the procreative element in the human body, the psyche or soul, was conceived in serpent-guise as a crystalization of the liquid and fatty vitality of the body as a whole: it did, however, have a different symbolic form in other contexts, notably a winged phallus, as will appear below. In some versions of ancient pre-Classical Mediterranean myth, Okeanos, the immense belt of water said to encircle and bind the world together, was conceived as a vast serpent with human head and horns. This is clearly a transposition onto the cosmic scale of our inner image of the liquid psyche, source of all vitality and fertility. It is the image which justifies much of the known snake-symbolism of primitive men, although in many cases the image is, so to speak, pre-phallic, and appears either as 'the possession of' or 'vitalizing' a female image. For example, both Astarte, the western Asiatic goddess of sex and fertility, and the bare-breasted Cretan Mistress of the Animals may be represented in their icons with snakes entwined around their hands and arms.

The enormous diffusion of the snake as a representation of supernatural vitality and power seems to be based upon various projections of this nuclear image. Many African peoples operate a symbolism of magical snakes. In Dahomey another Rainbow snake was worshipped, in the form of a clay image kept in a gourd (a female emblem); this Great Snake made young girls his own when they were once tattooed with his emblem and so possessed by him. Elsewhere snakes may be believed to fertilize barren women; snake priestesses give oracles; and the Haitian voodoo ceremonies of possession by the snake-spirit Vodunhwe were followed by an orgy. In Melanesia snakes have particular mythological functions. But in the Americas cosmic snakes inspired an immensely potent symbolism. The Mexican imagery became very varied and particularized, the most significant icons being those of the plumed serpent, whose feathers signify an airy, celestial connection. These icons can best be understood in relation to an imagery still surviving among the Hopi and Zuni, who reverence a supernatural snake as the spirit of the rain which fertilizes their fields; in rain-ceremonials they carry images of snakes from which water is sprinkled for initiates to drink.

Many phallic symbolisms and ceremonies recognized the importance of male insemination without succumbing to a predominantly male mythology. They represent, in different social contexts, the primacy of the generic female womb-function, whilst at the same time proclaiming the importance of this supra-individual male sexual energy-juice. In its most primitive form such a symbolism can be found among the many early farming groups in Africa, America and the Pacific Islands, whose women are the gardeners. The women identify themselves symbolically with their gardens; along with their crops they may also plant emblems of male and female fertility, such as small terracottas. They may also require of their men sexual intercourse in the planted gardens, either orgiastically, or more commonly, as a ritual preceded by a preliminary chastity which reinforces the power of the ritual sexual art. Emblems of the male organ, either realistic or purely symbolic, were often planted in their fields by agricultural peoples. The innumerable phallic images with which the countryside of the classical Mediterranean world was filled must have been derived from this ancient custom. Needless to say the same imagery underlies the many land-fertility ceremonials which Frazer and others have collected. Most involve either ritual sexual intercourse in the ploughed furrows, ceremonial public coupling, or the display of artistic substitutes for the act, such as the working models of a male and female coupling which some southeast Asian farming peoples carry round the rice-paddies in musical procession. Fertility images of the female in intercourse with one of the animals emblematic of celestial vitality such as an elephant or stallion have also been reported, notably from India.

In rather more sophisticated city contexts the primitive customs and imagery centred upon femininity were developed into established social institutions, even in the face of a general masculine dominance of the society. Many such institutions must, in fact, have contained vestiges of very ancient customs which had survived, modified, from Palaeolithic times. At the famous Greek female ceremonies of the Thesmophoria (fifth-fourth centuries BC), sacred to the Chthonic fertility goddesses

Demeter and Persephone, phalli were displayed and reverenced. In the Egyptian processions of Mother Isis and Osiris (fourth–second centuries BC) enormous phallic images were carried, and women as well as men participated in sexual songs and orgiastic behaviour. Some Greek vases illustrate festivals in which the huge phalli are shaped like fish – a recrudescence of a very ancient image. The modern Indian Holi procession at which coloured water was once squirted about was similarly orgiastic, before interference by the British. At the Cow Goddess festivals of Egypt female images holding their genitals open (like the Sheelagh-na-gigs) were carried; and Isis herself is often portrayed holding an emblem of the vulva called the Kteis. At the Roman festival of Flora the women stripped themselves naked and invited sexual attentions from the male citizens; whilst during the Roman festival of Venus an enormous phallus was carried to the temple and there presented to the sexual parts of the image of the goddess. In all these rites sexual enjoyment of every kind, not mere ritual act, played a part of paramount importance, and the ceremonies were magically very dangerous. The analogy between male semen and the seed-corn in female ceremonial was incorporated, especially in the phallic loaves which were made, for example, as offerings at springtime rituals in many parts of the ancient world, to be offered or sometimes ceremonially eaten. That the custom was widely distributed is borne out by the fact that even until very recently such phallic cakes were baked by German, French and Italian peasants at Easter to be carried in procession to the church.

Such symbolic ceremonies were supplemented by a number of archaic female sexual institutions which, so to speak, bridge the transition from a female to a male-oriented cosmic imagery. The chief of these is sacred prostitution, known in the ancient middle East, in Japan and in India, as well as in classical Europe. Women served at temples, either permanently or temporarily, as personifications of the female principle, representing both fertility in the Chthonic sense and sexuality in the erotic sense, the two being seen as interdependent and mutually enhancing. Such prostitutes would consort with all male visitors to the shrine. In Babylonia they might also consort with men in other parts of the city. For the epic of Gilgamesh makes it clear that each prostitute represented in some sense Astarte – the goddess who is represented naked with beasts in a number of well-known images. The rationale behind the institution can be seen very clearly if one takes into account all that has been said concerning older sexual imagery. It implies that for the good of the country on which the temple stands, and for the general good of the inhabitants, as well as distributing the benefits of the female energy to men (as in the Sahara rock painting mentioned above), the masculine energies of the population in the form of seminal fluid should be absorbed by representatives of the goddess of fertility. It is probably this aspect of the cult which gave rise to a later Roman image, represented in several reliefs, of the winged Lamia, an erotic dream-woman with clawed feet, who was fancied to drain off the semen of men at night and give birth to spiritual bodies. Such Lamiae survived to figure in the early literature of European witchcraft.

Benefits were also supposed to accrue from special customs of premarital promiscuity, either at temples or in the fields, practised by many primitive populations. In many cultures can be found traces of the overwhelming importance of matrilocal deity. In Frazer's *The Golden Bough*, R. Briffault's *The Mothers* and A. M. Hocart's *Kingship* can be found an enormous collection of instances which illustrate how the pattern of kingship depends, not upon male descent, but upon the king's marrying with one or more women who personify the earth and whom the king has to dominate and fertilize. Much has been made of the ceremonial slaughter of the old king by the new, both in comparative mythology and poetic thought. But however speculative the literary theories may seem, there can be no doubt at all of the fundamental truth which myth and legend convey: that at the root of this imagery and ritual lies the thought that a man is king by virtue of his ability both to control the female representatives of the earth and, by having continuous sexual intercourse with them as well as performing other ritual acts, to keep the land they personify continuously fertile. There is abundant evidence, especially from West Africa and the Pacific, that a palace full of royal concubines represents far more than the self-indulgence of a powerful individual. And numerous phallic images on palaces and shrines testify to the royal sexuality by means of which the metaphysical security of a kingdom is maintained. Parallel and analogous to such symbolisms may be the imagery common to cattle-herding peoples of the bull or goat as the male principle of fertility distributing his sexual favours and energy among female devotees and initiates. The early western Asiatic cult of Dionysus is one example, and another is the cult of the Celtic horned god Cernunnos, which survived as a principal element in the medieval witch-cult (this has been doubted; but there are far too many thoroughly documented survivals of ancient cults in medieval peasant Europe for such doubts to be justified).

The process whereby the underlying vital energy of the natural world comes to be reinterpreted in favour of the male principle can be seen at work in many different traditions of imagery. Different societies give a different emphasis to particular aspects. There are surviving peoples among whom ancestry and/or land-tenure is still reckoned in the female line, such as the Nayars of south India, and their imagery still features the creative female principle. In other cultures a balance between male and female may be struck, and the roles of men and women may be matched in both agricultural ritual and imagery as well as in ancestral symbolism. In yet other cultures an almost total primacy may be given to the male principle, leading often to a disproportionate emphasis being laid on the phallic cult, so that male deities take over the functions and even the names of older goddesses. This happened, for example, with the Norse god Frey, who took over into his own exaggerated phallus the sexual and procreative functions of the womb of the older goddess Frig. In historical India the custom of sacred prostitution usually came to be interpreted as practised by 'wives' of a male deity. And late classical legend has Aphrodite being born from the chopped-off phallus of Uranus.

From the point of view of art, which was primarily used by primitive people for ceremonial not personal reasons, the generic image always precedes the particular – maybe in the logical rather than the evolutionary sense. The individual tends to be seen as an example of the embracing class; the sexual man is a manifestation of male sex. Thus the art-made phallic emblem precedes the individual phallic ancestor image, which is characteristic of so many primitive art-traditions. At the same time we have to recognize that any major phallic deity, recognized over a wide area as cosmic prototype of the procreative male, is the result of relatively sophisticated syncretic activity resulting from some geographical and cultural mobility.

There are innumerable customs, recorded from all over the world, which involve a deep-laid image of generic male sexuality inhabiting sacred objects and places and manifesting itself in different ways in relation to the life of women. The commonest involves the defloration of girls or brides. Among many primitive peoples it is customary for young girls to be ceremonially deflowered by a spiritually important male, such as their father, a stranger from another tribe, a chief or holy man, or by means of a ceremonial instrument wielded by a male or female initiator. European anthropologists have tended to agree that this was done out of fear of the

21 (*Opposite*) Venus of Savignano. Prehistoric

54

2 (*Opposite*)
Tomb 'door' engraved with sexually symbolic circular designs. Bronze Age, Sicily

3 (*Right above*)
Branched antler head engraved as a double phallus, the left branch combining vulva symbolism. Gorge d'Enfer, Dordogne

4 (*Right below*)
Venus of Laussel, probably Solutrian

5 (*Overleaf*)
Carved body mask worn by male dancers. Makonde, southern Nigeria

26 (*Previous page*)
Chalk goddess. Grimes
Graves, Norfolk

27 (*Left*)
Venus of Willendorf.
Aurignacian-Perigordian
period

28 (*Opposite*)
Sheelagh-na-gig. Ballyport
Castle, County Clare, Eire

29 (*Left*)
Bronze female statuette,
Aust-on-Severn,
Gloucestershire

30 (*Opposite*)
Bronze phallic amulet, Bu
St Edmunds, Suffolk

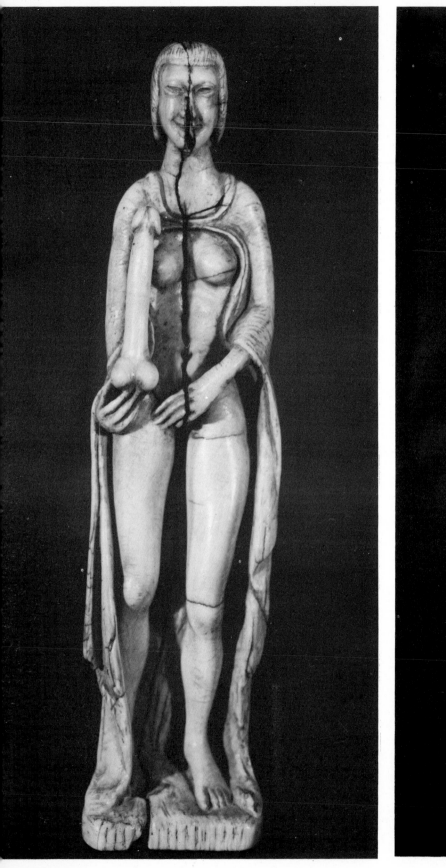 

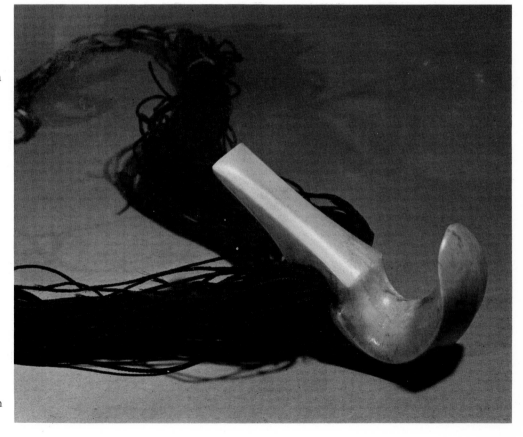

37 (*Above*)
Rock carving: the drama o
the seasons. Bohuslän,
Sweden

38 (*Left*)
Relief of nymph goddesses
bathing. High Rochester,
Northumberland

39 (*Opposite*)
Rock carving: the sacred
spring wedding. Bohuslän,
Sweden

'power' residing in the female genitals, thought to be particularly dangerous when they were first broached and the hymeneal blood flowed. This explanation does not now seem to be entirely adequate. For the help of such especially sacred people and objects was also invoked to cure sterility in a woman already married. In many parts of the ancient world, including Greece and India, sterile women would resort to intercourse with strangers or the priests at a temple to cure their trouble. In Christian Europe priests and monks used to perform the same office. In the Roman world young girls and brides would sit astride the phallus of a priapic image in a temple of Jupiter or Mutunus, to break their hymens. Barren women would have intercourse with similar images. This idea fascinated the erotic imagination of Baroque Europe. At the court of Louis XIV, for example, a large number of engravings (e.g. by Ertinger) made great play with the theme. In parts of India brides were often either deflowered with small sacred lingams, or seated on a large lingam as an act of symbolic intercourse with the divine principle. There is abundant evidence, especially from France, that in recent centuries country women would rub themselves upon ancient megaliths, or natural stones of suggestive shapes, for the sake of being married or obtaining children. These customs testify remarkably to the survival in Europe of an archaic transitional stage of belief in which the power dwelling in the stones, which was originally, no doubt, female, has come to be seen as masculine. The smooth-worn phallic stalagmite in the cave of Pech Merle springs at once to mind.

Among many other peoples sanctified instruments were and still are used to initiate girls into mature sexuality, very often by female initiators; and these may be in the form of sculptures with phalli. It is more than likely that some of the Hellenistic Egyptian terracottas which are shaped either as simple phalli or as phalli borne by disproportionately small male figures were also meant as practical devices for inducing both sexual pleasure and active procreation. In Europe through medieval times, even into the eighteenth century, it was customary for dildos (called 'love gods' or 'love birds'), which were roughly shaped as phallic-headed birds, to be sold openly in markets. These were descendants of the winged phalli of ancient Greece, such as those still standing in the sanctuary at Delos, which symbolized among the Greeks, as we have seen, the psyche or procreative soul. Such phallic birds, imagined either as live cocks (!) or geese, or realized as wood and leather dildos, feature large in the folk and erotic art of Europe. They explain the meaning of the girl who waits with her birdcage open, represented in so much eighteenth-century art. But behind them must lie a symbolic and religious intent related to the male energy which claims defloration and cures sterility. All these customs are not the product of mere dread though they may well be enveloped, among some primitives, in the validating force of taboo. They must have some such significance as the passing on into each maturing woman of a supra-individual spirit force, conceived as male.

The generic male power is, of course, universally represented by the penis, either in the form of a stylized emblem or as a naturalistic part of a male body, the part analogically symbolising the whole. The testicles are often relatively insignificant; for their role in paternity was not clearly understood by most primitive peoples, as it is not by many Westerners even today. The active penis is what is identified as the primary vessel of male sexuality, the visible embodiment of an abstract and intangible semen which propagates all things. On the cosmic scale it symbolizes that which generates the world and all its phenomena. On the human scale it symbolizes the spirit of family and tribe which is passed on by each individual and survives when he dies. In this guise it is represented on the houses of

Indonesia. The long houses of the Maori in New Zealand were once ornamented with wooden kingposts and lintels carved with male and female figures with large exposed genitals, and smaller images of coupling, executed in a looping, sinuous yet ferocious style – clearly images designed to assert the power imbuing human identity and continuity. The cosmic phallus may be represented by the standing stone, pillar or tower, often enough transposing and absorbing the originally female power of its material substance, the 'mother rock'.

In fact a feminine counterpart to a predominant phallus symbolism can always be found somewhere in the complex even of those cultures which are pronouncedly male-oriented, such as those of the Hebrews or the Norse tribes. It is, for example, conjectured, almost certainly correctly, that the Old Testament Ark of the Covenant contained a phallic emblem, thus becoming itself a female symbol.[22] A plan of the interrelationship of the archaic female personifications of the Fates referred to in Nordic literature, the prototypes of Macbeth's Weird Sisters, who live in a cave by a round, white well of water, has been composed by Professor Brian Branston.[23] It demonstrates quite clearly how the old underlying feminine significance of the abstract idea of Wyrd, or Fate, was overshadowed but not eliminated by the phallic, masculine and military gods of the north European tribes. It seems that there really is no such thing as 'pure' phallism, even in those cultures where female sexual symbols may not be very evident.

All over the world, however, to express the general intuition that a masculine energy is vital both to men and crops, phallic emblems that have no connection with a named specific deity have been used, sometimes with their significance reduced by day-to-day familiarity either to frightening away the evil spirits, or to mere generic Good Luck. In the archaic Shinto religion of Japan, which originated in the rice-farming culture of the pre-Buddhist period, the 'Heavenly Root' (i.e. the phallus) was worshipped as a sacred object in temples large and small, where large numbers of phallic *ex votos* were offered. It was in these temples that the highly revered priestess-prostitutes performed their duties. All over the rice-country phalli were planted among the paddies, and nude figures with enormous phalli were offered at village shrines to avert catastrophes such as famine or disease. In the fields of southern Italy crude phallic boundary stones survived long into modern times, descendants probably of the old Herms or Terms of the classical world. These were block-like stones with projecting phalli, sometimes also with human heads, which came to be 'named' as Priapus, Hermes, Liber, Tutunus or Mutunus. Phallic stones were likewise set up and worshipped in the Semitic middle East, including Palestine. In ancient graves, notably in ancient Egypt and in Norway, phalli were sometimes buried with the dead. Viking examples are in the Museum at Christiania. Among the Norse farmers domestic ceremonies involving the passing of a phallus from hand to hand through the household are mentioned in an ancient poem. In the Philippines large wooden phalli featured in funeral ceremonies. Innumerable versions of this cult will be mentioned in the later sections of this book, many of which are associated with sexual rites as assertions either of crop and animal fertility or of human immortality.

Often with these objective symbols of male power are associated symbols referring to the 'etherial', cosmically 'subtle' or 'infusorial' quality of the power itself. The open sky and the wind, although themselves unrepresentable in art, have prompted customs often related to a bird-imagery which has an underlying sexual strain. The sun, however, is perhaps the commonest of these; and joint sun–phallus emblems, combining a solar disc or wheel with a phallic image of some kind, often in human shape, are very common. The Shinto Heavenly Root was emblematic of solar energy. A striking artistic image of this equation appears in the long, white cotton sun-pennant which used to be erected by the natives of the Babar archipelago, under which their ritual orgies took place. It was cut out in the shape of a man, with a stuffed penis and testicles attached to it. But such a joint imagery is very commonly personalized in the dynastic-sky and father-gods with whom the chieftains of powerful tribes identified themselves. They often reinforced the identification, as we have seen, by rehearsing the sky-god's own union with the ancient earth goddess by ritual coupling with her live representatives.

The Slavonic solar sky-god Byelbog was hymned as broaching the earth and fertilizing her with his spear. This is closely reminiscent of Australian aboriginal dances referred to above. Other military objects can carry a similar phallic symbolism, swords and clubs especially. The club of Legba, the phallic god of African Dahomey now naturalized into Haitian voodoo, was often carved as a phallus. The giant prehistoric figure cut in the chalk downs near Cerne Abbas in England is ithyphallic and carries a club, as did Hercules, another solar hero.

Perhaps the most interesting of all the phallic emblems representing generic power is the wand. In Japan at festivals held on the first full moon of the year willow sticks were used to stir a special gruel. These were then whittled at the top into a bunch of shavings, and the village boys used to run about striking young women with these sticks. The Australian Arunda used similar wands; and in many parts of Europe, from classical to recent times, wands with bunches of leaves, thongs or feathers were used either at festivals to strike young women or at weddings to beat the bride. It is not at all difficult to associate these objects both with the feathered phalli painted in the Palaeolithic caves and with the bunched besoms which the medieval witches were supposed to straddle and ride to the Sabbat; supposed examples of witch-besoms even have handles carved as penises. The bunch attached to the end must be a graphic image for the seminal jet, a plastic analogue to the coloured water sprayed about at the Indian Holi procession and the rice or confetti thrown at modern Western weddings. Thus it is possible to recognize a special phallic symbolism in the foliated royal sceptres of Europe, and in the traditional staff of the medieval European fool with its captive bladder representing either sperm or testicles. Indeed the fool has many archaic fertility attributes, including his horned headdress and parti-coloured clothes.

Many books have discussed the vexed question of the common medieval symbolism of the 'vegetation god'. Some, such as Margaret Murray's *The God of the Witches*, have developed elaborate historical fantasies concerning the deaths of the English kings which cannot really be sustained. Jessie L. Weston's *From Ritual to Romance* had the distinction of inspiring T. S. Eliot's great poem *The Waste Land*, and Robert Graves has testified in several books, including *The White Goddess* and *Seven Days in New Crete*, to the inspiration he has derived from the many sections of Sir James Frazer's *The Golden Bough* which deal with the repeated sacrifice of temporary kings at the hands of a college of female representatives of the Great Goddess whom they have served sexually and energetically during their tenure. The great play by Euripides, *The Bacchae*, remembers the power, still deadly numinous in Classical times, once attributed to the Maenads. These were female devotees of Dionysus–Bacchus, a god who wears a leopard-skin; they tore animals to pieces in ecstatic frenzy, copulated with the Satyrs and destroyed male strangers who spied upon them, as did female goddess worshippers even in imperial Rome. In the play the Maenads circumstantially destroy the king. No pure history for such legends can now be authenticated, despite the magnificently realistic passage with which *The Golden Bough* opens, describing the incumbent of the Nemi kingship roaming red-eyed through the grove by night, watching for the successor who will finally slaughter him and take his place.

However, it is undoubtedly true that human sacrifice has been continually performed all over the world, expressly for the purpose of energizing the natural realm. It is also true that many animal sacrifices, such as the early Dionysiac and Mithraic bull-sacrifices, were done with the purpose of promoting crops. The blood which flows from the wound of the Mithraic bull in some Helleno–Roman images is carved as ears of corn. It is also true that animal and vegetable sacrifices were identified with the slain god to whom they were offered. Frazer collected numerous folk customs whose patterns seem to suggest that human beings identified, like bulls, with the masculine power of nature, had indeed been sacrificed in parts of Europe at unspecified times in the past. It is also more than probable that such humans, following customs similar to those carefully recorded among tribal peoples in nineteenth-century India, were also accorded special sexual favours from women representing the female power. Scholars who work in the field of the Medieval Romance have recorded numerous genuine reminiscences of ancient, perhaps pre-Celtic, cults. Sceptics like Geoffrey Parrinder are almost certainly correct in assuming that during the Middle Ages ritual king-slaughtering was not practised. But scepticism can be carried too far. There is abundant evidence from papal and ecclesiastical records that fertility rituals featuring representatives of animal and vegetation gods were indeed a common feature of European peasant life during medieval times. And it is certainly wrong to dismiss the fact that nature and fertility elements did underlie the ghastly extravaganzas contrived by the medieval witchhunters, whatever their political overtones.

The central figure in the putative rituals lying behind both the literary and the morbid manifestations is undoubtedly authentic. He appears in variant shapes all over Europe, and is called both benevolent and evil; he is seen as both king and sacrifice. He was certainly the patron of sexual orgies, in which human representatives of himself played a leading part. At bottom, no doubt, he was primarily a figure of myth, invoked in stories, sexy springtime songs, ritual chanting and seasonal festivals, who represented the concretion of the masculine sexual and cosmic energies so important to agricultural peoples; there can be no doubt that individual men did indeed personify him in England wearing the guise of Herne the Hunter, Robin Hood, Jack of the Green and so on, clad in garments of leaves or coloured patches, horned headdresses, and brandishing phallic batons. The descriptions of festivals and processions in which such personages figured are authentic and well known.

The old annual processions dedicated to Isis, Demeter and Flora with their phallic emblems have already been mentioned. They were accompanied by the singing of erotic songs and lecherous horseplay amplified by 'Fescennine' (i.e. erotic) joking. They were sophisticated versions of ceremonies carried out seasonally in rustic communities all over the world. In Europe, however, we know that during late classical times through into the Middle Ages a variety of ceremonies continued, notably in Greece, Italy, Spain and France, in which a leading role was played by characters also often dressed in leaves or patches, who had a kind of universal licence on those special occasions to ignore the taboos of society, and to lead wild, Dionysiac, orgies. It is often said that they inherited their licence by virtue of the fact that, sometime in the undefined but distant past, they were soon to be sacrificed as 'May kings' after coupling with 'May queens', and that the effigies known to have been burnt or hanged in trees were substitutes for what were originally human sacrifices. Perhaps this may once have been so. But more

74

important is the fact that these sexual figures inherited the freedom to sing erotic songs and indulge in lecherous horseplay and jesting from their ancient prototypes. In medieval Europe they survived as court fools; but their most important descendant was the Harlequin of the seventeenth and eighteenth-century Commedia dell' Arte troupes, who evolved the prototype of one of our principal forms of modern theatre sometime in the sixteenth century, from local Tuscan festivals. As can be seen from numerous engravings, no self-respecting Harlequin – before the nineteenth century – lacked his phallic club complete with huge dangling testicles.

Here we have the Patron of Fertility in his guise of fool. But there can be little doubt that he once also existed in Europe, secretly and under grave official disabilities, as a serious figure who performed an equivalent to the role of the officiant in the American Mandan Indian Sun Dance, copulating ritually with chosen women – Festival Queens – for the supernatural benefit of crops, cattle and men. Witchcraft reports referring to the use of artificial phalli by the Devil are often held to be fanciful. But the basic rite may well have been real, since we know that many ancient and highly objective rites *did* survive, revolving around the worship of spirits in caves, and May Day orgies with masked dancers, some of which are performed to this day, heavily bowdlerized, in the seasonal masked dances of Switzerland, south Germany and certain Spanish towns. There have even been vestiges recorded in Scandinavia, England and Spain of rituals in which a bull-masked dancer carries out symbolic coupling in the manner of a bull with his cows; so it is by no means unreasonable to suppose that one of the ingredients in the phantasmogoria concocted by the writers of the *Malleus Maleficarum*, the witchfinder's handbook which set the pattern for all the later questioning under torture, was some knowledge of genuine surviving cults which were still rivals to the Church as sources of supernatural benefit. A further clue to the genuineness of popular demand for serious sexual images and rites is the fact that the Church made its own concessions to that demand. There were many places in France, Germany, Italy and Spain where sexual rites were performed, and where phallic images of Christian saints which had taken over the functions of more ancient deities were revered in various ways. At Trani, by Naples, a huge wooden phallic image called Il Santo Membro was carried in procession annually until the eighteenth century. At other Italian shrines huge wax phalli were sold as offerings. In the sixteenth century there were many Protestant reports of phalli being found at Catholic churches, in worship especially by the women, at, for example, Poligny, Vendre and Auxerre. A huge leather example 'with appendages' taken from the church of St Eutropius was burned by the Protestants at Orange; whilst at Aix another, of white marble, was regularly garlanded by the women. At the shrine of St Foutin de Varailles at Embrun the saint's enormous phallus was dyed red with the offerings of wine the women used to pour over it and then collect as an aphrodisiac. The whole shrine was full of wax phallic *ex votos*. Elsewhere the phalli of saints were scraped into potions, either erotic or progenitive. There are, as well, numerous scabrous but true tales told of priests who willingly served urgent female devotees in time-honoured style.

Clearly, medieval popular Catholicism was far from the puritanical religion it became when it was gradually forced by the conflict with Protestants, Calvinists and Puritans to adopt a posture more puritan than they. Bishop Eude Rigaud (*c.* 1248-75) has recorded his own efforts, the earliest described of many made by the more high-minded elements of the ecclesiastical hierarchy during the Middle Ages, to reform and purge monasteries and nunneries. The vivid erotic life many of them fostered is reflected in a few small works of art made or kept in them. Properly they belong to the history of European erotic art, since few are primitive. One ivory is reproduced, however, from an Italian house, since it perpetuates a fine image closely related to this whole fertility complex. It represents a woman, her coat open on her nakedness, holding a large phallus with testicles.

There are numerous references and hints in European literature to the fact that not only art-made objects but actual human genitals were felt to have a magical power, especially in averting all kinds of misfortunes, but also in fertilizing the ground. Many customs have been recorded in which farmers or their wives walk naked around their fields, sometimes, like farmers in Indonesia and the Pacific, deliberately exposing their genitals. Evil spirits could be repelled by both men and women exposing their genitals to them; and at the famous Celtic solstice bonfire festivals women used to stride over the fire, exposing their vulvas to the beneficial influence of the flame, and blessing it with their own power. This must represent a survival of the once widespread but now degraded European belief in the power of all sexual phallic images. The Sheelagh-na-gigs and other little male phallic figures still found on churches probably shared this function, as did the large, aggressively naked male and female that were once carved by the doors of Servatos Cathedral in Spain, and similar figures in Spanish colonial churches. Such facts and customs, again, must have been important ingredients in the imagery of medieval witch-craft.

A related idea survives in the extraordinarily widely diffused custom of wearing sexual, but especially phallic, amulets. They may be shaped like single phalli, like complexes of phalli, like male and female genitals joined or like couples with grotesquely enlarged genitals, and were conceived to carry great power for good, averting disease, the evil eye, and all other supernatural disasters. They have been made and worn all over Europe, as well as in India, China and Japan, as super-natural energizers. In Italy as in India they have been buried with the dead to ensure resurrection. Even today in parts of Italy they are still used, though the erotic 'thumb through fingers' amulet is more common, probably because it is less overtly sexual. The same theme, somewhat degraded and misunderstood, as it must be in a culture which officially represses its own sexual roots so strongly as the Christian, appears in the many different kinds of erotic talismans used by European peasants and bourgeoisie from the Middle Ages down to the nineteenth century. They include walking sticks, snuff boxes, watch-movements, candle snuffers, cigar cutters, pipe bowls and matchboxes. More sophisticated owners may have found them amusing; more primitive owners certainly knew the true purpose of erotic amulets and were aware of their underlying force. The majority are no more than straightforward representations of the sexual organs, of men and women display-ing their organs, the women frequently in the posture of Sheelagh-na-gig, or of men and women having intercourse.

Individual European oddities have been recorded. One of the strangest was the 'Jack of Hilton' illustrated in Plot's *Natural History of Staffordshire* (1786). This was a metal kneeling figure of a man found in a house, who held with one hand his large penis shaped like a bunch of leaves. Through it the draught was blown to the domestic fire – a most complex imagery of vital spirit. Among nineteenth-century cast-iron door-stops can be found some which represent full and bare-breasted female figures lying on their backs with their legs apart; some, but not all, are chastened by skin-tight pants. Like the lucky female horseshoe over the house-door, which symbolizes exposed female genitals, these ladies must have been meant to sound in the Victorian home some remote echo of immemorial female mystery.

2 Celtic and Northern Art

Anne Ross

Paul Jacobsthal, the greatest historian of Celtic art, in his description of a rock-carving from the ancient sanctuary in the Val Camonica, northern Italy, says, in connection with the great Celtic stag-god: 'Beside Cernunnos stands an "orans" – phallic: this is a regional or tribal feature, because on the whole the Celts are "decent".'[1] The adjectives 'decent' or 'clean' have also been applied to the literatures of the Celtic world and, up to a point, this would seem to be a fair assessment of their character. We shall return to this question later.

All art must be an expression of the society which creates it, a social artefact; in order to understand anything about the art of a given people it is essential to know something of the people themselves, their language, their national temperament, their attitudes to religion and taboo. The Celts do, in fact, require particular study for their thought processes were (and are) subtle; and their art is a reflection of these – complex, symbolic, suggesting rather than directly expressing, devious, confusing. Although they were included among the great barbarian peoples of Europe by the classical writers, the Celts can by no means be regarded as primitive people. For this reason their art, although it bears, in some of its aspects, affinities with that of the more northerly inhabitants of pagan Europe – Germanic, Danish, Scandinavian – must be treated separately. One of the criteria of primitive peoples is the fact that, in general, they have not evolved a system of writing; early Celtic society, however, is, to some extent, text-aided. It is true that the Celts did not commit their sophisticated culture to writing in their own language under the pressure of the Roman army, but later under the aegis of the Roman Church. They were literate in Greek; and the classical writers, whose ethnographical observations add much valuable detail to what we can determine of the nature of their early social structure, tell us that their not committing their own learning and lore to writing was *deliberate*. They believed that the practice of reading and writing weakened the memory; and, of course, that it also made available to the laity the sacred lore of priest and poet. As a result they evolved a powerful oral tradition, teaching being passed on verbally from master to pupil; amazingly complex material was committed to memory, and it took many years to become a fully-qualified priest or poet. This power of assimilating learning by word of mouth is so deep-seated in the Celtic tradition that it has persisted down to the present day in the surviving Celtic-speaking areas of Europe, in spite of all the pressures which combine to operate against such discipline and individuality of expression. As Robin Flower, in his book on the Irish tradition, says:

The function of the poets was to keep alive this long-descended record in its full detail of genealogy and varied incident. It was inevitable that, when this mnemonic tradition met the Latin tradition of writing, it should be fixed in the new form which offered a greater guarantee of permanence. The kings and the poets and the clerics worked together to this end.[2]

The pagan Celts were an extremely interesting and complex people; and what is even more important to us today in our efforts to search back into the minds of the tribes who, at the height of their power, were masters of Europe, conquerors of Rome, threateners of Delphi and rulers of Etruria, is the fact that they did not and have not ceased to exist. Their direct descendants are still to be found in the most westerly corners of Europe, speaking recognizably similar languages and possessing an archaism of tradition, attitudes and values which provide an invaluable link down the ages with their more formidable forebears. This greatly assists us in our attempts to understand what is, and what is *not*, likely within their cultural context.

To return to Paul Jacobsthal's statement 'on the whole the Celts are "decent".' How far is this statement supported by their art and by the references to sexual custom in the classics and the insular texts? Celtic art can be divided into two distinct types. The first is that to which the term Celtic art is most usually applied, the art of the La Tène Celts. Its great flowering began somewhere about 500 BC and continued until the conquest of the Celtic provinces by Rome, although in Europe it was more or less decadent by this time. It was the art of a powerful aristocracy; Celtic society was intensely aristocratic, and also passionately devoted to religious practices. Caesar, for example, remarks: 'The whole Gallic people is exceedingly given to religious superstition.'[3]

Art and religion were thus inseparable; and, although this splendid art style of the La Tène Celts, which looks on the surface purely decorative, was derived originally from a variety of sources – naturalistic patterns based on plants and foliage which the Mediterranean world delighted in; the splendid animal art of Scythia and more easterly regions; the old indigenous Hallstatt and Urnfield designs based on geometric patterns and on the widespread European cult of solar birds in connection with deities of healing waters; and perhaps the old spirals found in such places as the Neolithic tombs of the Boyne Valley in Ireland, and elsewhere. It is full of magical and religious allusion; and fertility and sexual imagery may underlie the tortuous spirals and the strange swelling horns, or fruits, which emerge from the heads of many of the obviously divine masks used so effectively and frequently by the brilliant and inventive La Tène craftsmen. So, if we think of Celtic art as being purely the art of this La Tène phase and style, then it is true to say that there are very few examples of overt sexual or erotic expression. Jacobsthal himself refers to only one other in his corpus of La Tène art, and this itself is in question. It is a fibula from Niederschönhausen (Kr. Nieder-Barnim); a man lies on the upper surface of the bow; he would appear to be ithyphallic, unless the object which appears to be an erect penis is in fact the tongue or muzzle of the ram's head which forms the lower part of the body. Jacobsthal does, in fact, also illustrate two stones which are clearly phalloid; one is decorated with symbols, while the other is more starkly naturalistic. The first comes from Pfalzfeld, K. St Goar in the Hunsrück; dating from the early phase of La Tène art, that is from the fourth to fifth centuries BC and at one time over six feet in height, it was originally crowned by a male head which was destroyed in the seventeenth century. The glans rested on, or in, the ground, and the four sides of the pillar are decorated with male heads having swelling horns, or leaf-crowns, emerging from them. This stone is an excellent example of the fertility significance of the severed human head in conjunction with the stone pillar referred to in chapter 1. There were, no doubt, innumerable parallels to this stone fashioned from wood which has perished. The second phallic stone published by Jacobsthal, likewise of early Celtic date, comes from Irlich, near Neuwied, in the district of Koblenz – a region where there are many Celtic graves. The stone stood in the vestry of the old church, and was brought into the new church when its predecessor was destroyed. According to local tradition, it promoted childbearing. The same honour was not accorded to an equally pagan stone in Guernsey in the Channel Islands. The so-called 'Grand-mère' of St Martin originally stood inside the consecrated ground of the church-yard: when people going to church passed her they touched her head and made offerings to her. During the last century she was removed from the sacred territory and placed immediately outside the gate of the church; nevertheless, the local people continue to revere this mother-goddess, touching her and making offerings to her. It is believed that if certain rites are correctly performed at the proper time, she not only confers favours on those who seek them, but can be seen to move and 'come to life'. Many pagan stones concerned with old fertility cults still have names and ritual associated with them at the present day in the Celtic areas of Europe.

Otherwise La Tène art, based though it is on swirling, curving, spiralling lines and abstract patterns of a complex nature, is rich in portrayals of the animal and human world which emerge on close examination and, once detected, become obvious. Peering through the stylized foliage a human, or rather, superhuman mask can be seen, surmounted perhaps by a bird-head or that of a ram or bull or horse; or a whole complex of these. Contrary to popular belief Celtic art, even at this stage, cannot be said to have been aniconic – that is without images. And it also seems certain that the complicated and intricate patterns had, in themselves, some symbolic meaning, magical, even sexual in significance; but the key to these has long been lost and like the secret language of the Celtic poets, *berla na filed* 'the speech of the poets', they must remain forever a matter for speculation, not interpretation. Just as this language was a code known to the elite, so was the meaning of this art, no doubt, reserved for the members of the privileged and intellectual classes – and, as all the evidence suggests, common to man and woman alike if they had attained sufficient rank and education. When, however, we come to more naturalistic forms, which both preceded and succeeded these highly-complex designs and must have co-existed with them, we are on safer ground. We know that the severed human head, universally worshipped by the Celts, was symbolic of divinity, all-knowledge and fertility; the sacred birds, many of which had sexual associations were often the servants of the gods and sacred in their own right, the form adopted by deities for various purposes or forms of metamorphosis or of transformation as punishment for wrong-doing; the sinister owl had its role in sexual contexts as did the goat, the potent bull, the sacred ram. These things we have knowledge of because although, as we have seen, the Celts did not write down their own beliefs and traditions during their pagan phase, the classics commented on various of these; and because of the strength and fidelity of the oral tradition, when the native cultural record did come to be committed to writing by the Christian scribes, much of the old learning and belief was preserved intact and we get an amazing and remarkably faithful picture of the Iron Age Celts recorded at this later date.

Although there is little that can be described as straightforward erotic art in the repertoire of the pagan Celts, it would be unrealistic to suggest that they differed from other peoples in sexual habit, engrossment and portrayal. Sexual fulfilment and fertility clearly played as great roles in their society as they do in the entire sphere of humanity, and the use of magic to promote these activities must have been as prevalent in the Celtic world as elsewhere. It is with this activity that the second type of Celtic art is specifically concerned, in a frank and unequivocal way. This secondary, less-sophisticated artistic tradition is frank and direct, concerned with the naturalistic, as opposed to the symbolic portrayal of sexual objects and situations; a tradition which is shared with the peoples of the northern world, and indeed with mankind down the centuries. We can, therefore, say that over and above the highly sophisticated art of the La Tène aristocracy there was an archaic, and class-free art-form, with an impressive ancestry into prehistory, and a persistence equally powerful and lengthy.

Northern European, pre-Celtic and Celtic Miscellaneous Fertility Figures and Symbols

One of the most interesting and early fertility figures from the British Isles is the figure, fashioned from ash-wood, found beneath the Bell track in Somerset and dating from the Neolithic period. Excavated in 1966, the figure was found set within a group of pegs which suggests that it was part of a ritual during the construction of the track, and proves the figure to be contemporary with the original construction. The most interesting thing about this fetish, christened by the excavators the 'God-dolly', is that it is hermaphroditic in form. It had been placed upside down beneath the later track, known as Bell B. Six inches in height, it has a head, flattish but clearly demarcated breasts and an emphatic phallus projecting from below the left breast; the figure was carved from a solid piece of ash, so no projecting branch of the tree was used to create the male organ. A deep linear groove runs down the back of the figure, and there is a similar line down the left side of the torso. One can only speculate on the rites attendant on this bi-sexual figure; its position may suggest a foundation ritual, perhaps 'blessing' the trackway. It is certainly an early British example of a wooden fertility figure, of which several are known from a much later period, although they are not hermaphroditic.

There are one or two other emblems of fertility and sexual potency from this early phase of British and European prehistory. Representations of chalk phalli of a naturalistic kind come, for example, from Thickthorn Barrow, Dorset, and Windmill Hill, Wiltshire, and elsewhere. Chalk figurines of gross or pregnant women are also known from this early period: for example, the little chalk figurine from Grimes Graves, Norfolk, portrays a fecund female of a style found in other contexts of this date. Such images, descended no doubt from the Palaeolithic figures discussed earlier, continue the tradition of emblems of female sexuality and fecundity found down the ages. Another figurine of clay, in this instance, has the features depicted by means of deep holes, while there is a round hole in the centre of the forehead. The neck is as broad as the head, and the breasts are well-defined; the figure was allegedly found in association with pottery of a Hallstatt type – that is, dating to somewhere about 600 BC. Another representation, no doubt of some potent goddess, in the form of a bronze statuette, was found at Aust-on-Severn at the base of the cliffs there; it was discovered in association with a figurine of a horned god, now lost. The goddess wears a crescent-shaped head-dress; the eyes were inset with glass beads, one of which remains. The hands are rigidly pressed to the sides; the breasts are firm and pronounced. Lack of any contemporary documentary evidence must, of course, leave the true significance of these early figures perpetually in doubt; speculation can only be in the broadest of human terms.

Another type of early portrayal of the human figure, the sexual potency and fertility associations of which cannot be in question, is found widely in Europe. Many examples come from the Scandinavian regions and from Spain, and they form a link with the later wooden figures from the northern and Celtic areas. In general, they consist of representations of emphatically phallic men engaged in some activity such as hunting, fighting, sorcery or ball-games; they are not usually shown in company with women, nor is the sexual act depicted. One rock-carving from Bohuslän, west Sweden, shows men with erect genitalia engaged in a ball-game with sticks, reminiscent of shinty sticks. That the game had some ritual significance is suggested by the nakedness of the men and their ithyphallic state. Field or board games are often described in early Irish tales as taking place when some ritual or magical situation is in progress. Similar naked figures armed with stick and ball are known from the Romano–British iconographic repertoire, the main difference being that they are not phallic. Ritual nakedness is, of course, well-known and widespread in early religions, and many examples of it occur in the Celtic literatures. In the Irish mythological story, 'The Destruction of Da Derga's Hostel', the king-elect sets out on a bird-chase; he does not know that his mother was seduced by a supernatural bird-man, and that these birds are in fact magical – his father and his followers. It has been foreseen by one of the wise men that the king-to-be would be seen going along the road towards Tara (one of the most important pagan sanctuary sites in Ireland), stark naked, and having a stone and a sling in his hands. Conaire's bird-father told him of this: 'A man stark-naked, who shall go at the end of the night along one of the roads of Tara, having a sling and a stone, he shall be king.'[4] Hags, having strong sexual characteristics, are also introduced into this tale and are discussed later.

Three men, phallic and thus probably engaged in some sacred activity, are engraved on a rock at Zalavruga, White Sea, Russia; they move on skis and hold ski sticks in their hands. Another scene, involving naked, seemingly dancing figures, male and female, is engraved on rock at Addaura, Sicily, and probably dates from the ninth century BC. Much later, from about the first century BC and from a sanctuary site at Neuvy-en-Sullias, Loiret, therefore of incontestably religious import, are two superb bronzes of a man and a woman dancing. Their faces are rapt, their bodies exquisite and sensitively depicted; the man, however, is not ithyphallic. A magnificently phallic man, or god, is drawn on a rock at Skäne, Sweden; the figure dates from the eighth or seventh century BC. He holds a gigantic ritual axe, a weapon with strong religious associations. Again from Bohuslän, Sweden, a horned and phallic sorcerer, or god, fingers splayed and unequal in number, seemingly rides in a wheeled chariot preceded by a horned animal.

This leads us on to a series of phallic wooden figures dating from the late Bronze Age or early Iron Age. Some, like the superb male figure in the National Museum at Copenhagen, have a huge penis carved in one with the body; others, like those from Roos Carr, Yorkshire, of pine-wood, have deep holes for the insertion of the male organ, which may originally have been made of wood, or perhaps some symbolic substance. Four of these superb figures stand in a boat; one holds a circular shield in his left hand. Another similar figure was found with this group; he too has the hole for the phallus and holds a circular shield in his left hand again. One can only speculate on the magic and ritual that must have been attendant on the insertion of these phalli. Another, from Dagenham, Essex, shows similar features. An impressive male figure from Ralaghan, near Shercock, County Cavan, Ireland, likewise has a sinister aspect and a deep hole for the insertion of a penis; it was found earlier in this century in an area rich in traces of the supernatural and pagan Celtic cults in general. When it was dug up from the bog, by good fortune a local school-master, a native of the place, happened to be present: the man who chanced upon it not only failed to realize its archaeological importance, but viewed it with strongly superstitious eyes. He said that people had been turning up 'carved sticks' like this one in the same bog for a long time, but they didn't like them, and so threw them 'back into the bog-hole'. And this must have been the fate of numbers of cult figures in Ireland thrown back into the bogs, re-buried where they had been dug up in fields, or smashed up because of their known pagan associations. Another male fertility figure, the phallus carved one with the body, was found at Teigngrace, Devon. A pair of such wooden fertility figures, long and stick-like, was found at Schleswig-Holstein; one of these is male, with a carved penis; the other female, with breasts and genitals indicated. Another female figure, with a markedly fearsome and hag-like appearance and probably dating from the early Celtic period, was found at Ballachulish, Argyll, in Scotland. Preserved in the peat-soil, together with traces of wickerwork which must have been used to house her in her remote shrine, she must have presented a sinister sight in her full splendour. Exposure to air caused rapid shrinking of the wood, but even so, the menacing features, eyes inlaid with pebbles, and the well-defined sexual organs, place her amongst the category of powerful hag-like goddesses discussed below. However such wooden figures, distributed in Europe and the British Isles, are, on the whole, male and have a clear association with fertility rites involving male sexual power. Such images as these must be what Lucan had in mind when he describes the sacred places of the Celts so graphically: 'And there were many dark springs running there, and grim-faced figures of gods uncouthly hewn by the axe from the untrimmed tree-trunk, rotted to whiteness.'[5]

Somewhat later in date, belonging perhaps to the early Romano–British period, is the famous chalk-cut figure on the hill above Cerne Abbas, Dorset. Known as the Cerne Abbas giant, this British 'Hercules' with his all-conquering club, like that of the great Irish god the Dagda, and his huge penis and testicles, has survived through the centuries, dominating the surrounding countryside, defying the Church, and remaining down to the present day a powerful fertility symbol. Young couples, about to be married, still resort to him, and it was believed in the district that to have sexual intercourse within the hollow of the vast phallus could only have beneficial results. The Irish Dagda, the great god of the early Irish mythological race known as the Tuatha Dé Danann, 'People of the Goddess Danu', is described as possessing a huge, all-powerful club; and although there are no erotic descriptions of him, he is reputed to have mated with many powerful goddesses in a ritual manner. He had intercourse, for example, with the sinister war-raven goddess, the Mórrígan, whose sexual lust was as powerful as her desire for blood and carnage.

The Dagda had a house in Glen Etin in the north. Now the Dagda met a woman in Glen Etin on that day about the *samain* (Hallow-een) of the battle. The river Unius of Connacht roars to the south of it. He beheld the woman in Unius in Corann washing herself with one foot at Allod Echae to the south of the water and the other at Loscuinn to the north of the water. Nine loosened tresses were on her head. The Dagda conversed with her and they made a union. The Bed of the Couple is the name of the place after that. The woman mentioned here is the Mórrígan.[4]

Here we have a powerful, virile, pagan god: when he is sexually united with the highly dangerous, essentially female war-goddess, with her ominous crow-raven transformations, we do indeed have a potent coupling. And when, as in this instance, the union is carried out in association with a mighty river, then the erotic nature of the situation is very clear. The Celts worshipped water, and believed it to have strong powers of conveying fertility. An interesting link between this passage and the Gaulish tradition is found in the fact that the war-raven goddesses are also known from Gaul; there are examples of personal names such as Boduagnatus or Boduagenos, 'born or descended from the goddess Bodb'* showing her reputation as an eponymous ancestress. One of her names in Gaul was Nantosuelta, 'She of the Winding River', a name which again links her with the fertilizing powers of water. Her mate is Sucellos, 'The Good Striker', the European counterpart of the Irish Dagda, 'The Good God'. Sucellos has the mallet and his dish of plenty as his fertility attributes. But the Dagda, although he is reminiscent of the club-wielding chalk figure of Hercules at Cerne Abbas, is never portrayed in the literary tradition as exceptionally sexual or ithyphallic. There is, however, another hero or divinity who has more claims in this direction than the Dagda. This is the powerful Fergus mac Roich, 'Fergus son of Great Horse', the name itself being suggestive of virility. The name Fergus also means 'Choice of Men', and so his role as an Irish equivalent of the Cerne giant seems clear. His penis is described as being seven fingers in length; he mates with the great divine queen Medb, 'Drunk Woman', whose own sexuality is boundless. Her many husbands were mere passing bed-fellows; only Fergus with his tremendous sexual capacity could satisfy her; his mate was Flidais, goddess of the woodlands and wild things. She was mistress of the animals, provider of dairy produce and venery for the people, a Celtic equivalent of the classical Diana descended from and successor to the Palaeolithic prototypes. The virility of her mate is indicative of her own sexuality.

There are many tales concerned with amorous situations in which birds, especially swans or geese, are involved. These contain little of a sexually suggestive nature, however, and are rather distinguished by their restraint and delicacy. Birds are employed as messengers to facilitate communication between lovers, or as the form adopted by lovers of either sex in order to meet, mate with, or carry off the loved one, sometimes for the purpose of bringing about the conception of some superhuman hero.

The Horned, Phallic God of the Pagan Celtic World

There are two distinct types of Celtic deity depicted in the iconography and described in the literature, whose sexuality and powers of fertility are consistent and clear. The first of these is one of the most basic of the Celtic god-types, with an ancestry in Europe which takes us right back to the imagery of the Swedish and the Spanish rock-carvings, and beyond into an indefinable past. This is the horned, phallic god of the Celtic tribes – aggressive, fertile, bull-or-ram-horned; or antlered and non-phallic, his powers of fertility indicated by his branching antlers, symbolic of male strength, and his obvious concern with matters of fecundity and fertility.

* The names of this trio of fearful goddesses in Ireland were Bodb, Macha and the Mórrígan. Collectively they were sometimes known as the Mórrígna.

There is also another type of fierce and phallic divine warrior, but he is figured without horns.

The earliest Celtic portrayal of the antlered god occurs in the ancient sanctuary in the Val Camonica in northern Italy, where for centuries the evolving peoples of Europe gave expression to their religious ideas on the rock faces of this sacred place. The Celtic drawings must date from the time of the Celtic conquest of Etruria, that is from round about 400 BC. The antlered god is known from one inscription only as Cernunnos, 'The Horned One'; this may well not have been his name throughout the Celtic world because the Celts had few divine types but many divine names. The great god of fertility and prosperity of stocks, commerce and man himself, stands chastely in a full-length *chiton*; he is antler-bearing and has, over his right, bent arm, the sacred neck-ring – the torc – worn by gods and heroes alike. Over his left, bent arm are traces of the horned serpent, his most consistent cult animal. The relationship between the serpent and sexuality is widely diffused; to endow the beast with the horns of a potent ram would be to create a highly apotropaic and fecund symbol. The god is covered; but his worshipper, smaller in size and having his hands raised in the same *orans* posture as the god – a posture used by the Celts for prayer – is markedly ithyphallic. It is noteworthy that this great and ancient antlered god never appears in phallic form, but, as we have noted, his great branching antlers and his potent horned serpent companion are indications of his own undeniable virility. He is widespread in the Celtic iconographic repertoire of Europe; and there are traces of him in the vernacular literatures where he figures as a great warrior, connected with a mighty serpent, but never as a lover or as being symbolic of male sexuality, as does, for example, Fergus in Irish lore.

The second type of horned god is likewise associated with pastoral pursuits, with the rearing of stock, with war, and sometimes with venery. He is known in Europe, and he figures largely in north Britain where, in Roman times, he was sometimes likened to Mars the warrior. It is in this guise that he appears, for example, at Maryport (Roman Alauna), at Brough by Sands, and elsewhere. He is naked, strongly ithyphallic, holding shield and spear, barbarous and menacing, equipped for battle and prepared to deal death and to convey life. Sometimes both gods and horned animals are depicted with horns having knobbed ends: this is a problematic feature. It was customary to bind the horns of bulls being prepared for sacrifice, and this may indeed be the significance of these bulbous horns. It cannot, however, be denied, that in many instances the combination of horn and knobbed terminal gives the impression of a phallus, creating, like the addition of ram-horns to the sacred snake, a very powerful fertility symbol indeed.

Sometimes, in Roman contexts, the horned god was likened to Mercury, no doubt in his earlier role as the protector of the flocks and herds. Here too he is usually ithyphallic, but carries instead of weapons the purse and wand of the classical god. The sinuous serpent winding round the caduceus is once more in accordance with Celtic tradition. Again the horned god appears as a kind of native Silvanus, god of the woods, naked and without attribute apart from his huge penis. In north Britain another type of naked phallic god is figured, but without the horns, therefore presumably of the Cerne giant type, bearing arms or without attribute. A deity of similar type, fierce and aggressively phallic, comes from Maastricht, Holland. The male horned beast is fierce in combat and competent in the sexual sphere. It is not then surprising that in early societies the men, relying on their own physical strength in battle and their personal ability to increase the numbers of their tribe or group by their procreative powers, should have envisaged their gods as combining the powers of the male animal with their own anthropomorphic form and attributes.

Before leaving the direct imagery of the phallus for the sexual symbolism of the human head, we must glance at one monument where the two concepts most clearly meet and merge, and where the implied sexual significance of the stone is made implicit by surviving local traditions about it. It came originally from Maryport (Alauna), where there are several examples of the horned god. Now part of the Netherhall collection, it is known locally as the Serpent Stone; natives of the area believed it to have phallic associations, and fertility rites are said to have been performed in connection with it. One side of the stone is decorated by a thick serpent, crested – a variant of the male symbolism of the horn – and collared, in the act of swallowing a fish. On the other side is a fierce male head, the mouth seemingly in the attitude of shouting or screaming; the neck is adorned by a torc with knobbed terminals. The association of the severed head with a pillar stone had a clear phallic significance for a people such as the Celts. Before returning to the sexual symbolism of the human head and its place in Celtic religious art and life, we will look at another remarkable group of figures, from the Caucasian mountains this time, testifying to the widespread cult of ithyphallic deities or heroes in pre-historic Europe, as elsewhere. This group forms part of the remarkable Kazbek treasure, and has features which are also known in the Celtic world. The hoard was found when the military road was being made in the last century, and it has the appearance of a religious deposit in a pool formed by a spring, nine feet under the present ground. A silver bowl, filled with little bronze figurines and tied round with chains, was discovered, associated with a grave. Several of the figurines portray an emphatically phallic man, sometimes well advanced in years; in one instance he holds a double hammer and stands on the curly horns of a bull-head. Other figures disport themselves on goat-horns; one pair, both ithyphallic and naked, have their knees bent – one is actually engaged in decapitating the other. This group would seem to demonstrate admirably the sexual link between the severed head, the phallus and horns. Yet another naked figure, ithyphallic and with a shield in his hand, stands bent-kneed above the horns of a goat, and an ithyphallic old man plays a lyre. Prisoners and their captors are depicted in this re-markable deposit of bronzes, and the fact that all are phallic suggests the ritual significance of this material. Pendants also occur; some of these, in the form of men, are extremely interesting. One has a pair of twin spirals on the shoulders and on the buttocks; the penis is fully erect, and the testicles well-defined. Another figure, holding a drinking horn, has even more pronounced genitals. There is also an impressive series of horned animals, with the horns pronounced but the genitalia not emphasized. The combination of horned beasts, ithyphallic men and other symbols, together with the close association of a spring and probably a pool, indicate an ancient Caucasian fertility rite, somewhere between 1000 and 600 BC.

This leads us on to the most highly significant sexual symbol of all for the Celts, that of the human head, especially in conjunction with a pillar-stone or a sacred spring. The fertility powers of water are well-known; the severed head too was believed to be capable of conveying fertility. The combination of these objects was a very potent one. The Celts, like many barbarian peoples, were head-hunters; but the severed human head was no mere trophy of military success. They pre-served the heads they took in battle in oils and herbs, and either kept them in wooden chests in their houses, displayed them on stakes round their houses and hill-forts, or set them on pillars in their sacred groves and temples. They also made heads from stone, wood or metals; they must have carried these about as amulets, or as icons portraying some particular deity or power. The archaeology of the Celtic world supported by classical writers testifies fully to this belief in the powers of the head. But it is in the vernacular literatures of the British Isles that the full meaning of the severed human head for the Celts is illuminated. They believed it to be the seat of the soul, the very centre of being; this must include in it the powers, not only of prophecy, all wisdom and entertainment, but of generation itself. The head was a symbol of fertility and for this reason it is the head, not the phallus, that is figured most frequently in the Celtic iconographic tradition. Heads were believed to be capable of presiding over the feasts so dear to the Celts, and thus to provide all good things. Often the deity was portrayed merely as a head, with, or without, specific attributes. They took stones of suggestively phalloid shape and either surmounted them with a human head, or drew a face on the glans, thus creating a powerful fertility symbol. One such stone, from Broadway, Worcestershire, is so shaped; on the glans, which is in fact formed by the head, is a crude human face. From Eype, Dorset, comes a large pebble, again phallic in outline, on which is cut a sombre countenance; below this are four interlaced circles of obscure significance. A stone somewhat similar to that from Broadway comes from Roman Corstopitum (Corbridge, Northumberland); and such examples could be multiplied indefinitely. The setting of the head on a pillar is also a method of creating a special phallic image, which unites the powers of these two potent parts of the body. The heads of men taken in battle were given to the highly sexual and awesome raven-goddess, or rather trio of goddesses; according to the ninth century glossary of Cormac, such offerings were known in the Irish tradition as *Mesrad Machae*, 'Macha's mast'. This again stresses the sexual symbolism of the head and brings to mind the sinister statue from a grotto at Vence, near Marseilles, which depicts a seated woman with a sharp, beak-like face holding in her lap, not an infant, but a severed male head. A similar image is the woman, from a tomb at Espeyran in the Rhone valley, naked and voluptuous, who stands with her hand resting possessively on a human-headed and phallic stone pillar. This imagery is again strongly illustrative of the theme of fertility and regenerative powers. The qualities possessed by the all-fertile head are well illustrated in the insular literary tradition. One example is that of the head of the great warrior Conganchness; in his head three magical dogs were generated; and the skull of another divine hero used to supply the whole of Ireland with milk. The sacred head of the Welsh divinity Bran, 'Raven', had likewise all the qualities of a good Celtic head, both providing and entertaining at the sacred feast. Other stones, not decorated by heads but associated with fertility, occur widely in the Celtic world. One of the most famous of these is the Turoe stone from County Galway in Ireland. Of granite and nearly four feet high, it is decorated by spirals of a late Celtic style which dates it, or at least its decoration, to somewhere between the first centuries BC and AD. It has clear phallic significance, and it may have been one of the sacred stones known in Ireland to have been associated with the rites attendant on the inauguration of kings. The king was thought to be responsible for the fertility and prosperity of the tribe or people over whom he ruled. His inauguration was therefore extremely important and attended by rites of which we now have only veiled hints. It is clear, however, that his own virility was as vital as his powers of judgement and authority.

In this connection we must consider the Celtic goddess in her equine form. There is evidence that one of the most powerful and widely-worshipped of the Celtic goddesses was a deity having the horse as one of her attributes or metamorphoses. Her name varied throughout the Celtic world. In Gaul she was known as Epona,

42 (*Opposite*)
Wooden male sculpture. Broddenbjerg, North Jutland. 4th century BC

43 (*Left*)
Bronze Age fertility goddess
from the bog at Viksø,
Denmark

44 (*Right*)
Plate from interior of base of
silver cauldron. Gundestrup,
Jutland

45 (*Previous page*)
Silver cauldron, Gundestru[...]
Jutland. Outer panels depi[...]
individual gods and
goddesses, inner panels sho[...]
cult scenes. Early 1st
century BC

46 (*Left*)
Rock carvings, Vitlycke,
Bohuslän, Sweden. Early [...]
millennium

(*Right*)
ck carving. Litsleby,
num, Bohuslän, Sweden.
rly 1st millennium

48 (*Left*)
Grotesque Viking statue,
perhaps Freyer.
Rällinge, Södermanland,
Sweden

49 (*Above*)
Limestone Sheelagh-na-gig.
St Ives, Huntingdonshire

50 (*Right*)
Sheelagh-na-gig: female
fertility figure. Newtown
Lower, County Tipperary,
Eire

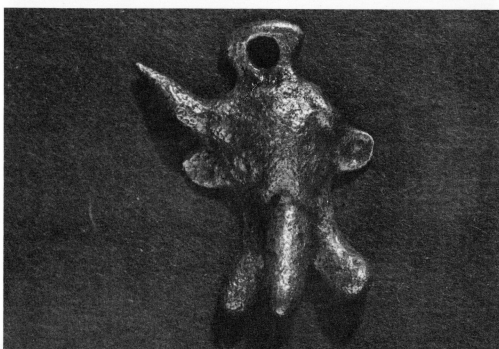

5 (*Right*)
Phallic amulet. Dorset.
Romano-British

4 (*Opposite*)
Fragmentary stone head.
Heidelberg, Baden, Germany.
c. 4th century BC

6 (*Right*)
'Swastika'. Meigle,
Perthshire. c. 9th century AD

'Great Horse'; she appears in Wales as Riannon, 'Great Queen'; in the Irish tradition she figures as Macha, the eponymous goddess of Emain Macha, the Navan hillfort in County Armagh. Sexuality is strongly marked in this deity, and there is some evidence that she, or rather her animal equivalent, played an important role in the inauguration of the kings of Ireland in pagan times. Even as late as the twelfth century AD traces of such a custom survived, to be recorded by the shocked and hostile Giraldus Cambrensis in his Itinerary of Ireland. He writes of one of the northern Irish tribes whose chief or king was made to simulate sexual intercourse with a mare – no doubt a memory of the goddess in horse form. Once this was enacted, the beast was immediately slain and ritually eaten. Giraldus describes the ceremony in the following terms:

A whole people of that country being gathered in one place, a white mare is led into the midst of them, and he who is to be inaugurated, not as a prince but as a brute, not as a king, but as an outlaw, comes before the people on all fours, confessing himself a beast with no less impudence than imprudence. The mare being immediately killed, and cut in pieces and boiled, a bath is prepared for him from the broth. Sitting in this, he eats of the flesh, which is brought to him, the people standing round or partaking of it also. He is also required to drink of the broth in which he is bathed, not drawing it in any vessel, or even in his hand, but lapping it up with his mouth. These unrighteous rites being duly accomplished his royal dominion and authority are ratified.[6]

In other words, the king has assumed the form of a stallion in order to mate with the territorial goddess and thus ensure her beneficence and his own virility, as well as that of his people and land. One wonders whether the chalk figure at Uffington, the famous White Horse beside the Belgic hillfort, is not in fact the Gaulish goddess herself in horse form. There are still current in the area traditions of the good luck that will accrue from urinating on the figure; and no doubt in earlier times sexual intercourse there would be regarded as an act bound to bring good fortune, as in the case of the Cerne giant. The similarity of the Irish inaugural rite, as described by Giraldus, to one anciently practised in India, another Indo-European country, is noteworthy. This rite was known as *asvamedha*, and likewise concerned a horse-sacrifice. Here it is the chief wife of the king who actually mates with a stallion which was then sacrificed. Horse-sacrifice is well-known in the Celtic world; the animal was only eaten ritually. One thinks of the innumerable horse-remains which archaeology brings to light; and of the carefully-placed horse-heads in the ritual pits, wells and shafts which were such a feature of pagan Celtic religion. These may likewise have been beasts used in inaugural customs and slain after union with the king. It is extremely interesting to note that it is only in the Celtic world and in India that horse-sacrifice has this strongly sexual association. This is not the only feature the two cultures have in common and some genuine connections must be assumed.

We must now consider a class of Celtic goddesses whose appearances in the literary tradition may help to cast some light on a series of enigmatic female figures known in Ireland as Sheelagh-na-gigs; they also occur in Britain and in German Switzerland. Their significance may be more subtle and archaic than their crudely sexual appearance would necessarily suggest. Some of these carvings would appear to be early in date; others seem clearly to be much later. All show similar characteristics although some are cruder and more unpleasant than others. They portray a woman with an ugly, leering countenance, naked, legs usually apart, while her hands indicate her genital organs; these are frequently grossly exaggerated, demonstrating her strong sexuality. In Britain and sometimes in Ireland as well, they are connected with churches, which seems strange unless one takes into consideration the evidence of the Irish tales. This is perhaps twofold – both the powerful group of war-goddesses with their bird transformations and their strongly sexual characteristics, and the territorial goddess herself, ritually mating with the king-elect, are on occasion described in the tales in a way which is an almost exact parallel to the imagery of these enigmatic Sheelagh figures. For example, the war-goddess, whose beauty can be astonishing, can figure as a dreadful hag. One typical description occurs in the tale 'The Destruction of Da Derga's Hostel', in which the fated king Conaire the Red, son of a divine bird-man, meets his death; all the forces of the supernatural gather to destroy him. On one occasion the three war-goddesses are described as being stark-naked on the ridge-pole of the house; they are red with blood. In the same tale, one of the three war-goddesses comes towards the king:

As Conaire was going to Da Derga's hostel, a man with black cropped hair, with one hand and one eye and one foot overtook them . . . A pig, black-bristled, singed, was on his back, squealing continually and a woman, big-mouthed, huge, dark, ugly, hideous, was behind him. Though her snout were flung on a branch, the branch would support it. Her pudenda reached to her knees.[4]

The war-goddess, the Mórrígan, wishes the semi-divine hero, Cú Chulainn, to have intercourse with her; he refuses, and she determines to destroy him. Likewise, the territorial goddess, when she wishes to test the king-elect, comes to him in the form of a most loathsome hag, seeking to have sexual intercourse with him; if he accepts her blandishments, thereby proving that he has the makings of a king in him, she turns instantly into a radiantly lovely woman, the divine sovereignty of the territory, and by mating with him confers on him his royalty and blesses his reign. Traces of such an encounter are found even in modern Scottish Gaelic folk tradition, when the man who is brave enough to take on the hideous hag finds himself in the presence of a young woman of unworldly beauty. It would seem to be a reasonable explanation for the so-called Sheelagh figures that they are, in fact, portrayals of the ancient goddess, war or territorial, long-remembered in the traditions and festivals of the people. Many of them have local names; and the goddess in her hideous and sexual form with her pronounced genital organs would be a highly apotropaic talisman; belief in the power of the exposed genitalia of either sex to avert evil powers is widespread. Once Christianity was established in Ireland, and elsewhere, the powers believed to be inherent in such pagan figures would be tapped, as it were, by the Church and used to keep malevolent forces away from the sacred dwellings, and from the tracks across dangerous country where many of them stood. One Sheelagh figure, housed in St Michael's Church, Oxford, would seem to date from Roman times; another early figure of this kind is built into the wall of Ampney St Peter; yet another was found in association with St Ives Priory, Huntingdonshire; one comes from Yorkshire and one from the church at Rodil, Outer Hebrides. One, which clearly belongs to the church, occurs at Kilpeck, Herefordshire, a building full of symbolism of a pagan nature. Another stone in Ireland, known locally as Cailleach Gearagain, another hag-goddess consisting of a head alone, has strongly evil and ugly features. Curiously decorated with lines, which add to its sinister appearance, it glares out from the wall of the church at Clannaphilip, County Cavan, once again, no doubt, holding evil at bay by means of its female powers. A splendid passage in the Irish tale, 'The Sons of Eochaid Mugmedon', will serve to illustrate this dual nature of the strongly powerful, highly sexual goddess, both in hag form and in her guise of womanly loveliness. When the brothers of Niall of the Nine Hostages encountered her at the well they saw:

> . . . an old woman guarding it. Thus was the hag: every joint and limb of her, from the top of her head to the earth, was as black as coal. Like the tail of a wild horse was the gray bristly mane that came through the upper part of her head-crown. The green branch of an oak in bearing would be severed by the sickle of green teeth that lay in her head and reached to her ears. Dark smoky eyes she had: a nose crooked and hollow. She had a middle fibrous, spotted with pustules, diseased and shins distorted and awry. Her ankles were thick, her shoulder blades were broad, her knees were big, and her nails were green. Loathsome in truth was the hag's appearance.

It is no wonder that each of them turned and ran when she asked them for a kiss in exchange for water. Niall finally goes to the well himself:

> 'Give me water O woman' said Niall. 'I will give it,' she answered, 'but first give me a kiss'. 'Besides giving you a kiss, I will lie with you'. Then he threw himself down upon her and gave her a kiss. But then, there was not a woman in the world whose figure or appearance was more loveable than hers. Like the snow in trenches was every bit of her from head to sole. Plump and queenly forearms she had; fingers long and slender; calves straight and beautiful. Two blunt shoes of white bronze between her little soft-white feet and the ground. A costly purple mantle she wore, with a brooch of bright silver in the cloth of the mantle. Shining pearly teeth she had, an eye large and queenly, and lips red as rowan-berries. 'That is many-shaped O lady' said the youth. 'I am the sovereignty of Erin' she answered: and then she said, 'As you have seen me loathsome, bestial, horrible at first and beautiful at last, so is the sovereignty.'[4]

The fertility aspect of wells is known; in conjunction with this powerful, divine hag, the water must indeed have possessed potency according to belief. One is reminded of the relief from Carrawburgh in Northumberland, from the well sacred to the Celtic goddess Coventina; the naked goddess appears with two companions – perhaps herself in triple form – in the act of washing; or of the relief from Corbridge of the same goddess in single form, floating on the water, benign and calm, guardian of the fertile spring in her gracious aspect. Her more rapacious character, however, is revealed by the male skull recovered from the well.

The same type of Celtic goddess, nurturer and destroyer, is figured on the silver cauldron from Gundestrup, Jutland, dating from the second century BC. Recovered from the site where it had been placed as an offering, but of more easterly Celtic manufacture, it portrays cult figures and cult scenes from the pagan Celtic world. One goddess, whose body terminates beneath the breasts, sits grim-faced and powerful; the fact that she holds a raven on her upraised right hand may suggest a link with the war-goddesses. Two eagles and a wolf-like beast are portrayed; one woman dresses her hair into stranded tresses and another, equally forbidding of aspect, sits rigidly on her right shoulder. The fact that below her bare breasts lie a dog and a man suggests that she was a great goddess of fertility, nurturer of beasts and men alike, a deity similar to the Irish Anu, mother of the gods themselves. Another goddess figures on one of the inner plaques of the cauldron. Her hair is similarly dressed and she too wears the sacred torc about her neck. Her breasts are bare; she is surrounded by beasts, and this places her in the same sort of category of goddesses as the Irish Flidais, mistress of wild things, queen of the woodland realms. Two other fierce goddesses adorn the cauldron. Torc-wearing and with the same hair-style, one has a male and female worshipper above her, their hands raised in the *orans* attitude; her breasts are likewise naked. The other has her arms crossed below small and very high-set breasts; above her left shoulder is a young man, leaping, or aiming a blow at something. Above her right shoulder another young man fights with a beast – scenes which we cannot hope to interpret today, but which must have had some bearing on the cult legends of these deities and the mythologies to which they belonged.

Celtic art, then, has two forms; that of the La Tène phase, aristocratic, cryptic and elusive, and that which it shares with the rest of barbaric Europe, naturalistic, crude, direct. The first may contain allusions to sex and fertility in its flowing curves and sharp, keen angles, but we have no documentation to assist in an interpretation of these forms. The second is concerned with matters fundamental to life and its continuity, with sexual symbolism and fertility emblems – phalli, ithyphallic and sometimes horned men, pregnant women and breast symbols. But the repertoire is limited. We must never interpret as mere erotica images which in these barbarian societies were related directly to their preoccupation with the struggle for survival and hence with their own fertility and that of their beasts and crops.

3 North America

Cottie Burland

As is usual among people without cities and with but little pressure on their lives, the American Indians had no eroticism of the hot-house variety common among civilized nations. For them the whole matter of sex and its manifestations was part of the world of nature, as happy as a capture of food animals, as dangerous as a mountain storm. Within all the immense range of tribal life in North America there was no group which disregarded the erotic spirit. The artist might paint or carve some representation of sexual coupling, or make a charm in the form of organs of sex which would allow some degree of erotic expression, but it was fenced in by tradition and accepted custom. 'The ancestors or the gods did it, but of course in these days we do nothing of the sort.' At least this was what they told the crazed visitors from another world where humans were pink or pale yellow. For they had no special category for eroticism.

There was no likelihood of American Indians coming together in large numbers in the days before the arrival of the Europeans. The North American continent is a vast area and the total Indian population was never as high as five million, and some authorities are of the opinion that it was more like half a million. The migrations from Asia which had peopled the continent were not a unified invasion, but infiltration by very small groups of people living entirely by hunting, at irregular intervals over a period of fifty thousand years. Thus we can only speak of American Indian art in the sense that it was produced by people having some slight common physical heritage, and a habitation within the confines of a great and varied continent. Their speech can be grouped together into over forty linguistic groups and hundreds of languages. Their customs were just as varied, and were usually adapted to the way of life of each individual group. Yet in spite of the immense diversity one often becomes aware of a specifically American Indian art style. The basic quality is an emphasis on linear pattern with a tendency to formalization.

Within all the tribes the overwhelming unity was that which is shared by all mankind in the physical and emotional fields; and part of that inexhaustible ocean of communication which works through the unconscious mind. So we must expect that the American Indian contribution to erotic art will be by local versions of themes as wide as humanity itself. Cultural conditions will always diffract the conscious side, the visible work and the spoken word, but below the threshold there is a unity. When compared with erotic art of civilized peoples the American Indian contribution is simple, direct and innocent.

However the American Indians also had their social restraints, and show all manner of moral attitudes, from strict puritanism to a regulated permissiveness, mostly for the benefit of young people and often to help young warriors before they were married. The regulations dealing with sexual behaviour vary from tribe to tribe. They were not in the earlier days connected with physical exposure of any part of the body. In all communities nakedness was the usual dress, and the purpose of clothing was either for display or protection from the weather.

The expression of sex in art is not necessarily a clue to the pattern of behaviour in daily life. The function of American Indian art is usually to convey a myth in concrete form. It is only rarely that it had any direct aesthetic intent, but beauty was achieved because of a quality within the artist which was always safely pinned down by tribal opinion. In general tribal custom demanded an expression of factual events through recognizable symbols. There was a bias in favour of sequential narrative. The artist contributed through rhythmic spacing of elements and a liveliness of expression in suggested movement. Sometimes, as in the decoration of the buffalo robes worn on the Prairies there was a historical purpose implied in the paintings. As time passed the tribal traditions were influenced by the realist ideas of the pale-skinned invaders. The new attempts at portrayal of fact in a recognizable form were still, however, made in strongly traditional methods.

The material used in art was naturally chosen from whatever lay at hand. But there was some trade in special materials, such as catlinite from the red-pipestone quarries near Lake Superior; special missions to acquire this were protected from molestation by intertribal agreements. The stone was considered a powerful reinforcement of life energy and its origin was imputed directly to the Great Spirit. Hence when this material was obtained it was carved with care, and often included symbolic figures of ritually important birds and mammals as well as human figures. Some show sexual activity as the stone's life-force was naturally connected with fertility. The sacred stone was used over the whole area of the Great Plains, though the sculptural style was derived from the ancient Middle Mississippi cultures. Early in the nineteenth century the United States Government unthinkingly gave the sacred quarries to the Dakota alone, thus depriving other tribes of the magic stone which was a source of life through its fertility magic.

Costume conditioned some artistic representations of the human figure. However in the whole of North America, except among the Eskimo, clothing in historic times was influenced by European fashion. The only indigenous articles of clothing were the moccasin and the big cape. Maybe the breechclout and woven blankets came into the southern part of the region from Mexico; otherwise the ornamental fringe and a little leather apron was all that could be truly called American Indian clothing. However the acquisition of clothing had practically no effect on sexual behaviour. Perhaps it emphasized the attractions of nudity, because what is concealed becomes the more precious by association.

Among the Eskimo, however, clothing was of vital importance. They were the only North American people to wear tailored garments before they came under European influence. Eskimo folk stories from Hudson Bay tell of primitive giants, the Tornaq, who were probably the Norsemen from Greenland; beings so backward that they bound their legs with strips of fur because they could not make proper boots. However, Eskimo domestic life was very naked. The conditions inside the igloo in winter and the skin tents in summer were warm and smoky.

Clothing was always removed indoors, although some women wore a tiny *cache-sexe*. With the coming of the wooden houses, motor boats and oil heaters in modern days this old life has disappeared. But a century ago it was normal. The small groups of people in the vast desolation of the Northlands were close knit, and their life was clearly so companionable that nakedness in company was without any special significance. There was a good deal of visiting in the long winter, when people would meet for telling stories or dances. To wear beautifully tailored skin clothing was a credit to the women of the family and often the dances were held in the open, but even in the largest igloos the heat and smoke from the big dish-like lamps made it necessary to strip. To the European visitor such gatherings were repulsive. The Eskimo were naturally heavily built, their women proud of the fat they accumulated because their husbands brought plenty of food; and the sensible habit of wearing a coating of grease and lamp black against the cold was unpleasant to strangers, especially as the grease smelt strongly of fish. But to the Eskimo of old this was redolent of a heavenly comfort. The dark blue dots of tattoo and occasional ornaments pierced through cheeks and lips were beautiful to Arctic eyes. There was also a good deal of erotic joking at such meetings, though formal relations between members of families prevented any licence beyond verbal familiarities. Even so there were occasional fights about women, and the occasional murder – though murder was always socially abhorred partly because it deprived the community of a hunter's contribution to the food supplies. In general women felt that it was important for a husband to bring them good food and fine skins. In return they made him splendid clothes and kept the food pots simmering gently over the oil dishes. If a hunter was very skilled he might find that he had a little cluster of loving wives around him. But a mean or cruel man could be completely deserted, and a bad hunter was neglected. In the grim world of the Arctic, life depended on regular supplies of food and furs. Romantic love may well have driven people to mutual dependence but as in many another community 'kissing goes by favour'. The first interest of a woman was the welfare of her children, and as for a husband, it was no great matter if a wife already had a child by some other man. The child was another member of the family who would grow up to help hunt or to cook; living people were precious.

There was little secrecy about sex. In the limited area of the sleeping bench in an igloo the need for intercourse was satisfied, while the family accepted it as nothing untoward. It was not strange or weird that a man should embrace a woman and that they should both enjoy a dance lying down, with at most a fur rug over them. And as nobody was ignorant of the details of intercourse there was nothing wrong in its display. In fact it was regarded as a social necessity which was kept in bounds only by the code of family behaviour.

The special occasions when sex became more obvious than usual were when visitors from some other settlement were received. Settlements were far apart, and visitors after the long journey were always welcome. They were given food and became the centre of attention. They brought news and listened to the tales of their host's adventures in the past hunting season. To comfort them after the journey, and indeed to enjoy a change in the dull routine of everyday, they were offered the fattest girls available for a pleasant bout of intercourse, and it was polite to give one's hostess the pleasure of a caress and complete enjoyment through orgasm. Such a change from routine was held a good thing for the lonely family group. Since the visitors were but passing friends there was no jealousy and no shyness. Afterwards the visit with its sexual details would itself become a story.

In art the Eskimo were skilled in scraping little figures from walrus ivory and drift-wood. It is usual for such figures to be naked, and the sex organs to be shown. They are rarely more than ten cm in height. The women have their vulvas marked by a single groove and the men have little somewhat conical projections left to represent their penes. Often dotted lines mark tattoo, and sometimes beads were set in the cheeks. Figures in the round representing sexual intercourse are very rare. But when the Eskimo had learned the art of scratching little scenes on ivory which were then filled in with soot and grease to make black outline pictures, they had no particular inhibitions. Thus among the hunting scenes and depictions of the village with its racks of drying food, one finds joyful little figures in erotic postures which are best described as bawdy. Occasionally black outline figures of erotic significance were painted on wooden spoons from the Alaskan Eskimo, and on a paddle in the British Museum the Eskimo artist has depicted a summer orgy on the sea, where people on shore and in boats are having a party with no obvious sign of restraint. How one got through a summer day in the Arctic without clothes is something of a mystery because of the myriads of midges and mosquitoes. It may be that the paintings illustrate a myth.

All the other peoples of America enjoyed a quite different life in the unglaciated forests and prairies. They suffered enforced seclusion to some degree in winter, and enjoyed more mobility in the hot clear summers. A very specialized cultural group lived along the rocky and well-wooded coastlands from southern Alaska to Oregon. The Tlinkit, Haida, Tsimshian, Nootka, etc., were peoples who lived by the sea, fishing and hunting but not making any use of agriculture. They cut down great trees of Douglas Pine and Atlantic cedar to make their magnificent canoes and large wooden houses. Because of their sea coast habitat they did not suffer from extremes of climate, and they found plenty of comfort in roomy houses around central fireplaces. Box beds lined the walls, but they were more in the nature of benches with rugs which could be used for sleeping. Clothing was linked with rank and family. In general people wore twined fibre cloaks and basketry hats. Some women wore fibre skirts and the men often wore a small apron. Everything they used was carefully prepared, and often decorated with totemic symbols. As with most people in such a stage of civilization clothing was more for social and decorative reasons than as modest cover. Their strong, square body-build and actively athletic musculature gave them an attractive physical quality which went with movements of natural dignity. Society was divided into chiefly families, ordinary clansmen and slaves. Only the slaves were without privileges. They were captives taken in war and were regarded as the property of the chiefs. There were no great numbers of them at any time. People were very proud of their descent from specific totemic groups. Because of this the marriage regulations were strict, and it was only within a limited group of people that the young could marry. However there were plenty of opportunities for love play in the outings to collect berries, or on the festival occasions when a great catch of fish would be celebrated.

The whole of nature was thought to be under the influence of great spirit beings who assumed human or animal forms at will. Sun, moon and stars were often respected, but most important were the great beings of the immediate world. There was the Frog Woman who lived in volcanoes, the Great Whale who commanded the sea creatures, Raven, a trickster figure who brought fire from heaven, and many others who were regarded as ancestors of the clans whose emblems they wore.

The fantastic adventures of these creatures who played their part in framing the world of men were the subject of many tales. The myths were recited while

61 and 62 (*Opposite*) Wooden figure of a fertil dancer. The painted symb represent the penis and testicles

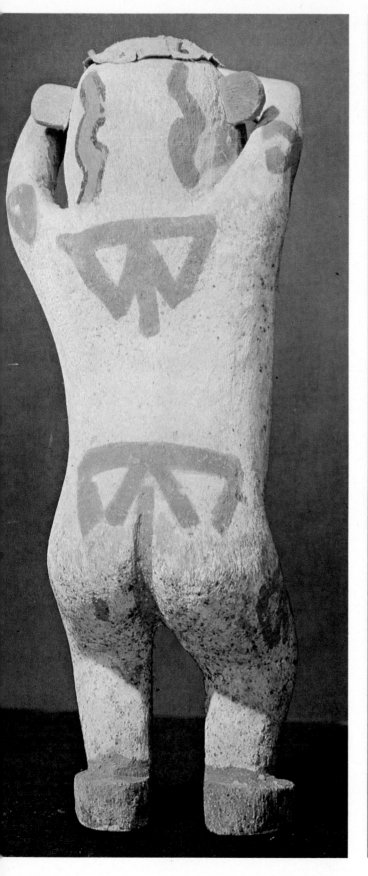

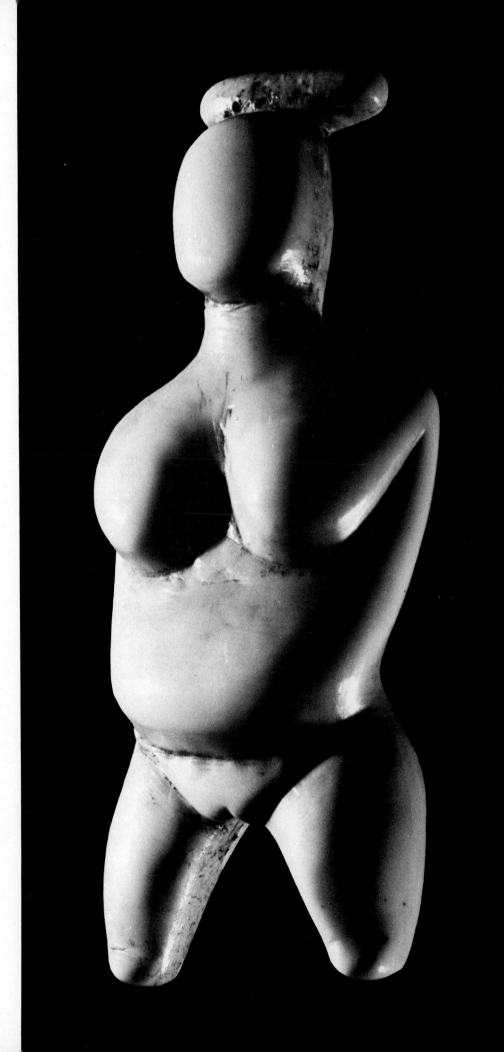

63 (*Left*)
Eskimo expression of the
essential feminine carved
from ivory. Alaska. 19th
century

64 (*Opposite*)
Pottery vase from the anci
site of Casas Grandes,
Chuhuahua, Mexico. *c.* AD
1000

65 and 66 (*Above and left*)
Sea Mother. Wooden
carving, possibly Kwakiutl
from the northwest coast of
America

67 (*Opposite*)
Partition wall of ceremonial
house. The entrance
represents the vagina of the
bear totem mother.
Northwest coast

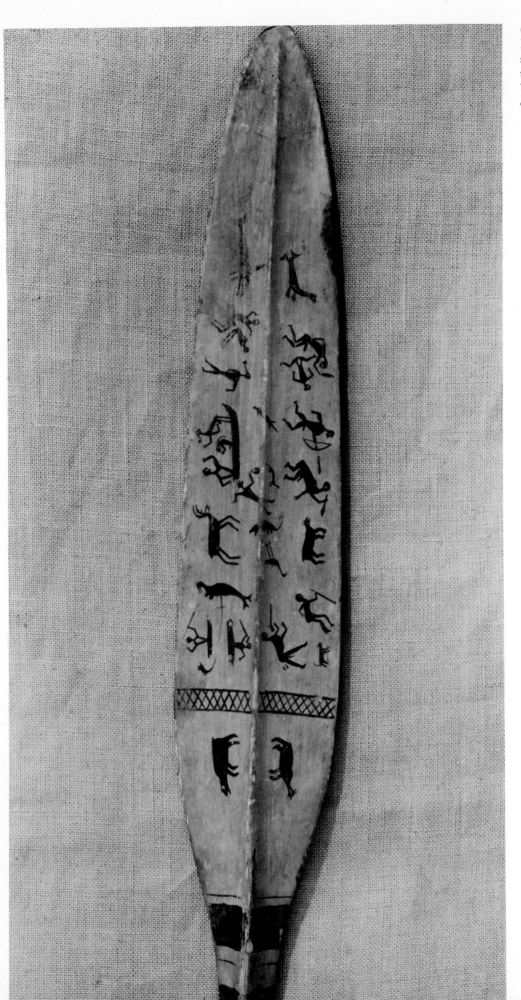

68 (*Left*)
Eskimo paddle with scenes o
sexual stimulation designed
to promote animal fertility.
Western Eskimo. Mid 19th
century

69 (Right)
Ritual prayer board to
promote fertility. Pueblo
Indians of Arizona. Late 19th
century

actors wearing masks and cloaks enacted them. The erotic events were mimed, and aroused ribald laughter, relieving tensions and bringing happiness. In fact no ceremony could have satisfactory magic unless people were in a good mood and laughing.

All the legends were represented in art, and once one is used to the symbolism employed the stories unfold themselves. Some of the small figures are quite explicit sexually, and merely illustrating tales which everyone accepted as fact. On the Queen Charlotte Islands the Haida Indians learned how to carve argillite to make figures, sometimes with details added in whale-tooth ivory. Occasionally these carvings show the sexual aspect of legends particularly associated with Bear Mother and the activities of Trickster, and even of historical events. But although the people were used to seeing each other naked without shame, they were usually reticent in art – perhaps because there were many events in their myths more exciting than such an ordinary event as sexual intercourse. The appearance of erotic images in the art depended partly upon the wishes of the powerful nobleman who commissioned the decoration of a horse or the design of its totem pole.

In some cases the artistic convention of showing a creature spread-eagled in heraldic fashion allowed the symbolism of ancestry to be shown, either by the elaboration of a phallus, linking totemic figures into a physical chain of descent, or by the use of the open vulva of an ancestress as a doorway, especially among those tribes who used a small oval entrance to their house. This was sometimes cut through the totem-pole when it occupied the centre of a house wall. Usually this kind of doorway is a feature of older houses where the totem-pole only extended a little beyond the roof-crest. One may compare the vulva-door pattern with the Sheelagh-na-Gig of some Celtic churches. However the Indian artists were not concerned so much with the womb of Earth Mother as with the thought of birth and the rebirth of the members of a clan descended from a symbolic ancestress. One beautiful princess went off with a handsome hunter (who turned out to be a bear prince in human guise). She quite naturally accepted him as her husband and was proud of her beautiful twin boys. They returned, after the self-sacrifice of the Bear Chief, to live with their mother among full blood humans, and became noted athletes. They were the progenitors of many a famous family. So to enter a house through the womb of Bear Mother was a repetition of the creation of the ancestors.

To accept the male penis as a design element was easy for people who never despised or concealed the normal centre of the male body. In the process of a day's working and living it was visible in many varying states, accepted and not particularly noticed. In the social milieu of the villages there was not much relief from the routine occupations of fishing, hunting, weaving and carving. There were erotic displays among boys, and both mutual masturbation and pederasty. But this was at once exciting and funny. It was more a subject for joking than disgust. Similarly everybody knew that women suffered from intense desire which could not always be satisfied, and so among women there were jokes and masturbation even where marriage regulations were strict. The mores of the ancestral society of these peoples were sound and adapted to their routine of life. Such stories as that of Bear Mother are expressions of the same reality of human nature as is found in the strange world of our own dreams. They are part of the universal human inheritance which has many local expressions.

A similar universal dream is the confused linkage of mouth-to-mouth contact with tongues and sexual congress. One finds it in ancestor figures in New Guinea, in European arts and among the Indians of the Northwest of America as part of mythology. On medicine-rattles for the Thunderbird one often finds the figure of a

(Opposite)
one pipe from Cherokee
dians of Georgia

shaman or young prince lying on the back of Thunderbird. His tongue is linked with the green frog who is the power of earth. The legend tells how the hero had to feed the thunderbird with his own flesh in order to make the great voyage to fulfilment in his future bride. However the frog goes with him, and somehow gives strength as well as taking it. She is a motherly figure, though in other legends she appears as a terrible mother under the earth who sets volcanoes in eruption.

In all American Indian societies the shaman is important. He is not a socially potent figure and never becomes a chief. His prestige derives from his unusual divided personality. He has the power to meet and speak with the spirit beings, yet he is most frequently a sexually unbalanced individual. Most shamans were transvestites and acted the female part in amorous adventures. They could be despised and become the butt of all manner of obscene jokes; but without a shamani's presence the legends may be forgotten and the powers not be available for contact between the human and spirit worlds. Hence the importance of the lonely wanderer who cannot live as other people and may be taken by the spirits into strange worlds where others cannot venture. Hence, too, the traveller on the back of the thunderbird and his ambivalent connection with the frog. He is also likely to be led around by Raven, the bringer of fire and the arts of civilization, constant victim and constant escaper, a picaresque character who looks rather like a painted and feathered version of Shakespeare's Puck.

Raven is the Spirit of uncertainty, patron of art, master of mischief. He is a traveller able to reach the sky and nearly independent of the sun and moon. He suffered after he stole fire by being deprived of his bright rainbow colours and made to wear the Raven's black smoky plumage. However he was also a great dealer in invisibility and shape-changing. In one adventure he fell in love with a chief's pretty young wife, so he went out, caught some birds and made their feathers all red. Then he came to the village showing the wonderful bird skins. The chief and all his young men went off to hunt in the valley where Raven said he found the birds. As a handsome young man he was able to visit his inamorata of the day. But the place where he had dyed the feathers was found. The chief returned in haste, and Raven was caught, beaten nearly to death and thrown into a canoe to drift off and die. Of course he escaped, and through another series of adventures became mixed with the whale clans. One sees Raven in art, sometimes as human wearing a raven skin cloak, sometimes as a black dusky bird carrying the speck of red charcoal in his beak which he stole from the sky, and sometimes with a bunch of the trick red feathers on his forehead. In many ways he is the human penis; and one of his myths describes him unwinding his own endless penis and sending it travelling to visit a girl. Thus through the medium of totemic art, often not outwardly erotic, fascinating obscene stories were retailed to gatherings in the wooden houses, behind paintings of Raven.

No doubt the Indians of the eastern states of Canada and America once had an interesting sculptural and symbolic art. Relics such as the symbols used by the secret society of the Midewiwin tell us a little of their graphic symbolism. However, almost all of their artwork has been lost; changing fashion, encroachments by Europeans, deportation and sheer neglect have contributed to the loss. The early European travellers drew pictures of them in their primitive simplicity of costume, which consisted mainly of a few fringes. But as the years go by we find them wearing first tunics and later trousers and jackets under their skin wraps. It was among the Iroquois peoples of New York State that women used to charm evil from the fields by walking naked around their maize patch, trailing a cloak behind them. The idea was to emphasize the relationship between Mother Earth and the fertility of all women. But this custom also belongs to old Europe and may have been adopted from some of the early Colonists. At an autumnal festival there were gay parties at which good luck was assured by men and women exchanging clothes. The custom still survives and is an occasion of merrymaking and laughter. In older times it was more important from the religious point of view, and probably much more stimulating sexually with the girls clad only in leggings attached to a belt and the young men in open fibre fringes which did duty for skirts. The ceremony was a symbol of the mutual dependence of the sexes on the great magic of the renewal of life. However nothing of it remains in art.

The most ancient art forms of North America, apart from the flaked stone arrowheads of pre-historic hunters, are to be found in the Adena and Hopewell cultures of the Ohio and middle Mississippi Valleys. In these we find pictorial representations of people and animals dating from the period from about 100 BC up to nearly AD 900. There are occasional sex symbols, and some male figures in strange postures suggest less normal kinds of sexual excitement. The most common of these shows a man crouching with open mouth apparently expressing sexual ecstasy. His anal region is lifted as if for an imitation of animal intercourse. It is impossible to say whether this represents a socially acceptable form of erotic enjoyment, or whether the man is a shaman in a characteristically deviationist situation. Female figures are rare, and this suggests that the middle Mississippi cultures were typically Plains Indian in type, the warrior playing the supreme part. Nevertheless this artistic tradition is worthy of study because of the elegance of the craft and the beauty of the figurative carvings on stone pipe-bowls.

Some evidence exists suggesting that the earlier phases of these cultures, around the beginnings of the Christian era were influenced by artistic traditions, already some centuries old, which originated among the Olmecs of southern Mexico. Certainly the skills in carving pipes from catlinite and soapstone became traditional. Some of these, from eighteenth- and nineteenth-century artists of the Woodland Indians, continue a realist tradition, somewhat simplified. They portray figures in sexual display, performing fellatio and normal sexual intercourse with a rather gentle expression. There is a notable absence of any sense of violent emotion about them. One could almost describe them as symbols of loving eroticism.

The direct descendants of the people of the ancient cultures of the middle Mississippi and the Ohio Valley mound cultures were probably to be found in the advanced tribes far to the south, such as the Natchez, of whom we know of a political system and some religious practices, but from whom no art has survived. Their arts of body-painting and custom of living in near nudity survive only in the charming, though romanticized, engravings of De Bry. There are some accounts of erotic ceremonies, but less important than those recounted in the nineteenth century of their neighbours to the north, the Creek, Cherokee and cognate tribes. From these peoples we know of a local version of the erotic trickster figure, who took the form of a rabbit. However we have no early representations of him which can be identified. In later times a number of Negro slaves from West Africa brought their own trickster, the amusing Anansi. He was in turn confused with the trickster rabbit, and so originated the series of innocent stories of 'Brer Rabbit' told to children all over the world. But this Brer Rabbit has lost his Cherokee and Akan erotic rascality.

On the Plains the Pawnee religion preserved something of more ancient customs which have a southern flavour, though little of their artwork has survived the period in which all Indian art was despised as the work of barbarians. On some great occasions when more food was desired from the heavenly powers the

Pawnee conducted a ceremony of arrow sacrifice on a girl stolen from another tribe. After a period of highly favoured treatment she was taken to be sacrificed to the Morning Star. Stripped naked and mounted on a framework to which she was tied with limbs spread apart, she was painted half red and half black and then slain by being shot with arrows. Her falling blood brought blessings to the fields and health to the people. The sad sacrifice emphasizes the American Indian realization of the unity of fertility and young women. To appease the divinities a symbolic offering of a part (one girl) for the whole (femineity in general) was consummated. The fact has been commemorated in model displays in some museums, but there seem to be no remaining Pawnee representations in art. In the whole of the southeastern States few settlements of Indian peoples remain. The older art is known by a few rare specimens in museums, some traditions have been recorded but all actual specimens of natural erotica have disappeared.

The tribes of the great Plains have fared somewhat better, since they survived into the times when European artists could record their appearance and customs and a few older objects could be preserved in museums. From all the buffalo-hunting tribes we have a great deal of mythological story-material. This is often supplemented by personal histories painted by great warriors on the inner surface of their buffalo robes. Episodes of raiding and slaughter are occasionally varied by a scene of wife capture, though the limitations of style restrict the erotic character of such scenes. In one case the artist George Catlin made a pencil drawing of a robe which showed an attack by white traders on an Indian camp.

The top-hatted white men rush on the camp, each with his flap-front untied so that a long white penis is exposed excitedly as they tumble the squaws over and rape them on the ground. It is not clear whether this realistic picture was on an actual robe or whether Catlin was using the theme as a protest.

None of the Plains Indians felt shame at being naked. Even into the nineteenth century in the summer time it was natural for people to go about their routine tasks without clothes. If sexual love was wanted it could be arranged, and among married people monogamy was respected, though often a powerful chief had many wives.

Many tribes had fertility symbols, and performed ceremonies to encourage the growth of crops and animals. A very important example was the Buffalo Dance. This has been depicted in many ways on stage and in film without understanding. The dance performed within the camp circle to the enjoyment of the populace was in reality a mime, and in spirit not unlike the mummers' dances of Europe, though it lacked most of their erotic play. Its purpose was to promote the fertility of the bison, and to remind them of their subjection to the human race. The whole affair was noisy, with the rhythmic beat of drums and shrilling of whistles as the heavily laden dancers with their huge buffalo masks stamped the ground circling around.

In a special pamphlet illustrated with a coloured plate, George Catlin describes a ceremony of the now much changed Mandan Indians. When the maize was ripe in the small plantations kept by the women in the river valleys, a party of women led by one of the most respected matrons went out to bring in the first fruits. They came back to the village bearing a sheaf of corn and laughing and joking. Every now and then their leader would press something under her arm, and a gigantic penis with a deep red glans would erect itself in the middle of the sheaf. This delighted everybody and led to an outburst of ribald teasing which was aimed at the men. Laughter and gaiety were characteristics of American Indian ceremonies. It was felt that when thanking the spirits one should show happiness. The woman who carried the magic sheaf was the wife of one of the more important elders.

This also was typical, for those in power had sometimes to accept that they were the butts of jokes, especially of sexual jibes and jeers. A few of the skin tubes which made up the artificial penes are preserved in museums. The apparatus was made from a long section of bison intestine, which was capped and covered with a sheath of fine skin. The stiffening agent was blood, kept in a bison bladder squeezed under the arm. All was realistically coloured so that as the blood was forced into the tube it erected and the glans was projected from the imitation foreskin. The whole depended on very careful needlework.

A more important ceremony for the men of the Plains Indians was the glorious and terrible Sun Dance in which brave men offered their pain under voluntary torture to excite the pity of the Power Above and so bring blessings on the people. As part of the ceremony there was a ritual in which the priest of the medicine pipe confronted darkness and chaos and drove them away from the sacred precincts. It was described by George Catlin, draughtsman, and friend of the Indians who travelled in the Great Plains in 1832 and 1833. We owe him a great debt for his faithful record of the people he met and the ceremonies they performed in the days before their culture had been subverted by the invading European. His most important record of the Sun Dance was made during his stay in a Mandan Village, housing most of the tribe which then numbered about 2000 people. After witnessing the four days of the ceremony he was so shaken by what he had seen that he commenced his account 'Oh! "*Horribile visu – et mirabile dictu*" Thank God that it is over, that I have seen it, and am able to tell it to the world.'

He was thinking of the terrible sufferings of the young warriors in the final ceremony of the Sun Dance in which they offered their pains to the Great Spirit, the One Above, by hanging themselves from the roof of the Medicine Lodge by skewers thrust through their flesh.

This offering of pain was, however, only the culmination of the long drama of man's escape from the Flood, of the appearance of the first man, the creation and conquest of the buffalo, and the escape from the Evil Power. This evil was a symbol of chaos. He did not appear in the ceremony until the fourth day. The warriors of the starry night had dances. The warriors of the sunrise had banished the ghosts. All seemed well and order was magically established, but the 'unexpected' occurrence happened. While the whole tribe were gathered around the sacred dance ground in which their holiest object, the planks of the Great Canoe which had staved off the Flood was preserved, a voice was heard calling from the hills.

Everyone turned to face the distant figure coming from the north. They soon realized who it was, and all showed signs of extreme fear. The women huddled together in knots, the men were horror-stricken. The dark shape did not travel in a straight line. He moved from side to side on a zig-zag uncertain trail. He came nearer and all saw he was painted black with white rings, and around his mouth were triangular patterns in white representing him as a devouring monster. He came nearer and they saw he had an enormous stiff penis (made of wood) some eight feet long and decorated at the end with a red ball as the glans. He pushed this along the ground in front of him. The women squealed and huddled together for protection as he came near, the men were silent in fear. He chased among the women pushing the fantastic penis towards them and under their skirts, rather like the lascivious hobby-horse in English folk custom. But the chief magician of the tribe came rushing towards him. He held out the sacred medicine pipe with its feather symbols of the union of earth and sky. At that the Evil One stopped and was silent. Four times this game with its sexual assault and sudden repulsion was enacted. Each in one of the four directions. As the dark power was finally held in an awkward posture with his penis entangled with his legs the assembled people shouted in triumph.

However the Evil One was released and he dashed into the ring in which a select group of warriors were dancing in bison skins. Into this Buffalo Dance the monster leapt, and imitated a buffalo bull leaping on the dancers apparently at random and attempting anal penetration. Having repeated this magical dance four times he had ensured that the real buffaloes would be fertile during the coming year. The performance was enjoyed both as a serious magic and a comic interlude by men and women.

At the end of the fertility dance the Dark Spirit acted as if he were physically exhausted, rolling around helplessly and demonstrating his inability to lift the fantastic penis. While he was in this helpless state the women realized that he had lost his dangerous potency. First they approached slowly and then one of them rushed at him throwing handfuls of yellow earth, powdered, into his face and all over his body. Since he was covered with grease and sweat the new colour spread and his darkness-paint became the yellow of daylight. He was then in great distress, howling and crying and seeking to escape. The women attacked and chased him round the enclosure. At last he saw an opening and broke through the crowd. Alas! Another crowd of women and girls were awaiting him and they chased him over the prairie, pelting him, beating him and shouting obscene insults. After a mile or so they left him to slink away over the hills whence he had first appeared.

This strange interlude was the preliminary to the great sacrifice of pain and blood by the young men who had dedicated themselves to the tortures of the Sun Dance to gain help from the Great Spirit for their people. It was a scene of agony and blood which made Catlin cry out in horror. He did not realize, as the Indians did, that the blessings of heaven are not obtained through easy prayer meetings.

This Okipa ceremony is best documented in its early form by Catlin's account of the Mandan version. In later times the United States Government forbade its enactment. The Indians were spared some pain, the white men were spared their own disgust, but the magic was gone and the Great Spirit sent mad foreigners to destroy the buffalo and drive the Indians into miserable reservations. Nowadays some sun dances are allowed as a picturesque tourist revival, without the self-torture and major ceremonial.

The episode of the Dark Spirit illustrates the Indian appreciation of the change in sexual behaviour when people reach full human status. The preliminary rituals and dances showed the travail of creation and the emergence of the earth from the four waters. The expansion of the early world, its submersion by the Flood and the rescue of the first man through the Great Canoe were a part of mythology of great importance. It was the final step in the emergence myth. The Buffalo Dance shows how men conquered the animals and succeeded to their position as earth rulers. Then we find an outbreak of darkness, not the usual starry night, but something else more frightening. This spirit of dark mystery is a fertility symbol, the unconscious strivings of sex and creativity of a chaotic kind returning to plague humanity. Its powers are subverted by the medicine pipe, the symbol of the road to the sun, with its duck feathers at the mouthpiece which referred to the earth being lifted out of the waters by sacred ducks, and the eagle feathers near the bowl which show the ascent through the realm of high-flying eagles to the heaven of the sun. It was a sign of the emergence of mankind from the animal past. It therefore restrained the powers of the unconscious animal side of nature and drove the Dark Spirit to its natural animal activities. In the final stage the being falls to the magic of the women. In the day-time paint it is impotent, and a woman rightly seizes its long penis and breaks it into pieces, thus driving away the mysterious instinctive force which rose from the darkness.

From our point of view this Mandan ceremony was an expression of art, in dance and mime. Little of it has been preserved except through Catlin's drawings. Even the false penis of the Dark Spirit is not to be found in museums. Some of the greater Mandan magic symbols used in the Okipa, however, remain to assure us that Catlin did in fact describe an actual ceremony.

Almost nothing remains of wood and bone carving by the Indians of the Prairie. Sometimes quite ordinary things had erotic associations, in particular, the bird-bone whistles and flutes with which young men called their girls. They would lie outside the ring of tipis in the long grass, kicking up their heels so that their moccasins could be seen, and play love songs on their whistles in hopes that the girls would slip out to them to make love under the evening sky. Romantic affairs differed of course according to the social code of each tribe, but the atmosphere was one of romantic amusement shared between boy and girl. Its expression was normally in poem and music, not in painting or sculpture.

The peoples on the fringes of the Plains and in the desert and mountains were in ancient times poor and culturally backward. They wore few clothes, and although skilled at basketry and sometimes in weaving, they have left little art. Erotic occasions were not often shown in any medium, perhaps because the people were always preoccupied with the sheer hard work of gaining a living from their harsh environment.

However in the heart of the semi-desert southwest there were civilizations with a history several centuries long. From some of the ancient sites frescoes have been excavated which express symbolically the relations between humans and the powers of nature. Their pottery assumes many forms, and in an early phase of the seventh to the tenth centuries AD, they made figure pots which sometimes show naked people, wearing their tribal face and body-painting, and with enlarged sexual organs. The majority of these works show fat girls who sit and hide nothing of their well-rounded vulvas. This corresponds with a custom once followed by the Pueblo Indians, by which girls went entirely naked until they married. The first duty of a husband was to weave a cotton blanket to clothe his new wife, and hide her beauty from other men.

Pueblo Indian religion includes a mass of ceremonials performed by men. The sacred underground rooms known as kivas were decorated with paintings not unlike the sand-paintings of the neighbouring Navajo people. However in these pictures, which deal with the sacred cycle of the sky and fertility, it is extremely rare to encounter an explicit representation of sex.

In historic times the nude female figure does not appear in Pueblo Indian art. However on painted prayer boards a formal shape of a pendant penis, reduced to a not very obvious geometric pattern, may be observed, and some of the kachina dolls were traditionally carved as naked males though with the penis small and curved much like a little boy's. The artists, whether Pueblo or Navajo, usually showed the female figures wearing a short skirt and the men with a loin cloth. This convention itself is a way of marking sex by an unmistakable symbol.

The most socially erotic ceremony of the Pueblo dwellers was the annual Corn Dance. Like most ceremonials part of this was for public enjoyment, including a procession of painted and masked figures of the Kachinas, the spirits of nature. Some of it was performed by the men secretly in kivas which were so sacred that only one old woman was allowed to enter them. Her function was mostly as cook and caretaker. One of the most important ceremonials included a ring dance by the priests, painted black and naked. Each had his penis erect, and it was usual to tie the penis to a wooden twig to keep the appearance of an erection, and to extend it to its greatest length. It was important to keep this fertilizing object as potent as possible during the dance for the good of the crops in the coming season. Again, erotic clowning was prominent. The people laughed to show their pleasure at the ceremony, though the actual participants were deadly serious.

The images of the more powerful spirit beings were kept by societies with exclusively male membership. The war god was often kept in fissures in the rock in sacred places, usually facing towards regions from which danger might come. In times when war parties were organized to repel expected raiders, the wooden figure of the god was taken out and chants were conducted to bring his powers to their highest potential. A symbol for this erect penis carved out of wood, sometimes with incised rings, was inserted in a prepared socket at the navel. Little seated clay figurines of him, prepared for Hopi warriors, show him in a kind of erotic ecstasy with head thrown a little back, mouth open, legs apart, as he squats with his penis erect. He inspires the warrior with a kind of ecstatic virility, displayed by the state of his penis, like that of the warrior engaged in personal combat. Just as the severely wounded hero would achieve an erection and ejaculate all stored semen before death overtook him, so the warrior in close combat experienced tumescence of the penis. This is experienced and remarked on by all peoples in a primitive state who still face their enemies in personal combat, though in civilized lands it is probably not a familiar phenomenon.

The Pueblos held one important and universal attitude to sex. They laughed about it. At major ceremonies the 'Delight-Makers' played a leading part. They were the clowns, often naked, with their little aprons carefully askew. Some wore false penes, or carried representations of a huge penis to amuse the spectators. They were selected from among the leading men, so important was their function to keep the people happy during the ceremonies, and show the gods how gay humans were at making contact with the powers of nature. Somewhat like the old European Hobby Horse, they were expected to prance about displaying sexual excitement, seizing girls and exposing their genitals, sometimes handling them to the point of arousal. This was all public, and never taken to a stage calling for revenge. Such horseplay was almost universal at spring festivals throughout the world, and is psychologically akin to the carnival and May day dance of old Europe.

71 (*Opposite left*)
Image of the god of war m
from pine wood. Zuni
Pueblo, Arizona. 19th cen

72 (*Opposite right*)
Small figurine of female i
the form of a frog, symbo
of the rhythm of sexual
intercourse. Eskimo

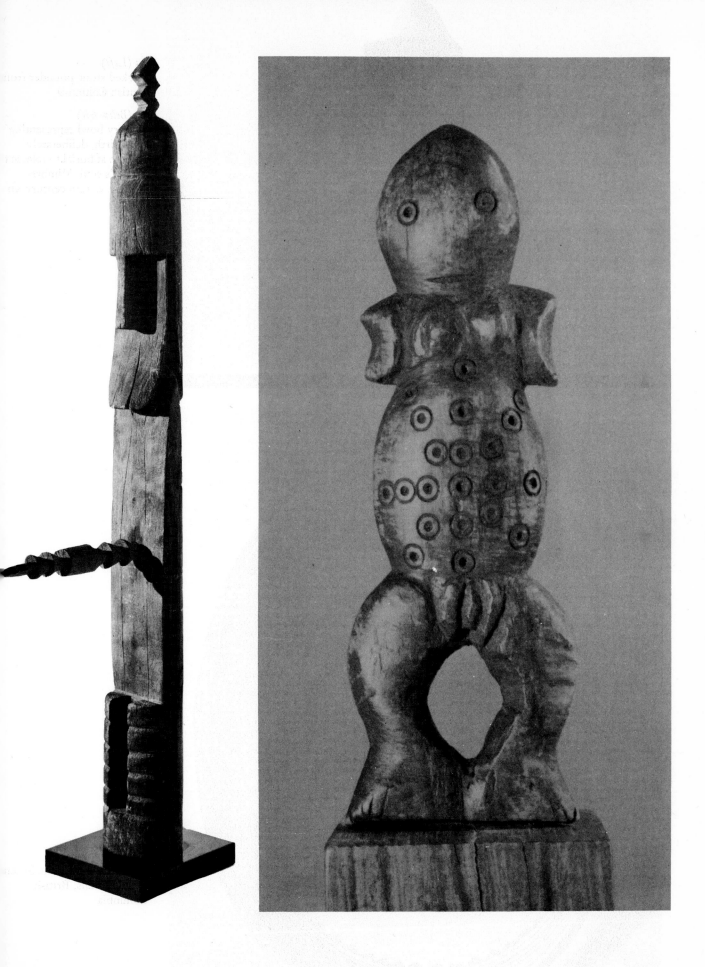

73 (*Left*)
Pecked stone pounder from
British Columbia

74 (*Below left*)
Pottery bowl representing
childbirth, deliberately
broken at burial to release t[he]
owner's soul. Mimbres
culture. *c.* 11th century AD

75 and 76 (*Opposite*)
Totem pole from the Skeen[a]
River Indians, British
Columbia

77 (*Left*)
Painted entrance wall of
Committee house of Tlinki
chief. Mid 19th century

8 (Right)
Eskimo figure of a young
girl. Late 19th century

79 (Right)
Carved walrus tusk figure of
a girl displaying her vulva.
Eskimo

80, 81 and 82 (*Left and opposite above*) Stone pipes from the Cherokee Indians of Georg

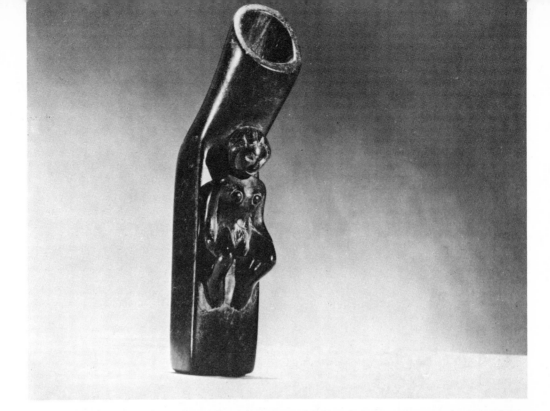

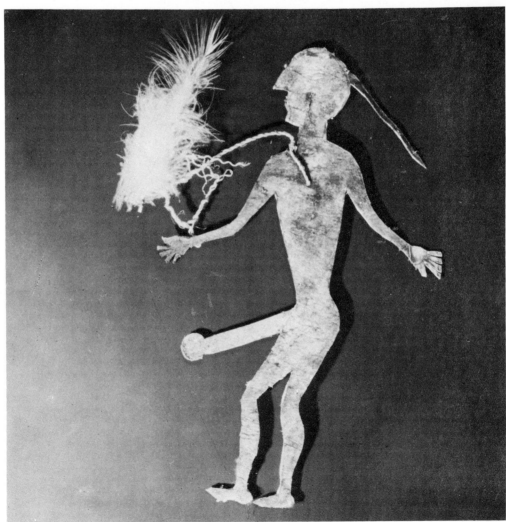

83 (*Right*)
Figure made from buffalo
hide of the 'Trickster', an
ithyphallic character
connected with Spring
festivals. Sioux Indians

84 (*Left*)
Ceremonial rattle. Tlingit,
northwest coast

85 (*Opposite*)
Pottery vessel in the form of
a reclining ithyphallic man.
Colima, western Mexico.
After AD 300

86 (*Left*)
Standing warrior in state c
erotic stimulation. Colima
Mexico City

87 (*Opposite*)
Fine ceramic whistle figuri
Maya of Jaina Island,
Campeche. *c.* 9th century A

88 (*Left*)
Pre-Columbian snuff table
emphasizing the theme of
feminine fertility. Arawak,
Jamaica

39 (*Right*)
Figure of squatting woman
preparing to give birth.
Colima. *c.* AD 900

90 (*Left*)
Maya carving of an ithyphal[
deity. Southern Mexico. 18
century

91 (*Opposite*)
Seated woman made of
burnished red pottery.
Nayarit, Western Mexico.
After AD 300

92 and 93 (*Left*)
Rim of a Maya dish show
spider monkeys, symbols
sexual excitement, fondli
women. Uaxactun,
Guatemala. AD 675–750

4 Middle America

Cottie Burland

From Panama to the Rio Grande, from the Atlantic to the Pacific, the area of middle America comprised primitive hunting cultures, agricultural villages and highly civilized city states. The area is one of cultural and linguistic confusion, but physically all the populations have been American Indian without an admixture of the somewhat aberrant taller peoples of the plains of North America. The sophistication of their art varies in direct proportion to their urbanization, but the degree of erotic expression is conditioned by local social structure.

In northern Mexico many groups of people lived by hunting or fishing with a small amount of agriculture, mostly maize cultivation, to support them. Something of the spirit of creative life was expressed in ceremonies and dances of the kind which survives in the Yaqui Deer Dance.

In ancient times traders from the great civilizations of Mexico passed through these regions with some trepidation. They went to the civilized Pueblo-dwelling Indians on either side of the present national borders. We know from some pottery of the eighth to the eleventh century that young people in those northern towns went naked, and ornamented themselves with body-paint in geometrical patterns similar to those on their pottery. These customs may well have scandalized the civilized Mexicans, though some of the Pueblo fertility dances were not unlike Mexican ceremonies. In particular there was a similarity in the midsummer festival in Mexico when certain priests carried bone rattles in front of them to represent erect penes. There may actually have been culture contact to explain this, but the idea is so natural for a fertility dance that it may well have been a convergence of ideas.

As one moves southwards signs of civilization increase. In the regions around Guerrero the Tarascos were the predominant people. They may have been subjugated by the Toltecs, but the height of their culture was around the twelfth century AD after the fall of Toltec power. The Tarascans produced a large amount of pottery of simple but most expressive artistic standards. Many of the vases represent human beings in all kinds of postures. Many represent erotic subjects, pairs in coitu, males with erect penes, and women with exaggerated vulvas. There seems to have been a special cult of the penis to judge from some of the more

M

143

elaborate figures. Unfortunately we have no records of the daily life of these peoples, and apart from a survival of tribal language there is little to form even a good guess at their religion.

Apparently the edible dog, a fattened version of the Mexican hairless dog, was regarded with some delight. Its figure, in hand-moulded pottery, is found in grave deposits. Naturally with such an important animal its continuation as a species was important. Hence we find occasional figures of these delightful creatures playing and copulating, beautifully made and very exactly modelled. Their ceremonial nature is made clear by one single figure which is modelled as a dog wearing a mask carved with human features. It is as if the dog represented the figure of a god which, in Mexican fashion, would be dressed with a mask to symbolize a ceremonial occasion.

South of the region of the pottery dogs we come to an area where human figures are found from a much earlier period; they represent men and women, some naked and some with little aprons. They raise the question of possibilities of use as fertility magic, or as representations of people with a tribal life which depended little on clothing. It is noticeable that in many cases the man wears a narrow loincloth which covers the penis but reveals the testes; there may well have been some social or ritual reason for this.

There is a similar situation when we go further back in time in central Mexico to the first millennium BC. There are many areas from which slightly differing groups of human figures in clay have been excavated. They are all small, and the great majority of them are feminine. By analogy they are taken to be fertility figurines, but no documentation survives. It is as easy to claim them to be goddesses of the maize plant as anything else. A particularly interesting feature of them is the insistence with which the artists have emphasized ornament. All have elaborate headdresses, mostly made from careful trimming and tying of hair. All wear large ear-flares, and most wear necklaces of beads and complete their ornament by body-paint. Their vulvas are sometimes a little larger than life, but are not specially emphasized. A curious feature is that one of the most popular forms of body-painting was a broad stripe with pendant fringing lines high on the thighs, giving the effect of the fashionable 'stocking-top' eroticism of the 1950s. Male figures wear more body ornaments, but are also naked without much emphasis. The village cultures which produced these charming little works of art show a few stone sculptures of a generally Mexican type representing deities, one of whom is the well-known Old Fire God. It still seems preferable to think of the figurines as symbols of young fertility rather like the later Aztec girl-goddess Xilonen who represented the young green cobs of the growing maize.

Within this village culture in the Mexican highlands we find other more sophisticated pottery of a type originating on the Mexican Gulf coast in the area of the Rubber People (Aztec: Olmec).

The Olmecs remain a mystery. They produced a cluster of 'towns' with religious monuments in stone in the southern coastal regions of Vera Cruz. They introduced a calendrical system with symbols which appear to have been the beginnings of syllabic writing (not alphabetic like the Egyptian hieroglyphs) and a method of writing dates using numeral bars and dots which later formed the basis for Maya calculations.

Olmec religion has left us with some fine sculptures which include symbols of a deity emerging from the jaws of earth carrying a baby in his or her arms. There is some curious sculpture. In one case a ceremony is shown in which a seated victim with erect penis appears about to be slain with paddle-shaped clubs. Throughout the region numbers of stone phalli have been found, and at least one sculpture in the regional museum at Hermosilla shows a human couple engaged in intercourse, which reminds one of the squatting figures in facing pairs in the later paintings of the Maya. Although there are intrusive, non-American features in some Olmec works, particularly of a few men with fully developed beards, the erotic aspects of their art seem to fit in with a universal pattern of the fertility magics of a male-dominated society. On the whole modern studies of Olmec iconography are more and more linking it with the much later manifestations of Mexican native religion in the painted codices which survive from the fourteenth to the sixteenth centuries AD.

In Oaxaca, at the ancient site of Monte Alban, there is a group of sculptures once shown to tourists as erotic art; they are popularly known as Los Danzantes. Dating from the second century BC they echo many features of the much earlier Olmec art. The subjects are men, some with place-name glyphs beside them. Each one is dead (with closed eyes) and the penis is treated with strange elaboration as if the flesh had been cut into foliate patterns. The reason why is a mystery. Judging from Mexican art in general they are an illustration to a myth, and because they line a passage under earth level they may have something to do with the self-sacrifice of the 'dead' maize seed personified in Aztec times as Xipe Totec who sacrificed himself for mankind.

In the great highland centre at Teotihuacan have been found many frescoes on the theme of fertility which hardly ever show an openly erotic theme. This was the city of weather magic, with the Rain God Tlaloc as its patron deity. The chilly highland climate made clothing a necessity, hence we may conclude that the representation of clothing of the appropriate type was as clearly indicative of sex as overt representation of the bare sex organs. This is the kind of convention used far to the north in Navajo sand-paintings.

In the early centuries AD the civilizations of the Totonacs and Huaxtecs developed on the humid coasts of the Gulf of Mexico. The more southerly Totonacs worshipped many gods who can be identified from later documents. In their sacred city at Tajin they have left sculptures which include a well-known picture of a priest sacrificing blood from his penis to propitiate a marine deity.

The more northerly Huaxtecs spoke a dialect of the Maya languages, but their artwork was much more simple and uncomplicated than Maya. The later Mexicans said that many of the oldest of the gods had come from the Huaxtecs. However, the puritanical Aztecs found them a problem since the Huaxtecs were a nation of nudists. They have left behind a number of statues around the mouth of the Rio Panuco which represent gods and goddesses all naked. The goddesses sometimes approach realistic treatment and are dressed solely in large sombreros. The gods are decorated with body-painting of a most elaborate kind. There are some sculptures of bisexual figures, male on one face, female on the other. They equate with other figures of life and death on the two faces of sculptured block figures.

The legends of Quetzalcoatl, the lord of the winds and of the breath of life, were said to have come from the Huaxtec region. Among his attributes was a round-ended loin-cloth which was thought to be designed to cover an extravagantly large penis. In the fifteenth-century document Codex Laud the god is shown as the breath in the waves of the sea to which a naked goddess offers her open vulva. This is apparently an early version of the legend of one aspect of the god. The later story of his temptation when he was ruler of the Toltecs in the seventh century AD is shown in the great Codex Vindobonensis, in which the divine king is tempted with pulque until he is intoxicated. He is shown carrying the goddess of the magic mushroom on his back in an action equivalent to a marriage. The codex, however, does not show the intercourse which was the reason the god-king abandoned his empire, lost all his possessions and set sail into the sunset, where his heart flew up to the sky as the planet Venus. In the codices there are a few pictures of such gods wearing the Huaxtec sombrero, but otherwise naked except for body-paint. One is shown perhaps ejaculating white curls of semen, apparently from some form of masturbation.

In Western Mexico the Zapotec people used to enact the temptation of the god once in the lifetime of each of their priest-kings, the Uija Tao. In this case the celibate ruler, brought up in a temple since infancy, was taken to the chief temple. There he was plied with food and drink while a selected group of maidens of noble birth stripped and performed enticing dances for him. Eventually the priest-king became intoxicated and joined in the sexual rituals with the girls. If one of the princesses bore a son at the appropriate season the boy was brought up as the new Uija Tao, and was himself involved in a similar ceremony soon after reaching full puberty.

Another legend linking the Toltecs and the Huaxtec gods is the one in which the demi-urge Tezcatlipoca, determined on the extinction of the empire of Quetzal-coatl, disguised himself as a Huaxtec merchant. Tezcatlipoca went to the market outside the palace at Tollan, and spread the mat on which he was selling his wares. As a Huaxtec he was naked, and his penis lay on the ground very handsomely. Seeing a disturbance in the market the princess sent a slave girl to see why the women were so excited. The girl returned with the story of the wonderful stranger, painted half red and half blue, who was quite naked and had so lovely a penis. The princess went out to see and became enamoured, so much so that when she stayed indoors she was sick with pining for more of that wonderful object of her pleasure. In order to save her life King Topiltzin Quetzalcoatl let her marry the stranger. Their son was Huemac, the king who saw the break-up of Toltec hegemony over Mexico – or so says the legend.

The best representations of the normal attitudes to sex in pre-Columbian Mexico are to be found in the beautiful Codex Zouche–Nuttall in the British Museum. On the 'green' side which tells of the history of the most important ruling families among the Mixtecs of Oaxaca there is a magnificent double-page picture showing a dynastic marriage at the Place of Reeds (possibly Tollan). In this the Lady Three Stone – Knife is married to the Lord Twelve-Wind, Smoky Eyes. The bride is carried in on the back of the 'marriage broker'. Then bride and bridegroom are stripped naked, placed under a matting tent and soused with water poured over them by their handmaidens. Finally they retire to the palace where they are seen behind a curtain (a symbol like 'going to bed' meaning sexual inter-course) where he commands and she receives as shown by their hand gestures. On the same side of the codex but two centuries later, there is a pleasant little vignette of the great Mixtec leader Prince Eight-Deer Ocelot Claw in his palace. He faces his new wife and she is shown offering him a bowl of frothed cocoa, which was regarded as the supreme aphrodisiac.

The rather shy way of representing sexual matters was typical of the art of Mexico under the Aztecs. As a people they were comparative newcomers to the high civilization of Mexico. Their language hints that they were descended from some of the tribes of the North American Plains, though the same language was spoken by their predecessors in Mexico, the Toltecs. Their civilized arts were acquired from other peoples and, although basically derived through the Toltecs, had a southern character. However their social system with its strict sexual regulations would be more characteristic of a small tribal society organized for the benefit of a warrior class. In such a society early freedom from marriage was important so that the warriors would be untrammelled in battle by family ties. Sexual restrictions on the young men were important perhaps on the theory that more energy would be free for face-to-face struggle with enemies. Later marriage was best, if carefully regulated so that quarrels over women would not weaken the strength of the community. The result was rather like the effect of strict Puritanism on the military societies which perpetrated many ghastly brutalities in seventeenth-century Europe. One is always faced by the risks that a transference of energy from the human emotional contact of sex may activate the human emotional contact of violence and cruelty.

The Aztecs, however, did not eschew beauty, colour and flowers. They condemned the use of intoxicants among people of possible military age, and drunkenness was punishable, like adultery, by stoning to death. A drunken Aztec seen by a man of another tribe was a symbol of weakness and lack of self-control, so he must be killed. Prostitution was sometimes allowed to ease the emotional strains of young warriors, but the girls were eventually killed and thrown away to rot in the swamps. Yet these people loved music, song and flowers. They produced great poets and teachers and were highly civilized in the context of their Chalcolithic stage of culture.

The emphasis on social morality of a very restrictive type produced the usual psychological confusions. There was a strong fear of sex and a horror of nudity. Emphasis was placed on glory. Equal with the warriors who died in battle or as sacrificial victims were the women who had died in childbirth. The bloody human sacrifices were surrounded by beautiful ceremonies and dancing parades. Similarly the few surviving religious books show a brilliant appreciation of artistic presentation, and then suddenly produce a shock of sudden death and blood. Yet they are delicate in the extreme in their treatment of sex. When the text is dedicated to the supreme creative duality *Ometecuhtli*, the vignettes in the book include a human couple in coitu. They are naked, touching only hand to hand, and linked not by their sex organs but by conjoined tongues which often take the form of a blood-drenched stone knife.

In the codices which deal with the gods, sex is depicted as a serpent, red with a few black bands across it. It protrudes from the loin-cloth of a lascivious man, is broken into pieces by the older gods, or becomes the constant companion of the Evening Star, the demon Xolotl, or of the strange witch-goddess Tlazolteotl.

Tlazolteotl has a whole section to herself in the beautiful Codex Laud, in Oxford. She is the four phases of the moon and the epitome of woman, closely akin to the Greek group of goddesses, the Kore, Demeter, Persephone and Hecate. The name of the Mexican goddess means Divine Eater of Dirt. Her mouth was painted black as a sign that in one aspect she could devour the sinfulness of men. However, as sins could only be eaten up once in a lifetime, most men waited until they were past middle-age before they made their secret confessions to the priest of the goddess. She was also the goddess who protected prostitutes. In a great international city like Mexico (Tenochtitlan means Beside Cactus Rock) there was room for a number of prostitutes whose function was to protect the purity of Aztec marriage by entertaining visitors from other tribes. At one of the great annual festivals these girls were allowed actually to touch the shoulders or waists of men during the dances. Otherwise, when dancing, men and women never touched one another.

Tlazolteotl begins her story as the young moon and is the lascivious maiden who tempts Quetzalcoatl. She is also depicted here as the one who breaks the symbols of penance, and as the protectress of the red serpent of sex. She is wearing a very short skirt and showing her breasts. In her second phase she wears a man's loin-cloth, and from her vulva projects a stream of magic power which swallows the red serpent. In this aspect she is the goddess of gambling. In her third phase she is modest and motherly; showing one breast full of nourishment, she makes offerings of incense before the fire of new life. Here she is in her cleansing and kindly aspect. In the fourth she is blind destruction. Naked apart from a very short skirt and sandals, she sits on the corpse of a young man and is the goddess of destruction and theft. To the Aztecs the wearing of skirts above the knee was but another of the catalogue of obscenities to which women might be tempted. They appear to have been somewhat afraid of femininity and acted cautiously, being ever ready to fly to the soothsayer for advice about fortunate days for marriage and so on. In several codices there occurs a series of pictures covering days numbered from two to twenty-six, possibly the days of the visible moon, each one of which refers to a matrimonial situation, ranging from a blessed old age together to threats of murder. The red serpent appears in only three of them as a warning of disaster on the male side. In one case of a happy prognostication the woman holds a quetzal bird, symbol of beauty and blessing, and the man grasps a lizard, symbol of the exciting rhythms of the penis in intercourse.

Festivals were occasions for a certain amount of flirtation among young people, especially where there was a chance of pelting each other with maize grains or popcorn. On one of the maize festivals the girls went topless, but that was to pretend they were small children again like the little goddess of the growing corn cobs. According to Codex Borbonicus, which is our best source for illustrations of festivals, there was one summertime festival at which some of the junior priests danced with bone rattles held against their loin-cloths like imitation penes. The bones were serrated and rubbed against other bones to give a rhythmic rattle. This was all part of a great fertility ceremony for the ripening of the first ears of maize. The goddess Lady Salt was impersonated by a splendidly dressed young woman. She was surrounded by priests dressed in the robes of other goddesses and given honour and adoration as the bringer of health. After four days of dancing and processions were completed she was placed back to back with a priest, who bent forward lifting her on his back. Her head-dress was removed, her limbs stretched out, and a swordfish snout was used to wrench the head back so that her heart could easily be removed at one cut. Then her head was cut off and the priest signalized the completion of the magic by dancing with the severed head swinging in his hand, sprinkling blood as one might swing a censer. Life for life, fertility of humans given to the goddess in return for the food she perfected for humans to live. The young priests with their musical bone penes all formed part of the presentation; life was thus represented by dead bones linking past with present and making rhythmic music to remind people of the rhythms of sex.

In Mexico one hears of sculptured sex organs on various pyramids, but they are not apparently very frequent sculptural objects. However, when pictured in the codices, where they appear with a rather unexpected frequency, the artists have tried to give some grace to the forms. The convention of a curved profile to the penis gives a rather special quality of verisimitude to the drawing. Women do not come off nearly so well. The bodies of feminine figures, even goddesses, show rolls of abdominal fat, and the vulva is shown as a single curling line. This is an art in which the painters were male and women were not normally seen naked.

In southern Mexico another culture flowered and followed quite different paths.

Basically the Maya-speaking peoples had the same theology as the northern Mexicans, but they expressed it very differently in art. The Mexicans thought of the Maya as drunken and immoral barbarians, but that may well be because they never conquered a Maya city.

The rise of Maya civilization began a few centuries BC, no doubt influenced in many ways by the neighbouring Olmec culture. They used a syllabary for written inscriptions and for books. Their sudden development of fine cities with great time-marker stelae occurred in the third century AD. Then for six centuries a great Maya art developed, which was somewhat baroque in style. There was great skill in the depiction of the human figure, but sexual subjects are rare. In some sites there are groups of phalli. In the pottery figurines one finds some representing pairs of people caressing or in coitu, but again these form a small proportion of the whole. The subject, however, is more important in painting, at first on pottery and later in the pages of the three surviving magical books.

In the accounts written of the late Maya in the sixteenth century by Bishop Diego de Landa they are shown as a rather gay and happy people, but with an unfortunate tendency to become very drunk on balche, a kind of honey beer. The result was that after the great and brilliant ceremonies in the temples there was a general orgy with very little restraint. It sound as if these occasions gave the opportunity of releasing pent-up emotions and finding some freedom which would not be penalized, because the usual rules had been relaxed.

One obtains the impression from Maya art that they were a well-balanced people with little need for any compulsive eroticism. What remains in the archaeological field is restrained and has obvious links with ritual. We have no clear information about social custom in the great days of the Maya in the period from about AD 400 to 900. Sculptures show us male and female figures of approximately equal social standing; though these may be deities, nevertheless there is a strong presumption that women held high sacerdotal office. The frescoes at Bonampak show a palace scene in which a baby prince is presented to the nobles. The ladies of the palace appear to be rich and well cared for. They obviously have social power. Their clothing covers them in fine white cotton cloth, and they have elaborate coiffures and wear jewellery. The simplicity of their white garments contrasts with the elaborate colours and fantastic form of male costume.

The sixteenth-century account by Bishop Landa in Yucatan shows an aristocratic culture with care for children and formal marriage, regulated against inbreeding. However only the first marriage was the subject of ceremony. It was considered that the woman should be a virgin. This was certificated through girlhood by a red shell pendant worn over the vulva from infancy until the girl was of a marriageable age. Then another ceremony was performed with some feasting at which the mother removed the shell pendant and the girl became marriageable. The marriage ceremony was performed by the priests, and organized through a professional marriage-broker, who arranged the amounts and quality of the gifts which were exchanged and saw to the whole of the arrangements. It was thought to be disgraceful not to use the services of this go-between. Nevertheless marriage was easily dissolved on mutal declaration. Second and third marriages were common but they were not accompanied by ceremony. Separated people simply arranged to live together. Sometimes they parted, but many couples stayed together for life. Powerful men had several wives, but the first wife was the head of the family household. Such a system allowed for much sexual freedom. However in the older culture the chiefs were obviously so important that the question of succession must have made a permanent alliance of great importance.

One can deduce but little from the painted religious books and sculptures. The men are naked when sacrificed or when taken prisoners in war, so it seems that nakedness was a kind of disgrace, perhaps because the insignia of rank were removed. Women are naked only in the context of religion. However there was an emphasis on figure fitting in the long gowns they wore, and the local ideal of beauty seems to have emphasized well-rounded breasts with dark nipples. Obviously an attractive sexual display was part of fashion. In later times when the bodies were painted the women had abandoned the old gowns and wore skirts only, though elderly women wore the Mexican quechquemitl over their shoulders. But even in the symbolic groupings which represent sexual intercourse there is some evidence that they retained the wrap-around skirt.

Something similar is to be seen in the late Maya buildings which inspired the first Spanish visitors, such as Isla de las Mugeres. The marble supports of a lintel are crude kneeling grotesques of half-naked women who appear to lift their skirts up beyond their navels.

In sculpture there were not infrequent representations of sex organs, and they are specifically mentioned by many of the early voyagers so we may conclude that in many cases Maya temples were decorated with symbolic sex organs in coitu. However one must be a little careful in accepting descriptions, especially those of the late nineteenth-century era of puritan gloom. Such an attitude has led a recent writer on the subject to describe a much battered stone games-ring in a ball court as a feminine vulva.

The painted books probably give one a better idea of the normal conditions of Maya representation of erotica. In Codex Dresdensis we find a group of paired figures of goddesses and male divinities in the usual Maya convention of squatting confrontation. The theme develops on page 25 where it is painted with the goddess apparently handling the sex region of the god, but not very explicitly. On page 47 there is an unusual scene with the rain god, Chac, caressing a goddess seated on his lap; rather a romantic concept for the Maya. On page 67 there is another petting scene with the goddess squatting between the knees of Chac, and on page 71 two elderly deities embrace. So in the seventy-four pages of the greatest of the surviving codices, which dates from the thirteenth century AD, we find that there are only four pages which include scenes we would interpret as erotic. That throughout the codex the ladies are topless must be attributed to the fashion of the period. The only male penis shown in the document is that of the male victim impaled on the magical tree in the centre of the four directions. In fact the overall picture presented by this oldest surviving Maya codex is of a treatment of the gods as the powers of nature with a very normal presentation of erotic features.

The fifteenth-century work, the Codex Troano-Cortesianus, is more crude and the subject matter much more concerned with everyday ritual magics associated with farming, bee-keeping, and hunting. On page 29 there are two horrific pictures of the death goddess spawning the different kinds of maize. On page 30 a goddess of wind and rain pours the rains from her breasts and vulva as she does again on page 52. On page 42 a magical deer displays a splendidly erect penis, which is numbered 11 for some magical purpose. He heads a series dealing with the trapping of deer, peccaries and alligators, so presumably he would be regarded as a power of animal increase, who gave new animals to replace those given to mankind in the hunt. On page 91 the death goddess again squats with open vulva, holding in one hand a flower and in the other a skull. In this aspect she becomes the universal Mother Earth figure, giver of flowers and nurse of the bones of the dead. In fact

150

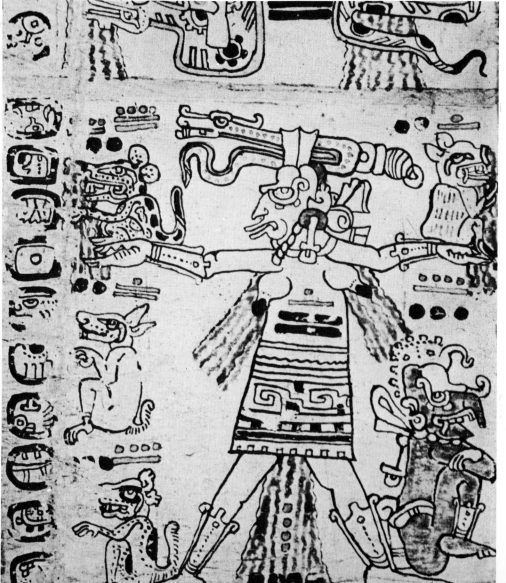

95 (*Left above*)
Pottery figure from the
borders of Colima and
Nayarit. 300 BC–AD 100

96 (*Left below*)
Maya storm goddess
projecting water on the earth
from her breasts and vulva.
Codex Troana Cortesianus

97 and 98 (*Right*)
Pottery figure of two dogs
copulating. Colima. 300 BC–
AD 100

99–102 (*Overleaf*)
The four phases of woman's
life shown by the witch
goddess. Codex Fejervary-
Mayer. Late 15th century

99 (*Above*)
The goddess as a violent girl,
the serpent of sexual sin
between her legs, squatting
naked to tempt the god
Quetzalcoatl

100 (*Below*)
The goddess dressed as a ma
projects magic power from
her vulva

101 (*Above*)
The matronly goddess
carrying the symbols of
subsistence and an incense bag
to kindle the spark of life

102 (*Below*)
Enthroned on the dead body
of a young man, the goddess
has turned her powers to
destruction and darkness

103 (*Left*)
Detail of a Mixtec
genealogical record. The
bride is handing her husban[...]
an aphrodisiac drink. Codex
Zouche-Nuttall

104 (*Below*)
Phallic stone idol, possibly
Guetar, from Costa Rica.
c. 10th century

(Right)
gure of an ithyphallic
cer from Colima. 100 BC–
250

(Right)
Mixtec dynastic marriage
the 8th century. Codex
uche-Nuttall

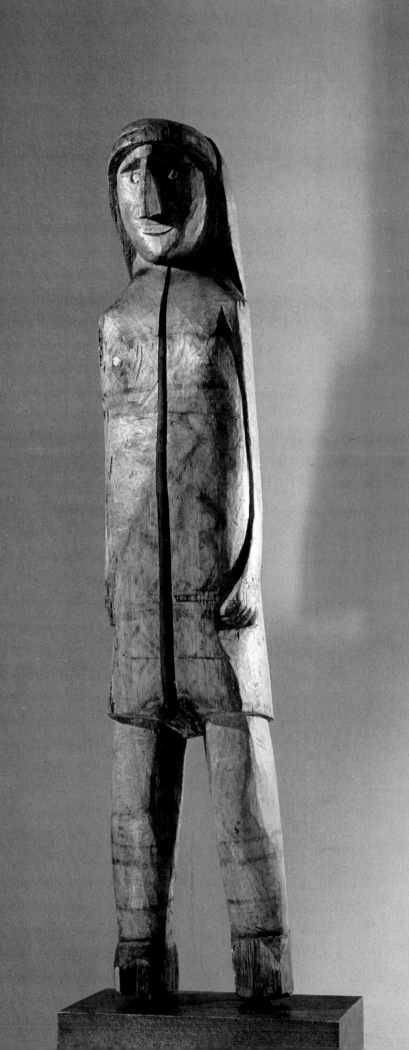

the picture is very nearly a parallel to the figure of an Aztec earth goddess giving birth to a flower in Codex Vaticanus B (Vaticanus 3773).

Thus the whole weight of the evidence about erotic art among the Maya points to it being comparatively rare. It always has a special purpose, and is most prominent where the work belongs to a temple of one of the fertility deities. Even the offering of blood sacrifice from the sexual organs among the later Maya was restricted to priests, who tore their foreskin into ribbons. Normal citizens did not pierce or cut their penes as the Aztecs did.

South of the Maya were a number of tribes, Moskitos, Chorotega, Nicarao etc., who were artistically influenced by Maya and Mexican contacts. They were all agriculturalists, all lived in towns, and all were in a state of war with their neighbours. European travellers in those rather backward countries of Latin America were suitably shocked by some of the ancient stone sculptures which were still standing neglected in ancient sites among the forest trees. They were almost without exception male. Bancroft, in his *Native Races of the Pacific Coasts of America*, tells us that they were particularly frequent at Zapatero Island in Lake Nicaragua. Some of these have survived and show the usual standing male figure with a huge penis in relief erect on the abdomen. A few were seated with projecting phalli. Some have headdresses in animal form, presumably symbolizing the nature of the deities represented. Even now these areas have not been fully investigated by archaeologists and there remains some hope that comparative material may give us a clearer view of the nature of these ancient towns and tribes.

Still further southwards the peoples of Costa Rica and Panama were mainly of different stocks. It is not clear who were the aborigines of the region.

Many of these peoples wore little clothing in their daily life. The Colombian Quimbaya held that nakedness was a social symbol of high class. Only people who had to work in the fields had to wear clothing, to protect the sensitive areas of the sex organs. It may well be that several of the tribes in Panama had the same idea. On the Atlantic coast the Cuna Indians used to do without clothes, though ornament meant a great deal. Even two centuries after the coming of the Spaniards the Indians of the hilly interior, among whom Surgeon Wafer lived for a while, went naked, covered only in elaborate painted designs. In the 1920s their descendents, the Cuna of the coastal islands, were wearing plentiful clothing but the old body-painting was replaced by multi-coloured appliqué textile designs. A number showing the serpent and turtle designs of the creation myths, and therefore having a phallic significance, are among those collected by the traveller and hunter, F. A. Mitchell-Hedges. The carved sticks, however, retain nothing of the ancient phallic carvings.

Among the welter of archaeological sites of differing cultures there have been many finds of erotic artwork. We have masses of pottery figurines of naked people, sometimes single, but quite often of male and female pairs. Only a few, however, represent them in coitu. Most of them are not well modelled and although some of the males are ithyphallic, the majority show the penis erect because the potter pinched up a small lump of clay and left it at that. As is common with all American Indian peoples there is a great deal of body painting shown on the figurines, but there is no evidence that any of the patterns had any erotic significance. This region also produced many beautifully painted plates with pictured deities of many kinds. The humans are quite scarce, but usually show their sex organs in a very natural and unemphasised manner. However these pots emphasize the sexual attributes of the chief animal figures, the alligators and jaguars. They dance their way across the vessels as if they were the powers of nature which inspired life.

(*Opposite*)
ved figure of a woman.
la Indians, Panama. Mid
h century

o

So we may conclude that these people differed from the northern tribes in worshipping the dangerous creatures of the tropical forest. One may find parallels in the art of the West African forest peoples where the dangerous creatures are treated with more respect than the sky gods whose planets are rarely seen from under the forest trees and steamy skies.

The artistic high spot of the area was the Chiriqui peninsula and nearby Nicoya. A very special product of this area is fine goldwork. Many techniques were used including surface enrichment of a copper-gold alloy, which burnishes up to a brilliant and smooth golden surface. Bells and decorative pendants were the chief products. The pendants may include single figures or groups of figures. Many of the feminine figures wear wrap-around skirts, most males are naked. Jaguars are usually ithyphallic. The figures are very carefully made and may seem erotic to the modern collector. They probably represent people in the normal costume of the region. In general they indicate a tribal reliance on fertility and a fear of power of a destructive kind which often has marked sexual aspects. It is a common psychological attitude represented in religious art all over the world. Sex is the unpredictable force which too often leads to tension and destruction. It is naturally analogized with creatures of aggressive power. This theme extends through all the tribal arts of Costa Rica, including the comparatively primitive Guetar of the area near the Atlantic coasts. Erotic monkeys and jaguars abound, male figures display small penes, and the whole is in a strongly rhythmic style reflecting something of the dance of life.

A third division of the Central American region comprehends the West Indian islands. Here the cultural pattern is clear. There was a little influence from North America, but it was not of great importance. The main invasions of the islands came from canoe men from South America. First by the people we know as Taino, who occupied all the Islands and who were the occupants of Jamaica when Columbus landed; and secondly by the Caribs, coming originally from the Brazilian coast and working their way through the lesser Antilles. They were the cannibal people described so well by Defoe in *Robinson Crusoe*.

The Carib erotic art may have been emphasized by the habit, when raiding an island, of killing the men and adopting the women as wives. It was important to make a sound sexual conquest in order to increase the tribe and hold the new lands. This may explain the reason for the appearance of naked figures in low relief on large stone objects which otherwise resemble stone axe blades. The figures, either male or female, are usually nude with exaggerated and tumescent sex organs. Some of them seem to be echoes of older Taino material. In general, surviving Carib artwork is not representational but we have no Antillean example of their wood carving. No doubt it was simple in form and covered in geometric ornament like more recent South American Carib work. A certain grotesque realism in the West Indian tradition was most likely inherited from the earlier Taino peoples.

We are fortunate in having a small collection of Taino wood sculpture, which was found in a cave in Carpenders Mountain in Jamaica. The find is no doubt a collection of sacred objects belonging to a shrine. There are a few more carvings known in museums, from these people, and they show the same erotic tradition. Typical of them is the small figure of a man in the Witt Collection of erotica, now in the British Museum. The man stands, legs apart, with hands grasping his hips the better to display his erect penis. No doubt he was a powerful Zemi (spirit) who fitted the traditional stories of the Zemis who were given to lascivious pranks, leaping on the wives of chiefs and giving them unexpected babies.

Most of our knowledge of Taino religion comes from Santo Domingo and Cuba where Father Buil, who was a chaplain on the Columbus voyages, recorded the strange idolatries of the natives of the new world. However one of his stories explains why one of the British Museum sculptures from Jamaica represents a one-legged bird which displays a human penis.

The story tells of a time long ago when the human race was first created. On the fertile earth there were all living creatures and men. The men were unisexual beings – there were no women among them – and they did not know why they were unhappy and not satisfied with what pleasures they could find in themselves. They petitioned the Creator to give them some beings who could do much of the work of the village and who would bring them peace of heart. This petition was easy to make because at that time the skies were supported by four great male birds holding them at the four quarters of the world. The creator thought and warned men that they might not like the change of circumstances. But they importuned, begging for the new helpmeets to grind the cassava, and make pottery and prepare woven cloths. They were not suited for such work they claimed, and they were tired of the half fulfilled needs which their sex imposed on them. So the Creator changed the four male birds into a number of women. Men now had their helpmates and comforters, but the corners of the sky were no longer supported and closed down around the earth as we see them today.

At first the men and women found much pleasure in each other's company. However, the men were overbearing and demanded too much from the women. There was a great quarrel. The women walked away and found themselves another region where they settled, cultivated the ground and built huts for themselves. But they had poor crops because the men were the only people who knew the magic chants which made the cassava, maize and sugar cane grow to their full strength. On the other hand the women knew the secrets of life, and were able to weave and pot, and even to make the feather ornaments which men desired so much. Thus the two separated sexes went on for a while finding material handicaps. The women were much more able to do without men than men were able to live without women. At length the two sides met and after a long discussion arranged that women should no longer have to perform the heavy tasks like house building and hunting, and that each woman should have her household under her own control. So they came to live happily ever after through a division of labour between the sexes. The women having stable homes took pleasure in having babies and bringing up the new people who would in turn run a bi-sexual world.

The other wood carvings have all the stylistic detail which is also found in ceramic decoration. One represents a bird on a turtle which may have reference to a creation myth. Otherwise all the surviving carvings are representations of ithyphallic male beings. The emphasis on an erect penis is important probably because the people normally went naked and nothing in a simple representation of a penis at rest would have any special significance to them. The spirit powers, whatever they might be, must have a function of creativity and this was the natural expression of the inner experience of such an idea. It is probably mere chance that female figures are not represented in the small number of surviving wooden figures from the Taino. They occur in pottery and are usually simply figures of naked girls.

It would be wrong to ascribe any general attitude to eroticism among the pre-Columbian peoples of middle America. As we have seen the decisive factor seems to have been the cultural level of the particular people involved. The simplicity of the West Indians who went nearly naked, apart from a tiny apron worn by the women, provided no place for inhibitions. On the other hand the strictness and militaristic tendencies of the Aztecs formed a puritanism which took refuge in blood-letting, and an occasional emphasis in religious art on the terrifying potentialities of sexual expression. It weakened the warrior and confused the family lineage. Between these extremes come the highly cultured Maya whose social life was much more free, and who found no special place for sexual representations in art apart from the needs of fertility ritual.

5 Central Andean Region

Harold Osborne

The pre-Conquest peoples of North and South America are of protomongoloid stock. There is well documented evidence of man's presence from the second time that the Bering channel became a land passage, that is approximately 11,000 to 8000 BC. Within the course of a few thousand years these first colonizers had spread from Alaska across to the Atlantic coast and down to the Strait of Magellan, bringing with them an advanced Palaeolithic culture. They were hunters and fishers, gatherers of wild plants and berries, without agriculture or the Neolithic crafts of ceramics and weaving. Distant memories of this pre-agricultural stage, when men lived without cities and without social comity, have survived in the native legends which were preserved, though distorted, in the official Inca histories and written down by the early Spanish chroniclers as examples of the follies and wickedness of people living without Christ under the dominion of the Devil. (See my *South American Mythology*, Paul Hamlyn, 1968.)

The development of these peoples from a hunting and food-gathering stage to the high civilizations of the Aztec and the Inca was accomplished without any cultural contact with the Old World. There is no credible evidence for trans-Atlantic migration or influence before the Spanish conquest in the sixteenth century AD. There is fairly convincing indication of contacts across the Pacific with the Polynesians from a rather early time, although the great voyages of the Polynesians are not thought to have preceded the Christian era and they probably did not reach Easter Island until about the fourteenth century AD, by which time the Peruvian civilization had reached its apogee. But whatever contacts there were were certainly rare and spasmodic, and insufficient to have had any appreciable influence on physical type, ecology or culture. One of the fascinations of studying the early history of the Americas is that it enables us to see how one section of the human race, virtually isolated from earliest cultural infancy, nevertheless developed cultures and crafts, beliefs, rituals and social institutions, even high civilizations, which despite differences of detail are all in their major features paralleled the world over. They also produced works of art and fine craftsmanship which evoke our admiration, proof that the aesthetic impulse is innate to all men, manifesting itself spontaneously without cultural influences in forms which postulate basic human kinship and identity beyond the sphere of practical needs.

An agricultural stage, when the typical American food-plants maize, beans and squash began to be cultivated, began about the middle of the third millenium BC. A pastoral stage, in which the llama, alpaca and cavey (guinea-pig) were domesticated, was roughly contemporary. Relics of a pre-ceramic culture have been studied mainly in the middens of Huaco Prieta, a settlement in the Chicama valley on the northern coast of Peru. The diet was mainly sea-food, supplemented by gathering wild plants and by very simple agriculture. Artifacts were of a Palaeolithic type. At this time dwellings were semi-subterranean, their walls lined with boulders or with adobe bricks. No weapons were found, and no ornaments. Baskets and mats were plaited from rushes and a simple technique of cotton weaving was known. From this very crude beginning the central Andean region became, during a period still almost entirely unexplored by archaeology, one of the world's great centres of plant domestication with more than thirty typical food-plants. Potatoes were indigenous to the highland plateaux, as also cereals called quinoa and canigua, little known outside, which are still cultivated there. In the milder lowland valleys cultivated plants included, besides those already mentioned, sweet potatoes, tomatoes, peanuts, manioc, avocado, chilli peppers, cocoa, tobacco, cotton and gourds. It was only towards the end of their period, about the middle of the second millenium BC, that these people began to make pottery.

From about 1500 BC until the Spanish conquest in AD 1532 archaeologists have drawn the main outlines of cultural development in crafts, technology and the arts of civilization. It was in craftsmanship that these people were supreme. For beauty of workmanship and design their textiles are by general consent the finest examples of decorative weaving that the world has known. And curiously enough some of the most splendid are among the earliest: the exquisite Paracas mantles from about 500–200 BC. Their architectural stone-cutting remains to this day something of a marvel and a mystery; great stone blocks so exactly cut and fitted together without mortar that a knife blade cannot be inserted between them. In certain departments of metalwork, particularly decorative gold and silver, and in their bronze weapons and artifacts, they achieved a very high standard. Their pottery, though it did not equal the mathematical precision of the Greek or the fineness of the best Chinese porcelain, surpassed the Greek in its variety of types and styles and has a beauty of craftsmanship which makes it now a valued acquisition in the museums of the world. It was all worked by hand without the use of the potter's wheel. Their technology was in advance of the contemporary technology of medieval Europe in most things. They were behind in the sort of constructional techniques which went to the making of medieval cathedrals and towns. But they were far advanced in megalithic stone building and for the rest most of their building in adobe has perished, although the imposing ruins of Chanchan, the capital of the pre-Inca kingdom of Chimu, still cover an area of eight square miles. They excelled in road and bridge making and in terracing and irrigation. In medicine they performed amputations and trepanning. While the mountainous nature of the country imposed formidable physical barriers between population groups and restricted agriculturally based settlements to a few regions on the highland plateaux, isolated mountain valleys and the coastal valleys of Peru, progress towards civilization was the outcome of sustained efforts to surmount a harsh and hostile environment. We know of two far-reaching religious and cultural dominions. The earlier was that of Chavin (1200 BC–500 BC) centred in northern Peru and named after the ceremonial centre at Chavin de Huantar in the valley of the Mosna. The other was the Tiahuanaco culture, whose religious centre was on the Bolivian Altiplano at the southern end of Lake Titicaca. Both have left imposing stone monuments. Confederations and kingdoms arose in the coastal regions, the most important of which were the kingdom of Lambayeque (AD 700–AD 1200) and the kingdom of Chimu, whose centre was near the modern city of Trujillo. The great empire of the Inca had its capital at Cuzco on the Peruvian Altiplano. It conquered the coastal states of Peru between 1450 and 1470 and by the time of the Spanish invasion it extended over 2,500 miles from southern Ecuador into Chile and northern Argentina. The Inca monarchs had the charisma of divine kingship fortified by legend and ritual in a manner that can only be compared to the ancient Egyptian Pharoahs. By a strange coincidence the Inca, like the Egyptian monarchs, married their sisters and were mummified after death. The Incas were not talented innovators but were able to adopt and exploit the skills of the peoples they conquered. Their talent, like that of the Romans, lay in organization and in warfare. But they were far more meticulous than the Romans in imposing their organization upon every detail in the lives of their subject peoples.

The peoples of the central Andean region were not 'primitives' in the sense that the other peoples who supply the subject matter of this book were primitive. There were many genuine primitives in South America: the peoples of the tropical forest regions of Brazil, the peoples of Chili, the Chaco and Patagonia all displayed the characteristic traits of primitives – as some continue to do to this day. But in their outlook and way of life, and in their conquest of what we understand as civilization, the central Andean peoples rank rather with the high civilizations of the Old World: Egypt and Babylon, China, Greece and Rome. Iron-based technologies were not developed. Perhaps because there were no draught animals (the horse was introduced by the Spanish and the llama was unsuitable for this purpose) they never discovered the wheel. They did not know the saw or scissors. Most important of all from the historian's point of view, writing was unknown. Records and statistics were kept by means of a sophisticated system of knotted and coloured cords called *quipus* and history and legend were preserved and handed down by a special class of 'wise men' or *amautas*.

The sources of our information are unprecedented in ethnological studies. The destruction which followed the Spanish conquest of the Inca was widespread and complete in both the material and the cultural spheres. The artifacts of the country, and in particular the vast stocks of finely worked precious metals, were systematically plundered and shipped to Spain. Production ceased from one day to the next. The carefully balanced economy was disrupted as the national effort was diverted to the mining of silver and gold for shipment to Europe, and within a generation the population which the land could support even at the subsistence level to which life had been brought was drastically reduced. The Spanish invaders kept them in existence as a reservoir of forced labour. But the disappearance of native traditions and learning had serious consequences. There were no written records, and the Spanish missionaries and writers were interested in recording only examples of 'error and folly'. Little or no light is thrown by a study of modern survivals, for the whole population was forced by conquering overlords, whose only superiority consisted of arrogance, horses and guns, into the rigid mould of an alien and intolerant culture still at the medieval stage. There has been no comparable example in the world's history of a fine civilization and culture so wantonly and thoroughly destroyed, without genocide, by stupidity and greed. Our present sources of information about the pre-Conquest peoples of the Andes are limited to the little that was recorded by the early Spanish chroniclers themselves and to the evidence of artifacts recently recovered by excavations and from the coastal burial grounds.

The Spanish treated the conquered peoples as beasts of burden in an age when the concept of humanitarianism towards animals lay far in the future; they set out to prove to themselves and to others that these people were in fact brute beasts, infidels, held in thrall to the devil and usurpers in the land. At a time when everything contrary to the literal meaning of the Old Testament was taken for blasphemy there was very little objective interest in local mythology and legend. The few shreds and tatters that have been fragmentarily conserved were quoted as illustrations of the errors which bedevilled these singularly evil and misguided peoples, who had been denied the Christian truth. Typical of the attitude in which these records were written is the title of a short manuscript left unfinished in 1608 by the priest Francisco de Avila describing the beliefs of the Huarochiri, one of the very few sources for the peoples of the coastal region. It is described by him as 'A Narrative of the errors, false gods, and other superstitions and diabolical rites in which the Indians of the provinces of Huarochiri, Mama and Chaclla lived in ancient times, and in which they even now live, to the great perdition of their souls'.

The greater part of the little that was recorded consists of legendary history, aetiological myths and myths of cosmic origin. There is singularly little of an erotic nature, but whether this is an accident of survival or whether the character of this mythology was always such it is impossible now to say. The myths of the Aymara on the Bolivian Altiplano tell of dreaded demons, who seem to be a memory survival of nomadic peoples of great antiquity who lived on the fringes in a hunting and food-gathering stage of culture and raided the more stable settlements. These demons were called *hapi-ñuñus*, or snatchers of female breasts, but the significance of the name is entirely unclear. The Spanish soldier-chronicler, Pedro de Cieza de León, records a story handed down among a people near Puerto Viejo in Quito about an invasion of giants, who having no women of their own and being shunned by the native women because the size of their members caused death, succumbed to the sin of *sodomía* and so incurred the wrath of God, who destroyed them with fire from heaven and an angel with a shining sword. 'And this story,' says Cieza, 'I believe to be true, because they say that very large bones have been found in the region.' The aetiological and cosmogenic myths seem not to have been of a sexual character. They tell how the various tribes were created from sacred mountains, rocks and caverns, rivers or trees, after an age of darkness or a destructive deluge. One of the myths of Inca origins traces the founders of the Inca monarchy to two children of the Sun, brother and sister, who were sent to earth to teach the arts of civilization to people living in a state of primitive barbarity.

Still less were the medieval and bigoted conquerors capable of an objective interest in the sexual habits of the peoples whom they had reduced to serfdom. In furtherance of their desire to show them as beasts entitled to no better treatment than was accorded to beasts, they accused them of homosexuality and bestiality as they accused them of cannibalism, human sacrifice and worship of the devil – and on much the same evidence. There is little more than this. Even the great mestizo, Garcilaso Inca de la Vega, and the Indian Guamán Poma de Ayala, whose manuscript *Nueva corónica y buen gobierno*, written about 1613, was rediscovered in the Royal Library at Copenhagen in 1908, have little to say about sexual customs. In *La vie quotidienne au temps des derniers Incas* his standard account of the everyday life of the Inca peoples, the modern scholar, Louis Baudin, finds something to say

08 (*Right*)
A Totonac priest offers blood
from his penis to a sea spirit.
Mexico. *c.* 12th century

(*Right*)
e sky god, Itzamna, is
ted with the goddess of
tility, Ixchel. Dresden
dex

110 (*Left*)
The naked goddess, Tlazolteotl, riding the serpent of sinful lust, symbolic of woman's temptation of man. Southeastern Mexico. 15th century

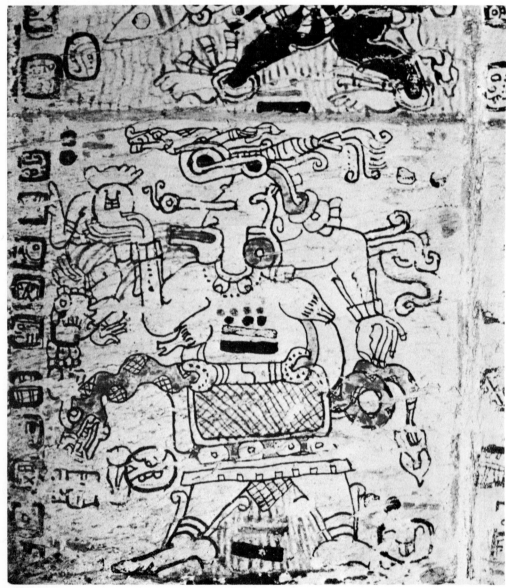

111 (*Opposite*)
Pottery group, probably depicting a birth scene. Jalisco, western Mexico. *c.* AD 100

112 (*Left*)
The storm goddess as the force of destruction. Codex Troano-Cortesianus

113 (*Left*)
Pottery figure of a warrior
masturbating. Colima.
300 BC–AD 100

114 (*Opposite*)
Pestle and mortar in the for:
of a phallus and a snake.
Northern highlands of Per

115 (*Left*)
Vessel with spout in the for[m]
of a phallus. Mochica

116 (*Right*)
Double vessel with male
figure of death. Mochica

17 (*Right*)
Vessel showing a married
couple and sleeping child.
Mochica

118 (*Opposite*)
Vessel with a square base on
which is depicted a couple
during intercourse. Mochica

19 (*Right*) Vessel in the form
of a couple modelled above
a square base. Mochica

20 (*Opposite*) Modelled
vessel depicting fellatio.
Mochica

21 (*Right*)
Vessel in the form of a couple
linking tongues in a kiss.
Mochica

122 (*Left*)
Vessel with the body in the
form of a couple in coitus.
Mochica

123 (*Opposite*)
Vessel in the form of a lovir
couple. Mochica

124 (*Left*)
Painted cotton textile depicting two prisoners on either side of a central ithyphallic figure. Northern coast of Peru

125 (*Opposite*)
Vessel with couple and sleeping child under a blanket modelled above a square base. Mochica

126 (*Left*)
Vessel surmounted by figure of dogs copulating. Northern highlands

127 (*Left*)
Wood carving with inlaid
mother of pearl. Northern
coast of Peru

128 (*Opposite*)
Ceramic ithyphallic figure.
Colima

129 and 130 (*Above and opposite*)
Carved top of a wooden staff
with inlaid mother of pearl
depicting intercourse
between a woman and a
jaguar (?) priest. Mochica

131 (*Left*)
Vessel in the form of a
monkey. Northern coast of
Peru

132 (*Previous page left*)
Vessel depicting fellatio.
Mochica

133 (*Previous page right*)
Moveable double doll.
Pre-Columbian

134 (*Left*)
Stirrup ring vessel with
engraving depicting gods c
demons during intercourse
possibly a ritual scene.
Mochica

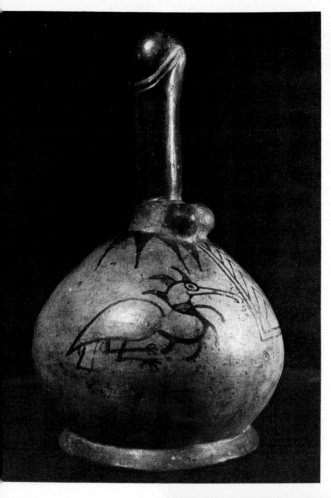

35 (*Above left*)
essel with spout in the form
f a phallus. Mochica

36 (*Above right*)
Popper' with handle in the
orm of a phallus. Northern
oastal Peru

(*Right*)
wl modelled inside with a
nan figure and two dogs
ulating. Northern
nlands

about marriage customs but not much else. It is certain that official sexual morality under the Inca was strict. Adultery and rape were punishable by death. Female virginity before marriage was not held in regard except in the case of the Ñustas, the sacred priestesses of the Sun. Puberty rites of girls and boys were designed to emphasize their assumption of the duties and responsibilities of fully adult members of the community (*ayllu*). Monogamy was normal except in the case of the Inca nobility, who had a plurality of wives.

Because of the paucity of other sources we are forced to rely heavily upon the evidence of the artifacts, chiefly ceramics and textiles. But in the absence of written records or continuous traditions, a very strong element of speculation must necessarily enter into our interpretations. These artifacts have been recorded mainly from burial grounds of the coastal valleys and represent the great coastal kingdoms and confederations and cultural centres about which other evidence is virtually non-existent. Some material has also been recovered from excavations in the highlands, at Tiahuanaco, around Cuzco and at Huari near Ayacucho. The whole of this material was entirely unknown fifty years ago and our knowledge of the very existence of flourishing civilizations in the Andes before the Inca goes back only two or three decades. North American archaeologists began to make a serious study of Andean pre-history only after 1940. In a science so young, in which the conditions for verification do not exist, interpretation must remain a matter of personal impression and in what follows this must be understood to be the case even though, for the sake of the reader, every statement is not individually qualified. And this uncertainty does not only apply to such matters as the purpose and significance of artifacts but extends even to less personal matters such as dating. When J. Alden Mason published in 1957 his now standard work *The Ancient Civilizations of Peru*, he gave two alternative systems of dating which could vary by as much as half a millenium. Even dating by the radio-carbon method has its limitations.

Design is highly conventionalized over the greater range of Andean art. The meaning was certainly patent to those within the cultures which produced it, but for us it is obscure. The same may be true of erotic symbolism. With the exception of one quite extraordinary tradition, the bulk of Andean art as we know it seems to be almost completely devoid of erotic implications.

The Chavin culture appeared fully grown and without apparent preparation about 1200 BC in and around the valley of the Marañon and the northern highlands of Peru. Its appearance is so strange that some archaeologists have speculated, though without evidence, as to a possible connection with the contemporary Olmec civilization of Mexico or the Chou dynasty of China. Its distinctive style of design features jungle creatures such as the cayman, jaguar, serpent and a bird of prey, combined with the human figure in highly stylized apparitions of great complexity and power. The style of symbolism lasted some eight hundred years and extended over a span of a thousand miles, northwards into Ecuador and southwards along the Peruvian coast as far as the Nazca valley. The Nazca culture, which lasted from about 200 BC to about AD 700, being influenced in the later centuries by Tiahuanaco styles mediated perhaps through a militant Huari culture centred at Ayacucho, produced some of the finest of the Andean pottery. Emphasis was on painted decoration rather than modelling and the craftsmen of Nazca changed from the resin paints which had been used at Paracas (1100 BC–200 BC) to the use of coloured clay slips. They achieved a superb mastery of coloured slip decoration, as many as twelve colours sometimes appearing on one vessel. Design was freer and less geometrical than the Chavin stylistic tradition. Motifs were derived from a large repertoire of animals, birds, plants and emblems combined with unbelievable

3 (*Opposite*)
ruvian gold pendant

imaginative fertility into a phantasmagoria of complicated but not menacing creatures. In the early Nazca period the badger head-dress and the trophy head were common features, the latter perhaps indicating a trophy head cult. Although this rich phantasy of symbolic design is clearly inspired by the animal and vegetable life of the fertile valley and of the sea, there is no obvious sexual symbolism such as might be expected of a fertility cult and nothing which is specifically erotic in implication. It is the art of an essentially urbane people, who have come to terms with nature and with life and who celebrate the immense variety of natural forms in designs of intricate beauty for their enjoyment and delight. There is one vase type modelled and painted with an almost classical restraint and reserve in the form of a female breast; on the back is what may be a sun emblem.

There are, however, some pots which represent what appears to be sexual tattooing. Urteaga-Ballón classifies this under the heading of exhibitionism and states that of a hundred pots 'of the exhibitionist type' which he examined, he found thirteen showing different types of sexual tattooing. Twelve of these belonged to the Nazca culture. But he adds: 'If we compare the meaning of the scenes and the sexual tattoos of our days with those that existed in Peru hundreds of years ago, we can observe that at present most of them are inspired in erotic feelings and drawings related to the opposite sex; while in ancient Peru sexual tattoos do not depict erotic scenes or, even less, symbolize sexual differences. . . . It is therefore fitting to ask whether at those times sexual tattooing had an erotic intent or not.' Sexual tattooing seems to have been performed for the most part on women and generally consisted of formalised or symbolic designs around the sexual zone. Rather than exhibitionism, the practice may well have been connected with the cult of the holy virgins or priestesses, fostered also by the Inca, and the tattooing round the sexual area may have carried an implication of taboo connected with divine virginity.

Other, less prestigious centres of culture are in the coastal valleys and the higher valleys of the Callejón de Huaylas and Chancay. Though their art styles were different, their outlook on life seems also to have been urbane. There are terracotta male and female figurines with arms upraised and fingers spread in what may be an attitude of adoration (though painted figures on an Inca *keru* in an attitude reminiscent of these are described as expressing amazement). One of these figures in my possession has the pubic triangle crudely marked in brown paint. But in others the sexual characteristics are so little marked that one cannot always be certain what sex they are.

While over the greater part of the vast Andean area a highly stylized art prevailed, there was one major naturalistic tradition of ceramic art. It seems to have begun with the Vicus culture of the extreme northern coast of Peru, which lasted from about 400 BC to about AD 700. This culture was entirely unknown before 1960, when vast graveyards were discovered and emptied in the upper Piura valley. The culture is now tentatively divided by archaeologists into two periods. The first, called classical Vicus, lasting from about 400 BC to AD 100, showed a development from a Chavinoid type of pottery design to a freer and more naturalistic style, which influenced the Mochica two hundred miles to the south. The second Vicus period (AD 100–700) is distinguished by a transition to negative decorated pottery. The Mochica culture (200 BC–AD 700), centred in the valleys of the Chicama and Moche near the modern town of Trujillo, produced what are probably the best known ceramics of ancient Peru and one of the greatest naturalistic traditions which the world has seen. Some of the so-called 'portrait' figures, and figures of prisoners sitting with arms bound behind them, ropes round their necks and genitals exposed, surpass almost anything except perhaps the Khmer for sculptural quality and expressiveness. The naturalistic tradition of Mochica was continued by the great kingdom of Chimu (AD 1000–1470), which represented in effect a renaissance of the Mochica culture after a period of decline, due perhaps to domination by the Huari conquerors. It is within these naturalistic traditions that the erotic art of Peru is found.

This naturalistic erotic art is entirely lacking in symbolic quality. It is eroticism naked and unashamed, blatantly sexual. With genuine primitives the erotic is deeply suggestive and pervasive, arising as the expression of profound human impulses and needs, connecting analogically with the fertility of the soil and of the animals on which man's existence depends, entering into his rituals and superstitions and extrapolated upon his deities, and creating a symbolism which – half symbolical and half real – penetrates his life, his religion and his art and impresses itself upon all that he does. It was not like this with the more sophisticated people of Mochica. Their naturalistic ceramic sculpture embraced every aspect of a rich and varied existence. There was nothing they did not depict – not for any recondite symbolic or magical reason but for the sheer joy in what life had to offer. Animals, birds, fishes, plants and every aspect of human existence – warfare, ceremonial, domestic scenes, portraits, even the diseased, mutilated and deformed – everything was grist to the mill. And the erotic activities of men and animals in all their multifariousness provided one theme for representation among others. Sexual activities were represented frankly, naturalistically, without *arrière pensée* or reserve. One has the impression of a wholly 'permissive' society which enjoyed sex without being dominated by it or allowing it to dominate other spheres of life and which took as much delight in depicting it, often with humour, as they took in depicting the other activities in which they engaged. The main forms which this erotic art took are described below.

There is a large and diversified group of ceramic objects in which the human sexual organs are employed for decoration or incorporated humorously into the structural elements of the vessel. The motive appears to be pure fun, akin to that which caused erotic scenes to be depicted on drinking vessels in Roman times or in the France of Brantôme's day, and indeed in our own day – though fun for frank enjoyment and apparently without suggestion of sniggering indecency. As Urteaga-Ballón says: 'The ancient Peruvians, especially the Mochicas, frequently included in their pottery sexual motifs orientated towards bringing about laughter or attracting attention.' There are poppers (ceramic pans for roasting maize to make pop-corn) in which the handle is a phallus, and some with the opening shaped like a vulva. Similarly, there are mortars in which the pestle has the form of a phallus. Closed vessels of many forms have a central spout in the shape of a penis or perhaps two penis-spouts linked by a strap-handle. In some cases the body of the pot stands upon a tripod of penes: such pots travesty a regular type in which the three feet are unshaped or modelled in the form of gourds or tubers. With this group I would also rank the many ithyphallic figures. In some cases the figure constitutes the body of the pot, which may then usually be a drinking vessel; in other cases it is a decorative adjunct standing above the pot body. In the former type a humorous intent seems to be indicated by the fact that holes are often pierced in the brim so that it is impossible to drink from it and the user is forced to drink from the end of the penis spout. The enormous erect penis in these figures seems to express an exuberant delight in this exaggeration of male virility.

The female pudenda were depicted with equal frankness. There are pots in which the body is, or incorporates, a woman in squatting posture with open vulva serving as a pouring edifice. In some examples the body of the pot is modelled in the form of a woman lying on her back with spread legs and one rib of a stirrup handle rising from the vulva. Where the female sexual organs are shown, the clitoris is usually well marked. In one humorous late Mochican vessel with a double bottom, the liquid is introduced into the body through the vulva and when the upper part has been emptied the remaining water or wine can only be drunk from the lower part of the vulva. What may be intended as representations of female organs occasionally, but very occasionally, occur in the elaborate symbolic painted designs on Nazca or coastal Tihuanaco vessels.

The interest of these vessels would be enormously enhanced if we knew why they were made or the purposes they served. But on this we can only speculate. As is the case with practically all the other remains of the pre-Inca civilizations of Peru, the examples we have were recovered from burials; and the disruption caused by the Spanish conquest and occupation was so complete that there remains no written record or continuing tradition of the usages which they served. There is no reason at all to believe that these were ritualistic or ceremonial objects and their appearance is against it. But we do not know whether they were ubiquitous or whether they were reserved for some particular sort of occasion. The fact that erotic vessels have been found in burials of children may be some indication that they were not regarded as a class apart. And certainly there is no positive indication that the people of Moche took up any different attitude towards what we think of as 'erotic' vessels or treated them as a special class distinct from vessels which, for example, depicted diseases, hunting or ceremonial scenes, domestic scenes, animals, birds, houses, and so on. There are known also detailed anatomical representations of the urogenital tract and of the male and female sexual organs, but these seem to belong more properly to the richly varied class of medical representations than to erotic art. There are some examples of such anatomical representations on Nazca pottery. Oscar Urteaga-Ballón devotes a chapter to the description of this type in his *Interpretation of Sexuality in the Ceramic Art of Peru* (1968).

Another and still more diversified group of ceramic objects shows human or animal couples engaged in sexual intercourse or in various forms of erotic play. The many ways in which the pot forms are adapted to the representation of these subjects evidence considerable ingenuity. Sometimes the coupled figures are shown on a rectangular or circular platform, which constitutes the body of the pot. Sometimes they exist as mere decorative adjuncts at the base of a stirrup spout or elsewhere situated on the pot. Sometimes the united bodies, whether modelled side by side or above and below, themselves form the body of the pot, a stirrup-spout or spout and strap handle being attached. The fusing of the bodies is often so complete as to form a single pot-body. But the theme may also be quite distinct from the pot formation: there is, for example, in the British Museum a large clay bowl within which stand a male figure and at his left side two copulating dogs. In the Linden Museum, Stuttgart, is a representation of copulating dogs (both of which have a double necklace of pierced stones) set upon a drum-shaped base.

The subject of representation is very varied and may be classified as follows:

(i) There are domestic scenes in which husband and wife lie together in bed, often with their heads on a bolster pillow and the upper parts of their bodies covered by a light blanket leaving the sexual parts exposed. The ordinary position in such scenes is for the woman to lie with her back to the man, who sometimes penetrates her vulva from behind. Often the woman is nursing a child.

(ii) Intercourse between man and woman is shown in many different positions.

The most frequent are: woman supine and man above; woman supine and man crouching between her legs; man and woman sitting face to face; *coitus a tergo* in the animal position. There are many groups which may represent homosexual acts between males. This has, however, been disputed and I know of no example in which both participants can with certainty be seen to be men. In some cases the presence of a young child appears to indicate that one partner is a woman and not a man.

(iii) Scenes showing copulation between animals are common and include monkeys, llamas, rodents, deer, toads, guinea-pigs, dogs, felines and owls. The representation is naturalistic, sometimes crude, and the characteristic attitudes are well observed.

Occasional representations of a woman being mounted by an animal would appear to have a ritualistic or symbolic significance. We know from Guaman Poma and other chroniclers that kings and chieftains of northern Peru enjoyed hereditary right to heraldic devices in the form of various animals – puma, jaguar, falcon, fox, etc. – and there is some evidence that priests in the cult of the jaguar, etc. wore animal masks. Bird figures are common and various.

(iv) The depiction of diverse forms of sexual play was a favourite topic. Representations include embracing, kissing often with intrusion or sucking of the tongue, stroking of the female breasts and genitals by the man and mutual masturbation. Fellatio or oral stimulation of the penis is very frequently shown. Cunnilingus is far less common and I do not remember having seen an instance.

Again it would be of great interest if we knew what role these erotic representations played in the social or domestic life of the people who made and acquired them, what their attitude towards them was and whether they were ordinary household articles or reserved for special occasions. But we are without evidence for this and speculation is vain. At least it seems that they are quite common both from the frequency with which they are found in burials and because many of them were produced from moulds.

These are pots from Mochica and Chimu and also from Chancay with scenes represented in low relief. Mochica drawing was less naturalistic than their modelling and a characteristic style was developed, less phantastical than that of Nazca but of great beauty with a manner of stylization somewhat reminiscent of Indonesia. The low-relief scenes on the pots have a somewhat similar style of conventionalized representation and it is sometimes difficult to be certain what the subject matter is. Many of them are battle scenes with the beheading of the defeated or the dragging away of roped prisoners. Some of the representations include zoomorphic figures or human figures wearing masks of jaguar, condor, etc. And some of them are erotic. Elaborate interpretations have been found for these as depictions of the god engaging in ritual intercourse with a woman in some fertility cult. Alternatively they have been taken as evidence of organized religious prostitution in a priestly state. All confirmatory evidence is lacking for such interpretations. The jaguar motif and the condor motif, along with others, persisted from Chavin (1200 BC) through Nazca (to AD 800) and into Inca art. But there is no evidence for a worship of animal gods, and we do not know whether these zoomorphic figures represented gods, priests wearing animal cloaks and masks, or civil chieftains wearing animal masks. But we *are* told by Guaman Poma (whose name means Falcon, Puma, and who claimed to be descended from native chiefs of northern Peru) that the chieftains of northern Peru bore hereditary emblems of the jaguar, the lion, the condor, the fox, etc., that they won entitlement to these emblems through valour in war, and that they jealously defended them by making

195

themselves fearsome in battle under these emblems. This is the only written evidence we have; and it seems adequate to explain the iconography of these pots, although it does of course fall short of proof.

There is not a shadow of evidence of the existence of a phallic cult among the Andean peoples; there is no evidence of an organized worship of animal gods, and there is no evidence of religious prostitution.

Finally – most curious of all and, I believe, unique to this culture – we quite often find moulded representation of skeletal couples, or couples with one living and one skeletal figure, engaged in sexual intercourse or in various forms of love play, mutual masturbation or kissing with the tongue. Where couples comprise one living and one skeletal figure either the man or the woman may be dead and the other living. Sometimes a third figure is included as onlooker. It is impossible to be certain what the implication of such groups is and in particular what is the signification of the onlooker where that occurs. One authority has put forward the absurd suggestion that these representations were intended as dire warnings against the consequences of sexual excess as leading to physical degeneration. Such moralistic implications are foreign to the whole temper of Mochica and Chimu art as we know it. Moreover, the lively and animated postures of these skeletal or emaciated figures, and the acts in which they are happily engaged, suggest the very opposite of physical degeneracy and exhaustion. And the explanation overlooks the fact that such skeletal representations were not restricted to erotic scenes. They were a persisting tradition, though unfortunately the implications have been lost, and I have in my possession pottery models of horses with skeletal riders made by contemporary Bolivian Indians. A suggestion which I regard as more convincing is one which occurs spontaneously to Indians in the region today. They are most likely to explain that the groups indicate the continuance of marital affection after one or both of the partners have died. There are many indications that the indigenous peoples of the Andes held a materialistic and concrete notion of life after death, analogous in some ways with that of the ancient Egyptians; and it is by no means unreasonable to suppose that such representations carried for them an indication of the persistence of sexual affection beyond the tomb.

The lively naturalism of the Mochica was continued by the Chimu people with no diminution of diversity, although there was a tendency for certain types to become conventionalized so that it is sometimes difficult to recognize, for instance, the species to which animals and birds belong. The tradition has continued to this day and rather crude examples of erotic subjects in *bucchero* ware are still sold to tourists on the international boats which put in at Trujillo.

6 Africa, South of the Sahara

Cottie Burland

Art in Africa is not a unity. This is an impossibility because of the immense variations between nations and tribes; between towns and villages; and between social groupings in different parts of the immense area. Linguistically too there is much division. Yet there is something underlying all African expressions, a quality for which one may use the once fashionable term 'negritude'. This reflects a quality of mind, a sense of the immediacy of events, and a deeply felt sense of rhythm characteristic of all African cultures. This arises partly from the naturalness of older African ways of life, and also from physical qualities, appearing in the way the people move.

The expression of eroticism in African art is as widely variable as any other aspect of African art and life. In modern times there is another overwhelming factor in the advance of the new social structure, religious belief and commercial activities which followed the impact of Arab, European and American ideas. Many old rituals and their associated complexes of art expression have gone. Systems of marriage and courtship have radically changed, and the sexual mores of the people have either assimilated to European or Islamic custom, or been totally disrupted.

In a modern African state there are not likely to be any of the old orgiastic festivals, or any concern with the propitiation of nature spirits. We can only therefore consider artistic expression from the past. In the vital matter of sex it was the product of societies close to nature. Even the elaborate ceremonial of the royal courts had its roots in a linkage between the forces of nature and the acceptable social structure. The powers of life and fertility expressed a universal necessity, but they took on local forms.

Another conditioning factor is the continual destruction of African art by natural forces. The use of stone, ceramic and metal was rare. Most sculpture was in wood and highly perishable. In fact some peoples deliberately made masks and figurines for use in a single ceremony, and prepared new ones for the next. Some preserved fairly old carvings for ritual reasons. But it is true to say that the history of old African Art is preserved in museum collections. Here the very process of selection was on the whole hostile to erotic art. In the Western world the period of inhibition of all expressions of overt sexuality resulted in much African carving being damaged or destroyed, although a few pieces were privately preserved by Europeans of more robust intelligence who recognized something of their genuine power.

African attitudes were only influenced for a comparatively short period by the curious anti-sexual aberration of nineteenth-century European behaviour. The Africans' sexuality had a triple conditioning; first by the natural drives towards sexual intercourse; second by the restrictions of tribal mores (of widely differing type), and third by socio-political patterns. Thus, as is usual in any human society, the uninhibited expression of sex was caged so that expression of this most powerful force ran more or less tidily in approved channels. As in all societies, there were elements of ceremonial freedom of the saturnalia type.

When we come to reconcile social behaviour patterns and art we find that types of erotic art match those of all human communities. There are paraphernalia of religious festivals to assist food supplies, which vary a little according to whether subsistence depends upon animal or grain husbandry. Then there is equipment for the sexual instruction and initiation of young people, revealing the magical influence of sex. Finally there are the fertility rituals which express the potency of the chief or king, giving important sexual aspects to courtly art.

Little has yet been written about any African pornographic art for personal titillation. This exists of course; the restricted lives of city dwellers demand sexual excitation as a release from drab life in the industrialized world.

Bushman art provides a background to the 'later' evolution of African art. The hunting tribes of whom the Bushmen and pygmies are the last remnants once covered all Africa. Even the Capsian art of the late Palaeolithic areas around the western Mediterranean has affinities with Bushman painting. Similarity between the ways of life and a common interest in figures in movement determined a parallel expression. It is current opinion that the Bushmen represent an early group of humans ancestral to the larger and darker skinned peoples who lived around the fringes of the Indian Ocean before they in turn spread to all parts of Africa except the far south.

Bushman art extends widely both in time and space, and is now no longer being produced. In the barren lands of the Kalahari into which the Bushmen have been hunted by European settlers, life is too hard for the few pure-blooded survivors to practise any art. However wall paintings and pecked boulders remain to represent life in southern Africa when the whole area was one vast animal preserve. They are the best possible testimony to the Bushman love of life. Small groups of human beings in copulation are not infrequent subjects, and some mythological scenes show strange animal men with erect penes ready for intercourse with women. The thought that the fertility of man and beast is an aspect of one great force is clear, but we do not know the myths which explained the illustrations.

The historic Bushmen lived in a rich environment, where food was easily obtained. Little unusual sexual activity seems to exist among the Bushmen tribes, though the first Europeans in South Africa noted the curious fact that the Bushman penis was usually semi-erect. There may have been magic involving sex, but neither early reports nor ancient paintings suggest anything like the Hottentot custom of excising one testicle from boys, or the manipulative hypertrophy of the labia minora among young women. As far as we know there are no remains of Hottentot figurative art.

Later African art developed against the background of Bushman art. The ways of life in tribal villages did not favour the continuation of either painting or narrative representation. It was not until comparatively modern times that the walls of houses were plastered and painted. So wood carving and pottery were the media available for most African artists. Tribal styles in any area varied greatly. However the cattle-keeping tribes achieved a kind of unity, partly because of a continuing need for artefacts of particular importance to their way of life. These included wooden storage vessels for milk and sour cream, and a type of stool which was suitable for use when milking. Once they had created sculptural forms for utilitarian purposes it was no great step to carving figures for ritual purposes.

This process is well shown by the arts of the peoples of southeast Africa. The Nguni clans, who early in the nineteenth century amalgamated to form the AmaZulu, were good wood carvers. Their way of life was that of patriarchal cattle keepers, travelling from place to place until they had found a suitable area for permanent settlement. Zululand was ideal, with perennial pasture and good streams. The usual plan for a village was a circular fence with a gateway. Opposite the gateway was the large hut of the headman, and on either side huts for his wives and grown-up children. At night the cattle were driven within the defended ring of huts for the night and in the morning they were taken out to pasture. Usually there was peace between villages. In many cases they were homes of relatives. So in quiet times the pathways were busy. Sometimes there was a journey to barter cattle for iron tools and weapons. Sometimes a group would travel to arrange a betrothal and marriage. Mixed groups would go to celebrate an initiation ceremony, or bring gifts and drink to a wedding festival or carry tribute to the naming of a new baby.

Sexual mores were strict; family pride demanded that girls be worthy of a good lobola (bride price). But nothing about sex was kept hidden from them. Very little clothing was worn. The girls had a little leather apron, or, more recently a beadwork flap, over their vulva. The boys might wear a fringe kilt, but they always had a case to enclose their glans penis. It was a matter of courtesy when they met for a girl to lift her covering to show her sex organs to a boy, and for him to expose his penis, but always with the glans covered. When they approached marriageable age girls and boys enjoyed a kind of petting party which was socially acceptable. The couple lay together on a sleeping mat masturbating each other; the girl never permitted penetration of her hymen and the boy had to keep his glans cap in place. There were regulations about who might share such pleasant occasions with whom. Also there were limits upon the grades of relatives who might joke about sex with one another. At initiation ceremonies and many other social occasions this taboo was important, since there was a great licence in language and song. Sexual decorum was, however, strictly observed, at least in public.

The social attitude towards sex is expressed in Zulu sculptures of the nineteenth century. Rarely, a pair of figures in copulation may be found on a staff carved for an elder. Human figures, conventional in form, are shown with sex organs larger than nature. The women are shown occasionally with vulva open to show the labiae minorae and vagina. The men usually have the penis only semi-erect or even pendant, with an apparently exaggerated glans – which actually represents its cover. These figures are direct statements of sexual difference. They have no pretence to charm or elegance. The people who lived by the increase of their herds of cattle were forthright about the human side of procreation, a familiar part of life constantly referred to in social conversation and displayed in the right society and at appropriate times with considerable pride.

It is hard to explain the origins of Zulu aesthetics. Their wooden domestic objects are often of great beauty and show a sensitive abstract style. Their human figures are heavy and formalized, at their best when they approximate to formal pattern, but never very easily understood. It may be that they reflect some artistic inheritance from the Kingdom of the Monomotapa which was centred at Zimbabwe. However the carvings from Zimbabwe are rough in the extreme. Their crude figures, soapstone amulets and ornaments in the form of sex organs do not suggest that the artistic standards of that lost empire were high.

East Africa has not been an area of great figure sculpture, and this is largely due to the influence of the Islamic trading cities on the coast. The Muslim feeling that there was something wrong in any representation of created beings seems to have influenced the tribes who traded in ivory, gold and slaves with the Arab merchants. It may be that they learned to avoid the label of Kafir (unbeliever) which stuck to their more southerly cousins until recent times. Yet here and there something survived. Perhaps a good example is to be found in the perishable clay sculptures of the Kikuyu in Kenya. The changing life of Africa has probably let this art slip into oblivion, though their value in social life could still be great. The curious little clay figures, meant purely for sex instruction, some fifteen centimetres in height, are as simple and ugly as the steatite carvings from Zimbabwe. The best ones have a kind of lovable teddy-bear quality, but most remain merely lumps of mud with symbolic protuberances. Every grown child had seen sexual behaviour, heard it talked about, and had some experience of an erotic nature. But as puberty approached classes were held to link them properly with the stream of life which had come down from the ancestors. There was a great deal of mystery and ceremony about it. In some areas the ceremonies included painful defloration, circumcision or clitoridectomy. But the function of the little sculptures was to illustrate the songs which described sex and mixed laughter among the grown-ups, with magic for the new initiates. By the ceremonies they were changed and given rights in their new status as sexually potent members of the community.

An initiation ceremony, with its artistic illustration, was a means of bringing the new emotional life of sex for the individual into harmony with the general tribal life. Young people were truly changed because the ceremony was linked to their biological processes.

This African attitude with its accompanying art found higher aesthetic expression in other areas, but the essential purpose was the same throughout Africa, a sexual initiation of a type sadly lacking among peoples of European culture for the last millennium. From the initiation ceremonies came a stream of erotic artwork. In areas which were free from Islamic and European pressure more artistic and elaborate figures were carved. Nevertheless the little mud figures from the Kikuyu represent basic African art form fulfilling a most important social need.

Usually the initiation ceremony was linked with a myth of creation and fertility. However in Africa there were many regions of dense woodland and swamp. The myths in these regions linked with stories of ancient heroes and heroines who conquered the devouring forces of nature. In such cases the letting of blood and taking of flesh became a token of the offering to the dark powers of nature. There are so many different African stories about the initiation ceremonies which bring young people out of the life of primitive ignorance into the full awareness of the responsibilities and full experience of sex that it is almost impossible to classify them. The best approach is to classify the spirit powers involved.

In the southern Zaïre area among the BaPende the main idea in the initiation ceremonies was to let the initiate die to the previous unrestricted wildness of life and be reborn as a responsible adult. In the arts of the BaPende one may encounter masks representing the unbridled licenciousness of youth as an antelope with a red and black face. There is no visually erotic note about it. But in the carvings of people in other tribal areas we find no censorship either of sexual organs or of their use. Imitation sex organs may be exhibited on maskers' costumes; but most important they may appear as symbols on the masks themselves. For example among the BaYaka, figures of tightly woven raffia with carved wooden features display detailed representations of the sex organs. Some of these figures convey a sense of uninhibited sexual excitement proper to youth.

Within the two aesthetic traditions these two types of mask from not very distant tribes give us a basic polarity of the psychological attitudes to sex. In one more obvious series the European mind may find a powerful pornography, but the other may offer it symbols that mean nothing unless one has some knowledge of psychology. Yet they have the same statement to make about sexuality. They represent two stages in development. One tells of the animal side of human nature, and ceremonially helps the initiate to escape from it. The other shows sex in its naked rawness as a fact of human life and tells the initiate that this is the way of the ancestors, of now, and of the future.

Although the masks may be very stimulating to the erotic inclinations of the spectators, they know very well where they all stand within the social structure of their village, and would not dream of transgressing customary rules. The stimulus will be enjoyed within the accepted degrees of relationship. The women at an initiation ceremony may well sing indecent songs, and dance some local equivalent to a can-can; but there are accepted relationships and the emotive responses are contained and canalized to be released at home or with the correct male companion in the privacy of the bush. The excitements and anxieties of an initiation ceremony are shared by all the members of the community. Even those who may be considered to be in some way inimical to the spiritual success of the occasion participate by their deliberate absence. It is characteristic of village life in general, and particularly in Africa, that even when an occasion is private everyone has some contact with it. The initiation is never a public spectacle. The sacred masks are not for exhibition to all. But each person in the community has some relationship with the event, which stands completely outside the dull round of everyday life. It is this community of 'atmosphere' which should give power to the ceremony. Its ambience should also have influence upon the artists in the community, those members of the societies who are selected to carve the masks. The carver must remember the quality of each occasion when he is making the masks and figures used in the various ceremonies. The legends of the spirits constitute the link with his own inner personality. Myth should provoke the attitude of mind which will condition the technical ability of the artist to produce a work which is at once an expression of the myth and a practical object. Where this is achieved the resultant work of art will stimulate the emotional life of those who look at it carefully with a receptive heart.

The people most to be affected are, of course, the young initiates. The masks are more than symbols to them; they are actual beings. The mask, the dancer wearing it, and the person in the myth are an amalgam. The power of the magic evoked is very considerable. The impact is heightened by the periods of seclusion, instruction, and deliberately harsh treatment which have preceded the ceremony. In itself the ceremony may include sharp physical suffering and in the blurred consciousness of the hopeful sufferer the teaching sinks deep. Usually it must be beyond the levels of clear consciousness and so will remain a powerful conditioning factor in the future life of the initiate. Sex will no longer be just fun but part of religious experience. It need not be at all consciously religious after the conditioning experience of the ceremonials, their magic remains implanted deep, part of the social 'instincts' of the individual. In fact the mask and the associated eroticism of sexual initiation are the foundations of a society which is natural enough and often bawdy, but never loosely permissive. In these circumstances eroticism in art has a social purpose of great importance.

To step from the cattle men of southeast Africa to the farming communities of southern Zaïre, with their elaboration of social life in large villages, points the contrast of ideas. Spirits of the untamed wild, of life and procreation, contrast with those of a world where the farmer cultivates the kindly earth.

It is in the agricultural tribes that sexual initiation is most rich in its ceremonial. Pastoral peoples, however, are not artists by inclination. The common occurrence of animal copulation provided laughter, and was also important since it would determine the nature of the calves which resulted. There was a certain amount of care taken to breed animal families of good stamina, but no elaborate rituals or scientific cattle management. One finds the pastoral life as far north-east as the southern plains of Ethiopia. Thence a band of tropical grasslands south of the Sahara harbours many herds of cattle looked after by various groups of people whose lives are interwoven with the ways of their herds. They have had a great influence on African civilization through their travels and trading. In the matter of art they have been steadily assimilating Islamic ideas from the North through the trade routes across the Sahara. The great cities which sprang up on the trade routes of the grasslands became Islamic cities of high culture. Here the old initiation ceremonies were replaced by Koranic teaching, with early circumcision, and the more isolated primitive tribes were left to their own ways.

In the southwestern quarter of Africa things were totally different. Only the nomadic Hottentots were entirely dedicated to cattle-keeping. The Ova Herrero lived by cattle, but laid some emphasis on agriculture. Further north the forests harboured cattle pests, which made the pastoral way of life uneconomic, and life was one of regular farming or gardening in which the rhythms of the seasons allowed periods of comparative rest. In ancient times the borders of southwest Africa, Angola and Zaïre were traversed by semi-nomadic bands of iron workers. Like the travelling foundrymen of the European Bronze Age these bands of smiths were well-to-do people, taking their cattle and grain with them but earning most of their food from the chiefs who commissioned them to make weapons and tools. Their own chiefs possessed many fine things and they were able to live in state in any place where work encouraged them to settle. The BaDjokwe, for example, were specialized in iron working, and had good tools, mostly knives and adzes, with which to carve. Their chiefs had thrones of which the back and front and side stringers were decorated with clusters of human figures, often illustrating a story of marriage and sex.

These BaDjokwe works of art were made because the chief carried within himself a power of fertility which was symbolic of the life force of his people. The thrones were symbols of that power. Sometimes they are amusing, openly erotic, and provide a visual manual of tribal sex practice. The intention was to link these ways of enriching life with the chiefly power. The special BaDjokwe contribution to erotic art was the so-called 'marriage-bed'. Such a construction sometimes represents a girl ready for intercourse surmounted by a young man ready to enter her vagina, or sometimes small groups of coupling figures. The purpose of these carvings was partly to illustrate the sex act for young people during their initiation ceremonies, partly to present it as a *fait* satisfactorily *accompli*.

The initiation theme produces erotic art in all parts of Africa. But within the more forested areas where agriculture constantly struggles against the forest, art deals with all manner of spirit beings. These are often a strange blend of human and animal characteristics. They take to themselves the power of terrifying creatures such as python, crocodile, elephant and hippopotamus, incorporated into the psychological complex. They recall the dangers of swamps in the rainy seasons, of deep black mud pools in the forest glades. In this world of the unconscious the creatures blend in a dream-like way, and the artists among the people project archetypal images known to the whole tribe. Such beings have power to do harm, and provoke unruly almost uncontrollable, impulses. So they are often shown as males with large and active penes. Their eroticism signifies that they are beings which hunger for activity and release a virtual orgasm of destructive energy when their powers are aroused. Among them are nail-fetishes from Angola, strange beings with mindless faces. They may be equivalent to the nightmare inventions of science-fiction, transformed by their aspect of grossly emphasized human sex, which suggests the driving force or inner urgency which will send them on their missions of black magic when the fetish-man releases them.

There are also female fetish figures from Angola, but they seem more protective, and mostly fall into the large class of figures with mirrors set into the abdomen, to reflect back evil powers. Sometimes they are given the form of attractive young women, but most often they follow the fertile mother-and-child theme. A few are nail-fetishes of the type to which most of the male figures belong, which seems to have derived from European wizardry introduced by sixteenth-century traders.

The fetish figures of Angola belong to a local group, and there is no record of a 'united fetishist church'. Within the tribal area there are many practitioners of magic, but they have individual variations of ritual. The spirits are given names which vary locally though they appear to have similar characteristics. But even though these characters are archetypal, and ultimately belong to the constitution of the human personality, they cannot so far be classified into anything like a united theology. The linkage between them seems to belong rather to the social constitution of the tribe than to any organised system of religion. There is a shared attitude of mind, a common language for describing phenomena, and an acceptance of ritual derived from folk-custom. And since there had always been an idea, especially among the BaKongo, that any spirit would inspire the carver to make the right image-body for its habitation, the visible continuity of style was really a continuity of fashion among the artists, and not a theological necessity. The inner African personality released archetypes naturally, among them those very important concepts associated with sexual activity.

In the deep forests there was very little art. Villages were widely separated, and depended for communication and trade upon the rivers. On the whole the forest was not a favoured land. Its inhabitants were the pygmy hunters who spent so much time just keeping alive that they produced very little artwork. What they had was traded by their larger BaNtu neighbours who had farming villages and even towns in the areas of grassland.

Once the area around the Kasai and Sankuru was the ancient empire of the BuShongo, whose ruling clan had migrated southwards from the Lake Chad area nearly two thousand years ago. By the middle of the last century there had been many changes. The tribes had mixed with each other. Local people intermarried with some of the migrants, first those from the North, and then those from East and West. Later there was a division of authority. The mid sixteenth-century state ruled by the great Shamba Bolongongo had broken up, though most people gave a painless honour to the spiritual overlordship of the Nyimi of the BuShongo.

Within this highly organized complex of peoples many art styles flourished. It was an area of productive agriculture and life had an easy rhythm. There was time for ceremony, and that meant time for art. Masks and figures were needed for communion with the spirit world, and the great Master in the Sky. Initiation ceremonies, betrothals and marriages, propitiations of the natural powers and mourning at death, all demanded colour and movement and the creation of wooden sculpture. The people reflected the cycle of life in their sculpture with a direct emphasis on sexuality.

The chief forms that erotic art has taken in the southern Zaïre region are carved wooden betrothal cups, initiation masks and pendants. The cups are finely carved from local wood, often so thin that they are very delicate, and coloured black. They were usually carried by means of a raffia plait attached to a toggle stuck in the belt. They were used for drinking palm wine, especially at social gatherings. A man would carve a cup to give to his wife, with his head on one side and hers on the other, just like the double-headed cups exchanged by blood brothers. A special style for marriage was carved simply with a girl's vulva on one side and the young man's penis on the other. The labiae minorae are understood as a sharp crest protruding just a little way beyond the enfolding labiae majorae. Initiated boys were circumcised, and hence the glans penis is emphasized.

Some of the cups show individuals, elaborated into fully three-dimensional statuettes. But even though the style of one carver might be recognizable within the traditional form, these cups do not amount to true portraiture. A few of them are tripod vases in which the tubby figure of a man is supported equally by legs and penis; this must be a joke. Similar cups showing women are supported only on the legs. The vulva is decorated by ornamental ridges across the mons veneris, reproducing the normal dark blue scar tattoo worn by girls, part of an overall decorative pattern which often formed the sole clothing of women of rank. Since they expressed some inner essence of the person one might almost describe these scars patterned all over the body as a form of erotic art. Though very painful in its execution, the social advantages bestowed by the artistic quality of such tattoos made it very popular in olden times. Nowadays not even the wives of chiefs submit to this enhancement.

In the later seventeenth century and throughout the eighteenth there were occasional southward outbursts of marauding bands of warriors from southern Zaïre. It seems that civil wars and pestilence sent whole tribes as refugees intent on capturing a new homeland. The panic which seems to have been the driving force behind invasions of Southeast Africa led to much cruelty. Many tribes were overrun, and the ancient kingdom of the Monomotapa at Zimbabwe was finally destroyed. The invaders from Zaïre also influenced the arts of many non-related tribes. Important among these were the Makonde of the region now divided by the borders of Rhodesia and Portuguese East Africa. They produced more woodcarving than any other tribe of Southeast Africa. A great deal of respect was paid to ancestors, expressed in curious globular masks. But for the initiation dances the young men who represented the ancestral spirits were required to impersonate women. Hence they invented a unique body mask, which consisted of a frontal cuirass of wood with the fashionable conical breasts and smooth well rounded belly of the MaKonde beauty. Sometimes these body masks were hinged just below the breasts, but most were made of a single sheet of wood stained to a soft coffee colour. Such a disguise allowed the maskers to copy the gait and actions of women, and even to simulate intercourse.

The MaKonde body masks are of great beauty. They reflect an aesthetic far more advanced than most of the ancient work of East Africa. The unusual feature is the care with which the surface qualities of youth and beauty are captured by the artist.

In other African art an emphasis upon personal beauty is found. An outstanding figure of a girl from the Baluba of the Kasai region is an example, where the smooth surface, round face, large eyes and interesting vulva all form a unity, which has been caressed and oiled regularly by several generations of owners. The work is in a tribal style, but it marks the point that many African artists have incorporated into their expression of physical beauty a sensuous appeal which goes far beyond simple sexual display. The physical attributes of beauty in itself have been given their own erotic appeal, unintentionally arousing desire.

The promotion of fertility, human and animal, is of course, the most obvious function of erotic art. Africans in general wished to have large families. There were thus more hands to do the work in a non-mechanised community; and while sons were socially superior there was also advantage in having girls who would bring in betrothal and marriage prices. In South African terms this bride-price was not paid in the sense of a purchase, but as a compensation to her own family for the loss of a girl's labour in looking after the household chores, potting, weaving and gardening. Among the South African pastoralists the lobola was paid in cattle, but in the agricultural areas of Africa a wider variety of goods were given.

In much figure-sculpture we find symbols of the social importance and wealth of young women, whether it be shown by cicatrization of the body, by hair style or necklaces and earrings. Because of the amount of hard-earned wealth which changed hands at marriage festivals the question of the sexual status of the girl was very important. The symbols for this of course varied from tribe to tribe, and even from village to village. It was by no means a majority that insisted upon true physical virginity. But even in the most unrestrained groups pre-marital intercourse was closely limited by kinship regulations. Thus it was only within a limited group that sexual relationships would normally take place. It was easy enough therefore to know just how a girl was to be assessed for her marriage qualities. In some regions girls were honoured by belonging to an organization which comforted young men while their wives were pregnant. The girls were bringers of peace, a social necessity. In other regions the permissive sex play of pre-marital days never went as far as penetration of the vagina.

Carvings for fertility ceremonies reflect the differing attitudes to pre-marital sex in their treatment of the form of the sex organs; but juvenile sex is never a very important factor to the artist, since in seeking inspiration from the spirits of fertility he is thinking of married people and their concern with producing beautiful babies. All things share in the ceremony which enhances life.

If one could mention any African belief as prevailing over the whole continent it is that which envisages the presence of a life force flowing through all existing things. It is expressed through all growth and change. Within the family it constitutes the chain of sexuality which links all generations through time. Time as such is not so very important because life is understood as a flow and not as a sequence of events. Because of this feeling for life practically all images used in ritual have some emphasis on their sexuality, though the head, hands and feet have always their special place in expressing the real structural facts about the being represented in the carving. Thus we may still grasp something of the significance of many figures about the use of which we have practically no information so long as they reach a high standard of artistic quality. One suspects that even first class figures may have had their origins after the decline of organized ritual, and have been made either for a specific occasion or even for the European market. Often such carvings are identifiable only because of their adherence to a tribal style.

The European collector has usually been interested in a work of African art because of the quality of the wood carving it displays. But to the African this may not be the most significant element, since in Africa a revered carving of importance may well have been covered with grime, or acquired the strange surface which often results from its being smeared with sacrificial offerings of chicken blood, palm wine, egg and other materials. These accretions were a vital part of the sacredness of sculptured objects. So a magical carving is likely to be most effective, in the African mind, if the traces of its magical use remain upon it. By means of all sorts of auxiliary symbolisms a solitary figure may thus convey vast conceptions in absolute simplicity. The whole fertility of the earth may be represented in a woman, the whole creative power of heaven in a head carved on a staff. Usually one is unable to interpret such a concept without an authenticated description of the myth with which the object is associated, or at least of the ceremony in which it was used. But in the great majority of cases we are confronted with figures having no verbal explanation.

There is, of course, no such abstract entity as 'African Art'. If at all possible every individual carving must be handled. All the figures in African free-standing carving are moveable, meant to be looked at from all angles, meant to be handled by those concerned in the ceremony. The tribal style can be identified. Decorations may well give a clue to the basic social meaning, because the spirits wear signs of rank and power just like living people. The head is large because it is the seat of the personality. One recognizes a person by the face, and the glance of the eye reveals the power of the soul. The sex organs are of lesser importance, but mark fundamental points. The penis is pendant or erect, for obvious reasons, though one cannot see the same functional variations of power in female figures. Sometimes however, an extra large vulva shows a more than human fertility-potential. The two are organs of projection and reception. The style will show a special relationship to general tribal style, and the ideal anatomical structure varies from tribe to tribe. Contrast the delicacy of a carved vulva in Fang art with a similar carving from the Kasai region. Each artist has been concerned with the depiction of what to him was essential fact, and was not given to distortion beyond the symbolic stylization of shapes. One may note the signs of initiation ritual by the state of the clitoris in females and the prepuce in males. That is all. The sex organs of the figures of power are symbolic of the sex organs of all humans in the tribe. Their unrealistic mass reflects their importance in life, not any real feature of a person represented. They may also express emotion in some way, though the emotional impact of the figure usually comes from its total form. Arms are not greatly expressive because each figure is usually carved from the solid. Legs and feet are powerful pedestals to support the figure, bent to illustrate function, showing strength, but not of more import. Thus we find that an unidentified figure can have a total artistic impact through the treatment of its special areas of head and sex organs, which adds power to the whole rather than any prurient interest or stimulation to the parts.

It is in this region of immediate impact that African and European arts can be compared. The quality of the strange expressive proportions of African carving can be compared to modern European sculpture which has broken away from classical realism. It was impossible for this to have taken place before the 1890s.

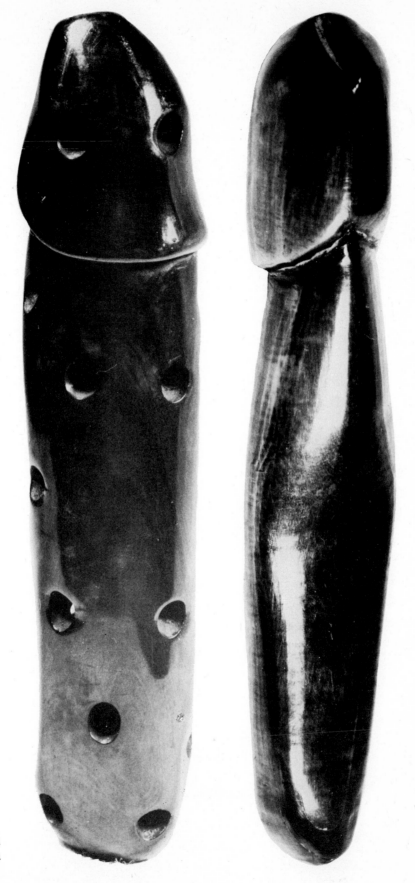

139 and 140 (*Right*)
Ivory penes used in
initiation rituals. Waregga
people of Zaïre-Kinshasha

141 (*Opposite above*)
rass gold-weight
epresenting a proverb about
nimal intercourse. Ashanti,
Ghana

42 and 143 (*Opposite below
nd right*)
rotic carving from the
oruba of Dahomey

146 (*Opposite*)
Yoruba wooden divining
board for the Ifa oracle.
Early 20th century

147 (*Right*)
A personification of the penis
carved from ivory. Waregga
tribe. Zaïre-Kinshasha

148 (*Far right*)
Ancient stone monument
representing the male and
female powers of earth and
sky. Sacred shrine at Ife,
southwestern Nigeria.
Yoruba

149 (*Left*)
Eshu Elegba, one of the
important gods of the
Yoruba people. Southeast
Nigeria. Early 20th century

150 (*Opposite*)
Cast and chased bronze
figurines from Dahomey.
19th century

151 (*Opposite*)
Mask for a young man's
society, symbol of the
ancestors' power of virility.
Zaïre

152 (*Right*)
Carved wooden board
representing water spirits.
Yoruba, from Ijebu Ode,
southwestern Nigeria

153 and 154 (*Far right*)
The male and female faces of
a Shango staff carried in
ritual processions. Yoruba,
southwestern Nigeria

155 (*Above*)
Masks worn by women in t
Gelede fertility dances.
Yoruba, southwestern
Nigeria

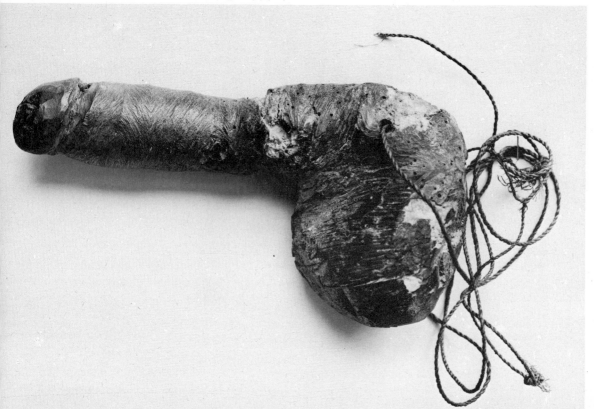

156 (*Left*)
Wooden penis made from a
tree root, used as a fertility
charm in the rituals of a
woman's society. Gabon

57 (*Above*)
mall soapstone figures,
robably fertility charms,
xcavated within the
lliptical ruin, Zimbabwe.
2th–16th century

58 (*Right*)
ail from a chief's throne.
adjokwe of the Kasai
egion, Zaïre-Kinshasha

61 (*Right*)
he dance of life from a chair
il of a BaPende chief. Kasai
gion, Zaïre-Kinshasha

59 (*Opposite left*)
arved ornament on a
remonial spear of a
aPende chief. Kasai region,
aïre-Kinshasha

6o (*Opposite right*)
arved ring in the form of a
eadrest surmounted by a
air in coitus. Baluba

62 (*Right*)
Iendi woman's mask. The
eaddress represents the
ulva. Sierra Leone

The impact of erotic arts was not felt in Europe until artists had first recognized that they embodied genuine but different means of communication. Europe had also to accept the natural completeness of a figure. The Africans never dreamed of concealing the sexual power of their figures until European commercialism and missionary misconception had made the carvers produce 'acceptable' work. The long period in which African carving had just been 'savage curiosities' to the European delayed the understanding between the peoples. This was just the period of the apogee of public puritanism, when Europe tried to divorce sex and its expression from social life and political thought, with dreadful consequences from which Africa has not recovered.

The single figure from Africa is commonly an ancestral symbol. People felt that part of the multiple personality was enshrined in a carving, as the ancient Egyptians felt that the Ka might inhabit the funerary statue. The total personality divided at death but contact was not totally lost. Some impalpable quality remained watching over the lineage. Most often the funerary figure is found in its purest form in East Africa and in the Nilotic region, where there were no great political pyramids of power which demanded a cult of royal ancestors. The ancestor was a more immediate relation in the spirit world under the power of the Sky God in the simple societies of pastoralists. Even in Uganda the powerful and holy kings were not represented by statues but by their dried umbilical cords beautifully wrapped and decorated. They were the physical symbols of the cord of life which united the generations.

In the forest areas of central Western Africa, however, the tribal chiefs were specially commemorated by carvings kept in the hands of the royal family. And as one studies art from increasingly developed cultures the importance of the single-figure sculpture emerges more and more. It represents a social development by which more people have the right to recognize their own family ancestors. In a way this can be seen as a degeneration of ancient African thought which concentrated power through the head of a lineage, towards a more democratic diffusion in individuals.

Symbolic carvings of ancestors stand firmly alive; in some regions they are lovingly handled, and smoothed over by hand until they shine dark and glossy. In other places they are painted white and associated with masks also painted white to symbolise the shimmering transparency of the ghost world. But one notes that the African spirit never loses a sexual connotation. These sculptured beings were ancestors, components in a physical seminal chain which goes back to the most remote beginnings. Even when an ancestor is represented by a real skull, the entity is felt to be complete. For the individual body did not count for very much in African thought. There seems always to be an acceptance of dissolution as part of a natural process. Death was as natural as birth, and was only different ceremonially because it needed rather more ritual to put the unity of the social group in order again. Life would go on, and the family chain would continue.

It is when one steps beyond the human that the great powers of nature manifest directly. Under their direction the carver may be inspired and driven to make an image which he has wished for but has not visualised. The hands work and individual ability is called into play in order to manifest the inspiration from the spirit. In the more advanced societies the carver is a specialist, having leisure for his work. The village may treat him with respect, but for his work he must find seclusion. He will be inspired, and not everyone is entitled to see the forms which the spirit world imposes on his work. In particular it is impossible to make an image in the presence of women, whose own great qualities do not mix with the

(Opposite)
ss finger ring with a
man and a man on a
codile. Dogon, Upper
lta

male artistic inspiration. In such a milieu of magical mysteries conditioned by straightforward tradition the artist is pre-eminent. That the artist is reliable is axiomatic, because he is working within the framework of his deepest beliefs. The gods drive him to make their images, and he has no need to discover that they live within him, closer than his own soul, because they are within it already. We may coldly describe them as archetypes, and identify them through associated stories and pieces of artwork, but we miss the essence. They are living and active parts of each person's inner personality. The union of opposites is brought about by them, the recognition of basic human drives is part of their work because they are in all people, though best expressed by the artist at work.

Among the archetypes are the various figures of woman, the charming maiden who has grown out of the old witch, the devouring mother who is but the fertile earth, and all the others found hidden in the male personality. The artists of Africa, as far as wood carving is concerned, are all male, and that makes it easier to understand their driving forces. To them the dance of life is something very much less complex than it is to women. But its expression is one whose power women feel. The dances and the stimulus given to the emotions by art may well raise erotic responses, even in the most staid of market women. Yet the contrasting quality of the feminine psyche may be so powerful that the men understand that women will cause magical collapse if they confront some of the spirit powers. This African attitude to the magical side of art is particularly interesting because it is the clearest expression of what seems to be a universal phenomenon.

Yet it is because of the archetypal understanding of the complementary nature of male and female that much African art is openly erotic. Each sex may have private magic ceremonies, but in many public places, particularly the palaces of chiefs, we find the two polarities set naked side by side. Unambiguous statements are to be found in the art of the peoples of the Cameroons Grasslands. The palaces of the Bamum and Bamileke chiefs are decorated with rhythmic carvings of men and women which are explicitly sexual. The carving is strong, simple and uncompromising. Doors and lintels are openly visible to the public. This art is not a matter of shame-faced eroticism, but a public statement of the chief's responsibility for life and fertility. The chief represents the life of his people. He is in himself a fertility symbol, and must have a fine collection of healthy wives not as servants or objects of pleasure, but to express the general life force in his control and fertilization of women.

There are less obvious erotic themes on the great wooden thrones which represent the kingly magic, in the Cameroons. Young women are shown carrying offerings, men and women stand around in pairs, the terrible leopard, and the cunning jackal decorate the seat, all to express the power linked with sex as the endless power of life. All such themes are avowedly and consciously erotic. The sexual powers of the inspired chief who is serving the purposes of the spirit world are to be maintained by sympathetic magic. They are real and natural powers and so the carvings are simple statements with no hint of shame, so that if people were inspired by the carvings to return to their homes to take sexual pleasure they become part of the process of life which inspired the sculptor; his function as a court carver was to express in his palace sculptures the abundance of life in the pairing of man and woman. But even in societies where sex is recognized as a great good one may also find that it is not a constant visible factor in life, and its erotic art forms may not be universal instant stimuli. Only when one is mentally attuned to the erotic implications can they take physical effect. Mind and body are linked in tropical Africa in a far more effective way than in chilly Europe.

The high artistic levels of African art were mostly to be found in private religious societies. The forest peoples of northern Zaïre, Gabun and the Cameroons lived in large villages. They were not greatly concerned with political powers, and organization was tribal depending on the observance by the extended family of agreed rules for each occasion. Membership of societies was always very important, partly for social reasons, and partly for the spiritual influences which enriched the life force. People did not just drift into adulthood, maturity and old age. Their societies were attuned to these natural stages of being, easing the transition from one to another. There was less individual freedom of choice in family matters, but much greater security. The individual followed his appointed path among fellow initiates. It was punctuated with places of rest and change so that each new enlightenment would lead to a further advance. Family relationships were paramount. The family was a sexual unit; and its welfare depended on the proper sexual life of each section. The more the family was in tune with nature the more the whole community felt at peace with the world. It was felt right that procreation should be reverenced in proper ways by each age group. Young women initiates could throng around a wooden ladle carved like a vulva, to lick a magic fertility medicine from it, and even in their ecstasy to bite at it. They knew well enough that what flowed into them at the ceremony would give them an extra 'lift' when they took their husbands into their bodies. Although their ceremonies were not seen by men, they relied on a man to make the carved ladle which they used.

Certainly the mind of the male artist dominates the erotic art of Africa. Sometimes in the case of sculpture in clay, women are the artists, but this derives from the practical monopoly of pottery-making by the women. But the women are also able to produce erotic sculpture and delight in the human comedy. They can paint secular themes of sexual diversions on house walls; among the Yoruba people they model sacred representations of Legba with his famous penis large and erect, for he is the Lord of Uncertainty who may act towards anyone like the penis acts toward girls according to the mood of the moment.

Along the whole West African coast, which has been in contact with Europe since the sixteenth century, there were trading stations where contact with Europe has been constant. The local kingdoms, mostly centred on individual towns, rose in importance. As they flourished their local religious cults prospered and art served them. Among the oldest wood carvings from Africa is a Yoruba divining board collected a little before 1600 and now in Ulm. The board was used for Ifá divination; a central motif is a West African mask of Eshu. Although the cult belonged as a whole to mother Ifá, it was the uncertainty of fate which was foretold, and that was the province of Eshu. He is what Jung called the archetypal Trickster figure. At first meeting he seems to be a sinister being, and something of a rapist; hence the decision by European missionaries that he was equivalent to Satan. However on further acquaintance he becomes an expression of fact and far less frightening. His devotees are protected from many accidents of life, and their real gain is their understanding of the nature of uncertainty. Though he stems from an inner consciousness he also reflects the experience of life and its uncertainties especially in the matter of sex. Hence he combines the elements of sexuality and the Trickster even down to his origins.

On the board in Ulm City Museum the carvings of the surround link the fate to be divined with sexual life. There are men and women, all stark naked, and with their sexual organs somewhat emphasized.

Eshu, however, is only one of the Orisha, or gods, of the Yoruba kingdoms. They all represent qualities of the human personality, and inspired dancers wear their masks in processions. In these highly developed mercantile towns there is also a secular art which in older times was seen mostly on the carving of doorways for chiefs and important citizens. Some of these tell amusing stories. There is one series about a young woman who made love to a porter, and had a very pleasant intercourse with his beautifully tumescent penis. She was arrested, and still naked sent down by the judge, to be taken away to detention where she managed to tempt the jailers. The details vary a little but the theme of the naked girl having her pleasure while standing with her man is found quite often. Small carvings were made for Europeans, and some of them have sexual connotations, since the carvers were amused at the lascivious ways of the inhibited white man. Sometimes, especially in Dahomey, he is shown without his trousers seeking a girl. This was not magic, but amused social comment, especially at the big pale pink penis.

In the steamy jungle of the Niger Delta about the turn of the century much magical art was being produced. It was not in those days a centre of culture, but a lonely land inhabited by hard-working farmers and fishers living in widely separated villages. Because of the natural conditions people wore little clothing, and were involved in religious societies which placated the terrible natural forces, represented by, among other symbols, python and crocodile. There was some trade, in special markets, but even then people moved in carefully separate groups for fear that inter-group fights would break out. Among the most intelligent of all African peoples, these villagers were also intensely superstitious. They made wonderful fetish houses with figures of the spirits, sometimes in painted clay. There was fear of flood and storm, of fever and sudden death; hence the un-subdued sexuality of many of their carvings. It countered with its own strength the violence of the wild, and no doubt was felt to ease the tensions of existence. Some of the beautifully carved masks worn in the ceremonies and social plays represent sexual organs as beings with a life of their own. Many complexes were figured in such masks. One representing a woman's vulva also has teats rather like a cow's udder carved on it, and was surmounted by a curved projection like the curved bill-hook used for reaping bananas. Sex and fertility are properly combined in one artistic whole.

The sexual frankness of many of the older carvings can be alarming, because they also represent the violence of the spirit powers in the country. One pair of wooden figures shows executioners in the service of a chief. They are black except for the vermilion glans penis. A carving representing a man's luck collected among the Ibo shows a householder of power sitting quite naked, with a skull on his knee, and in a row above a group of his wives. It is a large ikenga, a protective object for his life force, not unlike the small horned charm carried by most tribesmen in the past. Apparently the idea behind the sculpture was to show the quality of its owner as a person of power who was able to rest surrounded by wives when he was not actively engaged in trade or war. It was an essential part of the nature of its owner, not just a portrait, but a lodging for part of his soul. In time it would be his memorial until the white ants ate it away to dust.

To the west of the Niger Delta stands the ancient city of Benin. Because it was the centre of a powerful ruler and his court officials it enshrined a sacred complex of buildings dedicated to the lineage of the royal family. Bini art for the Royal House was not erotic; unless one finds an inverted eroticism in a few small bronze 'altars' on which we find the Queen Mother officiating at the beheading of human victims. The only occurrence of naked figures among the bronze plaques which once decorated the Palace in Benin are occasional naked boys. These represent the teenage boys who marched in royal processions and sometimes carried small cymbals to beat out a rhythm. They were traditionally naked, and the plaques show them in almost realistic proportions. They never have an erect penis, but the organ is always well shaped and shows the bare glans displayed through ritual circumcision. A gruesome story about them says that the boys must never during their period of duty have an erection. If they so far forgot their office as to let their mind stray on girls and physical desire they had no means of hiding the too proud flesh and were likely to be seized on and killed immediately. This was all part of the horror which surrounded Bini majesty. The Oba alone could make such a sacrifice of fertile life because it showed his power over the forces of nature. And such a sacrifice of life added to the reverence in which he was held, because no power of mercy or pity could stir the holy being. In any case on such sacred occasions he was in a semi-trance because he was inhabited by the ancestral spirit, sometimes even by the sea deity Olokun, and so ceased to be simply the present ruler of the state.

Another great West African State was the Ashanti kingdom of modern Ghana. Artistically and linguistically the Ashanti were linked with the people of the neighbouring kingdom of Dahomey. Here we should expect to find a much more restrained art, because of a tradition that the ancestors came down from the grasslands of the Sudan; we should expect these people to be more interested in sky deities than in the dark and convoluted spirits of the forest. This is, in fact, the case, and the name of Nyame or Nyankopon lord of the sky is well known. The court art of the Ashanti Kingdom has apparently always shown great restraint, though it is probable that clay sculpture on some of the Palaces represented historical events like those now in Paris from the palace of King Gelele of Dahomey.

In the popular art of Ashanti, however, there were forest deities, and all manner of spirit creatures, which had definitely sexual proclivities. The Sasabonsam image, representing a powerful demon who lurked in the trees, has been converted into a horned and bearded man with bat's wings, probably taken from a picture in a missionary bible. However the artists often show his large penis which derives from an earlier tradition. The proverbs of the land include many amusing references to sex and some of the figurative brass weights show erotic scenes. They are expressions of a particularly charming folk lore which has a great deal to do with a hero of mischief known as Anansi who is still much beloved in many places today. He is another of the archetypal Trickster forms who plays mischievous pranks including wife stealing, and sending his penis out on amatory expeditions on its own. So there must have been a good deal of eroticism in popular art in the old times, though little of it survives, as the expression of sex as seen by a farming community. The function of Anansi was to account for the odd events, the wayward love affairs which did not suit the usual marriage regulations, the sudden naughty escapades, and the accidents of love. He is a happy force, full of laughter, but not an easy companion. He makes the pompous into clowns, and the learned into laughing-stocks. However the folk-tales are not very often illustrated in traditional Ashanti art. Modern artists in Ghana have found them a source of inspiration, but the old people rarely turned words into shapes, except on a small scale in the brass gold-weights.

To the west of Dahomey the outward face of culture changes. There were no more great kingdoms. The trading ports were centres around which local tribal chiefs exerted influence. The men were often little more than factors engaged in accumulating ivory and slaves to exchange for the valuable cargoes of trade goods and intoxicants which came in the ships from overseas. The rich life of a trading port allowed leisure for good craftsmen, and from the ivories inspired by the first contacts with the Portuguese explorers, there is a continuous line of carvings down to the carved 'fetish' figurines and decorated mancala boards of today.

Perhaps the best known of the coastal art styles is that of the Mendi people of Sierra Leone. This is largely due to the interest aroused by the important 'Bundu' society, a woman's branch of the famous Poro, which protected the rights of those who had been initiated. This society made many masks for its protective wing. They represent initiated girls emerged from seclusion with the characteristic rolls of fat around their necks. Sometimes these masks display representations of a girl's vulva on top, but this is by no means compulsory. Probably it was more important in more ancient times. However there are a number of complete Mendi figures which represent the girls as rather elegant creatures, quite black, and naked except for the headdress and what appear to be boots used as a symbol of wealth. They display the usual rings round the neck, but the bodies are slender, and the sex organs realistic and rather demure. In spite of centuries of contact with Europeans there has been little development of eroticism. It was not a necessary part of Mendi culture. Sex and marriage were natural, and the well bred young lady had been through her finishing school in the Bundu House and knew all about the ways of men and how to keep her husband well content during his life with her.

Many of the figure carvings had no overt sexual meaning; they were representations of the spirit of the womens' society, and were used for divination. The inspired priestess would hold up the figure by an arm. If it stayed silent and upright it would indicate assent to a question asked; it would twist itself downwards to indicate dissent. There is no reason to ascribe this magic to conscious trickery, the force displayed is essentially similar to that which makes the movement of a divining twig so hard to resist. No doubt the figures were often used when seeking advice about sexual matters, so important to the conduct of normal life in any society. But in general these naked ladies were not thought of as erotic creatures, though they followed a feminine ideal, with ladylike fat in the right place around neck and buttocks.

On the southern fringes of the Sahara there is a band of grassland stretching from near the Atlantic to the Nile. It has for an unknown time been the home of travelling pastoralists. In some areas they settled and powerful states arose like the ancient Empires of Songhai and Ghana. Trade developed both with the peoples of the coastal forests and with the rich lands bordering the Mediterranean far across the deserts. In later times the teachings of Islam spread southwards and many of the Moslem states of Africa developed. The influence was of great cultural importance, and one must remember that the Moslem University of Timbuktu was founded in the ninth century, and is the oldest surviving University in the world. However many ancient pre-Islamic ways remained, particularly among the many small groups of people inhabiting the less accessible mountain regions.

It was natural for the peoples on the borders of the desert to develop rituals to encourage fertility and to bring rain, implying a study of creative existence and a deep reverence for sex. The natural force which brought life must be encouraged and helped, though of course in its manifestations it must also be brought under control. One finds the idea expressed in the so-called Tellem carvings from the Dogon country. Even the Dogon who now inhabit the region cannot give any clues to the identity of their supposed and elusive predecessors, the Tellem. Carvings attributed to them were preserved by the Dogon and later taken by ethnologists to many great museums and art collections. As is usual in African art the carvings do not conceal their sex. They are not usually found in combination, and more often than not are single figures, cut from roots and boughs of the tough trees of the barren lands. They are reputed to be bringing rain to the earth by their lifted hands reaching towards the sky. They are covered by a thick glutinous coating of offerings once poured over them by those who desired their magical aid, composed of some natural material not unlike lacquer. Their simple directness and imprecise form has made them appeal to art collectors. However, this is a case where in the absence of definite information beauty is in the eye of the beholder.

The Dogon themselves inherited an art style of great directness which is however much more harsh in its forms than the traditional Tellem art. Their most impressive works were horned masks and the doors of granaries. The masks are related to ancestors and fertility animals such as the antelope. The doors are covered with a simple pattern of massed blocks of simple figures 'pulling down the rain' apparently in a ceremonial dance. They also display so simple a cubic style that although the sex organs are often indicated they have practically no personal impact. Yet because of their association with the important magics of fertility and preservation they must be seen as among the least explicit variations on our theme.

The nearby Bambara people express their need for life and fertility through the series of carved wooden cap-masks worn by young initiates for dances to express the great events of life. Mostly they are intended to bring rain and fertility to the grasslands, and to increase all life. The antelope's mating dance is the inspiration for the leaping performed by the participants in the rituals. Rarely, antelopes are shown mating, but mainly this is expressed in the dance by the wearers of the buck and doe antelope masks. The does are very often shown with their babies, depicted as smaller figures on their backs. The elegant stylisation of the act of leaping incorporated into these masks has made them a great attraction both in the art world and in the souvenir market. The older ones have a certain strength and rhythmic construction of detail that emphasizes their purpose. But any direct expression of eroticism is an extreme rarity.

The antelope mask is an example of the use of a sufficient substitute for the direct symbol. The sculpture conveys ideas of life, movement and the communion of the sexes in a way which is perfectly explicit to the members of the tribe. But the societies which use the masks are the powers which protect social unity within the community.

Throughout West Africa the great secret societies such as the Poro overlap tribal boundaries. They are at once religious groups dedicated to the spirit world, and social groups keeping the material world in order. Initiation ceremonies are held, and fees are paid. As each stage of initiation is passed one rises to higher political responsibility and new masks are revealed. Thus the society and its hierarchy have a hand in all affairs of life. Among such peoples as the Senufo, whose artistic tradition is high, the society is well served by the carvers.

The fertility and initiation cults are served by maskers wearing animal heads as a poetic symbolism for the occasion and its spiritual quality. However the most attractive art style has been in the creation of wooden figures representing ancestors. Their simple forms directly echoing the quality of rounded angularity of the human body, and expressive faces decorated with marks of the grade of initiation reflect the power in the ancestral line through clear representation of the sex organs. The ancestors are shown as real people, though they have other spiritual powers to help their descendants. Nevertheless the power of life has flowed through their matings and its expression is as essential in a memorial figure as is the head. As usual, these African sculptors tell us that life is a unity.

Further inland the Baga people have also the typical organisation of men in a complex and powerful social society, with its related women's section. A very important being to them is the Earth-Mother Nimba. She is represented for ceremonial dances by a great helmet-mask which represents a half figure. The long pendant breasts are surmounted by a pillar-like neck and a head projecting far forward; rarely given additional support by the arms of the figure. The stylized face of the goddess is an epitome of creative sex. Her forehead is adorned by a vulva with erect exposed lips, and her nose is a long curved penis. Man-woman-life is the thought; and the entranced dancer leaps and gyrates for hours in his long raffia covers with the twenty kilo mask on his head. The dance is an offering of strength to the Great Mother.

There are other Baga symbols of the Goddess, but, although the bodies are often more realistic than one would expect, the traditional form of the head as shown in the great masks is retained. It is this which represents the symbol of creative life; the presentation of the body with breasts and vulva simply serves as a reminder of the generic femininity of the goddess.

Over the whole region from the Sudan to the sea shores there is an emphasis on the magical power of masks and figures. The expression of sex is important in all magic, but the other aspects of exerting power at a distance and of reflecting the future are all present. The members of the societies who fall into semi-trance are the contact, but the carvings are the foci which transform the idea into action. They are the tools of the magician. Sometimes they are used to scare away intruders more by the spirit power emanating from them than from their terrifying aspect, at least to the mind of the villagers. The figures of handsome girls among the Mendi will, as we have seen, bow and stretch in response to the inspiration reaching them. In Nigeria maskers will be inspired to answer questions in a state of trance, and in the Congo the shaman using the Itombe animal oracle figures will find answers to problems in the sudden stopping of the pad with which he rubs the back of the animal. In all this world of magic there are interrelated features which include sexual elements. Very often the power seems to come most strongly from women. Even in Western society the erection of womens' nipples at a seance may be a recognized phenomenon. It is this relationship of women in particular with sexual aspects of magic which has led to the importance of priestesses in many cults, and a stress on the role of the goddesses. The protruding breasts of many African figures signify the ecstatic erection of the nipples even more than the idea of motherhood. Yet the two are combined. The sense of giving out a stream of power from the nipples reflects the physical pleasure of lactation, and yet has a magical import because it is associated with states in which psychic phenomena are projected. One notices that the treatment of the vulva shows it more open and the clitoris more tumescent in the forested regions to the south, particularly in southern Zaïre, than in West African areas. Similarly the presentation of an erect penis is of roughly the same distribution; though in narrative carvings from West Africa the state of the organ corresponds with the action illustrated. The separate representation of either penis or vulva as a cult object is nearly universal, but the frequency is greatest in East and Southeast Africa. Such carvings are obviously erotic in intent, part of the idea of sex education for the young initiates into the adult grade of tribal life.

There is of course a difference in emphasis when we come to carvings representing ancestors. Here there is an intention to convey some solid remembrance yet not necessarily a physical portrait. The famous statues of the BaKuba Kings are a case in point. There is little physical variation even in the faces, but each has a symbol representing an important feature of his reign. The costume of the ancestral figures seems to have varied with local taste, but in most places they were naked and their sex was prominently displayed. After all what ancestor was with-

164 (Opposite)
Raffia and wood figures or mask intended partly as se instruction for the young. BaYaka, Zaïre-Kinshasha

230

165 (*Left*)
End of Eden stave of the
Ogboni society, representin
the male powers of nature.
Yoruba, southeastern
Nigeria. Early 20th century

166 and 167 (Right and far right)
Roof post from a men's palaver House, Mali Republic. From the front the penis looks like the female pudenda

168 (Right)
Ivory figure from western Zaïre representing the bisexual aspect of sex. Zaïre-Kinshasha

169 and 170 (*Left and oppos*
Carved wooden figures fro
a memorial post, Madagas

71 (*Opposite left*)
arved wooden figure of a
uardian spirit. The penis
etween his legs can be
oved from behind. Fon,
ahomey

72 (*Opposite right*)
Baluba carving of the ideal
f feminine beauty. Zaïre-
inshasha. Late 19th century

173 (*Right*)
Mother and son theme.
BaKongo of Angola. Early
19th century

174 (*Opposite*)
Brass gold-weight used to
illustrate a proverb. Ashanti,
Ghana. Mid 19th century

175 (*Right*)
Body mask representing a
woman in childbirth worn by
male masqueraders. Yoruba,
southwestern Nigeria

176 (*Opposite*)
Carved wooden figure life-size of a chieftainess signifying the continuity of power through the female line. BaPende, Zaïre-Kinshasha

177 and 178 (*Right*)
Phallic stones representing the male penis combined with the female sexual organs. Fertility symbols from Cross River, southeastern Nigeria

179 (*Left*)
Polychrome painted fertility panel. BaTeke. Zaïre-Kinshasha. Early 20th century

180 (*Opposite*)
Wooden shrine carving on the theme of fertility. Northern Yoruba, southeastern Nigeria

81 (*Opposite*)
shanti gold-weight
presenting a couple with
e man's penis rubbing the
rl's vulva

82 (*Right*)
ronze plaque showing three
rinces of the royal family at
enin. 17th century

out the power to transmit life? So we find they have the essential attributes. In parts of West Africa ancestors may become symbolic carvings like the BaKota figures from the ends of ossuary baskets. In others the ancestors are painted white to remind one that they are shimmering white wraiths. However one wonders if the white ghost is not a cultural idea taken from Europeans, like the Assyrian sasabonsam of Ashanti.

The cult of ancestors demands the development of figures as symbolic likenesses. It leads towards portraiture, and also towards the representation of living individuals. One notes that at least in ancient days, more than half a century ago, portraits as well as ancestors show the sexual organs in their natural context. Thus the artist is presenting the completeness of the human being in the sensory sphere. The taking and giving of influences and emotions at all levels of the personality are recognized. The facial features, the hands, feet, skin, and sexual organs are all part of this complexity which we know as ourselves, and the African artist is quite aware of this totality without having to reason about it. He can defend his point of view in any argument, but it stems really from the deep awareness of being which he shares with all who care to experience it.

One can experience this in African art at all stages. From Nigeria and Dahomey come the little Ibeji figures which represent twins. They are complete human figures with all their live strength and sexuality made apparent. If one twin dies the other has an Ibeji pair which enshrines their continuing unity. It is a kind of magic but expresses a reality of the unity experienced by twins in all nations.

Among the Baoule small ancestor figures, in the usual beautifully finished style, were made by specialist carvers to the order of patrons. This work by recognized artists naturally led to commissions for special sculptures representing important people, and even figures made for sheer artistic enjoyment. They were kept in safe places, and brought out for display to others, and for the pleasure of handling by the owner and his family. The figures were kept carefully, oiled and polished by hand, so that the surface became more and more beautiful. This is, of course, the best way to appreciate sculpture and indeed it must have had some reflex on the appreciation of human beauty. The act of handling the small sculpture must have been somewhat like a child handling a doll, but with the adult the appreciation of the whole quality of the work of art as a representation of a human body must be more complete. This has an erotic quality, though of that delightful special kind which is a pleasure apart from the violent sensations of physical desire and excitement. The Baoule small figure typifies much of a special quality of African art . . . its possibilities as a source of tactile pleasure, and a means of giving a material form to the imagination.

There is no attempt at hiding the physical aspects of sex, no desire to expurgate the erotic image of intense sexual pleasure, no shame at the pleasantness and joy to be attained through sex. Sex is the means of transmitting life. Its pleasure is the pleasure of earth and sky. It is so important that it is the subject of ritual observances. The whole thing is to be celebrated just because it is a unity with the whole personality of those enjoying it. One may find the whole gamut of sex in African pre-colonial art without finding any sign of shame or hatefulness. In that the African artists have given us a legacy of understanding of the wholeness of human life.

(*Opposite*)
e double Eshu Elegba,
al dancing staff, decorated
h cowries as a symbol of
inine sexuality. Yoruba,
thwestern Nigeria

v

247

The Afro-American Contribution

Many African cults went over to the Americas with the cargoes of slaves carried off to work on the plantations. Most were taken from the coasts of Guinea, Ghana, and Nigeria. Some also were taken from the Portuguese settlements around the mouth of the Congo. The condition of the slaves was utterly forlorn. To their new masters they were commodities. To die and be thrown to the sharks was not like being killed in some sacred ritual for the glory of a king. Death for the slave was as hopeless as life. The sheer misery of existence made sex in itself more important, and the uncertainties made it a necessity shared by all.

The treatment of slaves varied from one individual to another. However there were some basic cultural differences, mainly between Catholic and Materialist societies. In Brazil and also in parts of the Carribean the slaves were encouraged to join in church services and ceremonies. In the West Indies and USA there was a strong tendency to forbid slaves from any religion because it might give them an opportunity for banding together. Even marriage was not permitted because it might be commercially more profitable to sell members of a family separately.

Some slaves brought knowledge of the traditional arts from their home lands, so sculpture is not absent from Afro-American culture. However, most of the carving was of very small size so that it could be conveniently hidden. The slave owners lived in a kind of dream world where magic was around every corner. If they were frightened by the sight of cult objects they would kill the offender. Thus art was driven underground and the symbol became more important than the image or the mask. A twig of wood, an animal bone, a small stone, or some dried insect became the hook upon which magic was hung. It was secret, not talked about in the presence of the oppressor. Songs and dances survived because the slave owners thought that they were outlets for the 'high spirits' of the blacks. They did not realize that Erzulie and Shango were dancing in the midst of the slaves. They never realized that magic was there and brought peace of heart to the oppressed, as well as offering chances of telepathic revenge.

Amidst all the horror of slavery there were still kindly masters who treated their people well. Many a family had welcomed the household servants in to celebrations of the great festivals. Thereby the folk-tales of the slaves acquired a good deal of European folk-lore and custom. One finds the Latin people had their Carnivale, while the British slaves found pleasure in Christmas and Hogmanay. Some of the ancient mummer's plays like 'George and the Dragon' became part of life in the Caribbean. In America the process went further, and some slaves who had run away and lived among the Indians brought the Cherokee Rabbit spirit to supplement their own Trickster figure, Anansi, who came with their ancestors from Ghana. So arose the Brer Rabbit stories; though for Western ears they have been thoroughly bowdlerised.

Ancient African beliefs were reinforced from time to time by the importation of new slaves, so even in the most difficult circumstances there was a strong survival. Temples, sacrifice and ritual gatherings were difficult if not impossible to retain; but the traditions became folk-lore, and the ceremonies became popular festivals. People could meet in smallish numbers for a party and as the singing and dancing continued it was quite possible for some of the group to fall into trance and speak the words of the gods. For the white man there was in the old days no possibility of learning much, because the slaves resented his mindless cruelties, and because even the kindly white was unable to realize that anything good could come out of Africa.

The only regions where African religions could flourish in the new world were the places where runaway slaves could live in peace, like Surinam and Guiana, or Islands which had achieved independence in the late eighteenth century, such as Haiti and Santo Domingo. No doubt there have been important survivals of African thought in the Negro villages of Ecuador and Central America. In Mexico too, on the west coast there are quite important settlements of Negro people who have managed to build up efficient self-contained communities. However these Latin-American groups have not allowed visitors to interfere with their life because they have retained a suspicion of the motives of strangers. It is this natural self protection which has made studies of their life and beliefs very difficult. On the whole, like the people of Eastern Brazil, they have retained much of Catholic teaching, but with African cult material built up within their theology.

In Brazil there has grown up a strong Afro-Brazilian culture, which reflects material both from Angola and Dahomey. The people are strongly Catholic, but there are many cults within the normal religious life. There are prayer meetings with ecstatic dancing, and trance phenomena of many kinds. They are mainly a matter of seeking to know future events, and for the purpose of healing. The ancient arts of the calling of spirits and their exorcism are well known. The art work is mainly in Portuguese Catholic tradition though other figures sometimes appear. It has little overt erotic content. The most important group of Afro-Brazilian cults comes under the heading of Macumba, which included trance dancing, healing and prophesy. There is a curious survival of esoteric teaching in the importance of the rule that the inspired priestess has to wear a tight band over her solar plexus, so that the spirits can be controlled. Otherwise Macumba is normally a ritual for people wearing ordinary clothes. In many ways it has become a kind of Spiritualist ritual, though much of Africa remains in the dance and song. The binding of the solar plexus may indicate some European survival, since it was characteristic of some Celtic cults, and is not an African custom. Carvings do not represent any of the postures of the ecstatic dance, and are usually of Christian 'Santos'.

Throughout the West Indies there are a number of religious cults of strongly West African pattern. Art in connection with ceremonial flourishes in the form of the elaborate carnival masks and costumes, but where folk tradition survives in a cult the ritual objects are minuscule and secret. People are well aware of the existence of various ritualistic societies, and also of lonely sorcerers and black magicians. From what one hears there are resemblances even in small details with the old religious practices of Ashanti and Dahomey, which were the main sources of supply of slave labour. Some families came from the BaKongo of Angola, and something of their traditional art styles were handed down through many generations of carvers until modern times. In Jamaica in particular much was handed down in easily concealed small objects like images and masks. This survives in the work of modern artists like Namba Roy who was one of the Jamaican Maroons. In the remote villages in which the Maroons used to live away from the white men, a good deal of tradition survived. Some of the folk tales reflect the old aboriginal Arawak traditions, others tell stories from West Africa, including the important cycles of Nancy (Anansi) stories. All practice of occult religions is still prohibited in Jamaica, but there are semi-secret cults which seem to be tacitly accepted. Pocomania is the most frequently heard of, but there are also shadowy individuals who are reputed to practise widespread Obeah magics. Obeah is a West African form of magic, often used to direct spirit attacks against enemies, or people who have made themselves envied. However here there is now little artwork. The chant and the calling of spirits does not need a figure, though sometimes a small figure is plastered over with a black magical compound made of unpleasant odds and ends rather like the old English recipes used by the Witches in 'Macbeth'. But on the whole a twig from a special tree, or some leaves and seeds are sufficient to become objects through which energy can be concentrated and directed at a victim. In the widespread cult of Pocomania a few tiny masks were made and they personified the spirit powers of the woodland gods. However they were never made large and were kept very secret. It is doubtful if any remain. Although rituals included trance dancing, which naturally had a sexual exhibitionist side to it, there was no image made and no ceremonial carvings are known. The whole cult had taken a form which was not likely to arouse the attention of the slave owners. Nowadays it remains a minority activity in a free society, though because it is officially discouraged it tends to be a semi-underground movement.

In Cuba, the strongly Spanish character of the civilization led to the disappearance of the Afro-American cults, though stories of magic lingered on and the subject gave excitement to some of the night-club entertainments in the unpleasant days of the old regime. Now people are busy with a struggle for a new kind of civilization, and the old shadows have faded into insignificance.

The strongest survivals of West African religion are to be found in Santo Domingo and Haiti. The usual scarcity of artwork is still characteristic, but there are houses for the religious cults, and they contain carvings. Symbolic art is much more common, and the complex diagrams used in ritual may have strongly erotic meanings, but have no overt symbolism. The gods of Dahomey are present, and take the names characteristic of the western Yoruba. They are however worshipped in conjunction with Christian angels and saints. The main survivals of erotic art appear in the dances, where young people in trance exhibit an erotic activity which comes eventually from inspiration by the archetypal gods of the cult. As is common all over the world the dance in an ecstatic state produces more energy in girls than young men. This energy is largely erotic and leads to stripping and sexual display often including masturbation with cult objects. There are many rituals for divination, and for communicating with the dead. This side however is far less African than is supposed. Most rituals can be paralleled in Europe of the eighteenth century, and occasionally in modern times.

There is no doubt a strongly erotic undertone in the whole subject of necrophilia and necromancy. But in art it has almost no representation. The God of Death (Baron Samedi) is but a shadow who may reveal a corner of his black frock coat or perhaps of his high top hat. His image is a simple wooden cross with hat and coat draped upon it. Thus again we have an image which is almost aniconic. The whole of the Voodoo cult in the Caribbean is conditioned by the interactions between African and European cultures. The painful days of slavery muted many expressions of religion in art. It also led to the African shamans being taken to act as fortune-tellers to the whites. There was interchange, and many of the superstitions from Europe were fostered by the uncertain information which filtered through about Voodoo practices among the slaves. So from both sides a corpus of ideas was bound to grow into something strongly African in its basis but with many echoes of French occultist beliefs of the late eighteenth century.

The expression of erotic art is within the ceremony not in the surroundings. This has been as true of the Afro-American religious movements in the United States as in the Caribbean. There are many religious groups which practise rituals including trance worship and adoration of gods derived ultimately from the Ashanti and Dahoman areas. In any case those areas were lacking in erotic art, so there is no new artistic increase in the cults themselves. Dancing may be inspired, and all manner of trance phenomena occur. But again art is reduced to symbolism. It is only in modern societies that a kind of ecstatic eroticism is expressed in 'naif' painting; but that aspect of the subject belongs to the modern world rather than to the impact of African belief on eroticism in the arts.

7 Equatorial Islands of the Pacific Basin

Tom Harrisson

The two great tropical island land masses, Borneo and New Guinea, seven hundred miles apart, share a good deal in common climate and the basic equatorial 'facts of life'. Both contain elaborate river and delta systems, deep belts of rain forest jungle behind coastal swamp, and then harsh mountain ranges inland – to 20,000 feet in central New Guinea, over 13,000 in Borneo. Complex human populations, divided inland for centuries by geographical features previously almost unsurmountable, number millions. There is a rich diversity of cultures within a few broad bounds of physical similarity and prehistoric common tradition. The Borneo peoples are essentially mongoloid, with slender hips, pale brown skins and long hair, while the inhabitants of New Guinea are classed as Papuan except in the eastern end where they become more strictly Melanesians, in common with the small islanders further east and south. The New Guineans are heavier built, darker skinned and mostly with curly (Melanesian) hair. In both islands there are communities who are materially very rich. In Borneo this is nearly always based on irrigated rice growing, in New Guinea on root crops. Other peoples are extremely poor, some of them nomadic food gatherers at bare subsistence level.

A seasoned observer will again and again find parallels between these two vast islands, either of which will take him at least a month to cross – if he can do it at all. But once it comes to art forms, especially erotic treatment, parallels, though existent, are more difficult to trace out, dotted-in rather than drawn. Stretching back into the prehistoric, both share, for instance, localized concern with large rock menhirs of ancient megalithic cultures, directly related to the phallus and other physical conceptions. Similarly, female pudenda represented by triangles and other formal patterns are found in both, as indeed almost throughout the world, and conspicuously out as far as lonely Easter Island. The similarities are at that level. Further, as a whole both islands show a beautiful and extremely lively range of visual art expression, particularly in wood carving. Borneo has an exceptional and exclusive skill in textile weaving, often semi-erotically embellished. Both show an interest in decorating bark and bamboo.

Yet while techniques and often treatments are close, the mood, the temper, the tempo of artistic expression is strikingly different between the two islands. In New

Guinea at a first glance, much of the erotic art is rather crude in the way it renders the sexual organs, often exaggerating them, particularly those of the male; these reach drastic proportions with some cultures, such as the Asmat. In Borneo, on the other hand, there is a continuous and almost universal understatement. Though there are similarly exaggerated figures, they are exceptional. The general run adopts a more gentle, subtle approach. Nevertheless behind the New Guinea brashness there is a great deal of subtlety and complexity too. In both places, as well, there is an intricate relationship between man, animals and the universe generally in expressions of erotic and related (physical) ideas. In this analysis, the writer has tried to sort out some of the complicated ideas behind this eroticism, drawing on nearly four decades of wandering around this part of the world, but particularly on his experience during the thirties and World War II when virtually no white man entered these areas. Now that they are open to outside European influence, and are even becoming penetrated rapidly by tourism, this is having drastic effects on native art, specifically stimulating a sub-market in new, deliberately manufactured carvings outside the native tradition.

When symbolism becomes so elaborate and obscure that even the artists are no longer quite sure what they are doing, and when this is associated with mild treatment of the human figure within the context of total artistic expression, then the difficulties which always face the outside observer of any primitive culture become considerable indeed. This is, at one level, the situation for Borneo. First, we have a deeply established tradition, soft-pedalling (so to speak) the special characteristics of the human figure to such an extent that it is frequently impossible to identify the sex for certain, even by the ornamentation. This is not, of course, in itself directly an objection to determining erotic content, any more than it is to expressing erotic ideas. But it does make identification less than simple. This is secondarily accentuated by a characteristic of practically all native Bornean art, which elaborates the line, curving, curling, twisting, intertwining outlines and motives with something approaching a fear of a simple, straight line, let alone angular representation. One is reminded of the surrealist Paul Klee, who so elegantly expressed the idea of 'going for a walk with a line'. Even under craft conditions, where it is technically difficult to avoid simplicity in outline, such as in basket-making and hand-weaving, the Borneo artist manages to produce this undulant effect.

Even among the nomadic Punans, who have no sort of settled life, no crops, no salt, simple but beautiful black and white baskets reflect this mood. Moreover the people themselves seem to be extremely vague about what any particular pattern of lines and symbols is intended to represent. For in a sense it is not intended to represent anything in particular. Asked by an outsider, an individual weaver, carver or tattooer will probably be ready to give a name – perhaps the name of an animal or plant – to a particular sign. I have a beautiful Borneo tattoo, done on my twenty-first birthday in 1932, which was identified as 'dog' by the women of the Baram river who did it. But since then, travelling all over the island, I have had it identified equally as 'crocodile', 'scorpion', 'mythical monster', 'sleeping woman' and much else! Yet everywhere, in the remotest corners of the valley, Borneans invariably recognized it as unmistakably Bornean tattooing, Bornean symbolism.

This essential reticence, almost delicacy, among people who until very recently were head-hunters and 'savage' in the popular sense, is equally expressed in overt behaviour – and this is very much to the point. For example, during many travels in the far jungle, sometimes with wholly male groups, and even under the tense and difficult conditions of guerilla warfare of the Japanese occupation, I never once saw another man's penis exposed for one second; and only twice saw people defecate, both elderly women. What a contrast with New Guinea or Melanesia, where at times one seemed to be living surrounded by penises and pudenda. In Borneo you cannot – or could not until recently – bathe naked in the river without giving the greatest offence. Generally only the white man is, in the Borneo view, vulgar enough to expose himself. The idea has been captured in sculpture, by wood-carvers in interior southeast Borneo, who for more than a century have been making nearly life-size effigies as illustration. The Leiden Museum, Holland, even has one 8 feet high, (including a hardwood pedestal) cut from the solid log. This shows a Dutch burgher, with a full-length, frock-coat and a stiff collar, a sun helmet perched on his crown. In ludicrous contrast, a big, thick penis projects from under the frock-coat, held by his left hand. He is urinating. This was collected in 1884 but similar figures were still being made until after World War II. Now white men are so common that the joke has lost its innocence.

These urinating Dutchmen demonstrate also, incidentally, that there is no objection to showing the sex organs in a pronounced way in native art: but it is 'alien' to do so. The Kenyah people in the western interior of the island have rather similar but even cruder wooden figures, some attaining more than life-size, with a different sort of alienating purpose. These are placed outside the great communal long-houses, which may run over 400 yards long and are the normal unit of Bornean living. They are made when epidemics or other serious alarms threaten the welfare of the whole community. They may, exceptionally, have huge sex organs which are aimed outward, to repel the threatening hostile influences of evil spirits and of evil men (enemies). In the past, they could also be employed in connection with peace-making ceremonies, to end a long-drawn out head-hunting war which has exhausted everybody; then they drive away the beastliness and death, liberating the community which shelters behind them. Two enormous examples of this sort of sculpture are in the Sarawak Museum at Kuching, the capital, where I was curator for twenty years. The better than life-size penis on one became polished and shining during its long spell on display. There was a tacit arrangement by which sterile women could rub themselves upon the organ while the museum attendant on duty in that gallery politely looked the other way. Many miraculous conceptions are said to have resulted.

The simple fact (for Borneo) of obvious relative sexlessness, in other than exceptional and potentially alien form, is a first statement of importance. The physically anonymous or immature figure, very regularly spread-eagled in two-dimensional and also three-dimensional art forms with legs wide open, no sign of clothing, yet little or no sign of sex either, has remained persistent even into the present time.

This sexless or sub-sex situation is not by any means a recent development. It is equally frequent in prehistoric rock carvings. These occur in the remote interior, up to 5,000 feet high in the Kelabit Highlands, in now uninhabited areas, on high cliffs. The present inhabitants regard them as figures of mystery and wonder. In the wonderful Painted Cave at Niah on the west coast of Borneo, paintings at least 1,000 years old entirely lack sexual identification. On carvings at least 500 years old, discovered in caves further north in the state of Sabah (North Borneo), the sex is mainly indicated by the position of the hand over the organs, which are not visible. The male has the left hand over the groin; and exactly the same position is found amongst Stone-Age burials two thousand years and more back, from the Niah Caves.

The separated phallus is a more frequent Borneo phenomenon, mainly in stone, notably in single upright menhir megaliths. These, however, are restricted to three

84 (*Right*)
rass water-pot, the woman's
ulva forming a whistle on
he pressure of steam from
ithin. Brunei Bay

185 (*Far left*)
Golden phallus from a
probably Hindu hoard
found in Brunei Bay. 14th
century

186 (*Left*)
Phallic stone pestle in the
form of a bird. Prehistoric.
New Guinea

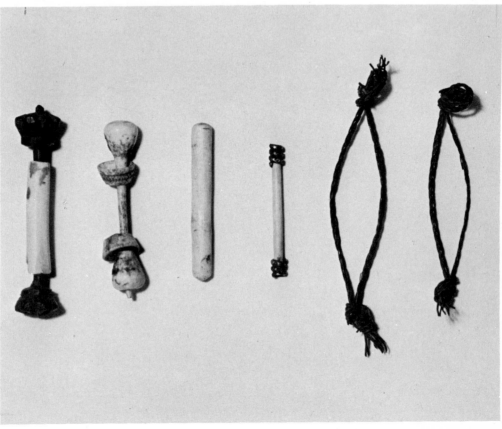

88 (*Right*)
Examples of penis bars

189 (*Left*)
Prehistoric rock carvings
a human/animal form. The
spotted triangle is believed
symbolic of female pudend
Sarawak river delta

191 (*Opposite*)
Adaptation of natural rock
into a semi-caricature of th
buttocks, clearly considere
fun by this native. Kelabit
highlands, central Borneo

190 (*Left*)
Asmat ancestor pole show
the base of the jemen carve
from the projecting root
mangrove tree

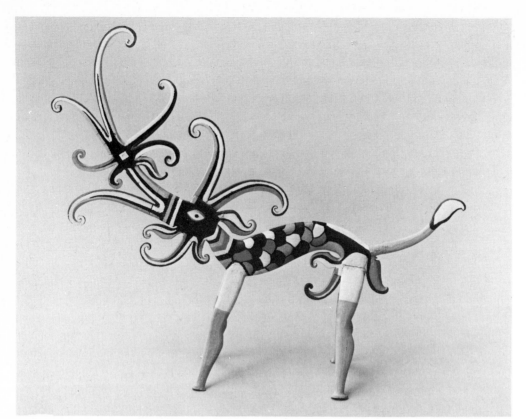

192 (*Left*)
Wood carving of animal w[...]
hooked phallic projection
directly reminiscent of the
penis bar. Kenyah tribe,
central Borneo

193 (*Opposite*)
Angoram figure with snak[...]
eyed (cowrie shells) penis a[...]
turtle belly

194 and 195 (*Left*)
Washkuk carvings showin[...]
facial androgyny taken to [...]
extreme stage

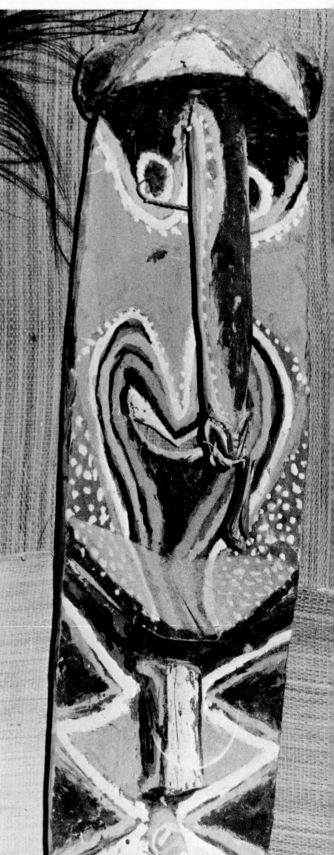

196 (*Opposite left*)
Angoram pole with a snake-penis gripping the mons veneris. Sepik river

197 (*Opposite right*)
Washkuk mask. The nose becomes the penis, the lips and black-coloured hair the clitoris and pubic hair. Photographed in situ, Sepik river

198 (*Right*)
Engraving of an archer with erect penis. Solomon Islands

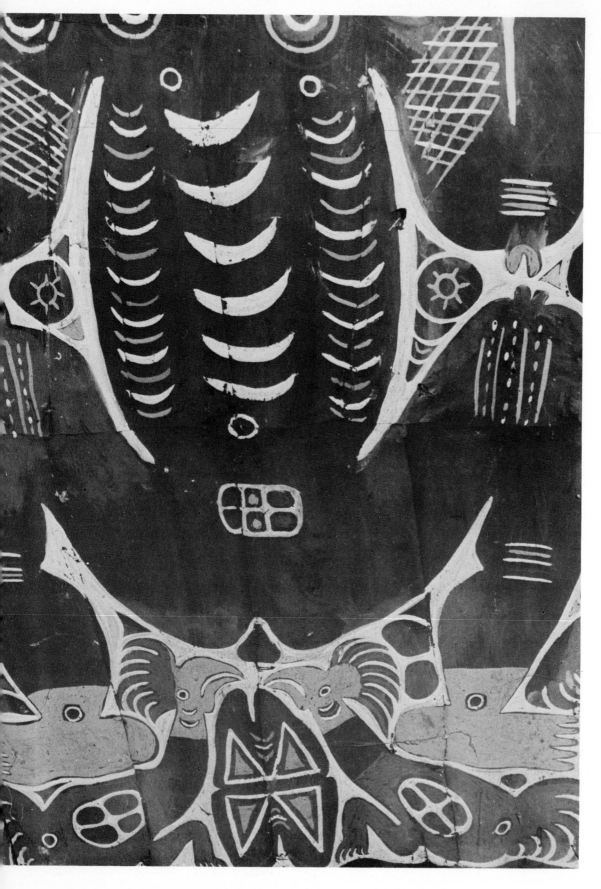

199 and 200 (*Left and opposite*)
Angoram bark paintings
photographed inside the
men's ritual clubhouse (haus
tamburan) at Angoram

201 (Left)
Angoram bark paintings photographed inside the men's ritual clubhouse (haus tamburan) at Angoram

202 (Opposite)
'Shark hooks' in the form of phalli. Northern Solomon Islands

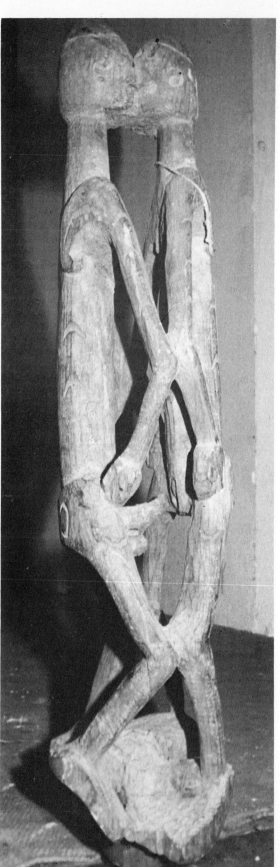

203 (*Far left*)
Phalli surrounding a female figure. Sepik

204 (*Left*)
'Kissing couple' – a rare carving of intercourse. Asma

205 (*Opposite*)
Traditional Trobriand Island carving of pigs in the act of coitus

parts of the islands with megalithic features continuing in historic times, although undoubtedly more widespread before. On the coast, Islam, which reached west Borneo after AD 1400 but never penetrated inland, took small pagan menhirs or broke large ones and used them as grave markers in Muslim cemeteries, especially on male burials. In much the same way, the Hindu culture of Bali, further south, incorporated the earliest menhirs into their great terraced temples where they sometimes became the most important religious symbols. In the Borneo highlands the people sometimes adopt and adapt natural rock-features as semi-caricatures of the human body, especially the buttocks, never the sexual organs.

Among the lost megalithics of Borneo is one we recovered by excavation, down in the Sarawak river delta on the southwest coast, in the fifties. It was associated with an immense ironworking industry, starting about AD 800 with an export–import trade to T'ang China and continuing until its sudden extermination about AD 1350 Ming. Extensive megalithic systems, including many rock carvings and petroglyphs were revealed under the roots of great forest trees and the earth of thick jungle along the river bank. Here again, life-size human figures are shown spread-eagled, without any visible sex or other physical or erotic characteristics. But the rocks are covered with what we believe to be the symbols of the female pudenda, triangles, loosely incised out of living stone, with circles or holes in the centre. Probably these are connected with some sort of Mother Earth idea known to have developed around the miracle of the discovery of how to smelt iron from out of the rock in many early metal technologies. Less common in this prehistoric megalithic context are indications of masculinity. But some of these are impressive, suggesting that the explosion of sperm in orgasm may have been a parallel idea, implied again in the presence all around these stones of tens of thousands of pieces of pellet-shaped iron slag which, to this day, the local population talk of as droppings from the gods.

Many of the things that archaeologists recover in temperate climates perish in equatorial, so it is not easy to reconstruct Borneo's past as one could that of a region with a temperate climate. Therefore this record in stone is helpful, especially as these rock carvings go back well before the advent of Islam in the fifteenth century (Islam never reached as far as New Guinea to the east). Imperishable, also, is gold, and around these carved rocks, many pieces of gold foil and symbolic gold have been recovered by excavation in recent years. Commonly, these come in the form of diamond-shaped pieces of thin, gold sheet with a cut in the centre, symbolising a vaginal form. Further up the coast, also dating from well into the fourteenth century, is an unmistakable gold phallus. This piece, and a small but solid golden *lingga* found in a silver box from a primitive but clearly Tantric shrine excavated in the same area, indicate the intrusion of Indian erotic ideas about that time. There are other signs, too, that a Tantric emphasis on sexual *behaviour* entered Borneo about the thirteenth century, and later developed a sort of underground effect, at least along the coastal plain. (Always, in these big islands, there tends to be a distinction between the coastal zone, susceptible to outside influences, and the mountainous interior, where it is very difficult for anything new to penetrate.)

It may well be that this Tantric influence did infiltrate inland. Certainly it has left an important residue underlying the native culture, and overlaid by the puritanism of Mohammedan faith in more accessible areas. It may well be, also, that this Tantric influence is partly responsible for the otherwise almost inexplicable erotic speciality of Bornean culture, though seldom of Bornean erotic art. This speciality is the *palang*, or penis-bar. Against the somewhat negative background for artistic eroticism, the palang stands out in extraordinary relief. It shows, too, how mis-

(Opposite)
:y rare instance of a
.llus symbol. Easter Island

leading the degree of visual expression for eroticism may appear in a primitive society. Here the sexual act itself has evolved – as in basic Tantric principle – to an erotic art of its own. The penis-bars are treated as beloved works of artistic craftsmanship. I have elsewhere defined the palang as:

. . . a cross-piece driven through the male penis. . . . The basic operation simply consists of driving a hole through the distel end of the penis; sometimes the determined man will have two (or more) holes at right angles. In this hole a small tube of bone, bamboo or other material can be kept, so that the hole does not grow over and close. It is of no inconvenience once the initial pain of the operation – always done by experts – has been overcome.

When the device is put into use, the owner adds whatever he prefers to elaborate and accentuate its intention. A lively range of objects can be so employed – from pig's bristles and bamboo shavings to pieces of metal, seeds, beads and broken glass. The effect, of course, is to enlarge the diameter of the male organ inside the female. And so to produce accentuated points of mobile friction.[1]

There is good evidence in native tradition that penis-bars were of still finer workmanship in the past and deteriorated (along with the whole attitude to sex) with the appearance of violently disapproving, even if distant, missionaries in historical times. Happily, however, the very first text in Spanish from the adjacent Philippine Islands, the Boxer Codex dating from AD 1590, proves not only the antiquity and distribution of the penis-bar even during the sixteenth century as far north of Borneo; but it also illustrates in the margin a beautifully worked palang in gold of an elaboration unknown today. The translated text of the codex, nearly four hundred years old at this point, is particularly informative.

The men commonly place on their genital member and ordinarily carry in it a certain wheel or ring with round spurs in the form (drawn) on this margin, which they make of lead or brass and some of gold. They have holes in the round part of the wheel or ring, one in the upper and the other in the lower part; through which they put a small pin or nail of the same metal as the ring, and with which they pierce the lower part of the prepuce, and thus the wheel or ring is placed on the very genital in the same way that a ring is put on the finger. Thus they have access with the women, with whom they remain for a day or a night in the way dogs do a similar act, after completing which they remain immensely satisfied, specially the women. Some wheels or rings are very large, there being more than 30 kinds, each with a different name, and in general a name sacred in their language. The Spaniards have had special care after coming among these people to abolish this abominable and bestial custom among the natives, punishing with beatings those who wear them, and in spite of this they continue to wear them and make them; and it is very common for them to carry the comb or nail which enters through the holes of the wheel or ring, and placing (the nail) in the member of the man continuously therein, so that the hole may not close or in order not to be bothered with the time in putting the ring or wheel – a custom invented by the devil so that men may offend more with this vice our Lord God.[2]

Despite four subsequent centuries of vigorous censure, driving the whole thing underground, the penis-bar remains popular in large areas of Borneo and the Philippines, even though the latter are overwhelmingly dominated by Roman Catholic influence.

Today in Borneo the operation preparatory to using the bar is usually undergone quite simply and without ritual at about the age of puberty. The proper tool for this work is a pair of finely made wooden forceps for holding the youthful organ in place, with a small wooden-handled drill-bore to drive the hole laterally. This is done by a single forceful stroke – sometimes by a blow from a stone. The initiate's palang is first generally tied to the handle of the forceps at each new operation. The result is a hard bar of bone, metal or other material, running right across the end of the penis. Wearers do not find it troublesome in normal life, though it can be taken out at will.

The bar may or may not penetrate the urethra; it certainly gives much increased pleasure to both the Borneo and Philippine women, especially after their inner organs are extended by childbirth. The southeast Asian penis, when erect, ordinarily tends to be rather smaller than it is in some other parts of the world, thus accentuating the difference that women find when the penis-bar is used. Once they have adjusted to this device, they will barely accept any unbarred alternative. Indeed in recent years, and despite growing outside disapproving contact, the palang has been secretly spreading within Borneo.

For men the pleasure is not so direct. On the other hand it underlines a sense of masculine domination in an important and emphatic way. Self-control and consideration are required, too, in inserting and successfully manipulating the palang – perhaps another echo of Tantric rather than primitive concept.

At least a million people live in palang-wearing societies in Borneo and the Philippines. But there is very little to indicate the existence of any such thing in the visual arts of either territory. There are, however, obscure references in the woven textiles of the Iban or Sea Dayak people, with whom the device is especially associated. As usual, it remains difficult to tell whether what one is seeing is intended to be a palang or just part of a general obscure treatment of the organ. And as usual, native informants can give a variety of solutions to any particular symbolism.

The origin of the palang remains equally obscure. The present writer believes that it has been influenced by the closely similar natural bar which occurs on the two-horned rhinoceros native to Borneo (not found in the Philippines). Anthropologists have recently made a similar suggestion that Australian sub-incision of the penis is an imitation of the natural form of kangaroo organs. Imitation of animal anatomy, whether rhinoceros or rhinoceros beetle, down to the levels of utmost intimacy, is absolutely in place in this cultural setting. These people are intellectually orientated into an intensely lively animism, individual and communal; human and animal entities are inter-related and at critical times interchangeable. The universe is alive with humanity, humanity with the universe. A cricket inside the palm thatch of the long-house can click one way to tell you he likes you, another way to spell out hate. Birds flying across the path will give the messages of good or evil luck due within the next few hours. Stones live and speak, as do the creaking branches in high jungle trees. In this setting, man is an animal, and his penis can be one, too.

Philip Rawson has speculated earlier that 'the whole vast world wide complex of spiral, maze and undulant ornament shares in this same underlying significance . . . the transcendent realm, a power identified at bottom with the sexual energy of the earth'. He attributes the origin of this to a female principle, a mother concept. In recent Borneo with its less differentiated set of sex concepts, one would be hard put to distinguish it from the equally significant theme of the thrusting male. Especially may this be so where, as often, the lines interweave through the bodily flesh in decoration, just as the palang cuts through the penis. It is so difficult for a Dayak to show any representative form, execute any idea visually, except in terms of the spiral, the meander, and what Philip Rawson so aptly calls the undulant ornament. Bamboo shoot, human foot, bird's beak, wild fruit, are turned and torn with a mildly tormented yet exhilarating look. Men spend weeks carving, women weeks weaving such exhilaration. Most of these designs are sensuous, and to that extent erotic. The metaphor is moving as well as confusing. Despite the sophistication of the penis-bar, sex and eroticism are not separate experiences in this 'primitive universe'.

There is a constant juxtaposition of the nearly male and nearly female which intermesh and merge in the interplay of volutés and curves. In some woodcarving and basketry, as well as on houseboards from the far Kelabit uplands, ecstasy is expressed with the line in this way, the masculine with the rounded spirals and the female with the centre blocked or hatched as a faint indication of sexual difference, the vagina.

Interchangeability of man and animal goes back to the oldest roots of Borneo folk-lore, just as it is expressed today in art forms. Each tribe has at least one plant or animal, especially bird, ancestry. Kayan people of the interior trace descent from the strong-smelling, spiky durian fruit, regarded as an aphrodisiac all through southeast Asia. In reverse the Muruts, further north, fear to pluck fruit from trees before they fall, lest in consequence the plucker's penis twists, bends and eventually drops off. Though bestiality and any form of sexual aberration is almost unknown among Bornean animists, in the metaphor of speech, dance, or carving, cross-identification is permissible and natural. Philip Rawson has earlier emphasized, for prehistoric Saharan rock pictures, the predominant importance of 'those which represent sexual intercourse either in the presence of animals or as hunters returning with prey', and shown how widespread this is, especially in primitive Africa. He suggests these images may symbolize 'the coupling of animals in some way re-enacted by their human representatives'. In contemporary southeast Asian animism such a definition might prove too definite. Any act of coupling is interchangeably human as animal, or animal as human. The Western phrase 'bringing out the animal in a man', underlyingly applies to just this situation. The act of sex is participation in the universe of life, be it as the upright menhir, the explosive semen on the petroglyph or, more obviously, an erotic interest in animals as entities from whom a more lucid sexual pattern may more acceptably be drawn or carved. (This 'animalism' interest is more fully considered for New Guinea in the text below.)

At one end of this scale, we have the spiralling animal of undetermined species, with its anus juxtaposed to doubtfully sexed, spread-eagled humans, partly dismembered, as in a fine panel belonging to the British Museum. At the other end of this scale, the Brunei Museum has a solitary three-dimensional treatment of a similar beast, with a hooked phallic projection, directly reminiscent of the penis-bar idea. The penis is almost sublimely represented in other wood carvings as a separate entity, crocodile animal, held by an elegant, humanized dog.

Among the southeast Bornean tribe known as Ngadju, who trace descent partly from the hornbill, a special association between the crocodile, the penis and the tongue is of the sort which is not closely paralleled elsewhere in Borneo, but surprisingly closely so, as we shall see, in much of New Guinea further east. The Ngadju make striking wooden sculptures, up to ten feet high, called hempatong, which are used in funeral rites and characterized by the exaggeration and elongation of the tongue. It is about the only feature of Borneo primitive art which outside observers have identified as in the ordinary sense phallic. Hempatong, which are generally male, sometimes show an ordinary-sized penis, lower down, though that is conspicuous in Borneo in any case. In some, the tongue leads down into, is clutched by or grasped at by a crocodile or large lizard, crawling right up the breast and covering belly and pubic regions.

It is rarely indeed that eroticism, whether humanistic or animalistic, is explicit in this island. One exception is a virile wood carving, again from the Baram river,

274

where a human couple copulate – characteristically without any visible sex organs. Characteristically, also, in a manner very seldom used in real life, where nearly all intercourse is prone. And, characteristically again, the couple are standing on the head of a mixed bird and monster, which has a kind of hornbill beak-hook coming out from the back towards the posterior of the woman, as the nearest thing to a manifest phallus in the operation.*

On the small oceanic islands further east, it is the mighty, piratical frigate bird which takes the place of the massive hornbill in the big, jungled islands, along with the rhinoceros, as representative of direct virility. The hornbill repeatedly occurs in Borneo art, often intermixed with crocodile, snake, or monkey-man as attendant. In the recent tendency to cater for outside, stranger or tourist demand, mostly in Sarawak, sex is transferred to the birds in this way. Catering for outsiders is not entirely novel, though. The same thing happened with the Muslim smiths who founded a splendid tradition of bronze casting, mainly of big, serviceable cannon, in the fifteenth century around Brunei Bay up the coast. Among thousands of thoroughly formalized, respectable Islamic products (banning the human form), once in a while appears a completely 'primitive' representation such as a gross penis attached to a straddled figure which forms the foresight of a cannon; or the extremely indelicate lid of a water pot, surmounted by a big breasted woman whose vulva whistles on the pressure of steam from within. Modern Mohammedans are rather embarrassed when asked about these pieces. But they are satisfactorily explained as having been made for the pagans further inland, who liked such alien curiosities – the obverse of the urinating Dutchman.

If one were to judge Borneo by the message of its artists, there would not seem to be much erotic life at all. That is far from being the real case. The folk-tale that describes the origin of the penis-bar, tells how a girl discovered that the use of certain harsh leaves rubbed on her organs increased her sexual pleasure. She fell in love with a young man who could not, however, satisfy her in this way. So, shyly, she introduced him to the possibility of applying greater friction to her vagina. Thus the penis-bar was devised. Some of the finest and longest folk sagas of the inland tribes (lasting all night) tell of past culture heroes falling madly in love with women, and pursuing them through every sort of hazard either to final achieve- ment or catastrophe. The lovely lady changes form in transit, becomes a be- jewelled wild pig or a golden-antlered deer, leading the hero past many perils, in, over and under the world of today, through the whole universe of fantasy feeling.

Among the mountain peoples post-marital adultery is very rare, though there is a great deal of pre-marital promiscuity. A young woman will commit suicide, by chewing poisonous vine leaves, if her desire for a chosen lover is frustrated by parental or class considerations – marriage is widely based on property exchange and social stratification. There are touching stories of married people, one dead, the other pining away for love. One version explains large prehistoric coffins in several caves as places where the bereaved widower insisted on being buried alive, mourning, there to dwindle away playing sadly a long projecting bamboo flute.

---

* The standing position is rarely used anywhere in the Pacific basin. This and other awkward positions are almost exclusively the ones shown in sculpture and any other form. See, for instance, the two-half-smiling figures in the Auckland Museum, New Zealand, as a perfect example of the Maori treatment, as illustrated in A. C. Ambesi, *Oceanic Art* (London 1970), Plate 52; or the intensely locked pair from Santa Anna, Solomon Islands, in the Basle Museum, illustrated by Jean Guiart, *Océanie* (Paris 1963), Plate 333. In many years I have yet to see representation of a couple in any form of prone position. The same applies right across the Pacific up to the peasant pottery of Inca ancestry to be bought in abundance through Peru and Bolivia. Noteworthy also is the Philadelphia Museum's delicate pair of female ear ornaments, showing two couples, in each one partner having the head of a frigate bird, illustrated in Guiart, Plate 381.

The island is rich in gentle love songs, too, as ever filled with the symbolism of natural history:

> Where now have I lost
> My favourite bird
> The bulbul sings so sweet. . . .
> The mouse with its trimmed claws
> Tears the shoot of the tapang tree.
> Where has it gone to
> The favourite pigeon
> Which shortens the day by its sweet voice?

This gentle tone may seem a far cry from the louder, tougher voices rising from the other great island of the far East, New Guinea. This is not to suggest that the Dayak peoples of Borneo are not themselves tough. They are very tough indeed. They express it differently.

The 300,000 plus square miles of New Guinea bulge with primitive erotic art, the work of mostly dark-skinned, curly-haired, heavily-boned pagans, many of them until recently cannibals and many living with stone tools into historical and even recent times. Artistically and technologically there is a sharp contrast. Borneo and the Indo-Melanesian archipelago in general received advanced metal-age methodologies more than a thousand years ago, in that respect at least passing from the 'truly primitive' well before the advent of Indian, Chinese and Islamic influences. These barely reached New Guinea at all. Not the least element in the contrast is that the more easterly island, 1,500 miles long, has attracted a very much larger Western interest and literature devoted to its primitive art, though there is nothing specific on the erotic aspects as a whole. New Zealand anthropologist Raymond Firth's *Art and Life in New Guinea* (London 1936) was a pioneer introduction, superseded by more detailed local studies in the past decade. The wood carving and clay-mat masks of the huge Sepik river and delta system in the northwest side of the Australian territory – which covers the eastern half of the island, with Indonesian–Irian on the west – has become especially and justly famous for over half a century.*

But the Asmat of the southern coastal plain in Irian, with passionately phallic wood and other art forms of dynamic merit, only came into prominence when Governor Nelson Rockefeller's son, Michael, was tragically and unnecessarily drowned in the sixties while collecting there. His work has since been deepened and elaborated by Dr Adrian Gerbrands of Leiden, whose *Wow-Ipits* (The Hague 1967) is a unique study of eight Asmat wood carvers at work. On the north Irian coast there is memorable though less intense erotic and related art, especially around Astralobe Bay and Lake Sentani, and further northeast again, on the large offshore islands of New Ireland, New Britain and the tiny Trobriand group to the southeast, made famous by Anglo-Polish anthropologist Bronislaw Malinowski with his *The Sexual Life of Savages* (London 1920).

It is notable that the greater, vigorous part of this erotic art is produced along the coastal plain and large rivers, among the people of the lowlands. In the densely populated central highlands, hitherto technologically backward, difficult for transport and major permanent structures, erotic expression has been more directly

---

* The Roman Catholic Mission at Wewak on the north coast has done much to preserve Sepik standards and ensure reasonable prices for artists as of 1971; over most of the rest of the territories this situation is rapidly deteriorating without adequate control, though new measures are promised soon.

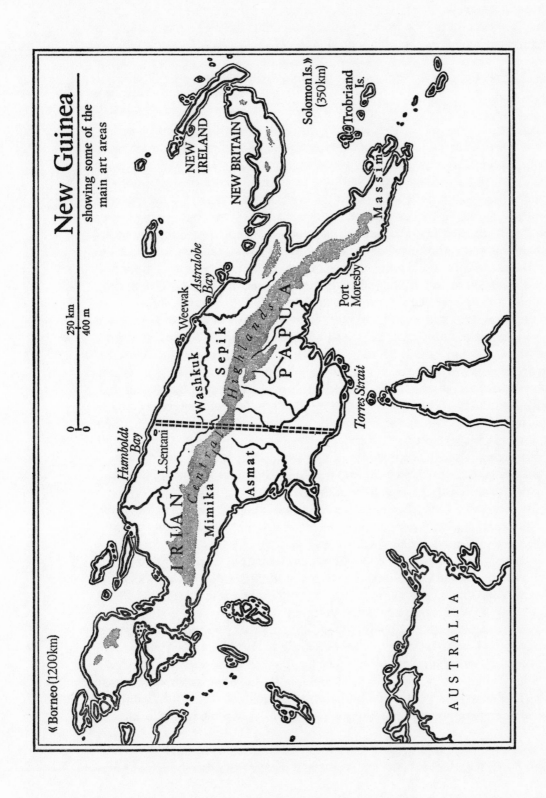

New Guinea

showing some of the
main art areas

250 km
400 m

0
0

« Borneo (1200km)

Humboldt
Bay

L.Sentani

IRIAN

Central

Mimika

Asmat

Washkuk

Sepik

Highlands

Weewak

Astrolabe
Bay

PAPUA

Torres Strait

Port
Moresby

Massim

NEW
IRELAND

NEW BRITAIN

Solomon Is. »
(350km)

Trobriand
Is.

AUSTRALIA

associated with the living person. So much so that the Mount Hagen craft-shop sells mostly things from the remote and culturally unrelated lowland Sepik!

The highlanders excel in self-decoration – with vivid and highly individual use of paint, flowers, cobwebs, mud, bark cloth, cowrie and other shells traded in from the distant sea, beads, bird of paradise plumes, parrot feathers and cassowary quills worn for visiting, feasting, dancing and in places a form of public petting. Unlike the rest of art-full New Guinea, these mountain folk have little or no art in the ordinary sense of that term. You will find no paintings or carvings from them in the world museums. The many collections in three continents visited for this study brought up literally nothing of theirs. Yet we cannot pass over this devotion to self-decoration in both sexes. It is in the true sense artistically erotic: a costly, creative mass effort directed towards two goals. One goal, more directly erotic, is to interest or excite members of the other sex with lavish display, as well as to elevate one's own physical status and virility. The other is to state specifically – by exactly what is worn and how – one's status socio-economically. The wearer's position is thus recorded and at the same time placed as one part in the great cosmological pattern to which all colours, creatures, concepts provide the clues.* Personal eroticism apart, there are also forms of relevant megalithic symbolism, as in interior Borneo. Thus the Duna people of the highlands worship stones of different sizes and shapes as representing different parts of the body, including the sex organs. But by and large, such activities are small.

Dr Simon Kooijman has succinctly put the montane background of giant festivals in an irrigated root-crop agriculture amidst organized tribal violence: 'In these cultures human energy is concentrated on the acquisition of personal wealth, particularly in the forms of wives and pigs.'[3] For the highlanders, eroticism is a moving part of immediate acquisition rather than something to be crystallized, let alone idealized, in any tangible lasting form. The same scholar effectively compares a lowland people from the south of Irian, Marind-Anim, famous for their man-sized hour-glass shaped drums, who: ' . . . could hardly offer a greater contrast (to the highlanders). Their country is so rich in sago and coco-nut palms (absent inland) that material cares are almost unknown. A desire for individual possession, if it existed at all, can hardly be said to be a dynamic feature of this culture.'

It is to the lowlands, then, that we must look for serious treatment of erotic themes in New Guinea. We do not have to look very far. In almost every village, the exclusive man's house may be richly decorated with expressions of masculinity, however wild the forms. This is a man's society, to an extent inconceivable in the pulsating community of the long-house which is the central unit, the essence of the Bornean pagan life style. This masculine emphasis finds its most marked and least artistic expression in the elaborate penis-wrappers worn by some tribes, using gourds or mats which attach the phallus to a belt or string, leaving the testicles dangling exposed. Along the outer side of the Victor Emanuel Mountains, and elsewhere, these penis-wrappers are the only male clothing and can be very elaborate, with tufted or curved out concave ends. And the practice extends sporadically right down the Pacific to Malekula and to the New Hebrides, southern Melanesia. Such display would be inconceivable in Borneo, land of the hidden pubis.

It is notable, too, in passing, that, in Borneo the testicles are nearly always omitted even when the phallus is shown, and often in New Guinea as well. This is

* A rich and valuable study of these themes is Andrew and Marilyn Strathern's *Self Decoration in Mount Hagen* (London 1971); for fine photographs and highland styles see George Holton and Kenneth Read, *The Human Aviary, a Pictorial Discovery of New Guinea* (New York 1971).

partly because they are not felt to be very important to the erotic life, and not even recognized as participating significantly in the act of sex. Rather exceptional is the Astrolabe Bay treatment where an already large curving penis surmounts testicles twice the size (7″ x 5″) while above these from an extraordinary fanged mouth hang two pierced cubes which again seem to symbolize the testicles. This in what is certainly one of the mightiest and toughest types of male carving for the whole island (now in the Leiden Museum).

Penis-wrapper people in the Pacific glorify the male organ less than average in their art forms. At the other end of this chain, the Asmat of southeast Irian go completely naked, seeing their own and everyone else's phalli all day long. Nevertheless the Asmat wood carvers devote a considerable proportion of their energy and their finest skill in carving monster phalli (*jemen*) out of mangrove trunks on ancestor poles (*bis*), essential furniture of the big ceremonial man's house (*yeu*) of which there may be several big ones, in the same village.

The mangrove tree has many projecting aerial roots by virtue of which it breathes, thrives and balances in the deep mud washed down from the central highlands to form the huge, malarial swamps behind the coraline coast. The tree to be felled is selected by the artist (*wow-ipits*) with a canoe party of companions, threading the labyrinth of steamy creeks. The roots are cut away on the spot, except for one, the most pronounced and probably most sweepingly upcurved, which is to become the 'pennant' (in most Western writing) on the ancestor pole. This projecting root is already, on that spot, there called the jemen, Asmat for penis. Isolated, projecting, peeled of the bark, otherwise as yet unworked, the whole trunk with the one remaining root is towed back to the village and placed before the temporary ceremonial house. Here the wow-ipits, assisted or alone, hacks out a rough form, in a single day completing much of the outline. The pattern varies from man to man, but always has a standing or semi-squatting human figure, surmounted by one or more above. In this human column cut from the main trunk each of the figures, normally masculine, may have normal sex organs. Some of the lower pole figures, though, may hold a human head between their hands over the phallus, since the whole structure represents, in the first place, an ancestor who has been killed by violence and had to be revenged by violence in head-hunting. Whatever the detail, invariably out of one of the figures, usually the topmost, the chosen root is chiselled out into an additional, two-dimensional swirling set of curves, cones and other projectile forms, sweeping upward in a great arc. This is the essential symbolism of Asmat, the art form which has made it esteemed as among the primitive world's finest.

This jemen need not begin from the ground: it may originate at the knees, from the chest, even from the head. It becomes the phallus of everything. Represented on pole after pole down the length of the masculine house, carved from the mangrove, each root branches out into the whole wide world of man's experience and doubt. 'Wood thou art and wood thou shalt become' is the tenet in Asmat, which is in turn defined in etymological terms 'we – the tree people'.[4]

For these prosperous, aggressive sago eaters (no root crops), only recently brought under control, the larvae of the capricorn beetle flowing from the sago palm stump are the symbol of fulfilling life. 'A tree is a man is a man is a tree', to rephrase Gertrude Stein. This is one remove further along the enigmatic labyrinth of animism, within the concepts so deeply implanted in Borneo life and art. But the Asmat also identify with animals, and prefer them to plants as symbols in visual art. For instance, the crocodile is especially identified with the penis, while both the hornbill (as in Borneo) and the big black cockatoo rank as what Dr Gerbrands has called 'undifferentiated ancestor-headhunter symbols', along with the praying mantis (the scorpion is the Bornean equivalent).[5] These are 'all heavily-loaded symbols from the headhunting complex, the central theme of the entire Asmat culture' – and frequently represented as end-pieces, heads to the great jemen phalli on the poles.* Among the Asmat in Papua (as among the Dayaks of Borneo) the huge beak of the hornbill is interchangeable with the head in head-hunting, charged with rejuvenating sexual life and identical in feeling with the mighty jemen out of the mangrove. This whole feeling should, I suggest, be seen as to do with more than the phallus or sex as a whole, more than even a super-virile sensuality; rather, it should be seen as the orgasm – and hard behind that, the ecstasy of life, albeit frustrated reaching for the stars, behind reason, behind comprehension even in the world of mind.

Every five years or so the man's house (yeu) with its big poles has to be rebuilt, as both poles and roof rapidly decay in this humid tropical island. Then is the time when the capricorn beetle larvae are crammed into sago logs signifying the tree of life, around which the women – allowed into the men's house for this enacted ecstasy – dance while the warriors wait outside. After as much as one full day of dancing, the men come back, the log is chopped open so that the beetle grubs (delicious eating, as I can certify) pour over the floor in a golden cascade to be shared by all. Over all this, the jemen stand spectators, as again when the women re-enter the yeu for the ritual adoption of men from another village, each man crawling through the tunnel made by the women's legs in an act of ritualistic re-birth.

The same male emphasis is also strikingly found in the phallus-beak association on Asmat canoes. So much so that they describe not only protuberant prows as jujemen (canoe penis), but extend that term to a wide range of sculpture in wood, mostly with beak ends.

There are, of course, other and almost as emphatic phallic art forms in New Guinea. Asmat is specialist, not exclusive. A huge penis projects from a big Humboldt Bay carving of the north, politely covered with a piece of new bark cloth, on display in the Royal Tropical Museum at Amsterdam. Important here is the big stone pestle in the form of a bird, but unmistakably phallic in detail, found ten feet down in the ground in northeast Papua. Though of uncertain date, the piece is clearly prehistoric, suggesting that the strong penis tradition is ancient here, just as the opposite tradition in prehistoric Borneo.

The Asmatic phallus is notably strong by comparison with the feminine pudenda which are more weakly represented. The feminine theme in Asmat tends to be treated as passive, ready, receptive – the necessary concomitant to the factual status of women in life. Where in some lands the tree of life is balanced towards the feminine, fruit-bearing concept, in Asmat even the grubs that cascaded from the sago trunk can only be seen as semen symbols of male orgasm. By the same token, the passive turtle (bu) is their common art symbol of pure virility by virtue of its ability to lay a hundred or more eggs at a time, putting any human female effort in contempt. The long wooden soul ships carved for the death rituals (uramum), a full-length classical Asmat form with canoes running up to twenty-five feet long, are elaborately covered with human and bird figures, but always with

* The finest New Guinea collections are in Holland, Switzerland, England, Australia, Hungary and the USA, in roughly that order of importance. There is an inadequate museum at Port Moresby in Papua which at the time of writing does not even have a permanently appointed curator, a distressing state of affairs under the Australian mandate. Nothing is organized on the Indonesian side in Irian. Contrast the poorer Borneo territories where there are three fine and fully staffed museums – at Brunei, Kota Kinabalu and Kuching (the latter approaching its centenary).

a turtle in the centre place. Hornbill and other birds regularly appear among death-ship figures, with the beak placed at the anus or elsewhere in the pubic region of a prostrate male human; and there are many variants of this theme, such as dogs and pigs merging into men at the pubic region. This is not, however, as dominant a theme in Asmat as it is in more northerly and easterly parts of New Guinea (below).

Lack of female emphasis includes, among the Asmat, a notable disregard for the breasts. If the lower organs are obscured for other reasons, such as the presence of symbolic birds, sex identification becomes almost as difficult as in Borneo. Dr Gerbrands, after eight months studying in one village, reports an incident which neatly reflects not only this situation in that part of New Guinea, but the whole problem of identifying these symbols in this part of the world. He writes of the artist Bishur bringing him a human head crowned with a bird as a prow head:

> The other end, which was the stern, bore a human figure, according to Bishur the representation of a female ancestor. Puzzled, since the figure seemed to me *entirely asexual*, I asked him how one could tell that; he answered by indicating with a resolute gesture a sharp, triangular indentation on the back of the figure's *head*. This represented the pubic covering made of sago leaves which the Asmat women wear pulled between their *legs*.[6]

Likewise Gerbrands was not able to identify any of more than five hundred wood carvings he saw made and then collected in the Asmat region as representing the act of sex. Curious are two crouched, facing figures, described by him each as an ancestor clamping a praying mantis between its legs. But re-examining this piece at Leiden in September 1971 it is difficult to avoid the conclusion that they are both equally human, the woman crouching on a long wooden pin, while the male is separate and detachable (points he does not mention) and fits perfectly between her thighs; his single, stiff, lifted arm, two-dimensional and flat, reaches from elbow to past her chin and surely can only be coital. Surely, equally, anything else!

The Asmat then, may be taken as one primary erotic pattern. Much attention is paid to male sexuality, but the feminine pudenda are not ignored, while the presence of related birds and other animals continues, though not too conspicuously. The rest of this teemingly cultured island with some eight hundred dialect languages shows many other facets which serve only to complicate rather than to contrast this base pattern. It will, in the available space, best serve to highlight these from a few of the many thousands of works of art from New Guinea in collections and illustrations across the world, as well as in our own and other field records. Of these the largest number undoubtedly come from the Sepik River, which runs right across the Australian part of the territory, on the opposite side of the island from the Asmat, a month's journey on foot, over the intervening highlands and the unbearably harsh barriers in between, defying any direct culture contact before the first white penetrations well inside this century.

Throughout the artistic variety of the Sepik River system the emphasis remains on the male. Much of the best art, especially erotic art, is centred on the man's house (*tamberan*) where the ritual-spiritual life of the people is ultimately fulfilled. High wooden figures, carved in the round rather than in the Asmat style of relief, masks of monumental proportions, elaborately painted bark and bark cloth, shields, stools, paddles, earthenware pottery decorated with shells and even dried plants, form part of the rich display. From the present point of view interest is centred on wood sculpture and bark painting. The whole Sepik situation is summed up in a superbly simple log-pile from the entrance of a big tamberan at Kangaman in the middle Sepik, bearing two male figures with greatly elongated faces, solidly one above the other, depicted with a firmness and lack of fussiness quite unlike Asmat and not projecting or in profile at all. From the upper face hangs a long tongue which starts *above* the upper teeth, between the gum and the lip, and drops down into the mouth of a shark, flanked by two sawfish, covering the chest and pubis. The figure below has a gourd-like stomach out of which projects downwards a long, thin penis with two unusual, nutty testicles, standing out on each side, with a turtle coming up towards the organ from between the feet.

Emphasis on the head is characteristic of the Sepik. Heads alone are popular, and assemblages of heads in which one or more are magnified, swollen as pumpkins. These put heavy emphasis upon the nose within an oval face. Noses – and to a lesser extent chins and tongues – become snouts, trunks, probosci, prongs, horns, hooks or double-hooked anchors, lizards and crocodiles, hornbill and cockatoo beaks. These sinister elongations press down to the chest or navel or, most strikingly, swing directly into the groin in unmistakably phallic design. Beside these Sepik forms, the hempatong of southeast Borneo pale into insignificance.

Thus in the Sepik, the male phallus is commonly lifted from below the waist and grafted onto the head, symbolically, without the exuberant extroversion from the body of the man himself as preferred by Asmat. The nose is the phallus is the nose – a concept given living context by what old-time Whites called 'the Sepik hand-shake', a peculiar form of greeting up river where men meeting after any considerable absence reaffirm their joint peaceful intent by each putting one hand to the nose and one to the phallus of the friend, forearms intertwined. Can there be a cleaner symbol of the man-mannered primitive position?

Among the rather remote Washkuk, the nasal theme reaches obsessive proportions, not so much in length but in thickness, virility, free of artistic frills. The nose here patently becomes the penis. At its simplest, a Washkuk mask or shield has a thick, banana nose starting above eyes as protuberant as nursing nippled breasts. This organ comes out over flat cheeks, passed a mouth with a tongue also protuberant, in a distinctly clitoris effect.

A rather more elaborate form gives the nose formidable, exaggerated nostrils, representing the glans penis. This may be carried over a mouth which has 'legs' swept up as lips and a black coloured beard representing pubic hair, while the eyes evolve from breasts to testicles in the sort of bisexuality so openly manifested further east (see New Ireland below). In a drastic further stage of facial androgyny, the upper lip develops from shadow clitoris to patently hanging penis with powerful glans projecting far below the chin.

This transference from nose to tongue to penis, by now becoming familiar for the area, is carried a remarkable stage further in another branch of Washkuk wood carving, which could be misinterpreted in erotic terms if this evolution were not traceable today. How often, over centuries, must the missing links have been lost in these dynamic yet localized, warring cultures, as patterns in one place or another become popular, the vogue, and were eventually adopted as essential, unavoidable, the only proper form to represent man, beast, dream or universal scheme. Thus are two big wooden house poles in the little Port Moresby Museum, believed to represent mythical beings and have supernatural powers to promote the fertility of yams (those phallic-shaped tubers) and the well-being of society.* On both, a pendulant-breasted woman forms the upper part of the solidly made house pole. Below her feet, facing the *other way* up, is a large human head, with a

* Information from Dr Dirk A. Smidt, Acting Curator of the Port Moresby Museum, Papua, 1970–71, who kindly extended generous research facilities for the present study. The two Washkuk carvings are catalogued there as E7285 and 7289.

heavy beak nose and hugely protruding tongue which penetrates her very long labiae. On one this could be taken for a real tongue. But on the other it is so long, at ten inches, as unmistakably to recall the penis-from-the-mouth of the masks already described. It is extraordinary for this part of the world, an act of seeming male submission as a lesser partner on the pole pecking order. Though it cannot, under Sepik circumstances, be interpreted as representing the act of fellatio, yet it remains an intensely significant treatment of insufficiently understood erotic relationships (cf. the Palaeolithic tongue images referred to in the Introduction).

This erotic Washkuk treatment of the female cannot, however, be put aside as purely symbolic. Much further down river, round Angoram, there are poles on the men's house which underline this point. One shows a full-breasted woman, topped by a beak-nosed male face, with a crocodile crawling all up her right thigh; with her right hand she takes its long, pliant tail and manipulates this towards her vagina.

The Royal Tropical Institute at Amsterdam has a related wood carving of a prone woman with (as so often) big falling breasts beside a large crocodile with a hornbill on its head and its tail firmly entering her vagina. In both cases we can postulate the penis as symbolized. This is less easy in another Angoram pole, still in situ, where a snake squirms up from below human feet to grip what appears to be the mons veneris in its spade-shaped mouth. 'Appears', because it is again possible that the mouthed organ is male, since there are no clear feminine indications above. And native informants for us as for Dr Gerbrands further south, did not or would not resolve such confusions of identity, which are strictly 'western' impositions anyway. This difficult erotic problem is further complicated by another delightful, though modern Sepik figure, at present standing outside the Roman Catholic Mission at Wewak. Here a penis shaped much like the Washkuk tongues is being approached by a shark in the usual animalistic way; but the chest above indicates a young girl.

The apotheosis of this Sepik 'animalism' is reached with the explosive bark paintings, brilliantly coloured but clothed in near-darkness, up the pole leading into the huge Angoram man's house on stilts. These make a kind of nightmare interior of posturing humans interspersed with crocodiles, snakes, turtles, fish, insects, wallaby, the inevitable hornbill and cockatoo, and hybrid myth-animals too. No amount of present interpretation can sort out this exotic and in part erotic chaos, where pregnancy and menstruation seem to merge with hermaphroditism and masturbation in all sorts of combinations, frequently focussed back into animalistic groups on or about human bodies.

The idea so violently expressed on bark at Angoram is taken up another way in the Maprik woodwork of the lower Sepik, usually flat and basically two-dimensional except (again) for emphasized heads in the round. Some of these show a kind of Papuan Prometheus, surrounded by pecking hornbills including two pecking at each side of a weakly shown phallus. We recently obtained one at Maprik with two hornbill beaks nibbling the phallus characteristically; but the exaggerated head is reversed on its shoulders to look the other way from this zone of torture – or delight.

Although, then, the female gets much more – if not 'better' – treatment in Sepik and northern New Guinea art generally, she is by no stretch of the imagination an equal partner in erotic art, whatever may remain in the erotic life. One is reminded of the old Christian question, raised forcibly at the medieval Synod of Mâcon, as to whether women should be termed human beings at all! And even where there is no erotic action, the options are clearly here with the man. Angoram wood carvings bring this out again in the round, like one where the male has a turtle on his chest in semi-copulating position over the navel, and his big hanging penis has two cowries as eyes in the glans – just as there are two cowrie eyes in a nibbling shark from Wewak. This seashell which appears all over the place is generally taken to be the vagina symbol (though it is probably not as simple as that).

With less refinement, another Angoram figure shows a truly vast circumcised phallus, semi-supported in a woven net-basket, the man holding a baby awkwardly across his belly above, in almost comic juxtaposition, perhaps to be taken as meaning female pregnancy over male potency.

A simpler, flatter Maprik treatment has the penis hanging to the knees. This insistence on size, though by no means always the rule in New Guinea and not at all in Borneo, will be familiar to the student of Japanese and other more sophisticated erotica, where the male member passes beyond size-belief.

Equally crude but more isolated are phalli presented separately. Often several are bunched together in the form of stands or pegs or simply as ornamental base supports, even for stools, especially among the Iatmul people. These reappear as 'shark hooks' in the northern Solomons. Such phallus symbolism is especially used around the much less common separate female figures, as if to state the ever-present, ever potent masculine promise.

Isolated or animalized, these and more ordinary representational treatments of the penis on other wood carvings in the Sepik add up to an extraordinary concern with the actual organs of male sex, but to a much lesser extent with the female. Psychiatrists may see here castration and associated menstruation fears, haunting ideas about the place of sex in the total animal universe as well. To pursue this more deeply on present information remains mere speculation or a play on words. Beyond dispute though is the aversion to direct, 'obvious' statements of sexual intercourse or other normal erotic experience, except under very recent influence. This is carried a stage further as we step firmly over the edge of New Guinea on to the threshold of Melanesia, at the Trobiand Islands, off the eastern tip of the main island, administered by the southern territory of Australian Papua.

The Trobriands became famous through the studies of the Polish–British anthropologist, Bronislaw Malinowski, who worked there during World War I. His best-selling, though scholarly *The Sexual Life of Savages* (London 1929) for the first – and perhaps for the last time – describes these matters in a primitive society with the insight of a first-class and deeply liberal mind plus adequate field work experience. He found that in the Trobriands 'love is a passion (that) torments mind and body to a greater or lesser extent; it leads to many an *impasse*, scandal or tragedy.' Yet the bodily functions involved were intrinsically misunderstood. He emphasizes, too, the limited range of sexual position and the rarity of even the least sexual aberration. The main erotic interest is fixed 'in the human head and face': this is as near as he comes to discussing erotic art.

For forty years, a debate has raged round Professor Malinowski's insistence on Trobriand's ignorance of any direct relationship between copulation and birth. The latest and most refined restatement has come from Dr Peter Wilson who confirms as basic 'two Trobriand articles of faith – parthenogenesis and matriliny'.[7] The child is, in this view, 'begotten' by a woman and her *brother* – with whom sexual relations are absolutely forbidden as incestuous, of course. On the other hand, only husband and wife can properly copulate; but they cannot thus beget children. Parthenogenesis, reproduction without sexual intercourse, logically follows as a satisfying explanation of pregnancy.

The present writer fully accepts this diagnosis. He has himself found, both among the highland Kelabits of central Borneo and some of the people of northern Malekula in the New Hebrides to the south, closely similar biological naivety regarding the sexual functions. This, in turn, liberates the orgasm from a whole range of connotations, quadruply birth-charged in established Westerly religions. It can now become an act almost as separate as vomiting, or as social as de-lousing your mate. Seen that way, much else becomes a good deal easier to appreciate, if not actually to understand, in the sorts of primitive eroticism and crypto-eroticism presently under review.

In only a few places, however, have outside scholars stayed long enough and gained deep enough insight to get at the roots of the fundamentally primitive and primitively modern problems of erotic life – and, especially, of erotic purpose as expressed both in action and (where that is frustrated or redirected from the 'savage') in art, whether visual, aural (song and folk tales) or muscular (dancing especially). Indeed had Malinowski not outraged accepted European thinking with his original discoveries, the Trobriand situation might well have passed unnoticed.

However, Trobriand sexuality is highly alive yet minimal in erotic expression in any immediate sense. All these Massim people (the term used for southeast New Guinea and the islands adjacent) pay great attention to the surface decoration in art form, covering everything with carved or impressed spirals and shapes sometimes reminiscent of Borneo. The human form tends to be weakly represented, notably so in contrast to the surrounding areas. This has been noted from the earliest records, so that Massim three-dimensional art is poorly represented in collections. It still has interest, as in the modern, simple, rather static yet insignificant feminine figures showing another, though remote parallel to the nose-tongue–phallus in the form of an object (perhaps symbolizing the fertile yam tuber?) curling up from the base into the pubic area, and characteristically surface ornamented.

But the impressive feature of Trobriand erotic art is the direct expression of coitus, so rare in the whole area, predominantly or entirely in terms of the only large mammal on the islands, the domesticated pig, which, like woman, is thought to be able to reproduce parthenogenetically.* The best traditional Trobriand sculptures today continue an ancient tradition of carving pigs half-seriously, half-comically perhaps, in the act. Sometimes two, sometimes three animals are in association; sometimes a man is gripping the rear one or appears to be sniffing at its posterior.

There are all sorts of deviants on this treatment – for instance, a small pig on a large one, with a third one of intermediate size sniffing the anus of the second. These figures are still being beautifully carved today, and the modern versions are almost inseparable from those which can be proved to have been brought from the Trobriands generations ago.† This anal rear inspection, indicated lightly in Asmat, carries over strongly southeastward into the Solomons and Melanesia proper. One virile work recently taken from the island of St Catalina, has a man clutching the rear legs of a running pig and making such an inspection, with the inference – in

* It should be realized that throughout New Guinea and the Pacific there is a scarcity of large endemic mammals. This can exercise a considerable influence on erotic symbolism, especially where the act of sex itself is so much less directly interesting and conspicuous for man in smaller forms.

† The best historical examples are in the Budapest Museum, two of these illustrated, one in Jean Guiart, *Océanie* (Paris 1963), Plate 313; and another in Tidor Bodrogi, *L'Art de L'Océanie* (Paris 1961), Plate 62. Compare also R. A. Rappaport, *Pigs for the Ancestors* (Newhaven (Yale) 1967), which further relates to the New Hebrides discussion of intersex pigs below.

the taut body lines expressed cleverly by the artist – of an urge to mount the animal himself. Almost the same idea – and tension – is shown in a well-known figure from eight hundred miles away, at Lake Sentani in northeast Irian, where a man similarly treated, handles, feelingly, the posterior of a cassowary.*

In the same mood is a wooden shark from St Anna Island in the Solomons, now in the little museum at Honiara, capital of the group. This has human thighs, legs, erect penis and testicles, while its fishy head presses breast level on a sitting, welcoming man. The god legend of Karimanua is background here.

Out in the Solomons, art is exceptionally frank – in the European sense – in a rather casual way. A very unusual basket design, transferred and engraved on to a wooden monochrome panel with almost Assyrian temper, shows an archer, arrow fixed aggressively forward, and below this his own penis similarly poised on a smaller scale. In the same mood is a striking, jet-black human, darker than any Melanesian, holding on each flank an upsweeping shark, standing above a gold-coloured band showing turtles and sharks in black. Head, chest and arm shell jewelry is pure white in vivid colour contrast, as is the dramatic effect suddenly achieved from a scarlet end to the long, pendulant black penis.

Similar in temper is a Solomons' couple copulating, the man standing and the woman with legs embracing his thighs in one of those extremely difficult positions which almost alone occur on coitus representations in all this part of the world. Straightforward, prone coitus is almost unknown in the traditional art, though utterly normal and locally often the only system practised in life.† Equally bold are the so-called 'shark hooks' already mentioned, derived from prototypes and also serviceable for spirit offering and other purposes. Some of these are beautiful in their simplicity.

In the rather more emancipated Solomons' atmosphere the women get a better showing. A woman may be nearly heroic and be completely her own person. Such is the splendid, black hardwood carving from little Rennell Island, at the southern end of the chain and with strongly Polynesian influences. She is pregnant, and holds her bulging milk breasts with inset shell white nipples. But her head is an owl's, the bird that sees by night, with great dark eyes protecting the pending mother from all kinds of accident and evil influence.

Less flattering but again extraordinarily honest and alive is another exceptional female wood carving, found at Honiara, showing a naked, black lady wiping her posterior with a large white leaf. Seen from the front, the leaf, as held, looks as if she had a penis below her pendulant breasts, thus obliquely repeating the familiar bi-sexual motive.

The lady cleansing herself with a leaf poses two themes closely and subtly touching on the erotic in much of Melanesia and most parts of New Guinea. The first, as an Australian anthropologist has recently demonstrated, shows that sex, faeces, food (especially yam and pork) may be very closely linked. The folk-lore of the Maenge people in southern New Britain – the three hundred mile-long island off New Guinea and north of the Trobriands and Solomons – deals heavily with faeces and mythology. The Maenge conception of the living world identifies, among other things, the sea with urine, lime with vaginal excretions, menstrual blood with manganese earth – which last is put on the teeth of young

* Lake Sentani figure in the Basle Museum, reproduced in Jean Guiart's *Océanie* (Paris 1963), Plate 130; and elsewhere frequently.

† There is a copulating couple in a difficult sitting position, from St Anna in the Solomons, in the Basle Museum, executed in stone, and illustrated in Guiart, 1963, Plate 333.

07 (*Right*)
Rare wooden carving from a
Batak staff. Sumatra

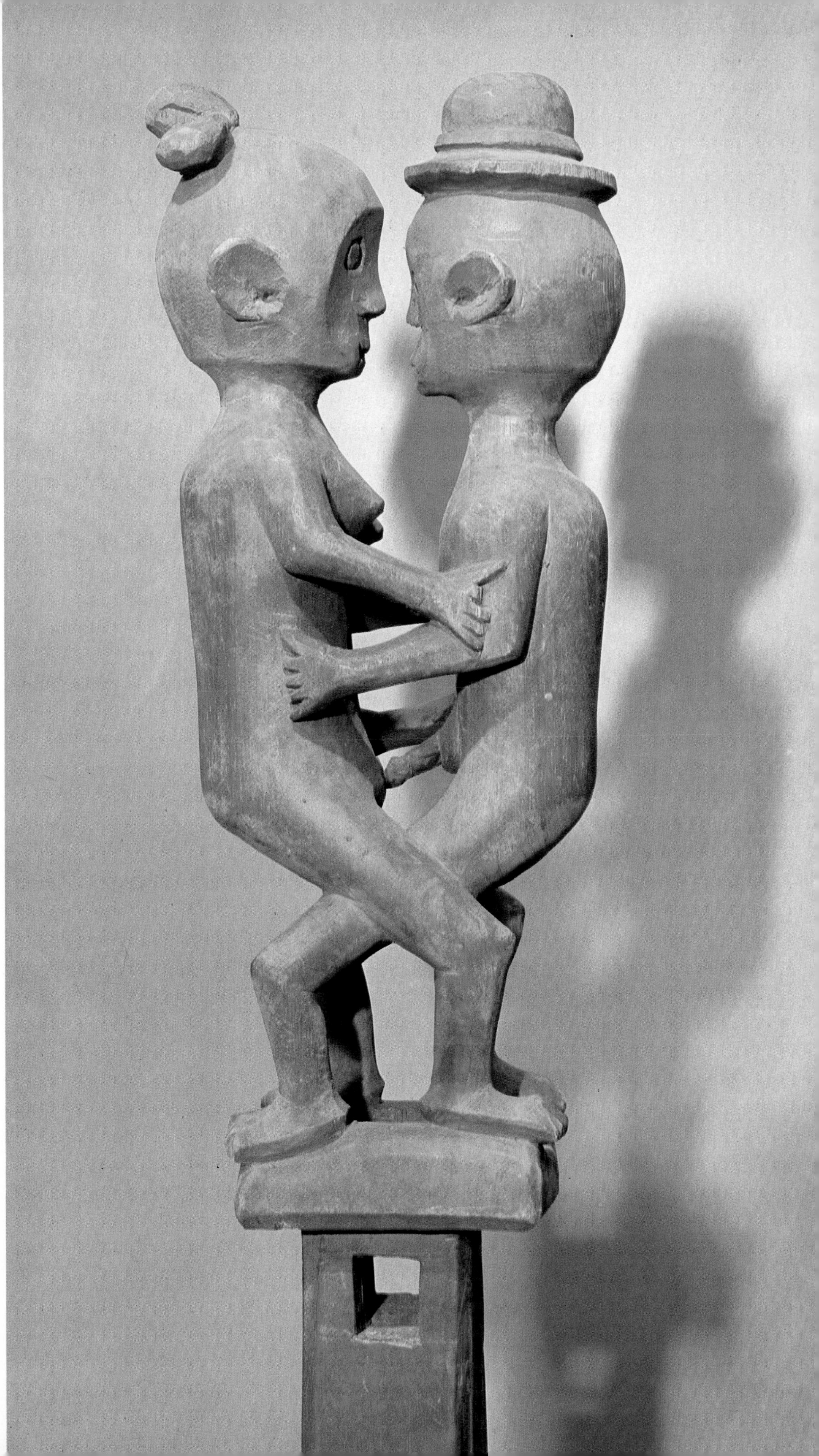

213 (*Previous page*)
Asmat ancestor poles with
their beautifully carved
jemen

214 (*Left*)
Fertility symbol from the
Torres Straits

215 (*Far left*)
Wooden carving of a woman
wiping her posterior with a
leaf. From the front the leaf
looks like a penis

218 (*Left*)
Sepik container in the shap
of a female

219 (*Left*)
Chalk figure. New Hebrides

men to accustom them to female influences and to prevent them falling sick after their first sexual intercourse.*

Second, an aspect which may have been noticed by the observant in this discussion, is the very small part which leaf and vegetable matter generally play in the erotic symbolism of the whole region. From this must be excluded, however, the gourd, sometimes incised with patterns repeating the same themes as those we have already seen; and used as a penis cover for men in parts of New Guinea. The gourd also plays an important part in Trobriand myth conceptions of the orgasmic role – itself a sort of reverse, negative mirror-image confirmation of the glorification of orgasmic ecstasy isolated from intercourse, as in Asmat. The gourd, a fruit closely related to the pumpkin, has a hard shell used over much of the area as a water-container. In Trobriand myth, gourd and woman are intimately inter-related: to such an extent that an act of male adultery can be extinguished by the breaking of the woman's gourds, enabling husband and wife to renew respectable (if unproductive) intercourse. Here and elsewhere in this scene we see that the vegetable world inclines towards the feminine, especially in conscious metaphor, whereas the masculine is more deeply animal and vigorous. This is much the same contrast as the Chinese yang and yin, and is found in other forms throughout eastern religions, both advanced and primitive in pre-urban life. Nowhere in the long range of islands here reviewed do we find a plant growing into the pubic regions of either sex, nor any botanical symbols of strong erotic content. There is nothing, for instance, to approach the similar use of strawberries and vines in so much western medieval paintings, finding its quintessential expression in the tropical palms of the orgiastic scenes painted in wild erotic fantasy by Hieronymus Bosch of the Netherlands, who died in 1516.†

The Maenge and other New Britain people have developed some variations on the New Guinea art theme, and these become really emphatic a little northeast, on the adjacent, equally elongate but narrower island of New Ireland. New Ireland provides the final link in the matted rope-chain of erotic form which binds, in a complex of knots past any present disentanglement, the art-styles from Malaysia across nearly 80° of latitude, a fifth of the world's width.

One feature, latent in much that has gone before, is highlighted with unmistakable intent and frequency in the erotic art of New Ireland: the androgynous or hermaphrodite statement of the male female body. This is best expressed in the almost life-size wooden sculptures in the round called *uli*, connected with elaborate fertility and animist rites similarly named. Uli figures are unmistakable. A big head with a wide mouth, but no special nose emphasis, is crowned with a high skull topnot or crest; from the chin, a tongue-like beard merges down to the chest, where there is sometimes a crocodile or other animal, but usually a baby girl (with cowrie as pudenda), held over the stomach in the familiar New Guinea way. The uli has a pair of large, very full, thrusting breasts, painted scarlet, emphatically those of a young woman; but lower down there is an equally emphatic penis, usually red with a black top, and without indicated testicles.‡

* See F. Panoff, 'Food and Faeces: a Melanesian Rite', *Man*, 5 (1970), p. 250; compare R. H. Codrington, *The Melanesians* (Oxford 1891), p. 370, etc. To pursue this little studied aspect further would take us beyond the bounds of erotic art defined in the volume. It has to be borne in mind in interpreting some of this complex visual material, especially the bark paintings of Angoram. The whole interest of pig and other anal zones may also be related here.
† Though Bosch, hell knows, indulged heavily in animalism as well, especially using birds and fish in connection with human erotic symbolism.
‡ A distinguished American art historian has suggested that New Ireland wood carvings have been 'derived from the Garuda' of Hinduism; Douglas Fraser, *Primitive Art* (London 1962), p. 94. Such stimulating theoretical projections become decreasingly convincing as one goes further and further into the western Pacific art, especially erotic art. It is particularly difficult, in this case, to see why such westerly influences should constantly appear with force in an isolated easterly island where some of the affinities (especially with the masks) might equally be theoretically derived from the American Indians of the Pacific coast (British Columbia in the north-west especially).

Nothing, even from the bisexually inclined Huon Gulf on New Guinea's north coast, can be more superficially straightforward than these uli. But that is not to say that New Irelanders are limited to a hermaphrodite insistence. There are several delicate, small, feminine figures, in limestone, in the British Museum, contrasting with the violence of the heavier work in wood. These chalk figures need not be female. A good male, 18 inches high, in the Rijksmuseum at Leiden, has a neat red line along the top of a curved drooping penis, over unusually well-shown testicles.

Another in limestone in the Hamburg Museum is a double-headed woman, recalling a notable double-headed wooden figure on display in Leiden which has a scarlet mons veneris protruding above a big vagina into which you can – and visitors do – easily stick a thumb. This comes from Mimika, west of the Asmat on the southwest side of Irian, with all of a thousand miles and the mainland blocking her from those New Irish cousins.*

In New Ireland, the capacity to think and to separate sex and bisex is further combined in powerful treatments of the penis, either carried over and past the knees in a lower form of maxi-tongue or uplifted to become a fish – one an evil-eyed fish with a cassowary's head sticking out of its mouth with the glans equivalent.

Hermaphroditism can, in a primitive sense, be taken to be one climax of erotic sensibility, the consummation of a certain confusion within the inner conflict of sex. In a difficult, deep way, a woman is hardly allowed to be just herself; the man unendingly unobtrusive, is very much around. This is the inescapable impression that we get throughout New Guinea on into Melanesia. The whole thing is much more gentle further west, as in Borneo; and again when you get out into Polynesia, it becomes more mild. In these conditions, eroticism becomes a tangled web, and there is no getting round or simplifying this state of affairs. To that extent, nearly all the erotic art of the western Pacific is, fundamentally, inhuman and to a certain extent even anti-human. Or, put another way, anti-normal – if by that term we accept that normality is more or less regular intercourse between male and female, associated more or less with the conscious procreation of children at least as a possible consequence. Without that consciousness, recognized or submerged, the woman ceases to be the whole end of sex for the man, just as the man's sperm ceases to be the essential beginning of childbirth for the woman. Sexual pleasure can then be, as it were, divorced from the sexual act alone, as in some supposedly advanced civilized situations.

Moreover, the extent of what we would call 'sexual frustration', which might here more closely be phrased as 'sub-satisfaction', underlies much that is otherwise baffling in a large amount of that which has been discussed here. Several observers have recorded degrees of such frustration for the area. There are records of sexually deprived bachelors having become possessed and uncontrollable, violent to the extent where such possession, often related to shamanism, has been classified as 'hysterical psychosis'.[8]

The native peoples themselves may diagnose nervous illness in strikingly similar, psychiatric terms. Thus what outside observers have described as 'fatal neurological disorders', such as the extraordinary and lethal form of seeming madness called by the eastern inland tribes 'kuru', they believe to be the result of semen or menstrual discharges, or the blood of parturition, obtained by an ill-wisher and mixed by a sorcerer.[9]

* The Hamburg double-headed limestone figure is illustrated in A. C. Ambosi, *Oceanic Art* (London 1966), Plate 30, as are also two very fine uli in the Basle Museum (Plate 29).

In viewing the visual expressions of feeling and taste in art form, this background of near-repression must be borne in mind. The sexual passion can find expressions other than sex. In Borneo sexual frustration was for centuries a major incentive towards manliness, expressed through head-hunting, thus leading to the possession of the desired woman: the bleeding trophy being, in effect, the phallus. Such action may negate the expression in wood, cloth or paint; acts speak louder than art (in the short term). This can give a false impression of the culture's deeper erotic content. But such difficult problems have barely been touched on in Pacific and Australasian societies, where the main disciplines of observation have come from social anthropology, preferring easier levels such as kinship, property exchange and ritual observance. Having lived among Melanesians in the New Hebrides over a third of a century ago, when the Malekulans were still cannibals, the present writer has good cause to know how overwhelmingly important, yet enormously intricate and largely secretive, sex life can be in such communities. In north Malekula, the adult men elaborate the phallus with penis-wrappers, testicles exposed for all to see. This fact is repeated mildly in their seemingly non-erotic visual arts, without special emphasis.

But although these same men practise polygamy and have a reputation for vigorous heterosexuality with folk tales and stories of affairs of the heart as well, they have a regular and organized system of homosexuality side by side. Young boys, prior to initiation into manhood, are the lovers of adult, married men. The man and boy commonly 'make love' in the darkness of the man's house, as dominant an institution here as in Asmat or Sepik.[10]

The same intricate bisexual attitude is shown, almost casually, in the repeated use of pigs' tusks in the clay and wood figures and masks from Malekula and other islands of the group. These tusks come from the domesticated pigs, centre of economic and ritual life, the same form as in the Trobriands. But some of the New Hebrides peoples have pioneered one of the world's oddest genetic experiments. These dark, fuzzy-haired eaters of root crops and pork (and previously each other), living on islands with no large wild mammals, trace their own origin from a boar which came from a vine, and a sow which came from the sea, the two mating to produce a human son, their ancestor. Many generations since, they – or nature – discovered how to breed intersex hermaphrodite pigs. This was developed in the first place almost by accident, but now with a high proportion of positively neuter results. The top incisors are knocked out, so that the lower canine, the tusk, can enormously elongate, making as much as two circles and growing clear through the lower jaw bone as it curves round back and then forward into the front of the mouth again. Such animals are of the highest value for sacrifice. Their tusks are transferred from the pig to the mask of an ancestral figure used in death and other rites. Nearly all of these tusked ancestor figures are masculine, but sometimes we find a more delicate, feminine figure, very much like the slip of a girl from south Malekula, her childish breasts below the tusked face (in the British Museum).

To underline the erotic complexity of these small islands in the southern Pacific, it should be made clear that marital devotion can be very high indeed. For example, among the Sakau people of Santo Island the widows of a polygamous chief committed suicide – hanging themselves – on his death (while I was there). On an adjacent island, as a special treasure before I left, I was presented with a numbetala, a large wooden tube filled with leaves which, according to their lore, was the original and only orifice penetrated by man for sexual purposes. They ejected their sperm inside the hollow wood, changing the leaves periodically. One day, a ship-wrecked stranger secretly initiated the women into the facts of sex, until they complained bitterly at the neglect of their husbands. The locals took on from there!

Such stories imply the same sort of ignorance as that first recorded by Malinowski about the Trobriands. Going back for a moment to central Borneo, the Kayans there have an equally 'ridiculous' belief: they too tell the folk tale at the expense of their own foolish ancestors, in this case some twenty generations ago. The Kayans, a wonderfully artistic and intelligent people, believe that at first their shapely women did not know how to have babies naturally. Pregnancy was regarded as an illness, and the swollen belly was cut open with a special sort of hard steel knife. Examples of such knives are still kept as objects of strange power, bundled alongside the human heads on long-house verandahs in the far interior.

It is only too easy to generalize for the erotic peoples of whom we have so little fundamental understanding. Generalizations at once expect exceptions, too. One final exception to the general rule of showing copulation simply must be cited to keep the record straight. From the Torres Straits Islands, between southernmost Papua and the northernmost tip of Australia – but thoroughly Papuan in culture and noted for careful three-dimensional carvings of both ritual and utility objects – copulation figures are not infrequent. Some of these were collected more than a century ago; they show women with big breasts reminiscent of New Ireland (though unpainted), legs in the squatting position to reveal a pronounced clitoris and labia and a big mons veneris. In the British Museum, one labelled 'fertility symbol' is of a full-breasted woman holding at the waist a much smaller but clearly human figure in between her thighs, arms along her ribs, head between her breasts, in a strange mix of sexuality and maternity, the larger woman placid, even flaccid, the smaller male eager, pressing, facially tense.

The Torres treatment reminds one, in a certain way, of the strange Maori couple copulating in the Auckland Museum, beyond the limits of Melanesia. As also the Maori 'godstick' with elongate tongue turning into a lizard overlying the human figure as if in copulation, only a step beyond the Sepik, or the tongue phallus and the animal on the uli chest in New Ireland.*

With such a leap in imagery we can leave the western side of that vast Pacific, and arrive across at the remotest, loneliest permanently inhabited island in the world, the twenty mile long Easter Island or Rapanui ('the navel of the world') for the Polynesians. Here, in a tiny concentrated community, erotic art is back at its simplest, with vulva symbols cut into rock and – very rarely – phallus symbols on the otherwise strongly 'naturalist' and nearly always sexless rock and wood carvings.

* One Maori copulating couple is illustrated in A. C. Ambesi, *Oceanic Art* (London 1970), Plate 52; also Plate 56 for the 'godstick'. However, normal 'godsticks' confine phallic symbolism only to the large tongue, if at all – see T. Barrow, *Maori Godsticks* (Wellington 1961), and the same author's *The Decorative Arts of the New Zealand Maori* (Wellington 1964).

References

EARLY HISTORY OF SEXUAL ART

1 R. B. Onians, *The Origins of European Thought*, Cambridge, 1951.

2 S. Giedon, *The Eternal Present*, London, 1962.

3 John G. Neihardt, *The Life Story of a Holy Man of the Oglala Sioux*, New York, 1932.

4 A. Lommel, *Prehistoric and Primitive Man*, London, 1966, p. 21.

5 A. Leroi Gourhan, *Bulletin de la Société Préhistorique*, LV, 1958.

6 R. Briffault, *The Mothers*, vol. II, London, 1927, p. 417.

7 G. R. Levy, *The Gate of Horn*, part IV, London, 1948, ch. 1.

8 P. S. Rawson, *Ceramics*, London and New York, 1971.

9 L. Frobenius, *Das Unbekannte Afrika*, p. 23

10 Briffault, *op. cit.*, under index entry 'steatopygy'.

11 J. Mooney, 'The Ghost-Dance Religion, and the Sioux Outbreak of 1890', *Annual Report of the Bureau of American Ethnology*, XIV, 2, Washington, 1896, p. 721.

12 A. Deierich, *Mutter Erde*, 3rd edition, augmented by E. Fehrle, Leipzig and Berlin, 1925.

13 R. M. and C. H. Berndt, *Sexual Behaviour in Western Arnhem Land*, Viking Fund, New York, 1951 (Johnson Reprint, London, 1963).

14 cf. M. Eliade, *Myths, Dreams and Mysteries*, London, 1960, p. 170.

15 W. F. Jackson Knight, *Elysion*, London, 1970, p. 105.

16 G. R. Levy, *The Gate of Horn*, London 1948, p. 50 and W. F. Jackson Knight, *The Cumaean Gates*, Oxford, 1936, pp. 122ff and *Elysion*, London, 1970, passim.

17 A. Lommel, *The World of the Early Hunter*, London, 1967.

18 R. S. Loomis, 'Morgain La Fée and the Celtic Goddesses', *Speculum*, April 1945, pp. 183ff.

19 Onians, *op. cit.*

20 See also A. van Gennep, *Rites of Passage*, London, 1960, pp. 170ff.

21 E. Fuchs, *Sittengeschichte*, Munich n.d., passim.

22 cf. George Riley Scott, *Phallic Worship*, London, 1966, 1970, ch. VIII.

23 Brian Branston, *The Lost Gods of England*, London, 1958, p. 65.

CELTIC AND NORTHERN ART

1 Paul Jacobsthal, *Early Celtic Art*, Oxford, 1944, 2 vols.

2 Robin Flower, *The Irish Tradition*, Oxford, 1947.

3 J. J. Tierney, *The Celtic Ethnography of Posidonius*, Dublin, 1960 (Reprint from Proceedings of the Royal Irish Academy, Vol. 60, Section C, No. 5)

4 Tom Peete Cross and Clark Harris Slover, *Ancient Irish Tales*, Dublin, 1969.

5 Lucan, *Pharsalia*, iii, 399f.

6 Giraldus Cambrensis, *Topographia Hibernica*, iii, 1185 (trans, Forester).

EQUATORIAL ISLANDS OF THE PACIFIC BASIN

1 T. Harrisson, *World Within*, London, 1950.

2 Reproduced by courtesy of Professor Charles Boxer. For other details see T. Harrisson, *Journal of the Malaysian Branch, Royal Asiatic Society*, 1964, 164.

3 Simon Kooijman, *Papuan Art in the Rijksmuseum*, Amsterdam, 1966, p. 38.

4 Adrian Gerbrands, *Wow-ipits*, The Hague, 1967, pp. 33, 53.

5 Gerbrands, *op. cit.*, pp. 90, 95 (cf. Kooijman, *op. cit.*, p. 86).

6 Gerbrands, *op. cit.*, p. 89 (my italics).

7 Peter J. Wilson, 'Virgin Birth', *Man*, 4, 1969, p. 288.

8 L. Langness, 'Hysterical Psychoses in the New Guinea Highlands', *Psychiatry*, 28, 1965, p. 258.

9 See R. M. Glasse, 'Some Recent Observations on *kuru*', *Oceana*, 40, 1970, p. 210.

10 T. Harrisson, *Savage Civilisation*, London, 1937; cf. A. B. Deacon, *Malekula, a Vanishing Race in the New Hebrides*, London, 1934, for details of homosexuality.

Acknowledgments

The editor and publishers wish to record their gratitude for permission received from owners, agents and photographers to reproduce the following list of illustrations (numbers refer to pictures; italic numbers to colour illustrations):

Aerofilms Ltd (51); Alinari (photo Josephine Powell) (1); Antikvarisk-Topografiska Arkivet (46, 47, 48); Ferdinand Anton (85, 86, 114, 117, 118, 119, 120, 121, 122, 123, 124, 125, 126, 127, 129, 130, 131, 134, 135, 136, 137); Arman Collection, Paris (140); British Museum (68, 88, 103, 106, 144, 152, 155, 156, 157, 172, 190, 210, 214); Brunei Museum (185, 188); C. M. Dixon (*26, 30, 35, 36, 38, 40, 41*, 49, 53, 55, 56, 59); Dumbarton Oaks, Washington, D.C., Robert Woods Bliss Collection of Pre-Columbian Art (87); Werner Forman (*25, 29, 61, 62, 65, 66, 67, 70*, 72, 73, 74, 75, 76, 77, 79, 80, 81, 82, 83, 84, *92, 93, 94*, 95, 96, 97, 98, *99, 100, 101, 102*, 104, 105, 109, 111, 112, 113, *128, 132, 133, 138*, 141, 151, 162, 163, *164*, 165, 166, 167, 168, *169, 170*, 171, 173, *174, 175*, 176, 177, 178, *180*, 181, 182, *207, 212, 213, 218, 219*); Frobenius Institute (5, 6, 8, 9, 146); P. V. Glob (37, 39, 42, 43, 44, 45); Goldman Collection, London (194, 195); Christine Harrisson (184, 186, 192, 204, 193, 196, 197, 198, 199, 200, 201, 202, 203, 204, 205, 208, 209, 215, 216); Tom Harrisson (187, 191); Jaeger Collection, Paris (142, 143); Kerchache Collection, Paris (62, 139, 153, 154); Klejman Collection, New York (145); Mission E. Anati (57); Musée de l'Homme (64, 69, 71, 91, 150, *179*); Musée Royal de l'Afrique Centrale (158, 159, 160, 161); National Museum of Ireland (28, 50); Nouvelle Librairie de France (58); Photo Meyer (27, *183*); Photographie Giraudon (90); Axel Poignant (7, 10, 11, 13, 14, 15, 16, 17, 18, 19, 20, 22, 33, 34, 52, 206, 211); Josephine Powell (54); Sarawak Museum (189); Scala (*21*); Snark International (60); University of Oxford, Pitt Rivers Museum (217); Achille B. Weider (2, 3, 4, 12, 23, 24); Joan Westcott (148, 149).

Index

New Guineans—*cont.*
280, 281, 283; Sepik River art 281, 283–4; turtle as art symbol 280–1, 282, 284; Washkuks 282–3;
nose, phallic equation 49, 282

objects, antler 11; bone 7, 11, 14, 19, 20–1; meanings of 4, 76; silver 105; stone 7, 17, 20; Venuses 7, 17, 18
Oceanic Art (A. C. Ambosi) 296n
Océanie (J. Guiart) 275n, 285n, 286n
ochre, red, relation with life-blood 7, 13; use of 7, 22
oculets 43
Oenpelli aboriginal culture 22, 39
Olmec culture (see Americans, Middle)
Onians, Professor R. B. 9, 47, 48
oracles 48
orgasms, experience of 5, 109; symbolism from 280
ornaments 19; equatorial 273, 278; Eskimo 109; manuscript 44; Middle American 144, 159; spiral 43–4
Orpheus, legends of 48
Osborne, Harold 163
Osiris 53
owl, protective role 286; role in sexual contexts 79

Pacific Island culture (see also Borneans, Melanesians, New Guineans) 252–298; animism of 273–4, 295; Balis 271; bisexuality in art 282, 286, 295–7; erotic similarities between 252; folk law of 286, 295, 297–8; gods of 286; ideas on sex frustrations 296–7; identification with animals 273, 279–80, 282–3; Philippines 272–3; Punans 253
Palaeolithic culture 6–22, 39–42, 49, 163–4, 283; female emblems in 13–16, 18, 42, 80; female pre-ponderance in 10; ignorance of paternity 10; incorporating many aspects 11, 12; labyrinth art 40–4
palangs 271–5
Panoff, F. 295n
Parrinder, Geoffrey 74

parthenogenesis, belief in 284–5
Pasiega, La, cave 13
Pech Merle cave, art forms from 9, 15, 19, 20, 71
Pembrokeshire, figurines from 17
peoples, migration of 6, 54, 107, 163, 198, 203
Persephone 53
Persepolis, pillars of 15
Petersfels, amulet from 17
phallus (see also symbols, phallic), analogy with agriculture 45, 76, 126, 143, 148; analogy with horns 85; analogy with severed head 79, 85–6, 148; animal 19–21, 150, 274; as Heavenly Root 72–3; ceremonial display of 53, 123–4, 126, 227; chalk 80, 82; dances incorporating 11, 75, 122, 126; effect of shape of 50, 71; experiences of 2, 126; false 124–6, 143, 148, 201; gold 271; humorous portrayals of 193, 194, 204, 225, 226; portrayals of 13, 20, 54, 75–7, 80–2, 85, 106, 110, 119, 125–6, 143–6, 148, 150, 159–60, 161, 193, 198–9, 203, 204, 206, 225–7, 230, 254, 274–5, 278–80, 282–4, 286, 295–6, 298; relation to crocodile 274, 279; representing male power 71–2, 126, 193; separated 254, 271, 284; spirit repellant 254; stone 145, 159; tongue association 274, 282–3, 298; tracing of cult 46, 54; winged 48, 51, 71; wooden 19, 72, 75, 123, 126
Picasso, Pablo 49
Pigs for the Ancestors (R. A. Rappaport) 285n
Pitjandjara Australian culture 39
Placard, Le, horn-staves from 20
Polynesians, voyages of 163
potency 2, 247; connection with antlers etc. 20; development of male 45, 72
pottery, African 199; Andean 164, 191–3, 195–6; equatorial 199; equine 196; Japanese 2, 3; Middle American 149, 159, 161; sexual Andean 193–5
Predmosti, art forms from 42
pregnancy, portrayals of 286;

sexuality expressed in 5, 39, 42; unconnected with Palaeolithic male 10
Primitive Art (D. Fraser) 295n
primitives, belief in 'spirit' 5; importance of sex to 4, 5, 22, 39; reaction to images 1, 2; sexual art of 3, 4, 7; snake symbolism of 51, 52; tactile memory of 3; thought processes of 4, 11–12
propagation, importance of feminine part in 11; paternal part in 10–11
prostitution 147; sacred 53–4
Pueblo Indian culture (see also under Americans, North) 125; Corn Dance of 125–6

Quina, La, cave 12

Rainbow Snake 10, 39, 51, 52
rape, portrayal of 122
Rappaport, R. A. 285
Rawson, Philip 273, 274
Read, Kenneth 278n
Red Indian, mime-dances of 8
reliefs, cave 10, 105
religion, cults of 249; occult 249; primitive 9, 40–1; West African survivals 249–50
rhinoceros, symbol of virility 275
ring-holes 12
ring-stones 12
rituals (see also journeys, ritual) 1, 4, 5, 7–10, 46; ancestry 45; birth 12, 13, 16, 22, 280; cave 13; creation 124; death 22, 48, 223, 280, 297; defloration 54, 71, 200; female 13; fertility 13, 15, 44–5, 49, 52–4, 72, 74–5, 79, 82, 85, 122–4, 162, 195, 225, 228–9, 295; Neolithic 48; orgiastic 52–3, 74–5, 149, 295; Palaeolithic 40–4; sexual 6, 9, 11, 18–19, 22, 39, 48, 52–3, 72–3, 75, 191, 195; tribal 203
Robin Hood 74
rock art 8, 10, 14–16, 18–19, 43, 50, 53, 77, 81, 84, 254, 271, 274; hunter 10; sexual 39; source of magical power 39
Roman culture 53, 71, 73

sacrifice, animal 74, 84, 103, 297; Dionysiac 74; human